W9-CKM-359

MOTHER
EARTH,
FATHER
SKY

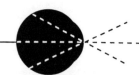

**This Large Print Book carries the
Seal of Approval of N.A.V.H.**

MOTHER EARTH, FATHER SKY

Sue Harrison

Thorndike Press • Thorndike, Maine

Library of Congress Cataloging in Publication Data:

Harrison, Sue.
    Mother Earth Father Sky / Sue Harrison.
        p. cm.
    ISBN 1-56054-093-1 (alk. paper : lg. print)
    1. Indians of North America--Fiction. 2. Man,
Prehistoric--Fiction. 3. Large type books. I. Title.
[PS3558.A67194M68   1991]   90-25536
813'.54—dc20   CIP

All of the characters in this book are fictitious, and any resemblance to actual persons, living or dead, is purely coincidental.

Thorndike Press Large Print edition published in 1991 by arrangement with Doubleday, a division of Bantam Doubleday Dell Publishing Group, Inc.

Cover design by James B. Murray.

The tree indicium is a trademark of Thorndike Press.

'

This book is printed on acid-free, high opacity paper. ∞

TO NEIL

WHO HAS TAUGHT ME SO MUCH ABOUT JOY AND LIVING
AND OUR CHILDREN
NEIL AND KRYSTAL
WHO HAVE TAUGHT US BOTH ABOUT LOVE

AND IN MEMORY OF OUR DAUGHTER KORAL

ALEUTIAN
ISLANDS
Area
enlarged

NORTH
AMERICA
7000 B.C.

Ice fields and glaciers

Bering Sea

ISLANDS OF FOUR MOUNTAINS

Kagamil Island

Tugix Mountain

Shugnan'
Beach

Chuginadak
Island

Whale
Hunter's
Beach

Yunaska Island

© A Karl/J Kemp, 1990

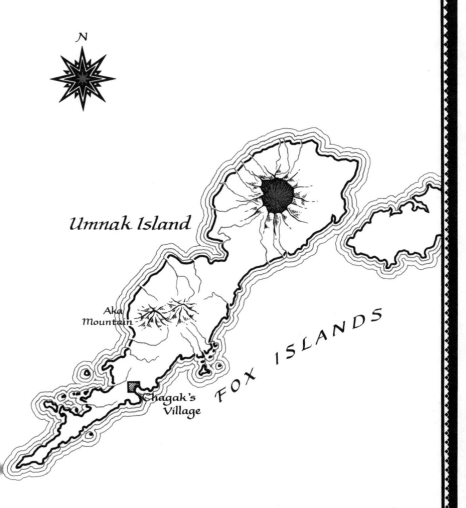

N

Umnak Island

Aka
Mountain

FOX ISLANDS

Chagak's
Village

PACIFIC OCEAN

Miles

0   10   20

PROLOGUE

The whalebone digging stick was cold in Shuganan's hand, but he leaned against it as he walked, and the end of the stick marked his path with a line of small holes in the dark beach gravel.

The stiffening of Shuganan's joints had deformed him. Once slender and tall, he was now bent, his hands gnarled, knees swollen. But when he was near the sea, the waves against his feet, he was young again.

At the edge of the water, where the tide had left a pool, Shuganan saw several sea urchins. He waded into the pool and used his stick to push them into his gathering bag. The bag was nearly full.

Then he saw the ivory. His hand trembled as he picked up the large whale tooth, a rare gift from some spirit.

Another sign, he thought. Something more than dreams. Shuganan closed his eyes and clasped the unfinished carving he wore strung at his neck. It was only one of the many carvings he had made, but this one had seemed to come from the ivory of its own will.

Shuganan had held the knife, but as he worked, it was as though other hands were holding his, as though he only watched while the blade brought forth the image.

"Soon," he said. In his joy he laughed and for a moment his laughter seemed as strong as the wind, louder than the sea.

PART ONE

SUMMER

7056 BC

ONE

Six days. The hunters had been gone six days, and during that time there had been a storm — rain and a roaring that seemed to come from within the mountains, and waves that swept the beaches bare.

Six days. Too long, Chagak thought. Too long, yet she sat on the low mound of her father's earthen ulaq and waited, watching the sea. She smoothed her hands over the dark feathers of her suk. Her mother had given her the garment that morning to replace the hooded child's parka Chagak had outgrown. The gift was a sign that Chagak was now woman, but she knew it was more than that. It was also her mother's way of speaking to the spirits, a woman's small voice that said, "You see, my daughter wears a new suk. It is time to rejoice. Surely you will not send sorrow to this village."

So Chagak spread her arms in the wind, a silent request for the spirits to see her, to notice the beautiful suk, for her mother had made it carefully, using more than twenty birdskins, and the cormorant feathers still held

13

the rich smell of the oil used to soften the skins.

"See me," Chagak wanted to shout to the spirits, to the great mountain Aka that watched over their village. "This girl is woman now. Surely, in her rejoicing you will bring our hunters back from the sea. Surely you will not let us become a village of women and children." But only men were allowed to call to the spirits. So Chagak stretched out her arms but held back the words that pressed full and tight between her tongue and the roof of her mouth.

A wind blew in from the sea, bringing the smell of fish and a coldness that made Chagak tuck her long hair into the suk's high collar rim. The suk hung past Chagak's knees, so that when she squatted down it was long enough to touch the ground and keep her bare feet warm. She drew her hands up inside the sleeves and squinted at the gray-white line between sky and sea where the black dots of the hunters' ikyan would first come into sight.

It was summer, but even in summer the skies were usually gray, the air thick and wet with moisture that rose from the sea. The wind that kept winters warm — with rain coming as often as snow — also kept the summers cold. And the wind blew forever; never, never stopped.

Chagak opened her mouth and let the wind

fill her cheeks. Did she imagine it or was there the taste of sea lion in that mouthful of wind? She closed her eyes and swallowed. Yes, some taste of sea lion, Chagak thought. And why would sea lions be here, this close to the First Men's island? Again she filled her mouth with the wind, again she tasted sea lion. Yes, yes. And if she tasted sea lion, perhaps the hunters were coming, towing sea lions they had taken during their hunt. But Chagak did not call her mother. Why raise hopes when perhaps it was only a trick of some spirit, making Chagak taste what was not there?

Chagak watched the horizon, holding her eyes open wide, until the wind filled them with tears. She wiped the wetness from her cheeks with her sleeve, and as the softness of the cormorant feathers crossed her face, she saw the first ikyak, a thin black line on the white edge of the sea. Then another and another.

Chagak called down through the square opening, both entrance and smoke hole, that was cut through the sod roof and driftwood rafters of her father's ulaq. "They come. They come."

As her mother emerged from the ulaq, other women climbed from the dark interiors of nearby ulas, the women blinking and shielding their eyes in the gray brightness of the day.

They waited, quietly, though Chagak heard

15

her mother's soft mumbling as she counted the boats. Ten ikyan had gone out. Ten had returned.

One of the women started a high chant of praise, a song of thankfulness to the sea and honor for the hunters, and from cliffs and ulas young boys and old men hurried to the beach to help the hunters drag ikyan ashore.

The women followed, still singing. Chagak, the newest woman, stayed at the back of the group, behind the women but ahead of the girls.

Sea lions were lashed to the sterns of the first two ikyan, the animals nearly as long as the crafts themselves.

One of the hunters was Red Sun, Chagak's uncle, the other, Seal Stalker, one of the youngest hunters in Chagak's village, but already that summer Seal Stalker had brought in six hair seals and now a sea lion.

When his ikyak was in shallow water, Seal Stalker jumped from the craft and began to pull it ashore. Then he cut the line that held the sea lion.

Chagak tried to keep her eyes on other hunters, to make her song as much for her uncle as for Seal Stalker, but it seemed something was forcing her to watch Seal Stalker, and twice, as he helped drag the animal up the slope of the gravel beach, Seal Stalker's eyes met Chagak's, and each time, though Chagak continued her chant, a chill coursed up from her fingers as if she and not Seal Stalker had brought in the animal, as if she were the one being honored.

Seal Stalker's mother came to take the hunter's share, the sea lion's flippers and the thick layer of fat under the skin. But suddenly Seal Stalker shook his head and instead turned to Chagak's father, handed him a long, stone-bladed hunting knife and said, "I need a wife. Let this animal be first payment on your daughter's bride price."

Chagak's father hesitated, and Chagak covered her face with her hands as the girls behind her began to giggle. But she watched her father through the cracks between her fingers, watched as he looked back at Chagak's mother. Her mother nodded, as if she had always known what Seal Stalker planned. Then Chagak's father sliced into the thick hide and began the dividing, to give each man a share for his family. Chagak glanced at Seal Stalker, then looked quickly away, her cheeks suddenly too hot, even in the cold wind. But her mother clasped her hand, pulled her toward the sea lion, and there, before everyone in the village, Chagak and her mother took over the butchering.

Chagak was thankful that her father had just

retouched the edge of her woman's knife so that the curved blade cut easily through meat and fat, Chagak's strokes so quick and sure that soon Chagak's mother sat back on her heels and let Chagak finish dividing the meat.

For a long time Seal Stalker watched her, and Chagak felt the warmth of his gaze on the top of her head and at the back of her neck where her black hair disappeared into the collar of her suk. And once, as she worked, Chagak looked up at Seal Stalker, her heart pounding, and smiled at him. But finally Seal Stalker turned away to help the other hunters and to take his share of the other sea lion.

When Chagak and her mother had finished, they folded and rolled the skin, flesh side in, then wrapped the bones in an old seal hide. Several women helped them carry the bundles to their ulaq.

Chagak had expected to begin the first scraping of the hide, but her mother pointed at the racks of women's boats near the beach.

"We must visit the otters," her mother said. So she and Chagak carried their women's boat, an open-topped ik, framed with driftwood, sheathed in sea lion hides, to the edge of the sea.

Chagak's mother climbed in and Chagak pushed the ik into deeper water, the coldness of the sea numbing her ankle bones until they ached. When the ik was far enough from shore, Chagak climbed in, too, and her mother handed her a paddle, motioning for Chagak to guide the craft near the kelp beds where the sea otters lived.

At first, Chagak thought her mother was going to tell of the time an otter had saved her father's life. It was a story Chagak had heard often, about the otter that had directed Chagak's father to land after his ikyak had been damaged in a storm. Since that time her father considered otters sacred and would not hunt them for their pelts or meat.

Sighing, Chagak closed her eyes and waited for her mother to begin the story, but her mother said, "Who are better mothers than sea otters? Did they not teach the first woman how to care for her children?"

So Chagak opened her eyes and watched the otters as her mother spoke to her of being a wife, of pleasing her husband. She spoke of the tradition of their people, the First Men. How the world was only water until the otters decided they needed dry land where they could hide during storms, and the seals wanted beaches where their babies could be born. So each animal dove hard and far to the bottom of the sea, and each one brought back mud until there was enough to make a long curve of land above the sea. Then mountains grew, pushing up in smoke and fire to guard the beaches. Green and shining grass rose to meet the mountains, to welcome them. Then heather and all plants grew; birds came and lemmings and last of all men until all the land was filled.

Chagak's people were the first to come to that land and so they called themselves First Men. The sacred mountain Aka protected their village and other mountains protected other villages east and west of Chagak's village, all down the long stretch of land that extended to the edges of the world, ice to ice.

And as Chagak's mother spoke, the otters, too, seemed to listen. One brought her baby close to the ik, the baby clinging to the mother's back, and another swam near enough for Chagak to touch. But when she reached out to it, the animal dipped into a wave, then wrapped itself with a long strand of kelp and floated, small gray face just above the surface, eyes closed as if asleep.

Then Chagak felt a tingling in her arm, a tightening in her belly, for some voice — perhaps the spirit voice of the otter mother — whispered, "Soon you, too, will have babies. Your own babies."

That evening, after Chagak and her mother had returned, Seal Stalker came to the ulaq. At first Chagak was shy. Though she had always known Seal Stalker, it was different to think of him as husband.

While Seal Stalker spoke to her father, talking of hunts and weapons, Chagak sat in a dark corner smoothing the skin side of a fur seal pelt with a chunk of lava rock. Chagak kept her head lowered, but the work she was doing was something she had done since she was a child and so did not require her eyes but only the tips of her fingers, checking the nap and thickness of the skin. So it seemed that some spirit directed her eyes to Seal Stalker and she saw that, though he was speaking to her father, his eyes, too, were wandering, scanning the ulaq walls, the curtains of the sleeping places, the pegs and niches that held digging sticks and sewing supplies.

Yes, Chagak thought, Seal Stalker should be interested in this ulaq. He and Chagak would live here with her family, at least until Chagak had their first child.

It was a good ulaq, dry and strong, and one of the largest in the village, high enough for a man to stand and stretch his hands above his head, and even Chagak, now grown to her full height, could stand in the sleeping places and not catch her hair in the rafters. Chagak's father could take five long paces in any direction from the climbing log in the center of the ulaq before he reached the thick earthen walls.

We will be happy here, Chagak thought, and glanced again at Seal Stalker. He looked at her and smiled, said something to Chagak's father, then came over to Chagak and sat down beside her. The seal oil lamps made yellow halos over Chagak's mother and father as they worked. Her father was straightening the shaft of a harpoon, her mother finishing a basket inverted on a weaving pole.

The ulaq was warm, so Chagak wore only a woven grass apron, her back and breasts bare. Seal Stalker began to tell her of his hunt, his dark eyes widening as he spoke, his shoulder-length hair glistening in the light from the lamps.

Suddenly he pulled Chagak into his lap, wrapped his arms around her and held her. Chagak was surprised but pleased, afraid to look at her parents and too shy to look at Seal Stalker.

He smoothed his hands over her arms and back, and Chagak, worried, glanced up at her father. He did not seem to care, to even notice that she was sitting on Seal Stalker's lap.

So Chagak said nothing but only sat very still, afraid a movement might betray her happiness and draw the envy of some spirit.

Chagak picked another salmonberry and dropped it into her woven grass bag. The bag was so full that the bottom berries were crushed, and juice dripped from the meshes to stain her bare feet.

Her mother had given her the day as a gift, to do what she wanted to do, to be away from the work of the ulaq. So Chagak had walked far into the hills, trying to find the patch of rye grass she had first found two summers before. It was coarser than the grass that grew near the sea, and it dried to the dark green color of dock leaves. Chagak used it to make border patterns when she wove dividing curtains and floor mats from the whiter, sunbleached grass that grew on the sod roof of her father's ulaq.

She looked up at the sky, and the sun's position in the northwest made her walk more quickly. Her father would be angry she was late, but the bundle of grass she had cut was worth his scolding.

The grass slung over her shoulder was heavy, but Chagak was strong. She thought of the weavings she would make — new curtains for the sleeping place she and Seal Stalker would soon share — and she began to hum.

It was an unusual day of cloudless skies and bright sun. The hills were crowded with plants: cranberries, cornel, pale-leaved roseroot, long waving fronds of joint grass, pink flowering stalks of fireweed.

Chagak stopped and moved the berry bag to her other arm. She was near her people's village. She could taste the salt that blew in from the sea, and the wind carried the smell of fish and sea animals.

She saw a patch of mossberries, the shiny black berries nearly hidden in a tangle of heather, and stopped to pick them. She lowered her berry bag to the ground and slipped the bundle of grass from her shoulder.

Chagak rubbed the muscles of her arm, sore from holding the bag away from her suk, then ate the berries slowly, savoring her last minutes alone before returning to her family's noisy ulaq. It was good sometimes to be alone. To have time to think and plan, to live in dreams.

She arched her back against the stiffness of her shoulders and strung the bag over her arm, but as she reached for the grass, she heard a cry, nearly a scream, that seemed to come from the beach.

Chagak clasped her amulet and, leaving both the grass and her berries, ran toward the village. Someone had died, she was sure. Probably a hunter.

Not her father, not Seal Stalker, she prayed.

As she neared the crest of the last hill, a glow lighted the blues and purples of the sky, and at the top of the hill she stopped, confused by what she saw.

A ulaq was on fire; the grass thatching of the roof blazed. Men were running from ulaq to ulaq, men with long hair, their bodies short and wide, their parkas not the familiar black of cormorant skins but a mottled brown and white as if made from the skins of many lemmings, sewn haphazardly.

They carried torches and were setting fires to roof thatching, then throwing the torches into each ulaq.

Fear fixed Chagak's feet to the earth and closed her throat so she could not cry out.

Two men, each carrying a large seal stomach container of oil, dumped the oil into her father's ulaq and threw a torch in through the roof hole. Flames leaped up from inside the ulaq, setting the heather and grass of the roof ablaze. Even above the noise of the fire, Chagak thought she heard her mother's screams.

Chagak's older brother lunged from the roof hole. Flailing her father's driftwood seal club, he knocked down one of the men, but the other caught him around the waist and pushed him over the edge of the ulaq.

The first man, regaining his feet, jumped down after, and when he again climbed to the top of the ulaq, he was waving a blood-tipped spear. Chagak felt the burn of vomit rise into her mouth.

Her mother came out next. Pup, the brother born that spring, was in her arms. She tried to run between the men, but they caught her. One man pulled the baby from her and flung him to the ground; the other cut the waist thong that held her knee-length apron.

At that moment Chagak's younger sister emerged from the ulaq, and her mother dove toward the child, escaping the men as she grasped her daughter. They stood together, two dark figures in front of the flaming roof grass, holding one another as the men advanced with raised spears. One of the men lifted his spear to the girl's face, and Chagak covered her mouth with both hands, sucking in great gulps of air to hold in her screams.

As the second man moved toward the child, Chagak's mother pushed the girl behind her. The man drew a knife from a scabbard at his waist, then slashed across the woman's breasts and reached for Chagak's sister.

"Aka," Chagak cried. "Please, Aka. No, Aka. Please . . . please."

In one quick movement Chagak's mother scooped the girl into her arms and threw herself and her daughter into the flames that rose from the ulaq roof.

Chagak dropped to her knees. The screams that she had held within her mouth burst out to join the cries of her mother and sister.

A roar of wind blew in from the sea, carrying the flames like orange waves into the sky, and the village was covered with smoke.

Chagak pressed her face to the earth and lay on the ground crying. She clung to the grass as the sea otter clings to the kelp, to keep the waves from pulling her away, to keep the waves from pulling her away.

TWO

Crouched in the tall grass, Chagak waited through the night. She clutched her short-bladed woman's knife, rubbing the smooth driftwood handle against her cheek. If the men came after her, she would kill herself before they reached her.

But finally, when the screams had stopped and the fires glowed only fitfully between the ulas, the men left. Chagak saw them load their ikyan with furs and oil from the village. She watched until they disappeared beyond the cliffs that bordered her people's sheltered bay.

Pain filled Chagak's chest from her belly to the tops of her shoulders, as if one of the attackers had also speared her, as if a knife were lodged within her ribs, cutting deeper each time she moved. And when she could no longer hold in her sorrow, she wept until her body felt dry and hollow, and her face was raw from the wind on her tears.

In the morning a thick fog swirled in around each ulaq, covering the village like a burial robe. Smoke curled up from the fog and carried the stench of burnt flesh.

Chagak watched the village for a long time but saw no movement, and finally she crept down the back of the hill and out of sight of the ulakidaq, then made her way to the top of the south cliff where she could see the beach.

The beach faced east and stretched in a wide bowed-in curve beyond the cliff. It was a good beach of fine silty gravel and many tidal pools where children and old women could gather sea urchins and small fish. The cliffs were a nesting place for auks and puffins, and in the spring Chagak and her friends scaled the cliffs or lowered themselves from the top in rope harnesses to set string traps at the entrances of bird holes or to fill gathering bags with smooth white puffin eggs and the dark-spotted eggs of the guillemot. A reef extended from the beach and in low tide the women paddled out in their large open-topped skin iks to pry chitons from the rocks.

On the brightest days of summer small boys would be at the top of the cliffs, their fathers in ikyan below them. When one of the boys saw a slow-moving sea cow darken the water, he would cry out and the men would guide their slim crafts to where the animal lay. Their spears were tied at the butt end to a long line attached to the side of the ikyan, and when each man had thrown his spear, they pulled the sea cow ashore with their many lines, then called the women to come prepare a feast with the sweet meat, a meat that held its good flavor even when old, even if covered with maggots.

Chagak stretched out on her belly, straightening the crushed grass around her so she was better hidden. She felt more vulnerable in the daylight. Perhaps some of the long-haired men had stayed behind.

The beach seemed to be empty. Chagak could see the lines in the gravel left by the keels of the attackers' ikyan. She waited a long time, afraid to move from the cliff. What if the men had only hidden their boats, what if they waited for those who had escaped them? Surely there were others from her village besides herself who were alive.

Chagak's mouth was dry and she wished she had brought her bag of berries with her. The tops of the cliffs were too rocky to grow anything but rough clumps of sorrel and grass. She cut a handful of the grass and chewed it, hoping to bring some moisture to her mouth, but the grass was rimed with salt and only increased her thirst.

Chagak stayed on the cliff until finally, when the sun was curling down the northwest side of the sky, she made herself get up, made herself walk back toward her village.

As she walked, she began to hope that all

she had seen had been a dream, that when she looked at the village it would be as it had been, each ulaq green with the grass that grew upon its roof; women sitting on the leeward sides sewing; men watching the sea; children running and laughing in their made-up games.

But the smell of smoke still rose with the wind, so when Chagak reached the top of the hill and saw the blackened ruins, she felt no surprise, only the heavy pain of hopelessness.

When she found her berry bag, she scooped a handful of the fruit into her mouth, and when she had sucked out all the juice, she swallowed the pulp. She watched for a long time, alert to any movement, but the only thing that stirred was the spirit of the wind, lifting torn bits of curtains and mats, blackened grass.

Chagak began to wonder if she was alone, if she of all her people was the only one alive. The thought made her shudder and suddenly she was weeping, though she thought she had used all her tears the night before. But though she wept, she began the descent into the village, her woman's knife in one hand, her amulet clasped in the other.

It is not a good sign, Chagak thought, when the first body she found was that of the shaman. He had been killed with a spear or knife, a deep gash in the center of his chest, but the fire had not touched him. The flames had left a circle of unmarked grass around him.

The attackers had not cut the body apart, and Chagak was surprised but glad. When a body was severed at all main joints, the spirit was robbed of its power and could not take revenge, could not help the living. Why had they left the shaman whole? Did they think their power was so much greater than his? Flies had begun to settle on the body and Chagak swatted them away. The shaman's face still held the grimace of his death, and his back was arched as if his spirit had escaped through the hole in his chest, drawing the body up with it as it went.

One of his hands was clasped around a carved staff, a sacred thing passed from one shaman of the village to the next. Slowly Chagak reached for it, ready to draw back if the touch of the thing burned her. For what woman was allowed to have a shaman's staff? But it did not burn her, did not seem to feel any different than other staffs.

Chagak tried to take it from the shaman's hand, but the hand was clasped so tightly, she could not remove the staff.

Hoping his spirit hovered near and would hear, Chagak whispered, "I do not want it for myself, but only to help my people's spirits." But still the shaman held the staff. "How will I bury them?" Chagak asked, the words coming out like a sob. But she turned away, and as she turned, she saw an amulet lying a short distance from the body. Larger than even a hunter's amulet, it was the shaman's greatest source of power. With fingers that shook, Chagak picked it up.

She lifted the amulet above her head and turned to face the mountain Aka.

"You see this," Chagak cried, lifting her voice above the noise of wind and sea. "If you do not want me to have it I will give it back to the shaman."

She watched for some sign, a glint of sun from the mountaintop, a change in the wind, but the mountain gave no sign, and so Chagak slipped the amulet around her neck, feeling some comfort in its weight against her chest, as though another heart beat close to hers.

Chagak wanted to run through the village, to see if by chance Seal Stalker or any members of her family survived. But a spirit could not rest, could not take its place in the joyous dance of the northern lights, until the body was honored, and the shaman should be buried first.

Chagak saw a sleeping mat near the closest ulaq. One end was burned, but the other was whole and strong. She laid it beside the shaman's body and pulled the body onto the mat. Then she began to drag the shaman to the death ulaq at the edge of the village.

The death ulaq was set aside as a home for the dead or any spirits who came to visit the First Men's village. The smoke hole was closed with driftwood logs lashed together in a square, and only the shaman and chief hunter were allowed to open the place to receive the body of one who had died.

Chagak had always avoided the death ulaq, never taking a path that led close to it, but with the amulet she knew she had some protection.

The shaman's body was heavy, and she could move him only a few steps before stopping to rest, but Chagak was strong, used to carrying a full water skin each morning from the fresh-water stream near the village.

She worked until, even in the cold wind, she was hot. Smoke tainted the air, and each breath seemed to add to Chagak's burden, but finally she had the shaman at the top of the ulaq. She pulled the cover from the opening and clasped the shaman's amulet, wondering what the spirits might do to her since she, a woman, dared to open the place, but then she thought, Which is worse, leaving my people without burial, or using this place of the dead? And the thought calmed her fears.

Chagak had no death mat in which to wrap

the shaman's body, no sacred herbs to anoint him, so she began the chant she heard at every death, a chant of pleading to Aka, a prayer of strength for the departed spirit. Then she rolled the shaman near the door and let him drop inside.

She fitted the heavy lid in place and looked back toward her village. From this side of the ulakidaq, more bodies were visible, mostly men, some burned beyond recognition. And suddenly Chagak felt a great need to find her father and Seal Stalker. What if they had escaped? What if their bodies were not here among the dead?

She went slowly from body to body. She was growing used to the smell of the dead, used to the stench that seemed to settle at the back of her throat, but often when seeing uncle or aunt, cousin or friend, she had to look away, hurry to the next body.

She found Seal Stalker's younger brother and, taking time from her search, also dragged him to the top of the death ulaq. He had eight or nine summers and so was not as heavy as the shaman, but Chagak's grief seemed to add weight to his body.

At the death ulaq, she again repeated the chants and lowered the body into the musty darkness. But after sealing the ulaq, Chagak realized the sun was near setting, and the thought of being in the village during the short, dark night quickened Chagak's heart.

Who could say what all the spirits might do? By now each should have been given some sacred rite, a good burial, but she had buried only two. How many people had been in her village? Three tens? Four tens?

"I cannot bury them all," she cried to Aka. "Do not ask me to bury them all. There are too many."

But then the thought came: Use each ulaq as a death ulaq. There are too many bodies for one ulaq.

And so, under the setting sun, Chagak went first to her father's ulaq.

The notched log that served as ladder to the interior was badly burned and so Chagak lowered herself with her arms, finally dropping to the floor below. She groped in the darkness until she found an oil lamp, then, using the moss, flint and fire stone she kept in a packet at her waist, she struck the stones together until a spark lighted the fluff of moss and started the circle of wicks. Most of the oil in the shallow stone basin of the lamp was gone, but there was enough to keep the fire going until Chagak could pull a storage skin from the cache in the wall. Nothing in the cache had burned, and as Chagak poured more oil into the lamp, and the wick flames grew stronger, she was surprised to see that, though the ulaq walls were darker than normal and some of the curtains had burned, little in the ulaq was damaged.

She searched the curtained sleeping rooms of the ulaq, wondering if by some chance a member of her family had escaped the fire. In her father's sleeping place at the back of the ulaq, Chagak saw a shape huddled against the back wall, and recognizing one of her brothers, Chagak cried out in joy, but then she saw that, though his body bore no marks of spear or burning, he, like all the people of the village, was dead, his eyes and mouth open to allow escape of the spirit, his belly already bloating.

What strange power did fire possess? Chagak wondered. How could it draw spirits from people without touching them? Did it take the breath, stop the heart, steal the blood?

Chagak set the lamp on the floor and rolled a sleeping mat around her brother's body, then laid him on the furs of her father's bed. This brother had been her favorite, his dark eyes always sparking with the mischief of a joke. Already, though he had only six summers, he had taken his first puffin, speared it with a small harpoon their father had made him. Chagak's mother had prepared a feast to honor the kill. They had all been together then, her mother and father, the aunt and uncle who lived with them in the ulaq, even Chagak's grandfather, who had died at the beginning of summer.

Again Chagak sang the death chant, filling the ulaq with the sound of her people's sacred song, and still chanting, she stacked bundles of scorched furs to reach the roof hole. Outside, she found the charred bodies of her mother and sister and pulled them into the ulaq, carried them, one at a time, to her father's sleeping place, not caring that the black of their bodies ruined the feathers of her suk.

The next time Chagak left the ulaq, she took one of her father's hunting lamps, for the sun had set and darkness filled the spaces between the ulas.

She remembered where her oldest brother had been thrown and found him there, eyes open in death, his chest dark with dried blood. She dragged him into the ulaq and laid him in her father's sleeping place.

Chagak walked through the village that night, finally finding her uncle and aunt and her father. She dragged each body to the ulaq and wrapped each in furs or mats.

When she no longer had the strength to climb from the ulaq, Chagak lay down next to the opening of her father's sleeping place and slept.

THREE

When Chagak awoke, her first thought was of finishing Seal Stalker's sleeping mats. But then she remembered, and with the remembering came a darkness that made her want to escape back to sleep. She began to tremble. Her hands felt too light for her body, her arms and legs too heavy, her chest so full of her sorrow that there was no room for anything else.

She rolled from her sleeping furs and relit several of the oil lamps. Then she dug up some of the eggs she and her mother had buried in sand and oil at the bottom of the food cache, and she made herself eat.

The food seemed to carry the taste of ashes, and Chagak gagged, but she knew she would not have strength to finish the burials unless she ate. She closed her eyes and thought of green hills, the wind that blew from the sea, and when she had eaten two eggs, she left the ulaq.

The night before, she had not been able to find her baby brother, though she was sure where her mother had thrown him. Now in the daylight she searched again but still found nothing. Fear began to grow, wedging itself into her pain.

Storytellers told of people who took children from other tribes to raise as their own. Especially sons. Perhaps her brother was not dead. Perhaps the attackers had taken him and would raise him to be like them.

It would be better if Pup were dead, Chagak thought, and for a time she sat at the top of her father's ulaq, doing nothing. But then it seemed as though the spirits of the dead called to her, and she left the ulaq to finish what she had begun the day before.

Chagak dragged bodies, chanted death prayers, and tried not to gag in the stench and the flies. The birds were the greatest problem. Gulls swooped and cried, trying to peck at death wounds and open eyes.

When the dim yellow sun lay at the top of the sky, Chagak found Seal Stalker.

At first she did not recognize him. His face was swollen and covered with blood from a neck wound, his belly slit from chest to groin, but then something deep within her brought forth a mourning cry and pushed it from her mouth, even as she looked at the body.

Seal Stalker gripped a spear in one hand. Another body lay nearby, the body of a stranger. There was a bloody wound in the man's shoulder and another at the center of his chest. His feet were painted black and he wore a parka of fur seal and lemming skins, yet it was not decorated in the manner of any tribe Chagak knew, not the traders who called themselves Walrus Men nor her mother's people, the Whale Hunters. Perhaps he was of the Caribou People, a distant tribe the Walrus Men sometimes spoke about. But why would caribou hunters leave their home to come to islands in the sea? The Caribou People were not traders. They knew nothing of ikyan or sea animals. And were not the Caribou People tall and light-skinned? This man was short and his skin, though discolored by death, was dark.

She looked at both men. Seal Stalker, the man she was to marry, and this stranger, an evil man. "They killed each other," Chagak said aloud to the wind, to spirits that might be near.

Had her people done anything to these men? Why had they come killing and stealing? Chagak took her woman's knife from the sheath she wore under her suk and began to slice through the dead man's joints. But each cut also seemed to add to Chagak's pain, as though her knife carried two blades, one for the enemy, one for her spirit.

Chagak dragged Seal Stalker's body to her

father's ulaq. She put him in her father's sleeping place, wrapped him in one of the grass mats she had made for him and washed the blood from his face and neck.

And when she had finished, it seemed as though she had no more energy to work, no desire to leave the ulaq. It was a large ulaq, large enough for the spirits of all her family and her own spirit.

Chagak was old enough to remember when her father had built the ulaq. He and several of the village men had spent three or four days digging an oval pit in the side of the hill. She and her mother and aunts and grandmother had hauled clay from the edge of a stream, worked it with just enough water to make it pliable, then plastered the clay over the dirt and stone floor. They had smoothed and leveled and packed the earth with their feet, all the time laughing and singing, listening to tales her grandmother told.

A whale had washed ashore earlier that summer and the chief hunter gave Chagak's father permission to use the jawbones as the center rafters for the roof. The men lined the walls of the pit with huge rocks and packed dirt around them. With the stones and driftwood logs as support, they set the whalebone rafters, then smaller driftwood rafters, in place. The women wove willow through the rafters and helped the men finish the ulaq roof with sod and thatching.

Chagak looked up at the light coming in the roof hole. There was still time enough to bury others, but Chagak thought, I am too tired. Surely the spirits will understand.

For a long time she sat in the main room of the ulaq, blocking thoughts from her mind, not even lighting oil lamps when light no longer came through the open roof hole. It had been a difficult day. Most of the bodies were cared for, only a few left to take inside, only a few more chants and mourning songs to sing.

Tomorrow I will finish, she promised herself. Then a thought came to her, something that had first come when she saw Seal Stalker's body: I, too, should be dead. What joy was there in living alone? She would never be a wife, never bear children. She would live in fear of spirits, in fear of strangers. And how could one person stand alone against the powers of earth and sky? It would be better to be dead.

And so that night, as Chagak lay in her sleeping place, she thought of death and the many ways she might die.

The next morning Chagak buried the last three bodies, and only the man Seal Stalker had killed was left to be eaten by birds, left to rot.

Chagak spent another portion of the day gathering any weapons she could find. There were few, not enough for all the hunters of her tribe. The attackers must have taken weapons with them when they left, Chagak thought, but it would not be good for the men of her tribe to be without weapons in the next world. How would they hunt?

Chagak spent much time in the storage places of the ulas, taking any weapons she could find, finally giving small-bladed crooked knives and burins, obsidian and hammerstones to the men for whom she had no spears. Perhaps they could make their own weapons.

It was time then for Chagak's death. She prepared herself carefully, first eating a good meal, then washing her face and hands in the still water of a tidal pool. The spirit image that looked back at her from the pool looked old and tired, not like Chagak, a girl newly a woman having lived thirteen summers.

She combed out the tangles in her hair and, taking off her suk, washed her arms and breasts. The suk was nearly ruined. The lifting and dragging of bodies had broken many of the feathers and blood dulled the sheen of those left, but she washed off the blood and straightened the feathers. Last, she washed her woman's knife and rubbed the blade with the shaman's amulet she still wore around her neck.

44

There were some things she needed for this death, and so she began a search of ulas, taking the necessary supplies: a lamp to guide her to her family, clean sleeping furs, a seal stomach of oil, and another of food. She did not know how many days it would take her, traveling alone, to find the Dancing Lights.

She crowded all her supplies into her sleeping place. Then she sat down, her woman's knife in her right hand, ready to cut the pulsing arteries of her neck. In her left hand she held a basket to catch the blood.

But then she felt a stirring within, a need as great as any need she had known, to once again feel the wind, to hear the sea, to have the sun on her face. And so she left the bowl and knife and climbed from the ulaq.

Chagak walked the beach, and in the midst of her sorrow she felt a gladness that she had given herself one last time to see the world, to hear the long sad cry of loons, the high-pitched *kik-kik-kik* of terns.

She began to sing, first songs of comfort, lullabies sung to her when she was a child, then, after the lullabies, songs of mourning, death chants for herself. Finally, as the sun was dimmed by clouds and a cold wind moved in from the sea, Chagak left the beach and returned to her father's ulaq.

She had climbed to the ulaq roof when she

heard a faint sound coming from the hill above the village, a sound as if someone besides her were mourning, as if another cry were being raised by one still living.

A child? How could a child survive the two, nearly three days since the attack? But a hope grew so large within her that it pushed up into her throat so she could not even call out. She moved toward the cry, listening carefully, always moving toward the sound, and finally made her way to the top of the hill.

First she saw only the woman's body — Black Wing — an old woman, someone who lived with a grown grandson, someone who would perhaps had given herself to the mountain in the next winter, thus leaving more food for her family. The woman was not long dead. She lay on her side, the body not swollen, the flies just beginning to settle in the eyes and mouth.

She wore a fur seal suk, something she had no doubt prepared as a death garment, the suk too finely decorated to be practical for everyday wear. Feathers and shells hung in wide zigzag patterns down the sides and around the sleeves; patches of different furs — browns, golds, blacks and whites — made a checkered design at collar rim, cuffs and hem.

Had Black Wing made the cries? Or perhaps it had been the call of gulls. Had Chagak, not wanting to be alone, imagined that bird cries were human?

Chagak sighed and thought of the long, difficult trip back to the village. Another body to put in a ulaq. She turned to go back down the hill to get the sea lion skin she had used to put under the bodies that had been some distance from a ulaq.

But when she was halfway down the hill she heard the cry again and she was sure it was not a bird.

She ran to the top of the hill and this time she turned Black Wing's body over. There was a bulge under the old woman's suk and again the weak cry.

"A baby," Chagak whispered and her heart quickened, beating so hard she could feel the pulse of it at her temples.

She reached inside the suk and pulled out the baby. It was Pup.

"I thought they had taken you," Chagak said. Then her legs were suddenly weak, and she dropped to her knees. And as though she had found her brother dead, not alive, sobs began to rip through Chagak's body, so deep and hard, it seemed they would pull Chagak's spirit from her chest. She clutched the baby to her breast and through her tears said to Black Wing, "You are a brave mother. Grandmother to all our people."

Chagak put Pup under her suk, cradling him in her arms as she walked back to her father's ulaq.

She laid him on a fur seal skin and cleaned his body with seal oil. There were berry stains on his lips, and whenever Chagak's fingers came close to his mouth, he tried to suck. In the four months since his birth, he had grown fat and round, but now he seemed smaller, his legs and arms as thin as they had been at his birth.

Chagak wrapped the lower half of the baby's body in moss and wads of seal fur, then bundled him in a sealskin, fur side in.

She chewed a piece of dried seal meat until it was soft, then, mixing it with water, made a paste and let the baby suck it from her fingertips. He ate slowly, and Chagak gave him frequent sips of water, though at first he choked since she gave him the water from the edge of a shell bowl. But finally he seemed content and so Chagak laid him in his cradle, the wooden-framed hammock that hung from the rafters over their mother's sleeping place.

When her brother slept, Chagak returned for Black Wing's body. She could find no wound, and so decided that the woman had died from sorrow and her great age. Chagak dragged the body to her father's ulaq, for though the distance to her father's ulaq was greater than to Black Wing's, Chagak saw the woman as part of her family now. Somehow Black Wing had found Pup and hidden him from the killers. It was right that she had a place with Chagak's family. They would care for her as she had cared for their youngest child.

FOUR

And now what is the best thing? Chagak wondered as she lay in her sleeping place that night. I cannot die and leave Pup alone, but should I try to live without our people?

What can I offer my brother? Who will teach him to hunt? Men who were neither hunters nor shamans earned no honor in the next world.

She had no right to end her brother's life, no right to send him to the spirit world, but perhaps the decision was not hers. Perhaps it was one that could be made by her parents.

The next morning, after feeding Pup, Chagak laid him back in his cradle and hung it in her father's sleeping place. Then Chagak left the ulaq.

During that long day she sat outside on the ulaq roof, giving the spirits of her family time to come and take her brother.

She did nothing but watch the sea and listen to her own thoughts. Why sew if she and Pup would soon die? Why gather sea urchins? Why weave?

But in the middle of that day Chagak realized that a part of her hoped the spirits would not take Pup, and she asked herself, Why do I want to live?

Guilt pulled at Chagak's soul, and she said aloud to the wind and any spirits that might hear, "I do not choose my life or death; my parents choose. If Pup dies, I, too, will die. If he lives . . ." She looked at the burned ruin of her village, smelled the stench of death that was beginning to leak from each ulaq.

She could not raise Pup here. This was a village of the dead. Besides, the attackers knew this beach and might return to kill survivors. She could find another beach, but she could not raise Pup without a man to teach him to hunt.

It will be best to go to my grandfather, Chagak thought. He was an important man, chief hunter of the First Men tribe known as Whale Hunters. Chagak had never been to the Whale Hunters' village, but several times her grandfather had visited their village and stayed in her father's ulaq.

Chagak had always been excited by his visits, had strutted proudly in front of the other girls her age. Their grandfathers lived with them in their own ulas; their grandfathers were only seal hunters, not chiefs of the fierce and proud Whale Hunter tribe. But she did not tell them that, though her grandfather always brought gifts for her brothers and told them hunting stories, he never even looked at Chagak or Chagak's sister, never brought them gifts, never told them stories.

So, Chagak thought, if I go to my grandfather, he may not want me. But perhaps he would want Pup, and it would be better for Pup there, with the Whale Hunters, better than on this beach with the spirits of the dead and a sister who could not teach him to hunt.

If Pup lived, perhaps their father's spirit would see the importance of Pup staying with the Whale Hunters and so would guide Chagak to her grandfather's village.

Pup's cry interrupted Chagak's thoughts, but she clasped her hands together and made herself sit still. She knew he might be hungry, but there was a chance that the spirits had come for him and that Pup was afraid of them. When his cries stopped, Chagak wanted to go into the ulaq, wanted to see if he was dead. But she made herself stay outside.

The grief that lay heavy within her chest seemed to wedge itself deeper into her spirit, and a sudden urge to cry made Chagak angry with herself.

Why do I cry? she asked. It is better if he is with our mother. And soon I will not be alone, but with all the people of my village. And so she stopped her tears, but they seemed to gather at the back of her throat, quivering there like drops of water at the edge of a leaf.

Finally, after the sun had peaked, she went inside. She looked into all the dark corners of the ulaq but saw no spirits. She had left the roof hole open to let in light and so did not light any lamps. When she walked across the ulaq to her father's room, she walked softly, as though her family were asleep.

She opened the door flap, and the fetid air made her hold her breath as she untied Pup's cradle from the rafters, but when she lowered the cradle, she tipped it toward herself and suddenly Pup began to cry.

The cry surprised her and she nearly dropped the cradle, and in that moment of dropping and catching, the tears that had hidden themselves in her throat moved up into her eyes and Chagak began to sob. For the first time since the death of her village, she felt some reason to live through the coming day.

It took Chagak three days to repair an ik the attackers had broken. The frame was undamaged, but the sea lion skin covering had been cut in many places.

Chagak took skins from another ik, even from the men's ikyan, to repair the boat. She sealed all her carefully sewn double seams with fat, then oiled the sea lion skins to keep water out.

She had found one of her mother's baby slings and wore it under her suk so she could carry Pup with her as she worked. The wide band of leather went over one shoulder and across her back. The baby lay against Chagak's chest, his head and back supported by the strap.

Chagak cut the neck opening in her suk a little larger, for since she was not a mother her suk had not been made with extra room for a baby.

When the ik was repaired, Chagak filled it with supplies: seal stomach containers of oil and water, baskets filled with dried meat and roots, two small hunter's lamps and moss wicks, mats, awls and needles.

She packed two extra paddles, knives and her mother's flat cooking stone, cutters, scrapers and packs of furs and grass mats. She also put in Pup's cradle, though while traveling in the ik she would keep him under her suk.

She would wear her father's chigadax, a waterproof hooded parka made of seal intestines, the garment a good protection against the sea.

But, as Chagak worked, doubts pulled at her mind. Perhaps it was wrong to take Pup from the island. She knew little of the sea. She had been given little training in paddling an ik, and even the small ik she had chosen to repair would be difficult for one person to control. What if she could not find her grandfather's village? What if she and Pup drowned? Would they find their way to the Dancing Lights?

"Perhaps our mother misses you," Chagak said to Pup. "Perhaps I should give the spirits another chance to claim you."

Chagak carried her brother back to the ulaq. Inside, it was dark but Chagak did not light an oil lamp. She walked slowly across the ulaq's big room and laid the baby at the door of her father's sleeping place. She placed her hands on Pup's belly and began to speak, her words echoing strangely in the empty room. "Father, here is your son. I want to take him with me to the Whale Hunters' village. I will raise him to be a good man. I will help him make an ikyak and tell him about our village. But if you think it is best for him to go to the spirit world with you, I ask you to take him now."

Her brother had lain still as she spoke, but when Chagak rose, leaving him on the bare floor, he began to wail. Chagak did not pick him up, did not look back as she climbed outside.

She stayed at the top of the ulaq, squatting on her heels, waiting, keeping all hope from her heart. Why try to influence spirits with hope? She cleared all thoughts from her mind, except for simple things like the color of the sea and the number of bird holes in the cliff. She tried not to hear her brother's cries.

Chagak did not know when she fell asleep, but when she awoke it was midafternoon. Pup was still crying.

Chagak climbed down into the ulaq. This time she did not try to see spirits in the darkness but hurried to where Pup lay, picked him up and held him close to her. She rocked him until he stopped crying, then slipped him under her suk and fitted the carrying sling around his small body.

Chagak began to sing a quiet song of thanksgiving and was surprised to find that her voice was weak with tears. Before she left the ulaq, she whispered, "We go now. Protect us. Please protect us."

FIVE

The paddle had become a part of her as had the rhythm of the waves. Chagak had been fortunate; the sea remained calm, the waves either giant swells or a quick, shallow chop.

When she looked back at her village, she saw that new green plants were already covering the scars left by the fire. So Chagak knew that, in spite of the killing, plant spirits still hovered thick and strong around every ulaq. And if Chagak could look back from the sea and mark the place of each ulaq by the green of plants, perhaps her people, looking back from the Dancing Lights, would also recognize their village by the green mounds of its ulas.

Once she saw the spouting of a whale. A whale was a sign of favor, but something within her could not rejoice. What favor could a whale give — new parents, a husband, her village whole and unburned? Even if the animal chose to cast itself on the beach, Chagak could not flense it without help.

In the moments after sighting the animal, Chagak nearly turned her ik back to her village. Why did she think that she, a woman alone, could ever find a place for herself and her brother? Why would her grandfather want them? An infant and a woman, two more for his hunters to feed.

But she continued to paddle west and, at the end of the first day, reached the point of Aka's island and the strait where north sea joined south. She paddled her ik to shore and pulled it high above the tide line.

The hunters of her village said that the waters of the cold north sea and those of the south sea used the strait as a place of battle. The south sea fought to flow north and the north sea fought to flow south. The battle had been since the beginning of time, they said, each sea strong enough to hold its place, neither strong enough to defeat the other.

The waters of the strait and even the wet sand under Chagak's bare feet seemed suddenly cold, and the wind coming from the north sea made her shiver. It was nearly a winter wind, though winter was months away, and reminded her of stories she had heard about a land at the ice edges of the world where snow piled as high as a man standing, and the people made their ulas out of ice. Chagak shuddered and drew her knees closer to her chest.

Perhaps she was too close to that place, she thought. But no, she told herself. I have traveled only one day. It is a year's travel to the edge of the world. And besides, who could believe snow grew so deep? Winter brought wind and icy rain, but only enough snow to weigh down the grass, to cover the low-growing mossberries. Then the rain came and left the ground bare until the next snow.

She wrapped her arms around Pup, felt him warm against her chest, then glanced up at the sky. The sun under its shield of heavy clouds was only a brightness in the northwest. "We do not have time to go on," she said aloud to her brother. "It is best if we stay here."

She turned the ik over to check for damage to the underside. Twice rocks had cut the oiled skin, but neither cut broke through.

She lashed down the ik, tying the rawhide ropes to boulders. She oiled the ik, then, opening a pack of supplies, she fed Pup and sliced up bits of dried meat for herself, eating while she cut handfuls of beach grass to make a bed under the ik for the two of them.

Chagak did not sleep well that night. It seemed as if she were in a new world. Even though she could see Aka, she had never slept beside the north sea, did not know the spirits that dwelt within that sea, did not know the proper chants of protection. So most of the night she was awake, singing to Aka, speaking to the spirits of her people, clinging to the shaman's amulet she had brought with her.

SIX

Shuganan speared another blackfish with his three-pronged leister and put the still wriggling fish into the basket at the edge of the stream. The sky was as gray as shale, petrels and black-legged kittiwakes marking the gray with their dark wings. Shuganan straightened and watched the birds, listened to their calls, then began to sing his own chant, something that seemed to keep his mind from the aching of his hands and fingers.

But then he heard the sound of another voice, the rhythm of another chant, cutting through the noise of the surf.

For a moment Shuganan could not move. How long since another person had come to his beach? How many years? He waded from the stream and hid behind a boulder.

He saw an ikyak. No, an ik. Inside, a woman alone. Shuganan's knees began to tremble. He clasped the amulet hung at his neck. Was this the woman the spirits had brought into his dreams?

Yes, Shuganan thought. But another part

of him whispered, This is not real. This, too, is a dream. You think you are on the beach, but you are on your sleeping mats. The spirits merely give you something else to consider. Something else to carve.

He thought of all the carvings, wood and ivory, that lined the walls of his ulaq, and of the unfinished carving he had hung around his neck: a man and his wife.

Shuganan watched as the woman in the ik turned her boat toward his beach. She seemed to travel alone, without other women, without a husband.

When she pulled the ik ashore, Shuganan left his hiding place. If he were in a dream, what harm would it do to help her?

The woman had her back to him, and she was pulling on the stern of the boat, mumbling a song as she pulled.

Shuganan reached out to help, but when he placed his bony hands beside hers on the ik, the woman screamed and jumped away from him. Her fright also startled Shuganan, making his heart squeeze tight into itself, and so at first he could say nothing to her, but finally he held his hands out, palms up, and gave the familiar greeting, "I am a friend. I have no knife."

She stared at him, a wariness in her eyes, but he also saw a tiredness there, and he said,

"The boat is heavy. Let me help you."

But the woman replied, "I am strong."

"Yes," Shuganan said, though to him she did not look strong. She did not even look like a woman, more like a child. But now that he was old, everyone looked young. The hunters who occasionally passed his beach, some distance out on the sea, always looked like boys to him, and so, of course, this woman looked like a girl.

Old eyes see youth everywhere, Shuganan thought. And when he was young, his eyes young, he had seen everything as old.

"I am strong," the girl said again, this time throwing her weight against the ik and pulling it an armlength up the bench.

"If this is your beach," she said, "I will stay only one night." For a moment her voice quavered, and Shuganan felt the echo of that trembling within his spirit. He looked at her more closely. She carried a great weight of sorrow, this woman-child. He could see it in her eyes, in the curve of her mouth. And already he began to see the planes of her face, the arch of her brows, the fine, sharp lines of her cheekbones carved in ivory.

"You may stay here," he said to her. "This is a good place. Safe."

The girl nodded and leaned against the side of the ik. She scanned the beach and Shuganan watched her, watched as her eyes stopped at the marks of high tide, at the rocks that bordered a fresh-water spring. And he also noticed the bulge under her suk. The form of a child, still quite small.

"Where is your village?" she asked.

"There is no village," Shuganan answered. "Only my ulaq."

"Your wife and children."

"I have no children."

"You do not care if I stay one night on your beach?" she asked. "I need to sleep."

"As long as you want," Shuganan said. "You and your baby."

At his words, the girl's eyes widened and she crossed her hands over the child.

"Where is your husband?"

She moved to face the sea and said, "He is there. Out there. Soon he will come for me." And looking back at Shuganan, she added, "He is very strong."

But her words were thin, as fragile as new ice webbed over the edge of a tidal pool, and so Shuganan knew the truth. The woman had no husband, and somehow that was part of her sorrow.

"If it would not make him angry," Shuganan said carefully, "you and your child may stay in my ulaq tonight."

But the woman shook her head.

"Then make your camp. I will bring you food."

"I have food."

"Then we will have a feast."

Chagak watched as the old man hobbled slowly up the rise of the beach. For some reason she was no longer afraid of him. He seemed to have the wisdom of a shaman but not a shaman's fierce, demanding ways.

She unloaded the ik and carried her supplies into the grass above the tide line. She pulled the ik to a flat, sandy place and turned it over, staking ropes into the ground and wrapping the ik so the wind would not blow it away. She stacked furs to make a sheltered corner under the boat.

She would not gather driftwood. She was too tired to tend a fire, to watch that it did not spread to the ik or her supplies.

She had spent the day fighting the sea, trying to force her ik west to her grandfather's island, but the winds worked against her, and finally she turned the ik north and followed the nearest island's coast until she found a cove, a place to wait until the wind again died and she could paddle west.

The cove was wide and shallow, dipping in toward cliffs that curled around the back of the beach. It was a shale beach, a good place to land an ik, a good place to make a camp, the shale easier to sleep on, easier to walk on, than round stones. A large tidal pool marked the center of the beach and a stream made a looping path from the fresh-water spring to the sea.

It would be a good place to live, Chagak thought. She could see why the old man had chosen it. But it worried her that he had no village. Sometimes spirits lived alone and pretended to be men. This old man — who could say what he was, why he lived here?

Using her fire stones, Chagak lit an oil lamp. It would give a little warmth. Perhaps enough for this night.

She unstrapped her brother from her chest, quickly wrapping him in sealskins as she pulled him from the warmth of her suk.

For the past two days he had been quiet, sleeping often, crying less. And now, as she laid him down, he did not even awaken. A tight edge of worry pushed into her mind, but she busied herself making a thin paste with water and meat.

She dipped her fingers into the mixture and put them in the baby's mouth.

He did not open his eyes, but he began to suck, and Chagak fed him until the paste was gone. She put the baby back under her suk, lay down under the ik and waited for the old man. She left out her grass bag of dried meat, the only thing she could offer him, and hoped he would not eat much.

The long, light evening was nearly past when the old man returned to the beach. A skin bag hung from each of his arms, and he carried a thin slab of shale with a steaming section of halibut laid out on it. Chagak was tired, wanting only to sleep, but she smiled at the man and thanked him. She stood to take the fish and then waited as he seated himself in the sand.

He slipped the bags from his arms and opened them. One was full of berries, the other of cooked bitterroot, the tiny bulblets something better served with rich oily seal meat, but also good with fish.

The old man broke off a section of the fish and handed it to her. The warmth of the food was good after a day in the cold spray of the sea. The man was watching her, and his watching made Chagak uncomfortable, so she said, "You must eat, too," and pointed toward her bag of dried meat.

He nodded and, fumbling through the bag, took a small piece of meat and began to eat.

"Your wife makes good food," Chagak finally said.

The man shook his head, swallowed and answered, "I live alone. My wife has been dead for many years."

Chagak waited, thinking he would say more, but he did not.

He was not a small man, though he was so stooped that he stood no taller than Chagak. His hair was thick and white and hung to his shoulders. His parka was make of puffin skins, and he wore the feathers turned in, but in the seams between the skins she saw that stitches were uneven, feathers sometimes caught in the sewing — something even an old woman would not do.

His hands were the large-boned hands of a hunter, but the joints were swollen, and his fingers, bent at odd angles, made Chagak think of pain.

He ate slowly, smiling and nodding often though he said nothing, but when they had finished eating, the old man said, "You may sleep in my ulaq tonight. It is warm, and if a storm comes, you and your child will be safe."

At the mention of a storm, Chagak stood and looked at the sky. All things seemed normal, the sky a smooth dome of gray. The sea showed no high caps of white, telling of wind coming from a distance. She was uneasy about going to the man's ulaq. She knew nothing about him except that he seemed to live alone. And a man alone was someone the spirits might control — for good or for evil.

"The sea is calm," she said.

"Storms come quickly from my mountain Tugix," the old man answered.

Chagak turned toward the white-capped peaks, trying to see if the wind pulled snow in long wisps from the mountaintop.

"If the wind gets strong," she finally said, seeing nothing unusual on the mountain, "I will come to your ulaq."

"You will not find your way in the dark."

"Then show me now and I will remember."

She walked with him up the beach and down a worn path to a small green mound that protruded from the side of a hill.

"There," he said, pointing.

"I will come if the wind starts," Chagak said.

Shuganan sat inside his ulaq, waiting. He had lit all the lamps and had laid fur seal skins in one of the curtained sleeping places. He hoped the storm would not come that night. It would be better for the woman if she did not have to find his ulaq in the darkness, but he knew Tugix.

Storms formed at her peaks, mist gathering until rain and wind scoured the beach. Today Shuganan had noticed the shimmering of the air near the mountain, a sign of spirits moving, and so he waited now to see if the storm would come.

Shuganan had dug his ulaq into the side of a hill and often, when he sat inside, he felt Tugix shake the earth. Sometimes she shook gently as a mother rocks her child, but other times she moved in anger, making dirt and moss fall from the driftwood rafters.

But since coming to this beach Shuganan had always considered Tugix a friend, a protector.

Once, while still a young man, he had climbed high up the side of the mountain and had brought back a small rock no larger than his hand. Each night for many nights he had used another stone to chip the rock into the shape of a man.

When it was finished Shuganan had tied a cord around the top of the head and hung it from a rafter in the main room of his ulaq.

As Shuganan had hoped, the little man still carried some portion of Tugix's spirit. Hanging at the top of the ulaq, the little man moved each time Tugix moved. Sometimes when Shuganan felt no trembling of the earth, heard no rumbling from the mountain, he saw the little man move and knew that Tugix's spirits were troubled.

So Shuganan sat carving a bit of ivory and watched the little man. The little man would be the first to tell of Tugix's storm.

★ ★ ★

Shuganan had not meant to sleep, and he did not know what woke him, but he realized that the wind had grown strong, loud enough for the sound to carry through the thick ulaq walls. And the little man was making a strange and jerking dance.

Shuganan's first thought was to go to the beach, to bring the woman and her baby back with him to the safety of the ulaq, but then the thought came, This is a dream. The woman is a dream.

But something was pushing from within his spirit, telling Shuganan to go, telling him the woman needed him. He rose slowly to his feet, surprised that for once the action brought little pain. Then he thought, Why not? This is a dream.

Dreams often left out some true part of life. Perhaps this time the thing forgotten was pain.

Shuganan pulled on his sealskin boots. The thick, ridged sea lion hide was hard and stiff on his feet. He climbed the notched log to the roof hole, then went out into the storm.

SEVEN

Chagak held onto the ik and tried to keep the wind from tearing it loose. Her arms ached and sharp pains cut down from her shoulders into her back. Pup, slung under her suk, had begun to make small, gasping cries.

Sand and pieces of shale blew into the ik and layered up against the piles of furs around her.

"Aka, Aka, please stop," Chagak begged, but the island belonged to Tugix, not Aka, and the wind took Chagak's words so she could hear nothing but the crash of the sea.

Then for a moment the wind eased, and Chagak shifted her grip on the edge of the ik. A crack like the sound of stone splitting came from the mountain. Chagak screamed and the wind ripped the ik from her hands, sending it end over end across the beach.

Closing her eyes against the stinging sand, Chagak began to crawl toward the old man's ulaq.

A sudden clattering of shale made Chagak turn her head into the wind, and one of the sharp-edged stones, skittering across the

71

beach, struck her in the mouth. She tasted blood on her lips and for a moment stopped, crouching on her knees. She covered her head with her arms, but then she felt a gentle touch, something not carried by the wind.

Chagak looked up to see the old man standing over her. His presence seemed to give Chagak strength, and when he reached down to help her, she was able to stand.

"Come with me," he said, and Chagak wondered how she could hear his quiet words above the noise of the storm.

Together they battled the wind, and when they came to the ulaq, the old man scrambled to the top, then helped Chagak up.

Inside, Chagak leaned against the notched climbing log and wiped the sand from her face. Her eyes felt scratched and swollen, and she blinked several times before she could see in the brightly lit ulaq.

Then she gasped and covered her mouth with both hands. Five shelves circled the ulaq, and every shelf was crowded with images of birds, fish, people and animals. They glowed in the light from the oil lamps, some of the animals smooth, golden like a walrus tusk that has been washed in from the sea. Others were white or gray, with feathers, hair or clothing detailed in fine designs. None of them were larger than a man's hand, yet to Chagak's eyes they seemed alive, watching her, watching her from the ulaq walls.

The old man followed her gaze and chuckled.

Chagak backed toward the climbing log, but he laid his hand on her arm and said, "Do not be afraid. They are only wood or bone; some are ivory."

"They have spirits?" Chagak asked.

"Yes, each holds some bit of spirit. Why else would I carve them?"

"You made them?"

The old man threw back his head and laughed. "This beach is a lonely place. What would I have done without my small animals? They are my friends. They will not hurt you."

He motioned to a floor mat beside an oil lamp, and when Chagak sat down, he asked, "You have the baby?"

The question made Chagak suddenly realize how long Pup had been quiet, and she slipped off her suk and pulled the child from his carrying sling. He whimpered but did not cry, his eyes focusing for a moment on Chagak's face, then wandering toward the brightest oil lamp. Chagak smiled, but when she looked up at the old man, he was frowning, his eyes on her chest.

"You are not the mother?" he asked.

Chagak looked down at her small, pink-nippled breasts. They were not full and hanging like the breasts of a new mother.

"His sister," she answered.

"He is sick," the man said.

"No, he is not sick," answered Chagak. A wave of dread made her shiver, and though the ulaq was warm, she reached for her suk and pulled it on again.

"Yes, he is sick," the old man said. He hobbled to a niche in one wall and pulled out a bag of something dried. "Caribou leaves," he said and, taking out several pieces, placed them in the bottom of a wooden cup. He filled a leather pouch with water from a seal stomach hung from the rafters, then held the pouch over the flame of an oil lamp.

Chagak waited, her arms tucked around Pup. Caribou leaves were good medicine but were difficult to find. The old man would not give her something so precious unless Pup were truly sick.

The baby's weight against her chest seemed to match the heaviness Chagak carried within, and she began to rock back and forth. Perhaps the old man was right. Perhaps her brother was sick. Had he cried harder before? Had he smiled more often and slept less?

During the two days' traveling Chagak had tried to block out all thoughts of her family. Otherwise she could not paddle, could not even rise from her sleeping mats in the morning, and now, thinking back, she found it difficult to remember how Pup had acted before their village was destroyed.

Chagak began to hum a lullaby, the song as much for her comfort as for Pup's. What did babies do? They could not talk or walk. And Pup already smiled. But how long since she had seen him smile? How long since he had laughed?

The old man brought the cup of caribou leaf tea to Chagak. She dipped her fingers into the pungent liquid and placed them near the baby's mouth. He turned his head away, but she pressed his lips open with her thumb and dripped the tea down his throat. He began to suck weakly at her fingertips, and slowly, drop by drop, Chagak emptied the cup.

When the baby finished, his eyelids fluttered, then closed, and Chagak pressed him to her breast. The fear he would die and the hope he would live churned with such force within her that even her breathing hurt.

The old man sat down beside her and, holding his hands out toward the baby, said, "Let me see him."

For a moment Chagak clung tightly to the infant. She was afraid of what the old man might find, afraid that even the small hope she carried would be pulled from her, but then she handed him the child.

He laid Pup on the floor and unwrapped the sealskin that bound him. The baby winced and moved his legs in quick jerks. The old man's hands moved over the tiny body, pressing against joints, belly and head. Finally he looked up at Chagak and asked, "Has the child been dropped?"

An image of her mother throwing the baby over the side of the ulaq came to Chagak's mind, the sight of flames and long-haired men killing her people.

"Yes," she said, but her throat tightened and the word came out as a sob.

"A child's bones are very soft," the old man said. "Something like a fish's bones. They bend instead of breaking." He wrapped the baby, tucking the skin carefully around the small body, then picked up the child and cradled him in his arms. "A baby will survive a fall that might kill a man, but sometimes, even if the child lives, there is damage." His eyes moved to Chagak's eyes and she saw the sadness there, and something within her seemed to tear open, spilling out the pain she had kept away from herself during the long days of paddling.

"Is there anything I can do for him?" Chagak asked, and her voice seemed small and far away, as though someone else had spoken from another part of the ulaq.

"Rock him. Comfort him."

The old man handed her the baby, the tiny form so familiar to Chagak's arms that he seemed a part of her.

"He will die?" she asked, unable to look at the old man when she asked the question.

He did not answer, and Chagak looked up at him, saw the answer in his eyes and began to weep. And in her weeping the story of her people seemed to flow from her mouth as the tears flowed from her eyes, one releasing the other.

"I was in the hills, gathering grass for weaving," she whispered, not caring whether the man heard her or not. Her words were for the many animals on the shelves around her, for the eyes that stared at her from the shadows of the ulaq, as if these spirits needed to know what had happened. "I do not know who they were. Not Whale Hunters or traders. Twenty, maybe thirty, men with long hair. They were burning our ulakidaq. I do not know why.

"My mother came out of the ulaq. A man caught her. She had my brother in her arms." Chagak shook her head as tears disjointed her words. "She threw my brother over the edge of the ulaq. But there was a fire . . . a huge fire in the ulaq's thatching. The man cut my mother with his spear. To get away from him she and my sister jumped into the fire. . . ." Chagak's voice broke.

She felt a hand on her head, heard a soft murmuring. First she thought the old man was chanting, but then she realized he was saying, "More deaths. I should not have tried to hide from them. They will destroy forever."

Chagak looked at him through her tears, saw the sudden veiling of his eyes.

"You and your brother are the only survivors?" he asked quickly.

"Yes," Chagak said, taking up her story as though she had not heard the old man's mumbled words. "I would have died, too, if Pup had not been alive. I would have gone with my people to the Dancing Lights."

Chagak clutched the baby and began to rock. "If he dies," she said, "I do not want to live. Please kill me if he dies."

"You will live," the old man said. "Even if he dies, you will live."

"No," Chagak answered, speaking not only to the old man but to the carvings that watched her, to the tiny spirits that huddled on the shelves of the ulaq. "No." And she closed her eyes and wept.

EIGHT

Chagak did not mean to sleep that night. She held Pup close to her, singing and praying, afraid that if she closed her eyes Pup's spirit would leave her.

Sometime near dawn the storm winds quieted, and in her weariness Chagak could no longer tell whether her thoughts were true thoughts or only dreams. The old man's carvings began to move, dancing together on the shelves, but it seemed a natural thing. Chagak watched them solemnly and did not know she was dreaming. She slept and did not know she was sleeping.

When she awoke, Pup's open, staring eyes told Chagak he was dead. Her spirit had not been strong enough to keep him and hold her dreams as well.

She lowered her head over the baby's still form and began her people's mourning chant.

Chagak washed Pup's tiny body and wrapped him in furs the old man gave her. She had no tears, but a weight at the center of her chest seemed to block all thoughts of anything but its presence.

The old man brought her a mat, one of her own, woven with the darker band at both ends. The mat was damp and full of sand, so Chagak lit two oil lamps and held the mat above them. When it was dry. Chagak beat it against the floor to dislodge the sand.

"Cry, little one," the old man said to her as she worked.

But Chagak looked at him, her eyes widening with surprise, as if she had no need to cry, and the old man turned away.

For a long time she held her brother, stroking the soft skin of his face, singing songs, but finally the old man brought in Pup's cradle. It, too, was damp, and one of the wooden sides was cracked.

Chagak was surprised that the old man had been able to find the cradle. Surely most of her things had been swept into the sea. Now Pup could take the cradle with him to the spirit world, and perhaps, since their father had made it, there would be some bond that would draw Pup to his people.

Chagak held the cradle in her lap as the old man walked the length of the ulaq, studying the many figures on his shelves. The ulaq was small, much smaller than her father's, and had only three sleeping places, their curtains breaking the line of shelves at one end of the ulaq. Finally the old man chose two carvings. A seal and an otter.

Chagak watched as he sat close to an oil lamp and tied a sinew string around each tiny animal's neck. Then, pulling a large basket from under one of the shelves, he took out several pieces of wood. One was only a sliver, as long and thin as Chagak's smallest finger; the other was larger, as long as her hand, but not as wide.

He worked on the smallest piece first, carving it with a crooked knife, the blade no longer than the last joint of his thumb, the handle the curved rib of an otter. He worked until he had whittled away most of the wood, until only the thinnest piece remained. But when he held it up for Chagak to see, she realized that it was a harpoon, tiny, but perfect, even the barbs of the spearhead in place. From the remaining discarded pieces of wood he carved an atlatl, a flat piece with a notch that fitted the end of the harpoon — a spear thrower to increase the distance and force of the hunter's throw. These two tiny pieces he tied to the string that hung from the seal's neck.

The larger piece of wood became an ikyak, small and perfect, and when the old man had finished it, he smoothed the ikyak with a piece of sandstone until, when he handed the thing to Chagak, the wood felt soft to her, like a newly tanned hide.

He tied the ikyak to the string on the otter's neck and then tied both strings, one with seal and harpoon, the other with ikyak and otter, to Pup's cradle.

"One to provide food," he said. "One to guide him to your people at the Dancing Lights."

Chagak nodded, but the old man's words had given form to her fears, and he felt the choking hotness of tears filling the spaces at the corners of her eyes. "He is so small," she whispered, and then her throat tightened and she could say nothing more.

The old man came and sat down beside her. "Why do you think I gave him a otter?" he asked. He held up the tiny ivory animal and Chagak saw the perfection of the features; the eyes, the curve of the mouth, even the separation of fingers and toes on the otter's feet.

"Have you ever seen an otter mother forget her young?" He turned the carving over and showed Chagak the line of teats on the otter's belly. "Otters do not get lost and they do not leave their young. She will be a mother to him until his journey ends, until he finds his true mother."

He handed the otter to Chagak and she held it in her hands. And somehow, as she held it, the otter seemed to grow warm. Chagak looked at the old man and said, "I am called

Chagak, a name my father gave me."

The old man smiled. The telling of names was not something done lightly, for someone who knew a person's name could control part of that one's spirit.

"A sacred name," he said to Chagak, thinking of the smoky translucence of the stone she had been named for. Obsidian, the spirit rock of the mountains.

"I am Shuganan," he said.

"Of the ancient ones," Chagak said. "A shaman's name."

"I make no claim to be a shaman," Shuganan answered, "But I will pray for your brother's safe journey."

That night they kept the body in the ulaq with them, but the next morning Shuganan carried the cradle to the place he called his death ulaq. Chagak followed him to the low mound. Aconite, tall and dark, grew at the edges of the ulaq. The roof hole was sealed with a square of driftwood chunks bound together with nettle twine, something, unlike babiche, birds and small animals would not eat.

Shuganan used his walking stick to dig away the dirt around the door, then pried up the square of wood. An odor of mold and dampness, of stale air, came from the opened ulaq.

Chagak tried to see into the darkness but could not, so finally she asked, "There are others buried here?"

Shuganan said nothing and so Chagak repeated the question, the old man finally looking at her as if surprised to see she was beside him.

"My wife," he said, then began a chant, something in words Chagak did not know, did not understand.

Shuganan's wife, now dead six summers, had been an old woman when she died, but was always young to him — young, so that in their last years together Shuganan had not seen her as she was but as the dark-haired girl he had given three seasons of sealskins to win.

He chanted, calling to her. Did she hear or had she found another man, a hunter who cared for her in the place of the Dancing Lights? Perhaps someone who would give her the son he had never given her. He chanted more loudly, hoping his words would carry the distance to the spirit world. This was a gift he wanted her to have and also something he could give Chagak, the safety of this child.

He set the cradle on the ulaq and carefully felt for the notches of the climbing log. He had brought an oil lamp, and when he was inside, Shuganan lit the lamp. The light threw arcs of yellow over the shelves of carvings that lined the walls. Chagak, looking down, gasped but said nothing.

Shuganan did not try to explain. Why should a man explain the gifts he gives to his wife? Who could explain feelings that did not die? How could he have lived without his wife if he had not spent the first year carving, giving her all the things she loved so she could take them with her to the Dancing Lights? Flowers, otters, bitterroot plants, sea urchins, sea ducks, geese, gulls. And shelf after shelf of babies to make up for the babies he had not been able to give her during her life.

But now I bring you a true child, he thought, then added the words to his chant, something spoken in his own people's language. For he did not want Chagak to be afraid that his wife would take the baby from Chagak's family. It would not be a taking but a sharing.

He turned, saw the bundle that was his wife's body, the knees flexed and bent to the chest, the body wrapped in mats. He reached up for the cradle, then set it beside his wife. Continuing his chant, he climbed from the ulaq.

He and Chagak replaced the driftwood door, tamping dirt around the cracks. For a long time they sat in the wind at the top of the ulaq, neither speaking.

Chagak's thoughts were on death, and as the evening darkened, she felt a blackness pressing in on her. In her mind she saw a wind like a storm wind blowing out the spirit flames of all those she had known until she was the last flame, bent and flickering against the dark.

But Shuganan said silent prayers of pleading: Please accept this gift, My Wife. All the years you wept because you could not give me a son, I also wept because I could not give you a daughter. It was not your fault but mine. I put all my power for making children into my carving and was not strong enough to create both. If you have found a young hunter, someone to give you children in that place you now live, go with him, but do not forget me. I give you this gift of a child. Take him as our son. Do not forget me. Do not forget me.

They sat until the sun set and the stars pushed through the clouds, until in the darkness Shuganan could not see the tears on Chagak's face. Did not feel them on his own.

NINE

For two days Chagak did not leave Shuganan's ulaq. She did not eat, and Shuganan was afraid that she had decided to join her brother and her people in death.

He rebuilt her ik, finding driftwood to replace the shattered ribs and keel, but he often returned to the ulaq, and hoped that his presence would bring some comfort. But she gave no sign that she noticed him.

On the evening of the second day she drank some broth, but it was as though she did not know she drank, as if her body moved without the knowledge of her spirit.

But the next morning Shuganan convinced her to come outside with him, to sit on the ulaq roof, to watch the sea for signs of seal.

And so they were both outside when the ducks came. They were large eider ducks: black and white males, reddish-brown females. Twenty of them landed on the beach as if it were their home, something Shuganan had never seen happen on this beach, something he could not explain.

"Look," Chagak said, speaking for the first

time since her brother's burial.

And Shuganan's heart expanded in a gratefulness that spilled into a prayer of thanks. For a moment they watched, but when the ducks entered a tidal pool and began to feed, Shuganan hurried into the ulaq and came back with his bola. The weapon was made of stones and sharp-edged shells tied to the ends of ropes. The ropes were fastened together at a central handle.

It had been more than a year since Shuganan had used the weapon, so he pulled at the ropes to be sure they had not rotted. They were strong. He tried to raise the bola over his head, but his shoulder joints had stiffened and he could not.

He sat down, discouraged, but Chagak said, "I will do it. I have watched the men of my village."

Shuganan, surprised, handed her the bola and watched as she raised it over her head, first swinging it tentatively, then with more power, the sound of stones and ropes swishing in the air. But when she slowed, Shuganan said, "Do not stop. Throw it. If you try to stop, the ropes will twist around your arm and the stones will hit you."

Chagak increased her speed. Standing at the top of the ulaq, hair caught back by the wind, she let the bola fly. The weapon traveled sideways from her hand into a tangle of heather.

"I wanted it to go straight," she said.

"It takes a long time to learn to throw a bola," Shuganan answered. "Do not be discouraged."

"But I want to get a duck."

"They will wait for you. Practice."

She looked at him, something, nearly a smile, shaping her mouth. "I will learn," she said.

For the rest of that day the ducks stayed on the beach and Chagak practiced with the bola. She threw until the rope had worn grooves of raw skin in the palms of her hands, but it was good to feel the bola's power, to watch as ropes and stones churned through the air, singing to her of their flight.

In the evening the ducks did not go back to the sea but crowded into a pond at the top of the beach.

That night, as Chagak lay in her sleeping place, she seemed to hear the whir of the bola like a soothing chant. And though she doubted that the ducks would be on the beach the next day, she had visions of the covering she would make from the eider skins, something for a baby, something that she could wrap her brother's body in, or perhaps, she thought as sleep pulled her into dreams, something to save . . . something for another child . . . someday.

Shuganan was awakened by the sound of ducks, the murmuring sounds of their feeding, and by something else. The sound of wings? No, a bola.

During the nights his joints stiffened, so he rose slowly from his sleeping mats. When he made his way to the outer room of the ulaq, he saw that Chagak had lit several lamps and laid out dried fish for him, but that she was gone.

Again he heard the bola, the thud as it hit some target a distance from the ulaq. He ascended the climbing log, calling to Chagak, "I am coming up. Do not throw your weapon."

"You are safe," she said, and Shuganan's throat began to ache, for there was an edge of joy in her voice that he had not heard before.

"Watch," she said and pointed to a jutting boulder in the grass beyond the ulaq. She spun the bola over her head, and when she let it go, it flew to the rock, wrapping itself around the pointed top, the bola stones hitting with sharp cracks.

"Chagak, you have learned quickly," Shuganan said, and he did not miss the snapping in her eyes, the acceptance of his praise.

"And look," she said. "The ducks stayed."

90

Shuganan shook his head in wonder. What had brought them? He had never had eider ducks come to this beach. It was too soon for them to be gathering for the winter.

"They are a gift from my people," Chagak said as if she knew Shuganan's thoughts. "They are a sign that I should live."

And since Shuganan knew no better explanation, he nodded, pleased with the idea.

"I am ready now," she said, and Shuganan, not sure what she meant, did not reply. But when she began a cautious walk to the beach, he knew she was going to try to take a duck, something he was not sure she should do. There was little chance she would succeed.

He wanted to call after her, to tell her that she should wait, but he was afraid his words would scare the ducks, and so he slipped down the side of the ulaq, moving slowly, his walking stick in his hands.

Chagak had dropped to hands and knees and was advancing on the ducks. She moved so slowly, Shuganan could scarcely tell she moved at all.

Shuganan's chest began to ache and he realized that he was holding his breath, just as he did when he hunted seals from his ikyak.

The ducks began a slow movement to the far side of the pool and for a time Chagak sat still. But soon they were again eating, dipping heads down into the water for shellfish. One drake raised up on the water, beating the air with his wings, but he made no move to leave the pond and Chagak crept closer.

Shuganan knew the bola would not be as effective on the water, the stones slowed in their flight by hitting the surface. He had often hunted ducks or geese with the weapon and wished that he had been able to tell Chagak the best way to kill a duck.

Would she know to make a loud noise, then to throw the instant the ducks began to fly, when water slowed their wings?

Chagak had the bola wrapped around her arm, the stones clutched in her hand, and now she rose, but only to her knees. Shuganan was afraid she would try to throw from that position and lose much of her power. But suddenly she jumped up, whirling the bola over her head.

Some of the ducks had noticed her and began skittering across the pond, but others stayed, eating.

"Yell, Chagak, so they will fly," Shuganan called.

"A-a-a-e-e-e-iii," she yelled. The ducks rose from the water, but the yell seemed to check the smooth circling of Chagak's arm. The bola jerked, and when she let it go, it fell short of the ducks and sank into the water.

Shuganan, disappointed, hobbled to her side. But when Chagak turned to him, he saw that she was laughing.

"I nearly got one. Did you see?"

"Yes, I saw," Shuganan answered and smiled.

Chagak started to wade into the tidal pool, but Shuganan caught the sleeve of her suk. "You will cut your feet on the shells," he said.

"The ducks will be back. I need the bola."

"Then wait."

Shuganan found a length of driftwood and started into the pond, clearing a path to the weapon. Finally, in knee-deep water, he reached out with his walking stick and pulled the bola toward him.

"Hurry," Chagak said and Shuganan was surprised at the urgency in her voice. But then he heard the ducks and, raising his eyes to the sky, saw that they circled the beach. He reached into the water, not caring if he got the sleeve of his parka wet, and grabbed the bola.

Handing the weapon to Chagak, he hid himself behind a boulder a short distance from the pond and waited.

Chagak backed slowly from the edge of the pond, then knelt, holding herself very still. "Thank you," she whispered, not knowing if her prayers were to Aka or to the spirits of her people. She was not surprised that the ducks had returned, but their presence was an affirmation to her that they were a gift, a sign that she should continue with her life, as ducks were a sign each spring that a village would soon be blessed with summer, a time of renewal, of all good things beginning.

The ducks settled into the water, their wings making a spray that Chagak could feel against her face. She waited as they preened and made small skirmishes, fighting for the best positions on the pond.

The rough nettle fiber of the rope pulled at the blisters on Chagak's hand, but the pain was good. Better than feeling nothing as she had for so many days: feeling nothing, seeing nothing, closing her mind to everything around her, the only way she knew to dull the pain within. But the pain in her hand made her feel as if she were again part of the things of the earth.

The sun was hot under the clouds, and its rays tightened Chagak's scalp. The strength of its warmth pulsed down her dark hair to her shoulders and back, coursing out to the rope she held in her hand.

Chagak crept toward the pond. What had Shuganan told her the night before? She must be close enough for the bola to carry to the center of the flock, but also far enough away not to scare the ducks before she was ready to throw.

The shale of the beach scraped her knees, but Chagak did not feel it. Her eyes were on the center of the flock, the place her bola must go to be effective. Then suddenly, in one movement, she lunged forward, yelling and whirling the bola over her head.

The ducks rose from the pond and Chagak threw.

The bola left her hand smoothly. One duck fell, then another, their bodies hitting the water. Shuganan was already wading into the pond to retrieve them, but Chagak watched the flock as it rose into the sky and disappeared beyond the island's curve.

They were her people's spirits, she had no doubt. She had taken two of them. Two spirits would stay with her.

Shuganan held up the ducks. "Two drakes," he called.

"Two sons," Chagak murmured. "I have won two sons."

She skinned each duck carefully, first removing all large feathers, leaving only soft down, then cutting at neck, legs and wings and pulling off the skin in one piece. She cooked the ducks that night, wrapping them in kelp and roasting them in a fire pit over a bed of hot coals.

Shuganan gave her many compliments for the meal, but Chagak's thoughts were on tanning the skins. The drakes did not have the fine, thick breast down of a hen, but the skins were thicker and so would be easier to scrape and tan.

When she had pulled off the first skin, she held it up and, seeing the size and shape, had been reminded of her tiny brother, and a sharp pain of grief rose within her chest, but then clearly in her mind she saw other babies who would someday be hers, and so she decided to keep the skins whole.

She would rub them until they were soft, using a mixture of brains and seawater. Then she would smooth each skin by rubbing it with sandstone.

"The meat is good," Shuganan said again. "Many years since I have eaten anything better."

Chagak lowered her head in acknowledgment of the compliment, and Shuganan asked, "You have kept a feather?"

Chagak reached toward the pile of her belongings. She kept her things in one of her mother's baskets, something Chagak had brought with her that the storm did not take. She showed him the handful of feathers she had saved.

"Could I have one?" he asked.

And Chagak, though surprised at the request, handed him a long black wing feather.

"As a pattern for my carving," he explained and tucked it into the hair at the crown of his head. "You should keep one also," he said. "Something for your amulet. I am sure the ducks were a gift to you. Perhaps from your people. Perhaps from Tugix."

Chagak selected a feather and tucked it into the leather bag at her neck, then something made her say, "I will save the skins for a suk. Something for a baby." Then she stopped, afraid to voice her hope that the baby would be hers. That she would someday be a mother.

But Shuganan said, "Yes. Soon we will go to a place I know. My wife's people, the Whale Hunters, live there. Perhaps we can find a husband for you."

Chagak opened her mouth to speak but for a moment could say nothing. Finally she said, "My mother's people are the Whale Hunters. I was trying to take Pup to them when we came to your beach. My grandfather is Many Whales."

"Many Whales," Shuganan said with a slow smile. "He is their chief."

"Yes. My mother told me."

"You will have no trouble finding a husband."

"He is not a man who values granddaughters," Chagak said. "And when I tell him what has happened to his daughter and his grandsons . . ." She shook her head.

All but one of her grandfather's sons had died in infancy. Many Whales was to have taken Chagak's oldest brother sometime during the next year and trained him to hunt the whale. But what would Many Whales say when he was told all his grandsons were dead and only Chagak, a girl, lived?

"My grandfather will not want me," Chagak said to Shuganan. "He wants sons."

"If he will not find you a husband," Shuganan answered, "then I will."

The words made Chagak shiver, and a sudden clear image of Seal Stalker came to her mind. A tightening of sorrow slowed her heart, but she looked up at Shuganan and made herself smile.

"Yes, I will need a husband," she said. "Someone who will give me a child. But I do not need a young man." And then, with a boldness Chagak knew must have come from the duck feather in her amulet, she said, "I would be wife to you."

But Shuganan smiled gently and said, "No. I am too old. But we will find someone. A good man. I will be grandfather. He will be husband."

TEN

It was the second time during that summer Shuganan had seen a boat close to his island. This time as before, he thought, they have found me. Even after all these years.

The first time, he had felt only a dark acceptance, and then, when the one in the ik had been a woman, relief. But this time, seeing the boat, knowing by the shape and speed it was not ik but ikyak, Shuganan was filled with anger. Why did they come now? He was an old man. He should be left in peace.

Shuganan squatted behind a boulder, hoping the man would pass the beach, would continue on, but the ikyak made a wide curve in the water. And as it came close, Shuganan's breath caught in his throat and his chest ached with dread. The marks on the craft, yellow and black, were the same, the narrow hull, the peaked ridge at the top. Yes. The ikyak was one of theirs.

Shuganan stood and watched the man pull the ikyak ashore.

The man gave no indication that he saw Shuganan, but when the ikyak was safely settled above the reach of the waves, he turned and walked toward Shuganan. When he was several paces away, he said, "I am a friend. I have no knife." His arms were thrust out before him, his hands open.

He spoke in the language of the tribe called Short Ones, and Shuganan, knowing the language from his childhood, answered boldly, "Show me your wrists. Then I will believe you have no knife."

But the man, his wide face made wider by a grin, made no move to do so. He was a young man, much shorter than Shuganan, but Shuganan saw the thickness of his arms and knew the man could kill him if he wished.

The young man's chigadax was well worn but spoke of a woman's careful work. His seal gut boots were in poor repair. Had he no more sense than to wear them on this shale beach?

"What do you want?" Shuganan asked. "Why do you come?"

"I have told you. I am a friend," the man laughed. "Have you no welcome for a friend?"

Shuganan glanced nervously over his shoulder. Where was Chagak? She had gone to pick berries that morning. Soon she would return. What would happen if this one saw her?

"What is the matter?" the man asked. "Do you watch for your woman?"

"I have no woman," Shuganan said, avoiding the man's eyes.

Again the man laughed, a deep boisterous sound. "There is a woman! Do not lie to me, old man. Do you think I would come to your beach not knowing who lives here? Do you think I am a fool?"

Shuganan backed away. So the man had been watching them. I should have been more careful, Shuganan thought. He had known by Chagak's description who had killed her people. And he had understood why but had not told Chagak. What good would it do for her to know? And how could he bear it if she hated him when she was told the truth?

"I am called Man-who-kills," the young man said.

Shuganan did not answer, would not return name for name. Man-who-kills thrust back his shoulders and asked, "Where is your ulaq? Why do you show me no hospitality? Perhaps I am hungry. Perhaps my ikyak needs repair." He stepped closer to Shuganan, his words nearly a whisper, his lips drawn back from his square white teeth. "Perhaps it has been many months since I have had a woman."

In that moment Shuganan wished for a knife, wished he could cut the man's thick dark throat, but he said, "My ulaq is small. You stay here. I will bring food."

"And have time to warn your woman? No,

we will go together."

He pushed Shuganan up the rise of the beach, but Shuganan walked slowly, limping more than necessary. At each step he was afraid he would see Chagak, afraid Man-who-kills would see her also.

Shuganan lifted his walking stick when they neared the ulaq. "There," he said. "My ulaq."

Rye grass grew long on sides and roof, the grass already bleaching in the late summer. Soon Chagak would cut it to use for winter weaving. She had promised him socks and shirts, even hand coverings, cunningly made with pockets for Shuganan's thumbs.

"Stay here," Man-who-kills said. "If you run I will catch you and you will run no more." Then, looking up to the entrance hole of the ulaq, he said, "If your woman is inside, I will greet her!"

Shuganan waited until the man was in the ulaq, and then he scanned the hills, searching for Chagak. He stuck his digging stick in the side of the ulaq, pressing it firmly into the sod. It was a signal among his wife's people, a warning to stay away. Did Chagak's people use the same sign?

The wind was cold against Shuganan's bare legs, and he squatted down until the edges of his long parka touched the ground. He tucked his hands up the sleeves and pulled up the hood, but he was still cold.

He heard Man-who-kills call him from the ulaq. "Come inside, old man. I have decided to accept your offer of food."

Shuganan wiped his hands on the feathers of his parka. How could hands that were so cold sweat? he wondered. But then he thought, If I give Man-who-kills food, he will stay inside a little longer, and perhaps Chagak will see my warning.

Shuganan lowered himself into the ulaq, his feet feeling for the first notches of the log. The oil lamp had gone out and the ulaq was dark. Shuganan left the door flap open to give light.

"Light the lamps, old man," Man-who-kills said. "Woman's work will not hurt you."

"No oil," Shuganan said and pointed to a heap of coals where Chagak had boiled water to soften reeds for weaving.

Man-who-kills made a face.

"Too old. No seals," Shuganan explained.

"Lazy or cursed in woman's work?"

Shuganan ignored the barb but thought, I took three seals last spring. I have oil enough to store eggs and light lamps for some days. But why waste it on you?

Shuganan squatted beside the coals, digging with a stick until he found a chunk of wood that still held fire. Carefully, he laid bits of dried grass over it, blowing gently to give the flame life, then added driftwood from the stack Chagak had brought from the beach.

As the fire took hold, Shuganan heard Man-who-kills hiss. Turning, Shuganan saw that the man was staring at the hundreds of small white figurines that lined the walls.

The man backed toward Shuganan, his eyes still on the ulaq walls, but he reached for the old man and, pulling back Shuganan's hair, revealed the left ear with its clipped lobe.

Man-who-kills dropped to his knees and crawled toward an oil lamp. He picked it up with both hands and thrust it toward the old man. "There is oil in this, and wicks. Light it."

"I do not have enough oil to waste. We have a fire."

"Light it!"

Shuganan found the braided piece of reed Chagak used to light the lamps and, taking fire from the driftwood coals, lit the circle of wicks.

Man-who-kills held the lamp before him as if it were an amulet. He walked the length of the ulaq studying the carvings. Twice he reached out, as though to touch one, but quickly drew back his hand.

"They are hot?" Shuganan asked him, feeling as he had not felt since he was a young man, knowing the power of his gift instead of its shame.

"You are Shuganan," Man-who-kills said, his voice a whisper. "The storytellers, the old men, they said you had died."

"Then perhaps you are also dead, and we are both in the place of the dead."

"Shut your mouth, old man," said Man-who-kills. "You think you have more power than I? How many animals have you taken in the last year? How many women? You are old. Your powers grow weak."

"Your storytellers told you that?" Shuganan asked. "They said my powers dim with age like a hunter's powers? They should have said my powers increase with age, like the powers of a shaman."

But then Shuganan realized the young man was not listening to him but was muttering to himself. He hobbled to Man-who-kills' side, heard the young man say, "I will be a chief if I bring this old man back with me."

Man-who-kills reached out for an ivory figurine, a man in an ikyak, two seals tied to the stern. For a time the young man's fingers only hovered over the carving, but then he grasped it. Eyes wide, he looked at Shuganan.

When nothing happened, Man-who-kills smiled, then, drawing a short knife from a scabbard on his left wrist, he held it, blade toward Shuganan, and said, "I will keep this one as a gift. It is mine."

"You may keep it," Shuganan replied, "but it cannot belong to you. Each carving has its own spirit and belongs to itself."

Man-who-kills moved his knife closer to Shuganan's neck and said, "You are a fool." But he put the seal carving back on the shelf and sheathed his knife.

Tossing his long hair back from his face, Man-who-kills said, "I am hungry. Get me food."

Shuganan went to the food cache and squatted down, using his hands to steady himself, then dug into the sand floor of the cache. He had buried many eggs, packing them in sand and seal oil to keep over the long winter. He dug out several, watching as Man-who-kills pushed into the ulaq's sleeping places.

Shuganan had knives hidden and did not want them found, so he held out the eggs and said, "Food."

Man-who-kills let a curtain drop and joined Shuganan. He took an egg, pushed his finger through the shell and scooped out the contents. Shuganan handed him another, but the young man squatted down, peered into the food cache, and pulled out a seal belly container. The belly, one of many Shuganan had filled that summer, was packed with dried halibut. The man took several chunks of fish from the skin and began to eat, asking between bites, "More eggs?"

Shuganan handed him several, hoping to keep him in the ulaq as long as possible, hoping to give Chagak time to see the signal. But soon Man-who-kills threw the seal belly back into the cache and motioned Shuganan toward the climbing log.

Man-who-kills patted his stomach and grinned, showing his many teeth. "Now we will find your woman," he said.

Shuganan hurried up the climbing log, but the man grabbed Shuganan's parka and climbed up until his head was level with Shuganan's. Man-who-kills stretched to reach the climbing log around Shuganan's body and said, "I would not want your digging stick through my throat, old man."

They reached the top at the same time, and Shuganan lifted his eyes toward the berry hills, wondering if Chagak had seen his sign, hoping she had already taken refuge. But as he looked, he saw her, and he felt Man-who-kills stiffen against his back and so knew that he had seen her also.

She had crested a hill, two berry bags hanging from each arm. The wind was blowing her long black hair, and the dark feathers of her suk ruffled as she walked.

Shuganan's heart pulsed in sorrow. "Look up, my Chagak," he whispered. "Look up and run, my precious one."

And as if hearing his words, she looked toward the ulaq and stopped, then suddenly she dropped her berry bags, turned and ran. Man-who-kills jumped from the roof hole and ran after her.

Shuganan hobbled after him, calling to Tugix as he followed, "Protect your child! Send your wind!" But the mountain did not seem to hear.

When Shuganan reached the hill where Chagak had dropped her berry bags, he could see both the young man and the girl. They were still running. Man-who-kills drew closer to Chagak with each step, and finally he reached out and grabbed her hair. He jerked her to the ground and Shuganan waited, thinking, If he takes her, I will kill him, even as he is upon her. But Man-who-kills twisted her hair around his fist and pulled her with him back up the hill.

Shuganan watched as they drew close, then he stooped and picked up the berries that had spilled from Chagak's woven bags and followed Man-who-kills back to the ulaq.

ELEVEN

They were together in the large room of the ulaq. Shuganan sat beside an oil lamp, a piece of ivory in one hand, a pumice abrader in the other.

Chagak was weaving a grass floor mat. The weaving was strung over a bare piece of wall near the climbing log. Shuganan had pounded hanging pegs shoulder height, about an arm's length apart, into the wall. Chagak had tied a piece of braided sinew between the pegs and to the sinew she tied the warp strands of grass, letting them dangle at the other end. She finger-wove the weft grass over and under the warp, using only a long needle to aid her weaving and a forked halibut bone to push the grass of the new row tightly against the rest.

Man-who-kills watched them, a knife turning slowly in his thick fingers. Chagak could feel the heat of his eyes against her back as she worked.

She had no doubt that he was one of the tribe that had destroyed her village, and fear and anger quickened her heart and made her hands cold and clumsy as she worked.

Shuganan called him Man-who-kills and spoke to him in a language Chagak had difficulty understanding. The words were clipped and rough; even Shuganan's voice sounded harsh speaking it. But as she listened, Chagak realized it was a language that had some similarity to her own, and she could occasionally pick out words and phrases.

Man-who-kills was not a tall man, but his arms and legs were heavily muscled and his neck was wide and heavy, making a straight line from his chin to his chest. His eyes were small, set deeply into the creases of his face, but when he looked toward an oil lamp, the light picked up the dark brown irises, the gray of the whites, pupils small and pinched like the pupils of a man trying to see the sun.

His parka, though old, was well made, sewn in small squares of many different skins, stiff panels of fur seal skins at front and back, soft lemming skins sewn together for sides and sleeves.

Chagak could not help but wonder about the woman who had made Man-who-kills' clothing. Was she wife or mother? Did she know the terrible things he would do while wearing the beautiful clothes she made him?

When he first caught Chagak, Man-who-kills had jerked her hair so hard, she had fallen and knocked the breath from her chest.

Then she had seen the square fierceness of his face, the scar that ran crookedly from the bridge of his nose across his left cheek, the thin growth of oiled hair that hung from his upper lip in two strands over his mouth.

Once in the ulaq, she saw the shabby condition of his well-made clothing and knew that he had not returned to his village for many days, perhaps months, so even if he had a wife he would need a woman, would expect Shuganan to give him the hospitality of nights with Chagak.

It was the custom of all people, Chagak knew, but in a village as large as Chagak's there were enough women so one such as Chagak's mother, who did not want to sleep with a strange man, did not have to. There were too many women ready to honor a visitor from another village.

Chagak herself had never slept with a man. Her father had saved her to get the larger bride price given for a virgin. This had never bothered Chagak, though sometimes she felt left out when other girls giggled and talked of nights spent with visiting hunters.

But after Seal Stalker asked for her, Chagak wanted only him and was glad her father had not given her as an entertainment for others. And now as she knew Man-who-kills' eyes were on her, she felt only revulsion and a

growing anguish, as though Man-who-kills'
touch would add to Seal Stalker's death
wounds.

When they had returned to the ulaq, Chagak
did not take off her suk. Although the garment
was made of fragile birdskins, it seemed to
be a protection against the man's probing eyes.

Man-who-kills took off his parka, but
Shuganan, glancing at Chagak, did not.

Soon after entering the ulaq, Man-who-kills
chose a carving from the shelves and strung
it on the amulet cord that hung from his neck.

The carving was of a man in an ikyak dragging two seals, and in taking it Man-who-kills
ruined Shuganan's village scene. For one shelf
had been set with tiny figurines in place as
though they were the parts of a village: men
and women fishing, children playing, old men
gathering sea urchins, boys climbing for eggs,
women weaving, sewing and cooking.

One figure in particular that Chagak longed
to touch, to hold, was of a mother nursing
a baby. There was something about the way
the mother held her head, the way she was
watching her baby, that reminded Chagak of
her own mother. And though the wanting was
deep enough within her to be an ache, she
had never asked Shuganan to let her touch
it. How could she ask to touch something so
sacred?

It made her angry that Man-who-kills had taken the hunter, but he seemed to be a man who respected nothing. Even when Shuganan and Man-who-kills were talking, Man-who-kills spoke with an insolence that made Chagak shudder.

Chagak reached into her storage basket for more grass and Man-who-kills said something to her. She glanced at him and said, "I do not understand. I do not know your language."

Shuganan came and sat beside her. His back was to the weaving, his face toward Man-who-kills.

"What did he say?" Chagak whispered without turning her head, her fingers still weaving.

"He thought you were my woman."

"Let me be your woman, then," Chagak answered. "I will sleep with you."

"No," Shuganan said, and Chagak turned and tried to see in his face the reason for his answer.

"If I told him you were my woman, he would take you to his bed as hospitality. It is that way among his people. He would not even have to ask."

"Who did you say I was?" Chagak asked, turning again to her weaving.

"Granddaughter."

There was a firmness in the word that lifted some of Chagak's anxiety. It was good to belong to someone again.

"And he cannot take me if I am your granddaughter?" she asked.

"Not without gifts," Shuganan answered, then added, "It gives us time."

Chagak nodded, then asked, "How did you learn his language?"

Shuganan's head jerked toward her, and even in the dim light of the ulaq Chagak saw the pain in his eyes.

But before he could answer, Man-who-kills said something, his voice low and angry. Chagak hunched her shoulders and pushed herself down into her suk, as though the folds of the garment could hide her.

"What does he say?" Chagak whispered, her voice so small she wondered if Shuganan could hear her.

"He does not want us to talk," Shuganan said, and he moved to a place near an oil lamp where his body blocked Man-who-kills' view of Chagak.

Shuganan wished he could sleep. The night spread its darkness in through the open roof hole, and the weariness that had begun at Shuganan's shoulders spread its weight to his fingertips.

How could he use the strength of his spirit to stand against Man-who-kills when the night took away every desire but to sleep?

Shuganan forced himself to watch Chagak, and he marveled that she still could weave, fingers guiding the weaving needle so quickly.

She is a beautiful woman, Shuganan thought, and remembered his joy when he had first seen her. The long eyes, heavily lashed, her small perfect mouth. She had been like a gift to Shuganan, as if Tugix, seeing his need for beauty, had given him the girl as inspiration for his carvings, but now her beauty was a curse, and he wished she was too tall, with broken teeth and misshapen mouth.

"So you do not have a woman?" Man-who-kills had said after dragging Chagak back to the ulaq. "And you sleep alone at night?"

"She is not my woman," Shuganan had answered. "She is my granddaughter."

"Why does she not speak our language then?"

"Her mother was from another tribe. From the village you destroyed."

Man-who-kills had laughed, the laughter coming from his mouth in short bursts, erratic and sudden like birds flying from cliff holes.

Now, as Shuganan sat watching Chagak, he thought of her question. There could be many reasons why he spoke Man-who-kills' language. But there was something in Chagak that would sense the truth. How would she feel when she knew?

It would have been better if she had found another beach, someone else to live with. He could never be a husband to her. He was too old to hunt well, too old to give her sons. Besides, he had never been able to give his wife sons or daughters, not in all the years they had been together. He knew this, yet he had not hurried to take Chagak to the Whale Hunters. Had there been something in him that had hoped Chagak could be his wife?

When she described those who destroyed her village, Shuganan had known they were the Short Ones. He had known they might come to his beach. He should have taken Chagak to the Whale Hunters. There were days wasted after Pup's death. Why had he waited?

Shuganan picked up his carving knife and a piece of bone. He looked at Man-who-kills, but the man evidently saw no threat in the short, small-bladed knife.

Shuganan had used the knife so often that the bone handle seemed to shape itself to his fingers, to the bumps and hollows left by the stiffening disease that caused so much pain.

Shuganan had ceased praying for release from the disease, realizing at last that the carvings he made while in pain had a depth to them unmatched by those he made without pain, as if the pain were also a knife, carving away what was not needed, revealing more clearly the truth of the people and animals hidden in ivory and bone.

Now the pain was as intense as anything he had known. The ache of his fingers traveled up his arms and joined the ache that pushed at the walls of his heart.

Chagak would suffer for his selfishness, she who had already suffered so much.

TWELVE

Chagak's eyes burned and her shoulders ached, but her fingers still moved over her weaving. It is better to weave than to be forced to Man-who-kills' sleeping place, she thought.

The oil lamp nearest her began to smoke. Chagak blew out the flame, pulled her woman's knife from the scabbard at her waist and trimmed the char from the wicks.

Man-who-kills said something to Shuganan, and Shuganan said to Chagak, "Leave it out. He wants to sleep."

Chagak looked at the old man, her eyes wide with dread, but Shuganan looked away. He spoke to Man-who-kills and led him to the honored back sleeping room, Shuganan's own room, closed off from the rest of the ulaq with curtains Chagak had recently made.

Chagak wrapped her arms around herself and began backing toward the climbing log. Perhaps she could be gone before either man noticed. She could take her ik, paddle all night. There were many places to hide along the coast — caves and inlets.

As Shuganan knelt and pulled the curtain

aside, he caught sight of Chagak, her back against the climbing log. Pain pressed into his chest, sorrow that she would leave him, but he pushed it aside, embarrassed that he could be so selfish, thinking of himself when Chagak had so much to fear.

"You see," said Shuganan, pulling Man-who-kills into the sleeping place with him, "there are places here for your weapons." The mats on the floor were new, woven by Chagak to replace the cut grass Shuganan had used when his wife's mats were beyond repair. During the month they had been together, Chagak had also made him feather-stuffed pillows with fur seal hide covers. Shuganan pointed to the pillows, but suddenly Man-who-kills shouted and lunged from the sleeping place.

In one skidding movement he grabbed Chagak's ankles, her feet on the top notch of the climbing log, and threw her to the floor.

Shuganan knelt beside her, but Chagak lay without moving, her long hair hiding her face.

Man-who-kills clasped a handful of her hair and jerked her head back, exposing her long throat. Pulling a knife from his wrist scabbard, he held it close below her left ear.

"Leave her alone," Shuganan said. "She does not belong to you."

"Tell her she will be dead if she tries that again."

"He says he will kill you if you try to escape again," Shuganan told the girl.

But Chagak began to laugh, the laugh high and yipping like the sound of an otter. "Good," she said. "Tell him to kill me. Tell him he should have killed me long ago, when he killed my people. It will be an easy way to die, this knife. I do not fear my own blood. It will be better than dying in fire as my mother and sister did, better than having my belly slit like my father."

She began to laugh again and Man-who-kills closed a hand over her mouth. "What did she say?"

"She says to kill her," Shuganan answered.

"What is wrong with her? Why does she laugh?"

"She wants to be with her people. She wants to be dead."

"She is your granddaughter. Our warriors killed your son, her father?"

"Yes." The lie came easily.

"She is too beautiful to be anything of yours," Man-who-kills snapped.

Shuganan shrugged.

Keeping his hand over Chagak's mouth, Man-who-kills pulled his knife away from her throat and in one quick movement slit the front of Chagak's suk.

Chagak had prepared herself for the pain of the knife, for the slitting of her throat. She held her teeth tightly together, determined she would not scream when he cut her, but when she saw what he had done to her suk — the garment precious because her mother had made it — she began to scream.

Man-who-kills laughed, and his laughter turned Chagak's horror into anger. She pulled her woman's knife from its sheath under her suk and slashed Man-who-kills' cheek.

"Chagak, no!" she heard Shuganan yell, but she did not care; if the man was going to kill her, let him bear the scars of her knife for a remembrance.

Man-who-kills grasped her hand and squeezed. Chagak felt the small bones begin to ache, then the man moved his fingers so Chagak's knuckles ground together until she could no longer hold the knife. Pinning her to the floor, the man spread the cut edges of her suk and dropped to sit on her chest.

"Do not kill her," Shuganan said.

Man-who-kills pressed a hand to his bleeding cheek. Shuganan leaned down, saw the cut was not deep.

"She needs to be dead," Man-who-kills said, the words coming from clenched teeth.

Chagak lay still, eyes closed, as if she slept, as if nothing had happened. But Man-who-kills raised from her chest and dropped back again, making Shuganan grimace for Chagak's pain. Chagak winced but said nothing and did not open her eyes.

"Do not kill her," Shuganan said again, this time making his voice firm, his words a command; not a request. He picked up a lamp, cradling the stone bowl in both hands, and walked slowly around the ulaq.

The light fell on the carvings that lined the walls. Tiny eyes, tips of ivory spears gleamed.

"These are my people," Shuganan said. "They have power." He turned to face Man-who-kills. "Do not kill my granddaughter."

Slowly Man-who-kills rose to his feet, and behind him Chagak scrambled to her hands and knees. She pulled her torn suk tightly around her and huddled against a wall.

"I do not care if he kills me," she said softly, her voice carrying across the ulaq.

"I care," Shuganan answered, then said in Man-who-kills' language, "If you kill her, I will kill you."

Man-who-kills snorted. "You are old. How will you kill me?"

In answer, Shuganan lifted his light, let it shine over the many carvings.

Man-who-kills rubbed his hand across his

cheek, wiping blood from the cut. "I am not ignorant. I know the stories of your power."

"I will not hesitate to use that power against you."

"Then perhaps I will marry the woman. I need another wife. I will provide well for her. Then I will be head man of this ulaq and all these carvings will be mine."

"You cannot own these. I do not own them. They own themselves just as a man owns himself."

Man-who-kills said nothing; instead he began to study the carvings, at first only looking at them, then reaching out, picking them up, staining their white surfaces with blood from his fingertips.

Shuganan watched him; a loathing rose in his chest. Man-who-kills is right, Shuganan thought. I am old, my arms are weak and I am slow.

He could tell Man-who-kills of his great power, of the power the carvings held, but Shuganan of all people knew the truth — that there was no great gift in making a likeness of something. What his eyes saw came easily to his fingers. The soul of each piece of ivory, each chunk of driftwood, whispered its existence to him. He himself did not find the lines of ikyak or woman weaving, otter or whale. The ivory, the bone, the wood told him. How else would he know? It was not through any great power of his own.

Once carved, revealed by the knife, the thing held its own beauty, not any beauty given by Shuganan. And if the carvings had great powers, those powers were their own to give and take; Shuganan did not control them. If he did, Man-who-kills would already be dead.

"Someday you will die, old man," Man-who-kills said, the words quiet as though he spoke his thoughts to the carvings and not to Shuganan. "You are old. But I will marry your granddaughter, and I will have this ulaq. But before you die, I will earn honor among my people by telling them I have found you. Perhaps by this marriage I will become chief of my people." He laughed. "Is there an easier way to become chief?"

Man-who-kills turned and pointed toward Chagak. "What do you ask for her?"

Shuganan studied the man's face, wide cheeks, dark, hard eyes, dried blood streaked from jaw to lips. If Shuganan agreed to a bride price, perhaps he and Chagak would have a few more days, time to plan the man's death or an escape.

"Five seals. Twenty otter skins," Shuganan said. A reasonable price, but something that would take a number of days' hunting.

"Too much."

"That is the price."

"Two seal. Ten otter."

"We need oil."

"We will be leaving this ulaq. You and I and the woman. All your small people." Man-who-kills' hand made a wide sweep of the room. "We do not need much oil. My people have enough oil."

"Four seals. Twenty otters."

"The days are growing short. Winter will soon be here. How will I take you to my people if I must spend many days hunting?"

"Four seals. Twenty otters."

"Two seal. Ten otter."

"Chagak needs a new suk."

Man-who-kills looked over at Chagak. He laughed, a short, hard laugh that pulled up his mouth at one corner. "Two seal. Sixteen otter," he said.

Shuganan looked at the man. Three days hunting seals, he thought. Four or five hunting otters. Time enough. Time enough. "Yes," he said.

THIRTEEN

"He will come to my sleeping place?" Chagak whispered to Shuganan before she left the large room of the ulaq. Man-who-kills had returned to Shuganan's sleeping place, leaving Chagak and Shuganan alone.

"No," Shuganan said. "He will not touch you tonight." But he would not look at her and kept his head lowered as if he were afraid to meet her eyes. His uneasiness made something cold and hard begin to grow in Chagak's chest.

She stood beside Shuganan, waiting for him to speak, but he did not until Chagak said, "There is something more you are not telling me."

Shuganan looked at her, saw the strength in her eyes. She is as strong as I am, he thought. More so. What she has lost was taken from her. I chose my loss and had little regret. "Yes, there is something," he said and then paused, trying to find the words to tell her. "Man-who-kills wants you as wife. He offers a price of two seals, sixteen otter skins."

Chagak shook her head.

"It is a good price," Shuganan said and felt foolish as soon as he had said the words. What honor would Chagak feel, whether good price or bad, if she hated the man who was to be her husband?

But Chagak said only, "My father did not take otters, and I must honor his belief. The otters saved his life once in a storm."

Shuganan was not surprised. He had heard of otters helping hunters before. "Do not worry about the otter skins," Shuganan said. "It will take him many days to kill sixteen otters. Sometime you will have opportunity to escape. There is an island . . ."

At that moment Man-who-kills came from Shuganan's sleeping place. Chagak glanced at him, then left her weaving and hurried into her own sleeping place. But Man-who-kills followed her, taking with him a rope of braided babiche. He tied Chagak's arms behind her back, then bound her ankles.

As he looped the rope around her ankles, Chagak tried not to shrink from his touch. She knew if she showed Man-who-kills she was afraid it would be worse for her. He was a man who took pleasure in another's fear. So she held her body tight and still and kept her trembling within the walls of her heart.

Shuganan is wrong, she thought. Man-who-kills will take me now. What will stop him?

Does he hold that much respect for Shuganan's agreement? What are sixteen otter skins and two seals to a man who needs a woman?

But when he finished tying her, Man-who-kills said slowly and loudly, "I go to tie your grandfather," and though he spoke in his language, he spoke slowly enough that Chagak understood what he meant. He laughed and pinched her legs but did nothing more.

Long after the ulaq was quiet, Chagak lay awake thinking of the words Shuganan had said: "There is an island . . ."

So there was hope, Chagak thought, but also betrayal in that hope. How could she go, leaving Shuganan to face Man-who-kills' anger? Besides, how could she ever find one small island in the great expanse of the sea? It would be better to go to her grandfather, Many Whales. He might not want her, but perhaps he would find her a husband. But what if Man-who-kills followed her? What if she led him to her grandfather's village? The Whale Hunters were powerful, but were they strong enough to stand against men who destroyed whole villages?

Chagak slept little, and early in the morning Man-who-kills came to her sleeping place. For a moment he only stood and looked at her, but when Chagak rolled to her belly and covered the gaping rip in the front of her suk, he stooped and untied her. He said nothing but laughed deep in his throat, then pointed toward the storage cache and made motions as if he were eating.

Shuganan was already in the main room, breaking spines and shells from the sea urchins he had gathered the day before. The sharp bits of shell littered the floor.

"He would not let me go outside to do this," Shuganan said.

"Then perhaps he will be the first to step on a shell," Chagak answered, picking up the pieces and putting them in a basket.

Man-who-kills said something and Shuganan told Chagak, "He said to light the lamps and that he wants eggs."

There were six lamps in the main room and Chagak lit all of them, using flame from the lamp left burning during the night. Then she crawled into the storage place where she found a length of babiche and tied it around her waist to hold her suk together.

She dug out three eggs and set them on a mat, then, taking water from the seal belly that hung from a rafter, rinsed the eggs and also a number of the sea urchins Shuganan had prepared. She gave the mat to Man-who-kills, but he puckered his mouth and said something to her, his words loud.

"He wants fish sliced and fried in oil," Shuganan said.

"Tell him I need my knife and that my cooking fire is outside."

Shuganan spoke and Man-who-kills grabbed a container of fish and pushed Chagak toward the climbing log.

The wind from the sea felt good against Chagak's face and seemed to clear some of the fear from her mind. She pointed toward the circle of stones that marked her cooking fire and slid down the side of the ulaq. Man-who-kills followed her.

The cooking place was on the leeward side of the ulaq so strong winds would not blow out new fires or cause old ones to spread to the ulaq grass.

Chagak started the fire with her fire stones, snapping her flint and the gold-flecked bit of iron pyrite together until a spark jumped from the rocks and caught on the dried grass at the center of the fire pit. She fed the fire patiently with grass and heather until the flames were large enough to take driftwood. As the wood began to burn, Chagak rubbed oil on her cooking stone. It was three handbreadths across, flat and thin, but in spite of its thinness it took a long time to heat. She set it on the four blackened stones that held it the right distance above the flames and waited.

Man-who-kills, squatting beside her, motioned for her to cook the fish.

"It is not hot yet," Chagak answered, reaching out to lay her hand on the stone so he would understand what she meant.

He snorted, but Chagak shrugged. What magic did he think she had that could make a stone heat quickly? If he had left her untied, told her the night before he wanted fish cooked in oil, she could have made a fire, put the stone over it and banked it with dirt. By morning the stone would have been hot, and his food would have cooked quickly.

But what man would think ahead to do that? she asked herself.

Pointing toward the fish and making slicing motions with her hands, Chagak asked Man-who-kills for a knife. For a moment he sat without moving, as though he did not understand her, but then he pulled Chagak's woman's knife from a pouch at his waist and handed it to her. At the same time he unsheathed his own knife and crossed his arms, holding the knife point up at the crook of one elbow, the blade toward Chagak.

She pretended not to see his knife as she sliced the meat into thin pieces, then rolled each in oil.

Man-who-kills said something, the words

rising like a question. Chagak understood some of what he meant, something about the worth of women and knives, but she pretended she did not hear. She laid the fish slices on the cooking stone and watched the steam rise from the heated surface.

Shuganan hurried into Chagak's sleeping place. He wondered how long he had before Man-who-kills returned to the ulaq.

Long ago Shuganan had hidden two knives in his sleeping place, one in the wall, another in the dirt of the floor. But now Man-who-kills used that sleeping place.

When Man-who-kills had untied Shuganan that morning, then for a moment went outside, Shuganan had hidden three knives in his new sleeping place, one a tiny crooked knife he had once used for carving until, after frequent retouching to increase sharpness, the blade had begun to gouge unevenly. Shuganan had hidden it in a crack between wall and floor.

He also hid a long-bladed hunting knife in a niche in the wall, a place that Shuganan packed with dirt and smoothed to match the smoothness of the rest of the wall. The third knife Shuganan placed on the floor, somewhere easily found, covered only by grass and sleeping mats, for he hoped if Man-who-kills decided to search the sleeping place he would be satisfied with finding only one knife and not search for the others.

Shuganan had hesitated before taking knives to Chagak's sleeping place. What if Man-who-kills found knives there? What would he do to the girl? But if Chagak were always tied, how could she escape? It would be better to take the chance, to give her opportunity to get away. And so he had found his wife's woman's knife, something he had kept in one of her finely woven grass baskets. The basket was as large as a man squatting and was filled with her belongings, old things that Shuganan had not buried with her when she died but that he could not throw away: skins she had tanned, baskets, needles, a cooking stone, floor mats, dishes made from driftwood and a pillow of goose down. At the bottom, a sheathed woman's knife.

Shuganan took it to Chagak's sleeping place. Measuring three hand lengths from the curtained door and using the knife to cut a hole in the floor, he hollowed out a place for the weapon, fitted the hard chunk of dirt carefully back into the hole and covered it with a mat.

Shuganan returned to the central ulaq room. He sat with his back to Chagak's sleeping place, for if he faced it, he knew his eyes would betray him, resting often at the curtain as if they could see through it to the buried knife.

He began to work at the figurine he had been carving since his first dream some months before had told of Chagak's coming. At the time it had been only a comfort for him, but now it would be a gift for Chagak, a protection. It was a carving of husband and wife, and since Chagak had come, Shuganan had made the woman's face like Chagak's, but the man was someone Shuganan still did not know. Now Shuganan used the point of an awl to trace in the details of the husband's clothing. He was not Man-who-kills; he belonged to some village of the First Men.

When Shuganan heard Chagak and Man-who-kills at the ulaq door, he tucked away his carving and sent a prayer to the spirit of Tugix.

Chagak was carrying a mat layered with fried fish. The smell lightened the heavy air of the ulaq. She knelt beside Shuganan and filled a wooden bowl with the meat, then handed it to Man-who-kills.

"Tell her to fill a bowl for you," Man-who-kills said as he began to eat. He looked at Shuganan and smiled, showing a mouthful of meat.

"He says to give me a bowl of food," Shuganan told Chagak.

"I understood," Chagak answered.

"Some for her, too," Man-who-kills added.

"I am a generous man." He laughed, but Shuganan did not smile.

"For yourself, too," Shuganan told Chagak again. And then in the same tone of voice, without moving his eyes from the fish, he said, "I have hidden knives . . ." Then, noticing that Man-who-kills had suddenly stopped eating, Shuganan pointed toward the man and said, "Thank him for the meat."

Chagak nodded at Man-who-kills but did not raise her eyes, afraid he would see the new hope there. She pointed to the bowl she had filled for Shuganan and the one she was taking for herself and said, "Thank you."

Man-who-kills mumbled a reply.

"He says you will be a good wife," Shuganan said.

Chagak lifted her head, "Yes," she answered, then, smiling, added, "but not to him."

Shuganan had carved the wooden shafts of his seal harpoons with scenes of hunting, and now, as Man-who-kills directed, he carved the shaft of one of Man-who-kills' weapons.

Chagak sat in a dark corner of the ulaq, one lamp burning beside her. She had removed her suk to repair it, and though Shuganan and Man-who-kills did not seem to notice her, she felt uncomfortable wearing

135

only her apron, so she held the suk close to her chest as she sewed, and it spread out over her lap.

Earlier that day she had decided how to repair the garment. She was afraid the delicate cormorant skins would not hold a long front seam, for usually her mother had sewn the birdskins in such a way that the seam between two skins met above and below at the center of a skin, the seams following a zigzag pattern. But the tear Man-who-kills had made with his knife went through seams and the centers of whole skins.

As she cooked sea urchins that morning, the thought had come: Why not strengthen the seam with a strip of leather, top to bottom? Why not make it the width of a hand and sew it securely at both sides? Then she had decided to make seams, carefully hidden under the feathers of the cormorant skins, that would divide the strip into seven or eight squares, each with something sewn inside: sinew, babiche, needles and awl, fishhooks, lamp wicks — things needed to stay alive, things that would help her escape.

When Chagak had finished seaming the birdskins, she unrolled a sealskin and laid the suk over it, measuring to cut the leather strip the length of the seam. But then she remembered she had no knife, and for a long time she sat without moving, wondering whether she should draw attention to herself by asking for it. But finally she crawled to Shuganan's side, holding the suk inside out in front of her.

"You need something?" Shuganan asked.

Chagak laid the suk on the floor between the men and pointed to the seam she had made. "It is not strong enough to hold," she said. "I need to cut a strip of leather to sew over it."

Shuganan spoke to Man-who-kills and then said to her, "Get the leather. He will cut it for you."

She brought the sealskin and traced the outline of the cut with her fingers. Man-who-kills picked up the leather and made a straight cut, using his teeth and one hand to separate the sealskin in two pieces, pulling from opposite directions as he cut so the seam was straight. Then he made a second long cut, measured the strip against Chagak's suk and cut off the excess at one end.

Chagak thanked him and stood, but he grabbed one of her ankles and held her, speaking to her.

"He says soon you will not need that suk," Shuganan said. "He will bring you otter skins so you can make a proper suk."

The muscles of Chagak's jaw tightened.

"Tell him I will keep this one also, since my mother made it for me."

"Chagak," Shuganan said, "you will have to make the suk. He is not a man who will turn away if you insult his gifts."

"I will be gone before then," she said, and did not miss the quick shadow of sadness in Shuganan's eyes.

"Yes," he answered.

Then, holding up the strip of leather and pointing to Man-who-kills' knife, Chagak thanked him. Man-who-kills grunted and released Chagak's ankle, and she returned to her place in the dark corner, laid the suk over her lap and, using an awl, punched holes down both sides of the leather strip.

Shuganan kept chunks of seal sinew in a dry wall niche just as Chagak's mother had. Since her seam was long, Chagak selected the longest sinew and, using her teeth and awl, pulled away a strip from the chunk. With her needle she teased a finer piece from the strip, tied it tightly to the end of her needle and began to pull it through the fine birdskins of her suk.

She sewed the leather strip up both sides and across the bottom but left the top open, then, being sure that neither man saw her, she curled several long strands of sinew around her fingers and worked them down the length

138

of the strip until they were at the bottom of her suk.

Using her awl, Chagak made a line of holes across the leather just above the coil of sinew, then sewed the coil inside.

Again, watching that Man-who-kills did not see her, she slipped a small ivory needle case down the length of the leather strip. There were several needles inside and the top of the case served as a thimble for forcing an awl through thick leather. She made another seam across the leather and sealed the needle case inside.

Working carefully, she filled the leather strip: lamp wicks; a packet of dried caribou leaf for medicine; a mesh berry bag, folded small; shell fishhooks and a fine line of nettle fiber; flint and a fire stone, each wrapped in a leather pouch. All things she would need when she had left this place; all things she would need when hiding from Man-who-kills.

FOURTEEN

The next morning Chagak made herself watch Man-who-kills, the way he ate, the way he stood, the way he walked. Though her spirit shrank from the man and her eyes fought against the watching, Chagak would not allow herself to look away. All men had certain ways of doing things, of speaking, of sitting and standing. She must know when Man-who-kills worked, when he slept, when he merely sat, doing nothing. How else could she plan the best moment for her escape?

That morning Chagak had her cooking stone heated. When Man-who-kills demanded fried meat, she cooked it quickly. She had water ready for him to drink, and when he left the ulaq, Chagak took a partially tanned hair seal hide and followed Man-who-kills to the beach.

Man-who-kills went to his ikyak, but Chagak stopped some distance away and unrolled the hide. She would finish scraping the hide, then cut it into boot tops for Shuganan.

She had done the first scraping, cutting the thick soft layer of fat and tiny blood vessels from the flesh side of the hide, then soaking it until the hair slipped off easily with pressure from a blunt-edged knife. Now Chagak would stake it out, scraping and smoothing the hide until it was clean of all remaining hair and flesh. Then she would let it dry.

Chagak spread the hide out on the beach and, padding her hand with a wad of leather, used a fist-sized rock to pound in the first stake. Staking was a difficult job, something that men of her village helped their women do, but Man-who-kills, though he turned from inspecting his ikyak and watched Chagak struggling with the hide, made no offer to help her stretch the skin or pound in the stakes.

Finally Shuganan came from the ulaq and helped Chagak. Shuganan gripped the hide and leaned against it to stretch the skin while Chagak pounded in the stakes. Once, when Shuganan's fingers slipped and he fell hard to the ground, Man-who-kills laughed. But Shuganan stood up and again clasped the hide, his crooked fingers white with the strain of pulling. Chagak's anger grew with each stroke from her pounding stone, beat into her spirit with the rhythm of stone against stake. But then she reminded herself why she was outside, why she had chosen to scrape the hide. She wanted to watch Man-who-kills. There was that chance that she would see something to aid her escape.

Finally Chagak pounded in the last stake. The hide was not as tight as she liked it to be, as it had been when her father or uncle had helped her, but it was not so loose that the scraping bone caught and tore the hide.

The scraping bone had belonged to Chagak's mother. It was made from a caribou leg bone her father had bought in trade from the Walrus Men. He had soaked it in oil to soften it, then cut off one end at an angle, dug the marrow from the center and serrated the cut end. Chagak had been only a small child then, but she still remembered him making the scraper, and she remembered how her mother had treasured it.

Chagak held the scraper at an angle with the ground, the serrated edge pressed against the hide and pointing toward herself. A leather thong tied at the top of the scraper and looped around her forearm kept the tool steady in her hand.

The hide was from a hair seal that Shuganan had taken just after Chagak came to his beach. It had been a small seal, but even so the hide was twice as wide as Chagak could reach, and she worked it in a circle, starting from the center and scraping back, moving around the entire skin.

Once she had removed the last bits of flesh, she would use a pumice rubbing stone to thin the thicker areas at the center of the back so the hide would not become stiff and useless.

The sun was warm, and in the monotonous rhythm of her work Chagak could almost forget Man-who-kills, almost believe she was on her own beach and would soon be Seal Stalker's bride.

She closed her eyes and imagined her mother beside her, telling stories of good wives and the joys of being a mother.

The memories brought pain but, for the first time, also joy, and the ache that had not left her chest since her village had been destroyed was eased by the closeness of her mother's spirit.

The sound of an ikyak did not startle Chagak, though she knew both Shuganan and Man-who-kills were on the beach. When she had lived with her people, there was always the sound of an ikyak, always the call of a man returning from the hunt.

But suddenly Chagak realized that the one who called was speaking the strange harsh words of Man-who-kills' language, and she opened her eyes, looked out toward the ocean to see a man nearly at the shore. Man-who-kills was laughing as he waded into the water to guide the ikyak.

Then Shuganan was beside her, standing between Chagak and the man in the ikyak. "Go to the ulaq, Chagak," he said, his voice low. "Stay in a dark corner. Set out food but do not take off your suk."

She stood up, then hesitated, looking down at the stretched sealskin. If she left it, the hide might harden in the sun.

"Leave it," Shuganan whispered.

She turned and walked up the beach. Shuganan hurried beside her.

Chagak had laid a long grass mat in the center of the room and arranged fish, eggs and dried whelks in piles on the mat. Now she squatted in the corner, saying nothing, waiting. Shuganan sat beside her.

Once the old man hobbled to an oil lamp, ran his hand along the edge of the oil bowl, pinched several of the cold wicks between his fingers. Then he came back to Chagak, his hands black with soot, and rubbed it over her cheeks and along the ridge of her nose.

Chagak looked at him in surprise, but when she started to speak, he laid his finger against her lips and said, "Say nothing. Do not look at Man-who-kills or his friend. Do not take off your suk. Do nothing to draw attention to yourself."

Finally the two young men came into the ulaq. Chagak glanced at the new man as he slid down the climbing log, but then she turned, pressing herself smaller into the shadows of the ulaq. She picked up a basket she was finishing and bent her head over the work and, using her teeth, trimmed the bits of grasses that stuck out here and there.

Man-who-kills said something to Shuganan and the old man moved to the center of the ulaq, neither offering open palms to the stranger nor squatting beside him.

Chagak kept her head bent. She moved her eyes toward the men and looked at them through the curtain of her hair. The new man was staring at Shuganan's carvings. He slipped off his parka and Man-who-kills did the same. They were about the same height, but Man-who-kills had wider shoulders, a more powerful build.

The new man had long hair but, unlike Man-who-kills, did not let it hang loose. Instead, it was bound at the nape of his neck with a strip of white fur. His face was flat, the skin drawn tight over his cheeks and nose so that his round nostrils always seemed flared and moved in and out with each breath. He had brown broken teeth.

His voice was harsh, like the grating of an ik against a gravel beach, something that had always made Chagak shiver with clenched teeth.

She bent so low over her work that her hair

brushed the ulaq floor, and she barely allowed her hands to move on the basket for fear the movement of one finger might attract the men's attention. She tried not to look at them. Why chance the catching and clinging of spirits that sometimes comes through the eyes?

Man-who-kills said something and pointed to the shelves of carvings, then he and his friend moved around the ulaq, occasionally picking up a carving, taking it to an oil lamp to study, then returning it to the shelf.

Shuganan tried to move so his body was always between the men and Chagak. Man-who-kills had offered a bride price for the woman, but who could say? Two men together often did things one would not. Perhaps they would both demand the hospitality of having a woman. He had never asked Chagak if she had been with a man. He knew she was to marry, so perhaps she had shared a sleeping place with her young man. His wife's tribe, the Whale Hunters, took their young women easily. An unmarried woman was allowed any man but her brothers, father or grandfather. Among many seal-hunting tribes, however, women were often saved until marriage.

It would be better for Chagak if she had some experience with men.

Man-who-kills' friend picked up the carving of a baleen whale, cupped it in his hands.

"This is something I need," he said to Shuganan. "Will you trade for it?"

Shuganan met the man's narrow eyes. "No," he said. "I do not trade for any of these things. They have their own spirits. They do not belong to me."

Man-who-kills lifted the corners of his mouth, showing his teeth, and the muscles of his jaw made knots along the sides of his face. "It will be a gift," he said slowly, his eyes on Shuganan. "Sees-far needs a spirit protector." Man-who-kills gripped the carving that hung from a cord around his neck.

Shuganan said nothing, but his thoughts were on his weapons, the knife still hidden in Chagak's sleeping place, the thin sharp blade of the knife he kept in the grass of his sleeping place. But he was an old man. And each night Man-who-kills tied his hands and ankles, looping the ends of the rope over the rafters above the sleeping place.

How will I kill two when I could not kill one? he asked himself. He wished he were a young man and did not have the swollen joints that slowed his run to a walk and stole strength from his arms.

The two young men continued around the ulaq, studying each carving. Finally Sees-far turned to Shuganan and said, "Your woman can make me a cord for this?" He held out the whale carving.

Before Shuganan could answer, Man-who-kills said, "She is his granddaughter."

Sees-far smiled and scratched under his apron. "Free to all?"

"No," Shuganan said, stepping closer to the man, but Man-who-kills moved between them.

"He asks a bride price," Man-who-kills said. "I have spoken for her."

Sees-far smirked. "So that is why you have stayed away from the fighting. Your father thinks you are dead." He laughed. "Now he will wish you were dead. Better dead than living in shame, tied to a woman's crotch."

"You are stupid," Man-who-kills said. The veins of his temples were suddenly round and pulsing under his skin. "The one who named you Sees-far should have called you Sees-nothing. You have studied all these carvings and you do not know who this man is?"

For a moment Man-who-kills turned away, but then he spun back, pushing Sees-far against the curtained opening of a sleeping place. "He is Shuganan. You do not remember the stories? Shuganan. I have found Shuganan.

"He is not dead, but he does not want to return to our people. How could I leave? He would disappear again. How could I take that chance? But now you have come. You must

148

return to my father and tell him I have found Shuganan and that I have married his grand-daughter."

Shuganan heard the words with dread. It was as Man-who-kills said. Before Sees-far came, there had been a chance Shuganan could kill Man-who-kills and thus he and Chagak would remain hidden, but now . . .

Man-who-kills took the whale from Sees-far and squatted beside Chagak. "Tell her to make a cord for it," he said to Shuganan.

Shuganan repeated the words in Chagak's language.

Man-who-kills grasped Chagak's hair, pulled her head up and looked into her soot-darkened face. "Stupid woman," he said.

He turned to Shuganan. "Tell her Sees-far will be leaving tomorrow morning and she must prepare a good meal for him. Tell her Sees-far will not need the hospitality of a woman since he is staying only one night. Tell her also to wash her face. I do not want an ugly wife."

That night Man-who-kills left Shuganan's ankles untied. "There are two of us, old man," he said. "You could never kill us both."

Shuganan, lying still as Man-who-kills tied his wrists together, said nothing. During the nightly ritual of tying, Shuganan made many plans for killing Man-who-kills, but each night he also discarded each plan, having come across nothing that would ensure Man-who-kills' death and Chagak's safety. This night, with two Short Ones in his ulaq, Shuganan made no plans at all.

The next morning Man-who-kills left him tied and Shuganan lay in his sleeping place, listening to the men talk, knowing from their comments that Chagak was serving them food.

"She is a good woman, that one," Sees-far said, his voice bulging over the laugh that he seemed to carry in his throat whenever he spoke of Chagak. "Too bad you are not man enough to share her."

For a time there was silence, then Man-who-kills said, "How can I share her when I have not had her myself?"

"Take her. Who will stop you?"

"You are a fool. You see the power the old man has. You see the statues around you. How old are the stories of Shuganan? We both heard them as children and our fathers say the same. He is too old to be alive, but he lives. You do not think he has power?"

"So you do not kill him, but you tie him each night. That does not make him angry?"

"His spirit knows I could kill him and do not. What is a little rope? Besides, I plan to take Chagak as wife. Any man has the right to fight for a woman, so I fight with ropes."

Shuganan closed his eyes. Power without power. It was as though he were a young man again, choosing to follow a way that displeased his father, that was against the teaching and customs of his tribe. The power of the spirit against the power of killing and taking.

In his frustration, Shuganan began to pull at the ropes that tied his wrists. With the rope looped up over the rafters, there was not enough slack for Shuganan to reach his hidden knives. Shuganan worked until his wrists were raw, but then he heard Man-who-kills' voice rise in sudden excitement, and Shuganan lay still, listening again.

"It is our plan," Sees-far was saying. "We will return to our beaches for the winter, then next spring . . ." There was a slapping sound as if Sees-far had pounded his fist into the palm of his hand.

"You have scouted their village? You know their defenses?"

"I was one of the scouts. They sent me this way before returning home to see if I could find you."

"You have found me. But you also see that I cannot leave here. There are too many statues for one ikyak, even for two, and I cannot leave the old man or he may find a new beach. Then who can say how long it will take to find him?

"Tell my father what you have seen. Tell him to have the men stop here first, before fighting, and I will go with you. By then, I will have Chagak filled with a son and the child will bind her to me."

"You are so sure you can make a son," Sees-far said and laughed.

"I have all winter to try," Man-who-kills said and he also laughed.

Anger pushed from Shuganan's heart down his arms and the ropes seemed suddenly tighter, harsher on the burned skin of his wrists.

There was movement in the other room; Sees-far spoke to Chagak, but the girl was silent. Shuganan heard the men climbing the log, then Man-who-kills said, "Show my father the whale carving. Show him and tell him I will make Shuganan carve many whales, enough so that each warrior may wear one. With each of us holding such power, how can they stand against us?"

Shuganan lay back on his mats. His wife's people. They would attack his wife's people. He must warn the Whale Hunters soon or he would have to wait until spring. An old man could not travel in the sudden storms of winter.

"I will warn them," Shuganan whispered. "I will kill Man-who-kills and then I will warn them."

FIFTEEN

"I said you could use a knife?" Man-who-kills asked, pointing to the small knife Shuganan held.

"It is my carving knife," he told Man-who-kills. "You have seen me use it before."

"I do not want you to have a knife."

"I am an old man. I must carve while I am still alive." He gestured toward his pile of ivory and bone. "You see how much I have to do."

"I do not want you to have a knife," Man-who-kills said again, his voice rising.

Since Sees-far had left, Man-who-kills had become more demanding, not as easily appeased. Shuganan pushed himself to his feet and handed Man-who-kills the knife. He glanced at Chagak. She sat near an oil lamp weaving a basket, her head bent over her work. For a moment Shuganan let himself study the checkered design of her weaving, the stitches so tiny and tight that the basket would be able to hold water without leaking. Then, slowly, Shuganan walked around the ulaq, studying the many carvings on the shelves. He selected one, a man holding a

153

long-bladed hunting knife, and brought it to Man-who-kills. "Take this," he said. "If you are so frightened of an old man with a tiny knife, perhaps you need some protection."

Man-who-kills lifted his head and Shuganan saw the glow of anger in his eyes. "Shut your mouth, old man," Man-who-kills said, but he took the carving from Shuganan's hand. "I take the carving, but not because I fear you, or anyone." He dropped the crooked knife at Shuganan's feet.

Shuganan picked it up, sat down and began carving.

"What are you making that is so important?" Man-who-kills asked.

Shuganan turned the figurine so the man could see it. "Husband and wife," Shuganan said quietly, then added, "It is for Chagak."

Man-who-kills bent close to study the carving.

"It is not finished yet," Shuganan said.

Man-who-kills grunted. "It is good you make it for her," he said. "It will give her strength. But there is something more that is needed. Put a baby in her suk. A fine fat boy. She will give me many sons."

Shuganan glanced up at the man, then began working at the woman's suk. He would enlarge the collar rim and carve a tiny head peeking from within.

After a time he handed the carving to Man-who-kills, waited as the man held it next to a lamp and examined the infant's tiny features. Man-who-kills laughed and nodded, then tossed it back to Shuganan. "It is good," he said. "Now finish it. Give the man a face. My face."

Shuganan picked up the carving but said nothing. He would finish the man, but not with Man-who-kills' face.

"You are clever," Man-who-kills said. He squatted beside Shuganan and rocked on the balls of his feet. "And perhaps one who is clever enough to find people in bits of bone and teeth can do other things. Perhaps a man who is clever at finding is also clever at hiding."

At Man-who-kills' last words, a chill pushed through Shuganan's body, tightened his chest and moved his heart to beat in quick, hard thumps. But he did not look up from his carving and continued to work on the small nose, the tiny eyes of the infant.

Man-who-kills picked up an oil lamp and entered Shuganan's sleeping place.

The light from the lamp made Man-who-kills' body look like a shadow behind the sleeping curtain. Shuganan could see him searching along the wall, running his hands up and down, pausing once in a while to pry at some irregularity in the surface.

The man made slow progress around the room and then dropped to his knees to search the floor. Shuganan looked at Chagak and saw that the girl's face was pale, her lips pursed.

"I have knives hidden," Shuganan said to her, his words low and soft.

Chagak nodded but said nothing, her eyes on the curtain of Shuganan's sleeping place. Suddenly Man-who-kills called to Shuganan, "You are not as smart as I thought, old man." And drawing the curtain aside, he held up the hunting knife Shuganan had hidden in the floor grass.

Shuganan waited, hoping the man would stop searching, that finding one knife would satisfy him, but Man-who-kills stayed in the sleeping place until Shuganan heard him exclaim again.

"He has found the crooked knife," he said to Chagak.

"You hid more than one knife?" she asked.

"Three in my sleeping place," said Shuganan. "One in the floor of . . ."

Man-who-kills cried out again, and then he lunged through the curtain. Three knives were in his left hand. He held the fistful of blades at Shuganan's throat and asked, "Are there more?"

"No," Shuganan said, unafraid. He was an

old man. What was death?

But then Chagak was at his side, her small hands between the knives and Shuganan's neck. "Do not kill him," she pleaded. "I hid the knives. Kill me."

"What does she say?" Man-who-kills asked, his voice a whisper, hot against Shuganan's cheek.

"She asks you not to kill me," Shuganan said.

Man-who-kills laughed, the points of his corner teeth pressing into his bottom lip. "I am not so stupid," Man-who-kills said. "Why should I kill you? There is not enough pain in that."

He jerked Chagak away and ran the points of the knives down Shuganan's neck, leaving three parallel scratches.

Shuganan gritted his teeth but remained still.

"You think you are a hunter, old man?" Man-who-kills said and, drawing back his right hand, hit Shuganan hard in the belly.

Shuganan curled himself into a ball, arms over his head, face against his knees, and tried to catch his breath. Man-who-kills kicked him. Chagak began to cry, the cries like small screams. Shuganan tensed for another blow, but when nothing came, he looked up, saw Man-who-kills had been waiting for him to raise his head. Man-who-kills hit Shuganan in the mouth.

Shuganan rolled away, stanching the blood from his lip with both hands. Then he saw Chagak throw herself against Man-who-kills, hitting with both fists as she rammed him with her head.

"Chagak, no," Shuganan said. The words, mixed with pain, were slurred.

Man-who-kills caught one of Chagak's hands, but she scratched at his face with the other. He dropped the knives and tried to grasp both Chagak's hands but, lunging forward, she grabbed the hunting knife from the floor.

Thrusting the knife toward Man-who-kills, Chagak sliced through his parka, and Shuganan saw blood welling up from the wound.

Man-who-kills screamed, a war cry that shook the ulaq, then he hit Chagak across the face. She dropped the knife and he was upon her, straddling her belly, slapping her face.

"No," Shuganan yelled. But Man-who-kills, still slapping and punching, did not seem to hear him.

Shuganan threw himself against the man. Shuganan's ribs ached when he hit, and for a moment he could not breathe, but he reached for the crooked knife laying beside Man-who-kills' knee.

Man-who-kills grabbed it before Shuganan

could and held it at Chagak's throat.

Chagak lay still, face bleeding, eyes wide, unblinking, and Shuganan's heartbeat was caught somewhere in his throat until the girl took a breath.

Shuganan saw the anger in Man-who-kills' face, but in the sudden quiet Shuganan said, "Kill her. She wishes to be dead. Then she will be with the man she was to marry and with her mother and father. Kill both of us and we will warn those who live at the Dancing Lights of the evil spirits you carry."

Man-who-kills curled his lips but rolled from Chagak's chest. He gathered the knives and stuck them in his belt.

"Go into your sleeping place," he said. "Take her to her place also. Tomorrow we hunt seal."

Man-who-kills stood and tipped the water skin that hung from a rafter. Water flowed into his mouth and over his face. Shuganan's body ached, but he bent over Chagak and lifted her to her feet. He put an arm around her shoulders and looked into her face.

She was not crying and in her eyes he saw a great glowing as if some light grew there. She leaned her head back on his shoulder and whispered, "Where in my sleeping place is the knife?"

But Man-who-kills shouted, "Do not talk!"

So Shuganan did not answer her.

In the morning Man-who-kills tied Chagak to the bottom of the climbing log. He laid a pile of sealskins at her feet. "Tell her to make babiche," he said to Shuganan. "Tell her we go to hunt seal for her bride price."

But before Shuganan could translate the words, Chagak said, "Ask him how I can make babiche without my woman's knife."

"You have her knife," Shuganan said to Man-who-kills. "How can she make babiche without a knife?"

Man-who-kills shrugged and picked up his harpoon.

Chagak said, "Ask him to give me the pile of skins there and my scraper." She pointed, and before Shuganan told Man-who-kills what she had said, the man had gathered the folded hides and laid them beside her.

"She needs a scraper and pounding stone," Shuganan said and hobbled to Chagak's storage corner. He brought back the stone and the scraper.

Shuganan knew Chagak preferred to work outside when scraping hides so the wind would blow away bits of hair and flesh her scraper shaved from the skin, but though she had to stay in the ulaq, at least she would have something to do.

Shuganan gathered a handful of stakes and spread one skin out on the floor. He used the pounding stone to drive the stakes through the edges of the hide and into the hard dirt.

"She can do that, old man," Man-who-kills said. "We must go now or we will not return before dark."

Shuganan looked up at him, surprised. "You go for seals and think we will return in one day?"

"I am a hunter," Man-who-kills said, lowering his eyelids, looking at Shuganan through the black of his lashes.

Shuganan looked away, took a breath and felt the pain of the night before in his ribs. "She needs water and food. What if we do not come back for three or four days? Why bring a bride price if you let the bride die?"

Man-who-kills strode to the center of the ulaq and untied the water skin. He brought it to the climbing log and tied it four notches up so Chagak could reach it when she stood. "Get her some food," he said to Shuganan. "Not much. I told you we will be back tonight."

But Shuganan dragged a seal stomach of dried fish to Chagak and propped it against the climbing log.

Man-who-kills stood with one foot on the log. He cupped his hand around Shuganan's chin and said, "You are generous, old man." His breath was strong with the smell of fish. "But let her eat. I like fat women. They make better sons."

He bent and pulled a handful of fish from the seal stomach and pushed them into the bag he had slung at his neck. "Get me eggs," he said to Shuganan and handed Shuganan the carrying pouch.

Shuganan filled the bag, then, as he passed Chagak, he pressed something quickly into her hands, for a moment felt the coolness of her fingers on his.

Shuganan thought that Man-who-kills had not seen, but the man took the pouch from Shuganan and said, "What did you give her?"

Shuganan smiled, hoping his face did not betray his nervousness. "The carving," he said. He wrapped his hand around Chagak's and turned the carving toward Man-who-kills, hoping the man would not look too closely, would not see what he had done with the face of the husband and with the base of the image.

Man-who-kills laughed. "We will bring many seals, maybe more than two. And while the woman waits, your little people will teach her to be a wife."

He pushed Shuganan up the climbing log, but Shuganan paused a moment at the top.

He looked down at the dark and shining crown of Chagak's head.

She glanced up at him, and he saw the understanding in her eyes, saw she had pressed her thumb over the face of the husband. She lifted her hand to him and Shuganan turned away, holding the memory of her eyes in his mind — something he would keep with him if he could carry out his plans, something he would keep with him even if he could not.

SIXTEEN

Shuganan kept his ikyak in a cliff cave at the edge of the beach. Even at high tide the cave was dry. Man-who-kills' ikyak was nearby, tied to several rocks to keep the wind from smashing it against the side of the cliff.

Man-who-kills began packing his ikyak, pushing bundles of food and an extra chigadax into the craft. His ikyak was longer and thinner than Shuganan's and Shuganan thought the hide that covered the wood frame, bottom, sides and top was walrus rather than sea lion.

"When did the People learn to make such ikyan?" Shuganan asked, remembering the wider, smaller craft they had used during his youth.

"We have learned much, old man," Man-who-kills said. "This one is patterned from the Walrus Hunters' ikyan. It goes faster in the water and is easier to turn."

"It must also flip over more easily," Shuganan said, seeing the narrowness of the frame. The craft was scarcely wider than the hole at the top where the hunter sat.

"For some," Man-who-kills said. "Get your ikyak."

Shuganan hesitated, hating to pull aside the grass and rocks that covered the entrance of the ikyak cave. It was a good place to hide, some place he and Chagak could go that Man-who-kills would not find them.

Man-who-kills was attaching a harpoon to a coil of babiche tied at the right-hand side of the ikyak. He reached out and shoved Shuganan. "Go."

Shuganan pointed toward the cliff wall. "It is there," he said. "Inside a cave."

Man-who-kills narrowed his eyes and left his ikyak to watch as Shuganan pulled away brush and loose rock.

"Some caves are deep," Man-who-kills called when Shuganan had uncovered the entrance. "Maybe you will go inside and not return."

Shuganan did not answer.

The cave was small, only as wide as a man's arms outstretched, and as long as a ulaq. The entrance was narrow, even for Shuganan, but he wiggled through. Inside was dark, but he could see the outline of his ikyak. It was where he had left it that spring, suspended from a strong driftwood beam Shuganan had secured at the top of the cave when he was a young man. Then, he had had the strength to lift the ikyak and tie it in place, above the reach of storm waves. But now, though the ikyak was light, it was difficult for Shuganan to lift. So he had tied it to ropes that ran over the beam and were fastened to wooden pegs pounded into the cave walls.

Shuganan untied one rope and let it out slowly until the stern of the ikyak rested on the cave floor.

"Old man, you take too long," Man-who-kills called.

But Shuganan did not try to hurry. The longer he took, the more time Chagak had. Shuganan lowered the bow of the ikyak and pulled his chigadax from the stern.

The chigadax was made of seal intestines sewn together in horizontal strips, each seam lapped and sewn double to keep out water. The chigadax was one of many that Shuganan had made for himself. It was not man's work to do such a thing, but if a man did not have a woman, what choice did he have? Who could survive the sea without a hooded chigadax?

The strips of translucent intestines seemed less apt to crack if he kept the chigadax in the cave. But after one summer, even if Shuganan oiled the chigadax every few days, the garment would mold, the skins weaken. Even now, as he unrolled it, he smelled mildew.

Throwing the chigadax through the cave entrance, Shuganan called to Man-who-kills, "I must oil my chigadax."

He looked outside, saw Man-who-kills pick up the garment, hold it to his nose and grimace. Man-who-kills spread it out on a patch of beach grass and untied a storage skin of oil from the side of his ikyak.

"You are stupid, old man," Man-who-kills muttered as he knelt and dumped oil over the front of the garment. "What hunter allows his chigadax to sit for days without oil? You think seals will come to us if you have no more respect for the sea than that?"

But Shuganan, pulling his ikyak from the cave, his back to the man, only smiled.

Chagak cradled Shuganan's carving to her chest and leaned her head against the climbing log. Her jaw ached where Man-who-kills had hit her, and her teeth were loose on that side of her mouth. She shuddered at the thought of being wife to him, and a faint hope came to her in a whisper: Maybe the sea animals will drown him. Maybe there will be a terrible storm.

"No," Chagak said aloud, and heard the word echo in the empty ulaq. "Shuganan is with him."

At first, after the men left, Chagak had

struggled with the ropes that bound her, but Man-who-kills had tied them so that if she pulled they tightened. Now her hands and feet were swelling, the ropes so tight at wrists and ankles that Chagak could not move without pain.

The rope that bound her wrists to the climbing log was long enough for Chagak to kneel and reach the floor, but even if there had been no pain, with both hands tied so closely together, it would be difficult to do anything, even scrape the hides Shuganan had laid out for her. And if she forgot her bonds and pushed the scraper too far, the ropes would tighten again.

Chagak held the carving to her cheek and thought about the old man who had given it to her. She often wondered how he had learned Man-who-kills' language. Had he been a trader?

Yes, Chagak thought, looking at the shelves of his carvings. Men would give many furs for even one or two of these pieces — ivory animals, bone people that looked so real that sometimes Chagak felt their spirits pressing against her, felt the need to leave the ulaq just to be alone.

She studied the carving Shuganan had given her. At first, when he handed it to her, when she saw Man-who-kills' sly happiness over it, the carving had made her angry. Yes, once, long ago, she had wanted to be wife, to have babies, but now she wanted only to be free from Man-who-kills. But then she had noticed the detail of the husband's face. His eyes were wide-set and cheekbones high. His smile was gentle. It was not Man-who-kills.

Chagak marveled that Shuganan had the courage to do such a thing. What if Man-who-kills saw it? He, too, would know the man was not him, was not even a hunter from his tribe. He would know Shuganan had used the power of his carving to call another husband to Chagak, someone good and gentle.

I must hide it, Chagak thought. But where?

There was no hiding place close to the climbing log, but if she wore it under her suk until the men returned and released her, perhaps she could hide it before Man-who-kills saw it.

Chagak reached into her sewing basket and found a chunk of sinew. She teased out three strands, twisted them together and tied them around the carving. Then she fastened the carving next to the shaman's amulet that hung at her neck.

Chagak clasped the carving. It was warm as if alive. She pressed it against her cheek and as she did she saw an outline in the smooth, flat base. She held the carving toward an oil lamp. The light showed a circle in the ivory, indented all around.

With fingernail and thumbnail she pulled until the circle popped out, revealing a long hollow space. Chagak turned the carving over and shook it but nothing came out.

Why would Shuganan drill a hole in a carving? Was it a place to keep sacred things? She slipped her finger into the hollow, felt something soft. She caught it with the tip of her fingernail and worked until she had pulled a fluff of puffin down from the hole. This time when she turned the statue over, though nothing came out, she could feel movement. She pulled out more feathers until finally, hitting the carving against the climbing log, she dislodged the last of the packing.

A small packet wrapped in a thin piece of seal hide and bound with fine sinew slid to the floor. Chagak carefully unwrapped it, then gasped. It was an obsidian blade no longer than the top joint of a finger.

The blade from his carving knife, Chagak thought, and gratefulness welled up to push away the pain in her hands and feet.

She gripped the blunt edge of the blade between her fingers and began to saw at the ropes that bound her.

How long would the men be gone? Most seal hunts were two or three days. How far could she go in her ik? Which direction should she go? Perhaps to the Whale Hunters. Man-who-kills might think she would go east toward other seal hunters' villages.

Yes, she decided. I will cross the next channel and go to my grandfather. Perhaps the Whale Hunters will come back with me and rescue Shuganan.

It was well into the morning before Shuganan and Man-who-kills pushed off from the beach. Shuganan sat in the ikyak, legs stretched before him, the hood of his chigadax tight around his head, the bottom of the garment laced to the skin covering of the boat in a waterproof bond.

The sky was heavy with clouds, and a south wind sharpened the ocean swells into waves that towered over the ikyak on both sides. The sea carried the gray of the sky, and the water took on a heaviness that made it seem thick and unwieldy against Shuganan's paddle.

We will have trouble finding seals, he thought. Man-who-kills had fastened Shuganan's ikyak to his with a long babiche rope, something that kept them together but hindered their paddling and made it difficult to keep the bows of the ikyan turned into the waves.

But Man-who-kills' problems did not bother Shuganan. His fear was that the rough sea would

171

make Chagak's escape too difficult. Would she be able to handle the ik in high waves? What if water slapped in over the open top? The ik was not a craft that could be righted easily like the watertight ikyak.

And if Chagak did not find the plug in the bottom of the carving, she would have no knife and could not escape at all.

But Shuganan had lain awake the night before, planning what he would do if Man-who-kills took him hunting. Perhaps it would not matter if Chagak did not escape. Perhaps Man-who-kills would not return from this hunt. The sea was dangerous, and every hunt carried the possibility that the hunter would not return. What man did not know that? What man, feeling the joy of the water under him—only the thickness of a seal hide between the sea and his legs — still did not turn, looking one last time to the shore, toward his ulaq and his village? What man did not clasp his amulet and ask the spirits of the sea for protection?

But what if, in killing Man-who-kills, I lose my own life? Shuganan thought and lifted his eyes toward the horizon. I have had many years and have no great need for more, but what if Chagak does not find the blade hidden in the carving? What if she does not get loose? She had a few days' supplies, water for perhaps four days, food for eight or ten, but then what would she do? Would it be worse for her to die in the ulaq without water, without food, or would she rather live as wife in Man-who-kills' village? As wife, at least she would have babies, children to bring her joy.

She will find the knife, Shuganan assured himself. Yes, she will find the knife. Then she will go to her grandfather and be safe. She will do that, and I will do what I must do.

Shuganan looked ahead toward Man-who-kills, at the man's broad back, his strong arms. He used the paddle easily, and it was difficult for Shuganan to keep up with him. More than once the rope grew taut between them, and Man-who-kills looked back with a scowl each time it jerked against Shuganan's ikyak.

Shuganan squinted toward the horizon. The gray of the sky melted into the edge of the sea and he could no longer find the dark line of his island. They had seen no seals' dark heads bobbing from the water, and Man-who-kills had not yet directed his ikyak toward any of the seal islands. Perhaps he does not know about those islands, Shuganan thought, and if he waits for a sighting on the sea, he could wait for days.

Shuganan lifted his head and smiled. Yes, Chagak will find the knife, he thought. She will find the knife and I will kill Man-who-kills.

SEVENTEEN

Chagak rubbed her wrists and ankles, then, squatting on her heels, tucked the tiny blade with its down packing into the carving and slipped it inside her suk. It had taken most of the morning to cut through the thick babiche ropes, but she was free.

For a moment she sat still, again going over the things she must take with her. Water, oil, dried fish, tanned sealskins and her sewing basket, perhaps a basket of dried whelk, a coil of rope, hooks, the bola, sinew for fishing line, her woman's knife, dried herbs for healing, grass mats.

She piled the supplies at the bottom of the climbing log, then went outside. She walked to the beach, her heart pounding with each step. What if Man-who-kills was there? What if he were waiting to see if she would try to escape?

But there was no one; the beach was wide and empty.

Her ik was inverted on a rack near the ikyak cave. She and Shuganan had spent much time since the storm repairing the ik, replacing wood ribbing and torn parts of the hide covering.

Chagak ran her hands over the covering, checking for any tears or punctures in the hide. A wave crashed in on the beach gravel, and the water hissed as it pulled itself back to the sea. The beach was colder, the wind stronger than on her people's beach.

Chagak thought of Shuganan. He had meant for her to escape. Why else would he give her the carving with the knife? Even so, she was afraid for Shuganan. What would Man-who-kills do when he found she was gone?

But she had seen Shuganan's power over Man-who-kills. It would take more than her escape to endanger Shuganan's life. And I will bring my grandfather, Chagak thought. Then, seeing the thought as a promise, she said aloud to any spirits that might be near, "I will bring my grandfather and his hunters. They will rescue Shuganan."

Then, remembering what little value her grandfather placed on his granddaughters, Chagak shivered and hurried back to the ulaq to get her supplies.

"Hah!" Man-who-kills shouted and, lifting his paddle, pointed with the blade toward something dark in the water.

Shuganan strained to see but could make out only a break in the water, something that could be driftwood or even a white and black sea duck, swimming the trough of the waves.

Man-who-kills began paddling toward the place, but Shuganan purposely allowed his ikyak to pull heavily against Man-who-kills' craft.

"You paddle like a woman," Man-who-kills called back to him, his voice cutting the noise of waves and wind.

"I am old," Shuganan answered, not caring if Man-who-kills heard him.

"You will be dead if you do not keep up," Man-who-kills shouted, his words carried to Shuganan by a gust of wind.

Shuganan thrust his paddle deep into the water, pulling his ikyak close to Man-who-kills. Then he held his paddle still, vertical in the water, and when Man-who-kills sent his ikyak ahead with a strong stroke, the rope between the two crafts stretched tight and jerked Man-who-kills' ikyak back.

"Stupid," Man-who-kills hissed, but Shuganan only shrugged and said, "I told you I am old." And this time he yelled the words so Man-who-kills could hear and perhaps, if the thing they had seen was a seal, it, too, would hear.

The object in the sea seemed to be moving away from them. Not driftwood, Shuganan thought. He kept his ikyak behind Man-who-kills, kept his paddling slow enough to be a hindrance.

"Two, there are two," Man-who-kills called to him, his voice low.

"I cannot hear you," Shuganan shouted, though he had heard, and he made his voice high so it would carry above the waves. "What did you say?"

"Shut your mouth, old man."

"Is it a seal?" Shuganan called.

"Shut your mouth!" Man-who-kills stopped paddling, and before Shuganan could stop his ikyak, he was abreast of the man. Man-who-kills whipped his paddle from the water and slammed the flat of the blade into Shuganan's side.

"Shut your mouth, old man," he said, his voice low.

Shuganan felt the sharp crack of a rib, heard the whoosh of air that came from his lungs. He sat still, trying to breathe, gripping the paddle as the pain tried to pry it from his fingers.

"Two seals," Man-who-kills said as though he had not hit Shuganan. Unlashing one of his harpoons, he checked the coil of sinew that linked the head to the shaft. "Two seals, and I will get both of them."

Chagak pushed the ik into the calm water of a tidal pool. The pool extended in a wide

177

arc, one end nearly at the center of the beach, the other dipping into the sea. It was a good place to pack a boat, to launch it when there was no one else to help.

She had her supplies out of the ulaq and piled on the beach by the pool. As she loaded the ik, she tied most of her things to the boat's thwarts to prevent shifting.

When everything was in, she went to the cave where Shuganan kept his ikyak. She took an extra paddle, babiche and oiled skins for repairs. She also took a bailing tube. The long, slender tube was carved from bamboo, a wood that often drifted to their beach. By sucking water into the tube and releasing it over the edge of her ik, she could bail with one hand yet still guide the craft with a paddle.

Chagak laid a seal hide, fur up, in the stern where she would sit, then took off her suk and threw it into the boat. Wading into the tidal pool, she pulled the ik toward the sea.

The waves caught her legs and sharp edges of shale cut her feet, but Chagak walked until the water was waist high. Then, grasping the edge of the ik, she hoisted herself in and grabbed a paddle.

She directed her ik into the waves, using all her strength to keep the bow slicing through foam and cap, but when she was in deep water, the waves only high swells, she laid her dripping paddle in the bottom of the ik and put on her suk, feathers in for warmth.

Shuganan crossed his arms over his chest and held his sides. Each breath brought pain, as though his ribs would fall loose from his spine.

Man-who-kills had guided their ikyan closer to the seal, and Shuganan, in his pain, was unable to fight against him. Shuganan's lungs ached with the need for air, so he braced his hands against his sides and took a long, slow breath.

Man-who-kills fitted the butt end of his harpoon into the hook of his spear thrower. The thrower was the length of the man's forearm and more than half the width of his hand. It was similar to Shuganan's spear thrower, with a hole for his forefinger and notch for his palm, but it was painted with designs of seals and hunters while Shuganan's board was carved.

Man-who-kills held the board at one end and allowed the other end to extend over his shoulder. The device lengthened his arm and, therefore, his throw.

They were close enough to the animals that Shuganan could see they were hair seals, valuable for their meat and for their tough hides.

Man-who-kills leaned back in the ikyak and cocked his arm. "Two," Shuganan heard Man-who-kills hiss, heard the man laugh to himself. And Shuganan wondered what had brought the laughter. The thought of Chagak, naked in his bed? The thought of honor earned by bringing Shuganan to his chief? And suddenly Shuganan's anger was greater than his hurt. He gripped his paddle in both hands and, forgetting his pain, dipped it lightly in the water, shortening the distance between the two crafts. He was close enough now to touch Man-who-kills' ikyak with his paddle, but he did not think Man-who-kills saw or heard anything except the seals.

Man-who-kills untied a second harpoon from his ikyak and held it in his left hand as he prepared to throw with his right.

They were in the trough of a wave, everything still and gray around them, sky and water. Shuganan grasped his paddle in both hands, held it before him like a weapon. Man-who-kills' ikyak crested the wave and he threw the harpoon, the man grunting as the shaft left the throwing board.

At the moment Man-who-kills threw, Shuganan raised his paddle, prepared to use it as a club against the man. But the beauty of the throw, the groan of the seal as it was hit, stopped him, and he sat still as Man-who-kills fitted the second harpoon into the thrower, hurled at the second seal. Again the harpoon struck.

But Shuganan still did not move. What spirit is working here? Shuganan thought. Why had the second seal stayed head above water even after the first was hit?

The seals dove, the heads of the harpoons in their flesh. The shafts, tied to the harpoon heads with lengths of sinew line, remained above the water, marking the seals' hiding places beneath the waves.

One of the seals surfaced. Man-who-kills drew his ikyak near, but the animal made no move to dive.

Man-who-kills pulled his harpoon shaft from the water and coiled the line around the holders attached to his ikyak. The second seal surfaced and it, too, waited as Man-who-kills tied the line to the ikyak.

Waited or is dead? Shuganan asked himself. Man-who-kills pulled each seal close to his ikyak. The bodies had begun to sink, held up only by their link to the ikyak.

They are dead, Shuganan thought as Man-who-kills attached drag lines to the back flippers. So quickly, they are dead. Where did Man-who-kills get such power?

Shuganan thought of the seal carving Man-who-kills had taken from the ulaq, but Shuganan could not give his own work that much power. It was too frightening, too horrible. What if other hunters came? What if they gained the same power by wearing his carvings and used that power for evil?

Again Shuganan took a shuddering breath. He lifted his paddle. He knew Man-who-kills would turn. A man who received his glory from self-praise could not make two quick kills without boasting.

"What do you think, old man?" Man-who-kills asked, turning his head, flashing his teeth.

Shuganan aimed his paddle as though it were a spear, as though the blade were harpoon, and slammed it into Man-who-kills' face.

The thrust was not as hard as Shuganan had hoped, but blood spurted from the man's nose and mouth. Shuganan drew the paddle back to hit again, but Man-who-kills caught the end of it, twisting the paddle until the muscles of Shuganan's sides felt they would rip from his ribs, until Shuganan's breath brought up blood from his lungs.

The pain spread to his fingers, numbed his hands. His arms strained so hard in their sockets that Shuganan thought the bones would break. Finally Man-who-kills jerked the paddle from Shuganan's hands and swung it hard against Shuganan's head.

Shuganan slid into the ikyak as far as he could. The wood supports protected his ribs and back, and he cradled his head in his arms. Man-who-kills swung again. The blow snapped a bone in Shuganan's left forearm, but he still held the arm over his head. Again the paddle came, and again. Blood congealed in a puddle on the drip skirt of his ikyak and spread thin wisps in the water like tails of red kelp.

Darkness edged Shuganan's vision, and each time the paddle hit, the darkness grew, blotting out the sea, the sky, until Shuganan saw only a pinpoint of light, until his only thoughts were of pain and the only thing he heard was some spirit saying, Do not die. Do not leave Chagak.

EIGHTEEN

Chagak turned her ik west. She knew she had at least a day's journey, perhaps more, to the Whale Hunters' island. Then she would have to search the coast for their village.

She hoped her grandfather would believe her and send hunters back to rescue Shuganan. But even if he did, Man-who-kills' people still planned to attack the Whale Hunters' village. Her grandfather's people would have a better chance if they were prepared, but could they stand against warriors who drew their power from killing? Chagak shuddered. Could she bear to live through another attack?

"No," she said aloud to the sea, then sent a prayer to Aka. "If all the Whale Hunters are killed, let me die, too. Choose someone else to bury the dead."

The sea rose in huge swells but there was little wind. At the top of each swell Chagak looked out as far as she could, keeping the land to her left, the sun to her right, and making a path in the sea between them.

She had packed the ik well, leaving a space in the stern for herself. It was a small ik but, even so, was difficult to maneuver. Chagak had to fight to make it turn, and she watched carefully so that, as she dipped the paddle in one side and then moved it across the ik to dip in at the other, she made strokes of equal force so the craft would not move in a circle.

She paddled steadily, not allowing herself to think of aching muscles, cramping legs as she knelt on the thick fur seal mat. The cliffs behind Shuganan's beach were so distant, it seemed they merely floated above the sea, a thin white-gray line separating them from the water.

For a moment the thought of Shuganan alone with Man-who-kills brought a tight, hard pain to Chagak's chest, but then she reasoned, Perhaps I can soon return to him.

But a quivering of fear settled into her belly, and she thought of Man-who-kills' anger and of Shuganan's old age. He had many summers, more than he could count. When a man was that old, who could say? He might live many more summers or perhaps only one.

She laid her paddle across the stern of the ik and at the top of the next swell surveyed the sea all around. She saw no sign of whale, of hunters or oncoming wind, but she waited for one more swell before putting the paddle back into the water.

At the top of the second swell Chagak directed her eyes to the north, out into the great walrus sea, a place Seal Stalker had spoken of, a place women from Chagak's tribe seldom saw.

And here I am alone in that sea, Chagak thought and wondered how the spirit of her mother felt, seeing Chagak use her ik as a man uses an ikyak. Chagak clasped the shaman's amulet and the carving she wore over it, and in that moment saw something dark in the sea.

Her ik dropped into the trough between swells and Chagak waited until the sea lifted her again. The dark place was larger. Perhaps an ikyak, she thought, but she could not be sure and so again waited through a trough and to the next swell.

"An ikyak, but too long to be an ikyak," she said, and at the words her heart jumped as though it had heard what she said and understood what Chagak at first did not understand: two ikyan. Shuganan and Man-who-kills.

Grabbing her paddle, Chagak pushed herself from the crest of the swell and kept her craft in the hollows, the walls of water protecting her from sight.

How in all this wide sea? Chagak thought. What spirits hate me? She moved along the trough, knowing there was some chance. If she kept the swells between them, Man-who-kills would not see her.

But if Man-who-kills were heading directly to the land, there would be that moment when his ikyak was in the same trough as Chagak's ik; it was a chance she must take. She could not try to outrun him; his slim, small ikyak was so much faster than her wide-bellied ik.

She waited, paddling only to keep herself in the hollow, and prayed that the men would not see her. Her spirit flitted, quick and agitated, within her chest, and her heart left a rhythm against her ribs like the sound of hunters beating the sides of an ikyak, a call for help.

Finally the pointed stern of Man-who-kills' ikyak rose above the crest of the wave. He was some distance away but close enough to see her if he looked west. Chagak sank the blade of her paddle deep into the water and pushed her ik farther down the trough.

Man-who-kills' ikyak slid into the trough. A rope attached to the stern stretched up over the wave, but Chagak could not see Shuganan's craft.

Her breath came in small gasps, pressing between her teeth in tiny hissing sounds. She watched as Man-who-kills leaned forward and the water rose beneath the ikyak, lifting it toward the next crest. Two fat hair seals were tied to the stern.

He does not see me, Chagak thought, but

at that moment Man-who-kills turned his ikyak into the trough. Chagak, paddle poised above the water, could not move. Man-who-kills shouted and pointed at her, then leaned back to pull against the rope that joined his ikyak to Shuganan's. Shuganan's ikyak slid into the hollow. He was bent forward, and Chagak could see that ropes crossed his shoulders and were knotted to harpoon holders at each side of the craft.

"He is dead," some spirit seemed to whisper, the words so blunt they drew the breath from Chagak's lungs as though she had been hit.

Chagak turned to paddle away from Man-who-kills, but at his shout she looked back, saw he had his harpoon pointing at Shuganan's chest.

"He is dead," the sea seemed to say. "Go. He is dead. You have a chance. Man-who-kills' ikyak is heavy with seals. Go."

But Chagak laid her paddle in the bottom of the boat. And with her back toward Man-who-kills, she untied the thong at her waist that held her woman's knife. Then, using the knife, she made a horizontal slit near the bottom of the leather strip she had sewn inside her suk and slid the knife into the strip.

She allowed the sea to lift her as it lifted Man-who-kills and Shuganan. Then, once more in a hollow, she slowly turned her ik and paddled toward them.

When she drew close, she could see that one of Shuganan's arms hung at an awkward angle, the hand dipping into the water. There was blood at his nostrils and mouth, some dried, but some still bright red. So Chagak knew that if he were dead he had only just died. But then as the ikyak moved up another swell and Shuganan's body was thrown back, Chagak saw new blood gush from his mouth, saw the blood bubble from his breath.

"He is alive," she told the sea.

Man-who-kills moved his harpoon from Shuganan to Chagak.

"Throw," she said. "Kill us both."

But Man-who-kills tied the harpoon in its place on the side of his ikyak and paddled toward shore.

With a deep stroke, Chagak sent her ik up the swell, following Man-who-kills and Shuganan.

"You will be dead!" some spirit screeched at her. "You will be dead."

"No," said Chagak. "I will not die. I will live and I will save Shuganan."

When Chagak beached her ik, Man-who-kills pulled Shuganan from the ikyak and left him crumpled on the beach, then he cut the lines that held the seals.

Chagak dragged her ik ashore without help, and when it was out of the reach of waves, she ran to Shuganan.

He still breathed. Each breath brought blood from his nose and mouth and a groan from his throat. She knelt beside him and tried to loosen his chigadax but Man-who-kills grabbed her by the hair and jerked her to her feet. He held his hunting knife at her throat.

"Kill me," Chagak shouted at him though she knew he could not understand her. "Kill me. Then I will be with my people and not with you."

Man-who-kills released her and, shouting, pointed at the ik and at Shuganan. Chagak saw the welt across Man-who-kills' face. A sudden pride in Shuganan's daring filled her chest and gave her courage to turn away from Man-who-kills and kneel beside Shuganan.

Chagak had packets of herbs, caribou leaf she had taken from Shuganan's supply.

She ran toward her ik, but Man-who-kills blocked her way. "You fool," Chagak yelled, "get out of my way." She lunged past him and began ripping at the cords that tied her supplies to the ik.

Pulling up her suk, she stuffed the packets of herbs into the waistband of her apron, then untied a heavy sleeping robe and carried it to Shuganan.

She did not look at Man-who-kills, did not care what he thought, what he was doing, as long as he did not try to stop her. She unfolded the robe and laid it, hair side up, beside Shuganan. Then, as carefully as she could, she moved him to it.

Again Chagak went to the ik, glancing at Man-who-kills as she passed him. He stood, his arms folded across his chest, saying nothing, only watching her. She grabbed a pile of tanned leather strips from the ik and turned back to Shuganan, but Man-who-kills caught her arm.

He said something to her and pointed at the two seals lying in the sand. Chagak knew he wanted her to take care of them, to remove the skins, cut up the meat, wash the bones, but she pretended she did not understand. She jerked her arm from his grasp, ran to the edge of the sea where she dipped one of the strips in the water, then came back to Shuganan and knelt beside him.

Chagak raised his head and laid it on her lap. Wiping away the blood on his face, she realized that some of his teeth were broken; their jagged edges tore his lips. Shuganan's face was discolored, one eye badly swollen. A long cut ran from his right ear to the top of his head.

His hands were also bloody, but when

191

Chagak washed them, she realized there were no wounds, that the blood was from his face. Shuganan groaned whenever she moved his left arm.

A gust of wind whipped her hair into her eyes and sand into Shuganan's wounds. I must get him to the ulaq, Chagak thought. She glanced up at Man-who-kills. He curled back his lips and spat into the beach gravel.

Chagak tied the top corners of the sleeping skin together, making a handle, and began to pull Shuganan up the rise of the beach toward the ulaq. He was not heavy, but the slope of the beach made the pulling difficult, and shale caught at the edges of the robe like hands trying to keep Shuganan near the sea.

Man-who-kills suddenly stepped in front of her, blocking her way. Chagak began to pull Shuganan around him, but Man-who-kills shouted at her and again pointed at the seals.

"I am not your wife," Chagak said, also yelling. "I do not have to do what you say." And even though she knew he did not understand her, she thought it was good to say the words, to let nearby spirits decide by listening who was right and who was wrong.

Chagak waited a moment, sure he would let her pass, sure he would see that she must tend Shuganan before worrying about seals, but he did not. And her anger was replaced by fear.

Shuganan was an old man. If Man-who-kills did not let Chagak help him, he might die.

Chagak turned her back to Man-who-kills and tightened her grip on the robe. But he grabbed her wrists, and his hands were so tight, Chagak could feel the crunching of her wrist bones.

He squeezed until Chagak let go of the robe, then he dragged her to the seals.

Chagak looked up at him, her teeth clenched. "No knife," she said, and when he did not seem to understand, she said again, louder, "I do not have a knife. How can I butcher them without a knife?"

She made cutting motions over one of the seals, and Man-who-kills nodded. Using his hunter's knife, he began to slash open the packets in Chagak's ik. He threw furs, food, even her mother's cooking stone to the beach, scattering the things close to the reach of waves.

"There is no knife there," Chagak screamed at him, anger bringing tears.

Finally he returned to her, holding a crooked knife, a small blade set in the side of a seal rib, a knife good for fine work, but something that would not cut through the thick seal hides. He threw it down beside her, then jerked her to her feet.

Before Chagak could stop him, he pulled

up her suk and ran his hands down her apron, dropped the suk and pushed up her sleeves. "I told you I do not have a knife," Chagak said, pushing her sleeves up farther, holding her arms out for him to see. She waited, her breath hard and full in her throat. The knife in the pocket at the bottom of her suk seemed too heavy. Surely he would notice the bulge, or perhaps even catch her thoughts and know she had hidden it.

He stared at her for a long time. Chagak met his eyes and did not look away. Finally he murmured something and turned toward the ulaq.

"Yes, you will find knives there," Chagak called after him, then she went over to Shuganan. He seemed to be breathing more easily. She gripped the robe and pulled, slowly moving him across the beach, out of the reach of the highest wave, against the cliff where he would be protected from the wind as she skinned and butchered the seals.

NINETEEN

In Chagak's village skinning and butchering
a seal was always the work of many women.
Two, perhaps three, would peel the hide from
the body; another would take the fat, still others cut away the meat. Then the hunter would
divide fat, meat and bones among the families.
The hunter's family got the hide, flippers and
first choice of the meat.

But here, Chagak had to do the work alone.
The animals were each as heavy as a big man,
and it was difficult for her to move them.

Man-who-kills had brought a woman's
knife and another crooked knife from the ulaq,
as well as several tanned hides. Chagak spread
out the hides, and when she had finished taking the skin from the first seal, she began
butchering. She sliced off the thick layer of
fat that covered the body and piled it in slabs,
then cut the meat from the bones and removed
the edible organs.

Carefully, she cut away the thick cord of
sinew that ran up the seal's spine and laid it
aside to dry; later she would twist the fibrous
strands into various thicknesses to use for sew-

ing. She tied the small intestine at each end before cutting it free. When she had finished the rest of the butchering, she would empty the contents into the sea, pull away the inner and outer layers, dry the intestine and roll it for storage. When she had enough saved she would slit and flatten the strips, then sew them together into a chigadax.

Chagak washed and scraped the stomach so it could be used as a storage container for fish or oil.

Finally only the bones were left. Some she would save for needles and small tools, but most she would boil for oil to light lamps and prepare food.

In her village the boiling of bones had been a time for feasting. The men started a line of fires across the beach and the women erected driftwood frameworks and hung large bags of hide filled with water. Rocks were heated in the fires and boys dropped the rocks into the water until the water boiled. Then seal bones were dropped in.

Old women who knew how much oil the bones should yield watched the layer that formed at the top of the water and, when it was thick enough, called the young women to remove the bones.

The bones were set on hides laid over the beach, and even before they were cool, the men came from their games of throwing and lifting and began to crack the bones with heavy stones.

For once, the hunters did not eat first. This time the men served the children, cracking bones and passing them to the youngest first so they could suck out any remaining oil or marrow. Then the men served the old ones, the women who tended the fires and finally themselves.

Chagak remembered all these things as she worked. And though her remembering brought pain, it kept her thoughts from Man-who-kills, for he stood above her, watching as she worked, and he did not offer to help her move the seal, but only smiled each time she had to roll the animal to a different position.

Chagak could hear Shuganan moan, but his moaning, though it tore at her spirit, gave her assurance that he still lived. And she forced herself to work faster, hoping that, once the seals were butchered, Man-who-kills would let her tend Shuganan.

It was dusk when Chagak finished the butchering. While she worked, Man-who-kills had taken all the supplies from her ik. For a time he had stood over the ik, knife in hand, and Chagak had been sure he would cut the hide covering and smash the frame, but he had not. Finally he had kicked her supplies into a tidal pool. But Chagak said nothing and pretended not to see.

He was the hunter. He was responsible for bringing food and hides. If he wanted to ruin what had been stored, it was his worry, not hers.

When Chagak finished piling the second seal's bones, she stood and stretched, arching her back. Man-who-kills shouted something, but she did not look at him.

Chagak laid down the knives and gathered up the hides that held the fat and began dragging them back to the ulaq. She would keep the fat in the cool storage chamber until she had time to render it to oil.

She noticed that Man-who-kills had picked up the knives, but he did not offer to help her carry any of the hides. He stood and kept the gulls from the meat as Chagak made the many trips back and forth to the ulaq. Her fear for Shuganan forced her to move quickly, though her arms and legs were weighted with fatigue.

"I am not tired. I am strong," Chagak whispered to the wind. "I am strong." The words seemed to strengthen her body, seemed to lighten the load of meat she dragged.

Finally only the skins she had used under the seal carcasses remained. Chagak pulled them to the sea and allowed the water to take the blood and the few scraps that were left. She dried the skins with handfuls of fine gravel and rolled them for storage.

Then Chagak walked past Man-who-kills and across the beach to kneel beside Shuganan. The old man breathed heavily, his eyes closed. Bruises discolored his face and, though he seemed to be asleep, he clutched his broken arm.

Chagak looked up at Man-who-kills. He was smirking and the smile on his face made her hate him more.

He needs to be dead, Chagak thought. But killing was what men did, and even the men of her own village did not kill men, only animals. But the thought came again: He needs to be dead. Then in words that pulsed like a hunter's chant: Someday I will kill him. I will kill him. Someday I will kill him.

The storytellers told of times long before Chagak's birth when the men, to protect their wives and children, had fought and killed other men.

Yes, Chagak thought. Man-who-kills does not need to live. And the weight of the knife in the front of her suk filled her with a sudden surge of power.

As she knelt beside Shuganan and called his name, the power seemed to gather itself within her breast and reach out to the old man. For a moment he opened his eyes, but he said nothing and Chagak was not sure whether he saw her or saw only the images of a dream.

"Be still," she said to him. "I will get you to the ulaq and give you medicine."

He closed his eyes, and Chagak looked over at Man-who-kills. Again she felt power coursing up from her knife and she said, "I must take him to the ulaq. Help me carry him."

And though Chagak knew he did not understand her words, he walked over to her. She gestured toward the other end of the robe, then picked up her end.

Man-who-kills spoke. Angry words. He lifted his hand to the welt on his face. Chagak looked closely at it. "I have medicine," she said, making motions with her hands of smoothing on a salve. "Help me carry Shuganan and I will make you medicine." Again she used her hands to illustrate the meaning of the words.

Man-who-kills grunted and picked up the other end of Shuganan's robe and together they carried him to the ulaq.

They laid him outside, in the lee of the ulaq. It would be better, Chagak knew. Outside, spirits of sickness did not settle into a body so quickly.

Chagak piled dead grass and driftwood into

a heap, then she climbed up the side of the ulaq, glancing only once at Man-who-kills as she descended the climbing log. He made no move to stop her.

Chagak took the packet of caribou leaves from the waistband of her apron, filled a berry bag with a small container of rendered fat and several wooden cups. She also lit a hunter's lamp, then, with the berry bag slung on her arm, she carried the lamp up the climbing log, shielding it against the wind when she went outside.

She started the fire, blowing on the flame until it took hold of the wood, then she returned to the ulaq. This time she brought a container of oil and one of water and a boiling bag. She hung the bag on a tripod over the fire and filled it with water. She worked quickly, making sure the flame did not touch the bag above the level of the water.

It was better to set the boiling bag a distance from the fire, to heat stones first and drop them into the water, heating and reheating stones, adding them to the water until it boiled. That way boiling bags lasted longer. When the bag was hung directly over the fire, the outer layer of the skin was charred and weakened. If the flame reached above the level of water in the bag, the bag would catch fire. But Man-who-kills had made Chagak wait too long and she did not want to wait longer. This way the medicine would be ready more quickly.

While she waited for the water to boil, she poured some of the powdered caribou leaves into one of the wooden cups and mixed them with fat, working the mixture with her fingers until the leaves were evenly distributed. Then she bent over Shuganan and began to smooth the medicine over his bruises, but Man-who-kills pushed himself between Shuganan and Chagak and gestured toward the mixture.

Chagak was angry. What were Man-who-kills' wounds compared to Shuganan's? But she smoothed the paste over Man-who-kills' cheek and clamped her teeth shut to keep her anger from creeping up to show itself in her face.

When she had finished with him, she turned back to Shuganan, and Man-who-kills did not try to stop her. She washed away the blood that matted Shuganan's white hair then covered each cut with salve.

There were no cuts on his face that needed stitches, and though the cut on his skull was long, it was not deep, and Chagak decided not to stitch it. Her mother once told her that scalps were difficult to stitch. The skin stretched so tightly over the skull that it was difficult to pull the edges of the wound together, and hair was apt to get caught in the stitches. And so Chagak only washed and salved the cut.

When she finished, the water was boiling. Chagak emptied the rest of the packet of caribou leaves into the water. It must boil for the time it took Chagak to count the number of her fingers and toes ten times.

When it was ready, she dipped out a cupful and set it down to cool. Man-who-kills watched but said nothing. Carefully, Chagak raised Shuganan's head and pressed the cup against his lips. At first much of the liquid spilled, but then he began to drink.

"Good," Chagak murmured to him. "Good. Drink this. It will make you strong again. It will make you well."

When the cup was empty, Chagak pointed to the robe and said to Man-who-kills, "I need another robe, something to keep him warm. I must remove his chigadax and parka."

For a time Man-who-kills did nothing, his eyes hard and dark, but finally he nodded and Chagak again went into the ulaq and this time she brought back the heavy fur seal robe from Shuganan's sleeping place. She laid it over his legs and began to pull up his chigadax. Each time she moved the garment, Shuganan cried out. Man-who-kills began to laugh, and Chagak felt her hatred harden and grow, spreading from her chest to fill her body.

"I need your knife," she said, teeth clenched.

She looked up at Man-who-kills and said again, "Knife."

"Knife?" he repeated, saying the word in Chagak's tongue. He drew his hunting knife from its scabbard on his left forearm.

"Knife?" He held it out to her, but when Chagak reached for it, he drew the weapon away. Chagak stood up and held out her hands, waiting as a mother waits for a child, until finally Man-who-kills gave her the knife.

Chagak slit open the chigadax and parka, one long cut down the front from hem to collar, slashes down each sleeve. She gave the knife back to Man-who-kills, then carefully pulled the garments from Shuganan's body. A wound extended from the center of his chest to his neck, and purple bruises outlined his rib cage.

"Some of his ribs are broken," Chagak said aloud, speaking not to Man-who-kills but to any spirit that might hear — perhaps helping spirits of old women who might know something of healing.

Chagak's grandmother had once told her that broken ribs must be bound tightly, but if a rib had punctured a lung, there was little chance a person would survive. What were the signs? Foaming blood at the mouth, coughing. And though Shuganan had been bleeding at the mouth when Chagak first saw him, she was sure it was from broken teeth that cut his tongue and cheeks.

Using strips of sealskin, Chagak wrapped Shuganan's chest. He cried out several times, and each time he did, Man-who-kills laughed, but Chagak still worked and pretended she did not hear the laughter.

When she had finished, she stitched the cut on his chest, then smoothed caribou leaf salve over the rest of his cuts and bruises.

Chagak sat back on her heels, but Man-who-kills leaned forward and prodded Shuganan's left arm with his toe. Shuganan's eyelids fluttered.

Man-who-kills spat on the ground, then spoke in his own language, pointing often to Shuganan's arm.

"Yes, it is broken," Chagak said, no longer trying to hold back her anger. "You are such a brave hunter. You are so strong, hurting an old man. The spirits tremble." And she, too, spat on the ground.

Man-who-kills grabbed the top of her head, his fingers digging into her skull. He pushed her face close to Shuganan's arm, then said slowly in her language, "Fix arm. He must carve. Fix arm."

Chagak shuddered. Man-who-kills had lived with them too long. He had begun to learn her language, a language too sacred to be spoken by one who destroyed villages.

"I will fix his arm," she answered.

Man-who-kills released her and Chagak began slowly moving her hands down Shuganan's broken arm.

She had never set an arm before. Once she had seen her village's shaman do it. But he was a man with great spirit powers.

I wear his amulet, Chagak thought, and clasped the leather pouch with both hands. She began a chant. Not a shaman's song, but a woman's chant, something to bring healing spirits to children and babies. It was the best she knew.

The shaman had used a long stick, something that spoke to the bone within the arm, something that told of strength and straightness.

There was only one thing Chagak knew to be that strong, something that at most times she would not think to touch: Shuganan's whalebone walking stick. For a long time she only chanted, looking at the arm, purple with bruises and bent where there should be no bend.

While she chanted, she tore Shuganan's chigadax into strips, long enough to wrap around the arm. Shuganan's stick was in his sleeping place and again Chagak told Man-who-kills she was going inside. This time he merely grunted, so she left quickly and returned with the walking stick.

She laid the stick along the arm and began to wrap the first strip above the point of the break.

But Man-who-kills knelt beside her and motioned for her to hold Shuganan's arm at the elbow, then he grasped the wrist and said something to her. And though Chagak did not understand what he said, she gripped tightly, remembering something she had forgotten in the shaman's ceremony, the straightening of the bone.

With steady pressure, Man-who-kills pulled.

Shuganan screamed, and for a moment his eyes opened, but Man-who-kills did not stop pulling. He motioned for Chagak to wrap the arm.

She worked quickly, wrapping the strips around both the arm and the stick.

When she had finished, Man-who-kills picked up Shuganan, holding him as if he were child, not man, and carried him into the ulaq.

TWENTY

For two days Chagak stayed in the ulaq with Shuganan. She left only in early morning to empty the baskets of night wastes and to fill the water skin from the spring near the south cliff.

By the second day Shuganan opened his eyes more often, though he did not speak to Chagak. He began taking broth in slow, careful sips, and he seemed to be breathing more easily.

They were usually alone in the ulaq. Man-who-kills stayed outside, and Chagak, glad to have him out of the ulaq, did not spend time wondering what he was doing.

The third morning, while Man-who-kills ate and Chagak washed Shuganan's wounds, Man-who-kills began to speak to Chagak. He spoke for a long time, sometimes gesturing toward Shuganan, sometimes toward her. Once he stopped to pull the two fresh sealskins from their storage place at the front of the ulaq.

After he had spoken, he waited, watching Chagak, until Chagak, uneasy, finally said, "When Shuganan is well, I will scrape and cure the sealskins. I will make you robes for your sleeping place."

But Man-who-kills cut off her words with an impatient gesture and pointed to the roof hole.

"Do you want something more to eat?" Chagak asked and started toward the storage cache. But Man-who-kills grabbed her arm and pushed her toward the climbing log.

He slipped on his chigadax and picked up two harpoons. A sudden fear clutched at Chagak's throat. Where was he taking her?

"Shuganan . . ." she said as Man-who-kills pushed her up the climbing log.

"Shuganan," Man-who-kills repeated and laughed. "Shuganan," he said again as they climbed from the ulaq. And Chagak heard the taunting in his voice so said nothing more.

I have fed Shuganan and cleaned his wounds, Chagak thought. He will be all right alone. He needs to sleep.

She squinted against the brightness of the day. The sky was blue. Cloudless days were rare, and most of them were shrouded through the morning with fog. When was the last time she had seen cloudless blue sky? Before Man-who-kills had come. Before she had found Shuganan.

Then she remembered. The gift day her mother had given her had been cloudless and hot. The day had been beautiful until the fire, until . . .

Man-who-kills grabbed the sleeve of Chagak's suk and pulled her toward the beach. She saw that his ikyak was near the stream and that he had tied gathering bags to the craft.

"Wait," he said to her as he set the ikyak into the water and climbed in. Chagak was surprised that he knew the word in her language. But she waited, noticing for the first time that the ikyak was different, now with a larger opening, the hatch no longer round but oval.

"Come," he said, again using Chagak's word.

Chagak hesitated. Did he want her in the ikyak with him?

"Come?" she asked and pointed to the ikyak.

Man-who-kills nodded.

Chagak could see that Man-who-kills sat in his ikyak like the hunters from her village, with legs flat. To fit in the ikyak, she would have to sit between his legs. She did not want to be so close to him.

"No," Chagak said and backed away. "I must stay with Shuganan."

"He strong enough. We not be gone long."

Chagak's chest was suddenly tight and hard with dread and she opened her mouth to speak but could not. How long had the man

known her language? Had he always understood what she and Shuganan said?

"You surprised I speak your words," Man-
who-kills said and laughed. "You think I know
nothing. That you make plans and I
know nothing.

"I have other women from your tribe. You
think I not learn talking from them? Sometime
best way to be enemy is be friend first."

Chagak felt a sickness within, as though the
spirit of the man were darkening all things
around her.

"I talk now so you can learn my words.
You wife must talk my words."

He grinned, showing his wide, square teeth,
then motioned for Chagak to get into the
ikyak. When Chagak did not, Man-who-kills
grabbed her arm and twisted it.

"Get in," he said.

Chagak slid into the craft, moving as far
forward as possible. Man-who-kills climbed
in after, grabbed her at the waist and scooted
her closer to him, tight between his legs, then
he drew up the hatch skirting and fastened
it around both of them.

He pushed the ikyak into the center of the
stream, and Chagak felt the jerk as the current
caught them and thrust them into the sea. She
had never been in an ikyak before, had never
realized how close the water would feel under

her legs, how cold.

For a time Man-who-kills only paddled, but then he began to speak, pointing to his weapons, the ikyak, the sea, cliffs and kelp, saying each word in Chagak's language, then another word that many times was similar but that Chagak had not heard before.

Something angry and hard rose up in Chagak's chest and she said nothing, would not repeat his words. She did not want to be so close to him. The smell of his sweat and the fish smell of his chigadax blotted out the good smells of wind and sea.

"Talk!" he finally yelled at her, slapping the side of her head. "Say words. You are stupid woman."

Chagak braced herself for another slap. But he only dipped his paddle more deeply into the water and the ikyak sped toward the kelp beds that spread out from the east cliff.

The tide was low and the kelp lay over exposed rocks and at the top of the water like long twisted ropes of dark babiche.

"Take limpets," Man-who-kills said and handed her a woman's knife, one she had seen in the ulaq, one that perhaps had belonged to Shuganan's wife.

Man-who-kills moved the ikyak close to a large boulder and Chagak leaned over, using the flat of the blade to pry limpets from the rock. It was hard work but something Chagak was used to.

Man-who-kills moved the ikyak slowly among the rocks, checking the water's depth often with the butt end of his harpoon.

When they had first come into the kelp, the sea otters disappeared, but as the ikyak moved slowly, making little noise, they began to surface, some following the ikyak and watching Chagak as she worked, others swimming in the kelp. Chagak threw limpets to them and more otters began to follow. Several wrapped themselves in the long strands and lay on their backs, anchored in the waves, and closed their eyes. Storytellers said the otters had their own villages under the kelp.

Chagak tried to watch the animals without moving too abruptly. Mothers cradled their babies in their arms while swimming on their backs. Others played, their sleek dark heads dipping and reappearing through the strands of kelp. Some caught fish, one brought mussels from the sea bottom and, laying a stone on his belly as he floated on his back, cracked the shells open against the stone just as hunters crack shells against stones and eat.

Chagak had claimed the sea otters as brothers and sisters when she was in the time of her first bleeding, a girl newly woman.

Then, in the custom of her people, her mother

had helped her make a shelter of driftwood, mud and grass. Chagak had stayed there thirty days, eating little, using her dreams as ideas for designs. Hunters knew a woman in first bleeding had special powers, and any man who brought Chagak's father sealskins had the right to ask Chagak to make a belt for him, something to give him good fortune in his hunting.

And so Chagak had worked during those thirty days, seeing only her mother or grandmother. She had been lonely and afraid of the spirits she knew had come to her, drawn by her blood.

Once after a long night when Chagak was kept awake by a cold rain that had seeped through the walls of her shelter, soaking her bedding and her small supply of food, Chagak began to sing, the song a comfort in the rain, the words coming to her from bits of remembered songs and chants. And as she sang, Chagak began to see images in her mind, a village of sea otters living beside the village of her parents, and she began to understand why her father called the otter brother, why he was so careful not to kill otters or disturb them when they fished among the kelp.

And then the otters had seemed to speak to her, telling her the stories her grandmother told, keeping Chagak's mind busy as her fingers wove a hunter's belt.

Now, as Chagak worked in Man-who-kills' ikyak, the otters again seemed to bring comfort, to speak to her of the joyful things of life.

Chagak dropped another limpet into the gathering bag at the side of the ikyak. The bag was nearly full.

She stretched out to reach the last shell on the rock and Man-who-kills said to her, "Be still."

She looked up at him, saw that he had untied both his harpoons. And before Chagak could move, before she understood what he was planning to do, he threw both weapons, one after the other.

"No!" Chagak screeched as the first hit a mother otter, baby clinging to her belly. The second hit an otter sleeping in the kelp. But as quickly as Chagak screamed, Man-who-kills clamped his hand over her mouth.

"Be still. Then I kill them all," he said to her as he drew in his harpoons, coiling the ropes that attached them to his ikyak.

He moved his hand from Chagak's mouth and she said, "Please, they are sacred to my family. Please do not kill them. They are my brothers."

But Man-who-kills threw back his head and began to laugh. He laughed as he cut the dead otter from the kelp, laughed as he brought in the mother otter, the small one following, laughed as he wrung the small one's neck.

Chagak thought she heard a quiet voice, the voice of the dead mother telling her, "Be still. Do not try to fight him." But Chagak's anger pushed her to move, and she turned on Man-who-kills, the woman's knife in her hands. She slashed the ikyak and the ropes that bound the harpoons to the craft, and finally slashed at Man-who-kills' arms.

"You be dead if I not need your grand-father's power," he said as he caught her arms, forced her to drop the knife into the sea. Then, with both of her wrists in one of his hands, he picked up his paddle and slammed Chagak on the side of the head.

The sound of the paddle against her skull made an echo in Chagak's head, a sound that drowned out Man-who-kills' laughter, that drowned out the fear callings of the otters as they tried to help those who had been killed by the spear.

Escape, you can do nothing for your dead, Chagak wanted to call out, but her mouth would not form the words.

Like the people of my village, Chagak thought, and the pain in her head became the red flames that had engulfed her people's ul-akidaq, and she heard their cries as Man-who-kills brought otter after otter, young and old, to the ikyak. He killed some with his spear, some with the paddle blade, caught some in nets as they swam among the dead ones hanging from stringers beside the ikyak.

And Chagak, caught in the darkness, could not move, could do nothing but watch and listen and weep. Watch and listen and weep.

TWENTY-ONE

Chagak did not want to skin the otters. She wished she could build them a death ulaq, give them burials as she had for her own people.

Man-who-kills would not eat the meat and did not expect Chagak to prepare it. "Meat no good," he had told her. "Taste like mud." And Chagak had agreed, though she had never tasted otter meat. It was difficult enough to remove the sleek, heavily furred skins, to stretch and scrape them. At least she could fling the bodies back into the sea and hope the animals' spirits found them.

On the third day after Man-who-kills had taken the otters, Shuganan opened his eyes and smiled at Chagak. She was washing his face, trying to coax him to open his mouth to swallow some broth. He smiled and then pushed away the broth, whispering, "Water."

Chagak, laughing, crying, gave him water. He drank in great gulps, making Chagak afraid he would open some of the wounds on his cheeks and throat, but when he finished, the color seemed to have returned to his face and a measure of strength to his body.

The old man looked around the ulaq and said to Chagak, "Man-Who-kills? He is gone?"

"On the beach," Chagak answered and saw the look of hope leave Shuganan's face.

"I could not kill him," he whispered, then, laying his hand over hers, asked, "You are his wife now?"

And Chagak, before answering, considered the fact that she was not. How strange that he had not forced her, that he had instead fulfilled the bride price. "Soon," she said. "He has taken the otters, and the skins are ready. He says I must make a suk for myself, but I do not know if I must do that before or after I am his wife."

"There is a knife hidden..." Shuganan began, but Chagak heard Man-who-kills at the top of the ulaq and she covered Shuganan's mouth, stopping his words. If Man-who-kills heard, he might hit Shuganan, and weak as Shuganan was, one slap, one kick might kill him.

"You are awake," Man-who-kills said and he spoke in Chagak's tongue.

Shuganan blinked and stared.

"He understands and speaks my language," Chagak said, and wished she could remember all the things she and Shuganan had said in the man's presence when they thought he did not understand.

"It is something a man should know," Shuganan whispered, struggling to sit up, and

Chagak did not know if he meant the language or the fact that Man-who-kills spoke it.

She tried to push him back against his mats, saying softly, "Lie down."

But Man-who-kills said, "No, he should sit. Make him sit and wait for me."

Man-who-kills climbed from the ulaq, and Chagak looked after him, wondering what he would do, angry that he would expect Shuganan to sit up.

"I will hold you up," she said to Shuganan and moved behind him, lifting him to lean against her. His breathing seemed harder, and he began to cough. He moved his arms to grip his sides, then looked down at his bound left arm as though seeing it for the first time.

"Be still," Chagak said. "You have broken ribs and a broken arm." He lay heavily against her and she felt him relax, then stiffen as another spasm of coughing took him.

He fought against the coughing until he gagged, until Chagak, thinking his struggle was causing him more pain than the cough, said, "It hurts, but let yourself cough. It will help you breathe."

Then again he relaxed and the coughing gradually stopped. He spat a gob of dark-colored phlegm from his mouth and whispered, "You are right. It helped."

Then Man-who-kills came back down the

climbing log, and to Chagak's surprise, he carried a bundle of otter skins on each shoulder. He laid them out in front of Shuganan, counting as he did so. He dragged two seal stomachs from the food cache, each filled with dried seal meat, then said to Shuganan, "Bride price for your granddaughter. Two seal, sixteen otter skin. Tonight she my wife."

He looked at Chagak, and even though she held Shuganan against her, even though she wore her birdskin suk, she felt the heat of his eyes. She shuddered as she thought of Man-who-kills' hands on her, thought of being wife to one she hated.

"You have met the price," Shuganan said, his words a whisper, and Chagak felt him tremble even as she held him. "But if she does not want to be your wife, I will not force her."

Man-who-kills squatted before Shuganan and laid his hands over Shuganan's ribs. He looked into Chagak's eyes and squeezed. Shuganan did not cry out but Chagak heard his sudden intake of breath.

"I will be your wife," Chagak said to Man-who-kills and willed all the strength of her spirit to show in her eyes, willed him to see the hate and anger she felt.

"No," Shuganan said.

"I must be his wife," Chagak said. "If I am not, he might kill you and then what will stop him? I have no knife."

Man-who-kills laughed. "Perhaps you need knives, old man. Then you would kill me?" He drew his long-bladed hunting knife from its sheath at his waist and forced it to the hilt into the hard-packed floor.

"It is yours for the night. Kill me." And grabbing Chagak's arms, he pulled her away from Shuganan and pushed her into her sleeping place.

Dread filled Chagak and gave her no room for breath, made her heart beat hard like waves against rock. But then she seemed to hear her mother's voice, a remembrance of words once spoken: "It is not a terrible thing to become a wife. There is pain the first time and some blood, a little blood, nothing bad enough for tears."

Then Chagak heard the whispering of some spirit, perhaps the spirit of one of the otters Man-who-kills had taken: "Do not let him know you are afraid. Do not let him know."

So when Man-who-kills entered the sleeping place, Chagak remained standing and held the muscles of her legs stiff so she would not quiver.

"Sit," he said to her.

Pressing as close to the curtained door as she could, Chagak sat, her hands clenched over her knees.

"Take off suk."

Except for the time she had repaired it, Chagak had not taken off her suk in Man-who-kills' presence. But now, as wife, she must do as her husband said and so pulled off the suk, gathering it to her as Man-who-kills crept close and began running his hands down her arms.

He jerked away the suk and dropped it to the floor. But it was within reach of the sleeping mats and Chagak felt a hope growing within her. If she could reach the suk, she could reach the knife hidden in it, but then, as though Man-who-kills knew her thoughts, he picked up the garment and passed it from one hand to the other.

"Heavy," he said and laid the suk on the floor. He ran his hands around the bottom edge until he came to the placket Chagak had sewn, then, ripping the seams, he pulled out the woman's knife and held it to Chagak's face.

"You sew knife in this suk," he said.

"It is the custom of my people," Chagak said, her voice coming from her throat like a child's whisper.

"What in here?" he asked running his hands down the placket.

"Needles, an awl, sinew for thread. Things a woman should carry."

"A knife?"

"It is a woman's knife."

Man-who-kills laughed. "Only woman's knife," he said. "Not hurt anybody." He cupped one of her breasts in his hands and pressed the flat of the knife blade against her flesh. "It not cut too good, this knife?"

He drew the edge across the breast and a thin line of blood beaded up on her skin. "Some people, they mark women for beauty," Man-who-kills said. "Must cut deep." He drew another line across the other breast, ending with the knife blade at Chagak's throat. He paused, smiled. "But not my people," he said and suddenly threw the knife into the far corner of the sleeping place.

"Stand up," he said.

She stood. Man-who-kills took off his parka, drew a knife from his wrist scabbard and cut the thong that held her apron. He laughed deep in his throat and reached out to touch her. He ran a hand between her legs, his skin rough, his touch harsh, then tasted his fingers. "You are salt," he said. "Like sea."

He pulled her down to the sleeping robes and spread her legs, poking and prodding, sniffing and pinching, and Chagak felt the welling of hate within her. She did not feel like a wife but like one traded as slave.

Tears pushed into her eyes, but then a voice seemed to whisper, "Come with me; come with me." And suddenly Chagak was not only with Man-who-kills but was also walking the cliffs, feeling the joy of new summer, warm air blowing in from the sea. And to her surprise, Seal Stalker was beside her, holding her hand, and they had no taboos, no reason to wait, she with no bride price keeping her virgin.

Chagak felt his hands on her, and she sank to the grass beside him, Chagak pulling off her suk as he pulled off his parka, removing her apron as he thrust his aside.

But then suddenly the weight of a body was on Chagak, pressing the breath from her lungs, and she was no longer with Seal Stalker but with Man-who-kills.

Man-who-kills was forcing her legs apart, pushing into her with hard thrusts, pressing until Chagak bit her lip in pain.

"You never had man," he said to her and she hated his laughter.

He pushed again, and Chagak felt as though something within her was breaking, was tearing.

"You do not want me," Man-who-kills said and as suddenly as he had rolled upon her he rolled off, giving Chagak space for a great gulp of air.

"You do not want me," he said again, slapping her. The blow took Chagak by surprise and she gasped. He slapped her again, the sound high and sharp. He hit her face, her legs, her arms, punching and slapping, hitting until Chagak rolled herself into a ball, drawing her knees in to protect her belly and crossing her arms up over her head.

"You will learn to be good wife," he said. "You will learn to be good wife."

Shuganan lay on his mats and wished he could not hear. It had been hard enough listening to Man-who-kills laugh, but now the man was beating Chagak.

He has left me a knife, Shuganan thought, and rolled from the mat. The weight of his body seemed to crush the wind from his chest and he could not breathe, but he moved closer to the knife, using the fingers of his right hand and his knees.

Chagak screamed three times before Shuganan reached the knife, and as he wrapped his hands around the hilt, her screaming changed to sobs, but with each of her cries Shuganan felt himself grow stronger.

He lay still for a moment, then rolled to his back, taking in great swallows of air, his ribs aching so badly he wanted only to lie still, to do nothing that would cause him more pain.

Darkness began to creep into the edges of his mind, blotting out thought, bringing sleep, easing the pain, but then Shuganan heard Chagak's cries once again, and he rolled back to his belly, gagged as the taste of blood came into his mouth. He grasped the knife and pulled, but Man-who-kills had thrust it too deeply into the floor and Shuganan could not move it.

He pushed his thumbs against the flat of the blade, and finally the knife moved. He jerked the handle back and forth and pushed with his thumbs once again. With each push, the knife moved, and then Shuganan felt the blade slip, as if the earth had released it.

Then Shuganan pushed himself to the curtain of Chagak's sleeping place. There was still movement inside, the rhythm of man with woman, and Chagak was crying. Shuganan rolled again to his back and waited. He was not strong enough to do anything until Man-who-kills slept.

Man-who-kills had hit Chagak until the blood poured from her nose, until her teeth cut the insides of her cheeks, then he had used his sleeve knife to cut the membrane that covered her woman's passage and open a path so he could enter her. The cutting had been a small thing, but now with his long man part still inside her and Man-who-kills moving, rubbing against the wound he had made, the pain broke over Chagak with each thrust.

It took all her concentration to stay above it, and she lost the thought of her people, lost the voice of her mother.

It seemed the pain had been with her forever, something she had always lived with, always known, like the rhythm of the sea, the crashing of the ocean. Her cries were only the cries of gulls, soaring above. So when Man-who-kills stopped moving, the quiet caught in her throat — the dying of the pain like the dying of the wind, a surprise, and something that brought fear. He did not move from her but seemed to lie more heavily upon her, and finally she felt the part of him within her grow small, felt it slip from her and rest against her thigh.

Man-who-kills murmured something and then Chagak heard his snores and was surprised. How could he sleep? But his sleeping was a relief. Then, except for his weight pressing against her, she was alone.

Her nose still trickled blood and she groped in the darkness for her apron, something to stanch the bleeding and wipe the crusted blood from her face. She moved her hands as far as she could, coming up with nothing. Finally she grabbed the edge of a grass mat, but as she pulled it toward her, she felt a ridge in the packed earth floor. She traced the line of it with a finger.

It was a rectangle, perhaps as long as her

hand, and when she pressed on it, it moved as though there were something beneath it.

Then came the whisper of a voice, perhaps that of her mother or grandmother: "Shuganan has knives hidden."

Chagak pried at the dirt with her fingertips. She had to stretch her arm out full length, and her hand quickly tired. She tried to move closer, but Man-who-kills moaned and tucked her more tightly beneath him, and so Chagak dug at the edges with her nails. The dirt was like a wedge, separating nails from fingertips, but finally she had worked her fingers down far enough to grip the chunk of cut floor and lift it up.

There was a soft thud as she forced the clump of dirt up, then, reaching to the bottom of the hole, Chagak found the knife. It was not large, but was a hunting knife, perhaps something a boy would carry. And at first it felt strange in her hand, a man's weapon, something she should not have, but then she remembered the night her village was burned, remembered her mother and sister in the fire, remembered the sight of Seal Stalker's body, the slit across the belly, the spilling of intestines, and as she remembered, the knife became more and more a part of her until finally it felt as though it had grown from her hand.

She drew the knife to her side and tucked it under the edge of the sleeping mat. She wanted to keep it in her hand but knew that she must first know where to strike.

She lifted her left hand, running it lightly over Man-who-kills' face, then into the indent of his neck. She laid her fingers against his skin and held her breath, not moving until she felt the slow beating that was his heart. She trembled and it seemed as if her whole spirit were crowded into her fingertips.

She moved her hand to grip the amulet at her neck and in her mind spoke to Aka, to the sea otters and to the spirits of her people. "Do not let me fail. He will kill others if I do not kill him. Guide my hand. Guide my knife. Let me kill him."

She lowered her hand and groped at the edge of the mat until she found the knife. She gripped it tightly, and it seemed as though the spirit of the knife reached out to her own spirit, caught and held. She raised the knife and used her little finger to find the pulse and then, clenching her teeth, pulled the knife hard across Man-who-kills' neck.

For a moment there was nothing, no blood, no movement, and some spirit whispered, "You did not cut deep enough."

But then Man-who-kills' hands were at Chagak's neck, squeezing until Chagak thought she could feel the inside walls of her throat touch.

She stabbed at him with the knife, slicing his arms and shoulders, and then someone else was with them in the sleeping place. At first Chagak thought it was a spirit, her father or perhaps Seal Stalker coming to get her, to take her with him into the spirit world, but then she knew it was Shuganan.

He had a knife. Chagak saw the old man raise himself to his knees, saw him hold the knife above the center of Man-who-kills' back. She felt the force of the weapon as Shuganan thrust it between Man-who-kills' ribs, as he leaned against it, driving it deeper. And suddenly Man-who-kills' hands were no longer on her neck but around Shuganan's waist, lifting him high, slamming him to the floor.

Shuganan lay still and Man-who-kills pulled himself to his knees, vomiting blood and gripping his neck with both hands.

Shuganan could not move. The pain in his side was so intense, he had to clench his teeth to keep from crying out. But it was not the pain that filled his mind.

Man-who-kills was kneeling, knife in his back, blood spurting from the wound in his neck. Shuganan watched until the bleeding stopped, until the man fell forward and lay still, his face pressed into the dirt floor. Then Shuganan closed his eyes. The darkness separated him from the dead man, and Shuganan felt nothing, heard nothing until Chagak's high, thin wail broke through to him and he opened his eyes.

The girl was curled on the floor beside him, her hair pulled over her breasts like a black curtain. Even in the dim light of the ulaq, Shuganan could see the darkening of bruises on her arms and legs. But he did not have the strength to hold her, to comfort her.

TWENTY-TWO

Chagak gripped her shaman's amulet with both hands and watched as Shuganan climbed down into the ulaq. He insisted that he go alone, but she worried that he would be too weak to climb down safely, and she closed her eyes in relief when the old man reached the bottom of the climbing log without falling.

It would take him a long time, he had said. She should wait and pray. And though Shuganan's injuries hampered him, it seemed that some of Man-who-kills' strength now belonged to the old man.

Why should that be a surprise? Chagak asked herself. The hunter always gained some portion of power from the animals he killed. Why else would a young man after his first seal kill suddenly be so bold, so sure in his actions? Why would he suddenly be so much more skilled in the ikyak?

Chagak had not slept the night before. Ignoring the pain of her bruises, she had covered Man-who-kills' body with old hides and packed everything in the ulaq. She had wrapped Shuganan's carvings in soft skins and packed them into seal stomachs and baskets. Last, she had hauled everything — food, supplies, weapons — to the center of the ulaq and carried them outside.

She had nearly left the otter skins that had been her bride price, but then had heard her mother's voice whisper, "Do not let the skins stay with him. It is better that you throw them into the sea. Perhaps the otter spirits will claim them and come back to their homes by the shore."

And so, when the ulaq was empty save Man-who-kills' body and one lamp, Chagak had taken the furs to the top of the cliff and thrown them over, one by one, and Chagak asked the otter spirits to claim them and live again near Shuganan's beach.

While she worked, Shuganan had lain beside a fire he had made with dried heather. She heard him chanting, his words something that Chagak did not understand.

And now she waited for him. He is strong enough, Chagak told herself, but fear pulled at her thoughts. What if Shuganan could not drive Man-who-kills' spirit from this beach? It was one thing to build another ulaq. Difficult, but possible. But to find another beach? One without people, one with protection of cove and cliff, with rocks for chitons, kelp for otters.

Chagak shivered and pulled her hands up into the sleeves of her suk. Her work the night before had crowded out worried thoughts, but now the dark moments with Man-who-kills came back to her.

She wished she had disobeyed her father, had given herself to Seal Stalker. At least she would have some hope that, if a baby grew within her, it would be Seal Stalker's son and not Man-who-kills'.

But then her thoughts returned to Shuganan and to the prayers she should be making. She began a chant, and when worries of babies or thoughts about the night before interrupted her praying, Chagak whispered, "I have had greater sorrow than this. This will not kill me," and continued to pray.

It must be done, Shuganan told himself as he climbed down into the empty ulaq. He had spent the night speaking to the spirits, clinging to his amulet, making small fires with sweet heather. He wished that he and Chagak were not alone in this thing, wished that he knew more of the art of the shaman. But there was no shaman and Shuganan wondered if he had chosen the best way, if his actions would be stronger than Man-who-kills' spirit.

Chagak had done all the work. Shuganan had been too weak to help her. She had taken all their supplies outside while Shuganan waited, bundled in furs, on the leeward side of the ulaq.

Now the ulaq looked large and bare, a strange place, no longer their home.

Man-who-kills lay on his face in the center of the ulaq. The blood had begun to settle in the body, and Shuganan could see that the stomach and chest had begun to darken.

He gripped his knife. He was not strong enough to finish quickly, but he had told Chagak not to worry if he did not finish until night.

She had asked if she could help him, and there was a fierceness in her eyes. But Shuganan had never heard of a woman doing the ceremony. It was enough that he, a man who was not shaman, would do it. What curse would a woman bring to them? It would be better to do nothing at all.

Shuganan plunged the knife into Man-who-kills' body, into the joint between the shoulder and arm. He wanted to follow the tradition of his wife's people, to sever the body at each joining: shoulder, wrist, hip, ankle. Last of all, head.

Then Man-who-kills' spirit would have no power. Then Shuganan and Chagak should be safe.

PART TWO

SPRING

7055 BC

TWENTY-THREE

Kayugh turned the bone needle in his hand. He had been working for a long time. He had cut a long splinter from a cormorant's leg bone, shaped the point, then smoothed the needle with sandstone so it would be easy to use. He had made it with a bulge at one end so his wife, White River, could knot a sinew thread around the needle and the thread would not slide off.

When he had finished, he sat for a moment, waiting to see if Crooked Nose would come to him. Surely it had been long enough for the baby to be born. But then perhaps the child was a girl and the women were afraid to tell him.

Yes, it would be good to have a son, he thought. What man did not want a son? But he had seen his own mother die in childbirth and since that time any safe delivery had been a relief to him, whether the woman gave boy or girl.

Kayugh had welcomed the birth of his daughter, Red Berry, three summers before, and though most men would have asked their wives to kill the child and thus eliminate the years of nursing when few babies were conceived, Kayugh chose to keep his daughter.

He picked up the bone and gouged out another splinter. He would make another needle, bargaining with White River's spirit. Surely her spirit would not allow White River's body to leave the earth knowing there were gifts waiting. But the gray of the sky, the heaviness of rain in the air seemed to reflect the foreboding he felt within. It was not a good month. It would have been better if White River's labor had not started until after the full moon, until after one full month had passed since Red Leg's death.

Red Leg had been Kayugh's first wife, a good woman, though old. Before Kayugh took her as wife, she had been a widow and childless, unwanted, a woman who in winter might have given herself to the mountains, to the winter spirits. Why should she take a share of food when she had no husband to sew for, no children to raise? There were others in the village who deserved the food more.

But Kayugh saw Red Leg as a strong woman, one who knew many plants for healing and who could sew fine, straight seams. Who could deny that it was Red Leg's chigadax that had saved her brother's life when he tipped his ikyak and could not right himself? What other chigadax could last so long in water, all seams keeping out the sea, keeping a man's parka dry so when the ikyak was righted the man was not cold or wet?

Kayugh, seeing the value of the woman, had asked her to be his wife and left his parents when he was young to build a ulaq of his own.

She had been a good wife. She came to his bed whenever he wanted, filled the food caches with dried fish and roots, kept his parka and boots in good repair. But when, after two years, she had given him no children Red Leg had come to him and asked that he take a second wife. She needed help with the work of the ulaq, she said. Then Kayugh had found White River.

White River belonged to a family from another village. She was a beautiful woman and, unlike most women, tall. Her skin was light, and her eyes were rounder than the eyes of women in Kayugh's village.

He had seen her on a trading trip and had traded a pack of furs and his fine ikyak to get her. But Kayugh had wanted her, and so had suffered the taunts of the other men when, without ikyak, he had used a woman's ik to bring his bride home.

And she, too, had been a good wife, though not so gifted at sewing and cooking as Red Leg.

But Red Leg had been dead now ten days.

She had fallen from her ik while cutting limpets from rocks, and though Kayugh had gone after her and had dragged her to shore, water spirits had sucked away her breath before he could get her to the beach.

There was no burial ulaq, so they left her at the edge of a beach, rocks piled over her body. But often in the days that followed, Kayugh had felt her spirit close to him, and though he knew Red Leg's spirit would not hurt him, he wondered if perhaps she were seeking a companion, or knew that death would soon take one of them so waited for that one instead of making the trip to the Dancing Lights alone.

But then perhaps it was not White River who would die but one of the others. Kayugh thought of the people who made up his small group. He, through no spoken word but only on his abilities as a hunter, was leader. The others waited for his decisions. Eight adults: three men, five women. Two children. No, thought Kayugh, four women now Red Leg is dead. And, of the four remaining, were there any he would not grieve for?

Kayugh rested his arms across his upraised knees and stared out toward the sea. It was early summer. They needed to take seals, to put aside something for the winter. How else would they live?

Then the thought came, sudden and unexpected: Why should we live? Kayugh rubbed his hands across his eyes. He was tired, worried. He had lost one wife and feared the loss of another. That was all. There was no spirit enticing him to join the men and women of his tribe who had climbed the mountain, refusing to eat, and waited for death after the great wave destroyed their village.

The wave had taken Kayugh's father, three brothers, a sister. Who had lost more than that? But how could a hunter decide it was time to die when he was still young? Others needed his skills to bring food and to help them find a safe beach.

So he had led the people west, but he crossed to the beaches of the north sea rather than the south. The winters were harder, but the hunters who spent time there said there were fewer large waves — waves that came during the night, destroying villages, killing people.

"Less for the women to gather, less eggs, less roots," Gray Bird had said. But Kayugh seldom listened to Gray Bird. He was a small man, not strong, and his spirit, too, was small and weak.

But though Gray Bird had argued with Kayugh, Big Teeth had agreed. Big Teeth was a good man, full of laughter and the telling of jokes, and content to let others speak of his hunting success. Kayugh valued his judgment.

Kayugh could see Big Teeth from where he sat. The man was repairing his ikyak. The craft was turned on its belly and Big Teeth was rubbing fat into the seams.

Big Teeth was a man with narrow shoulders, wide hips. His arms were long, and he of all the hunters of the village was able to throw his spear the farthest.

First Snow, Big Teeth's son, worked beside him. The boy had nearly eight winters. Soon he would be a hunter. Big Teeth was not blood father to the boy but had taken him as his own when, years before, another wave destroyed their village. That wave had taken Big Teeth's own son and drowned First Snow's parents. Unlike Big Teeth, the boy was short and stocky, powerful even for a boy. But though built differently, First Snow mimicked Big Teeth's swinging walk, his voice and the way he watched a man through squinted eyes.

Seeing the two together made Kayugh's hope for a son stronger, but then his small daughter skipped out to the edge of the water. Kayugh stood and called to her, and when she came, he sat cross-legged in the sand and pulled her to his lap.

She leaned back against him, and her tangled hair smelled of the wind. It would not be terrible to have another daughter, Kayugh thought. And then he saw the woman Crooked Nose walking from the sheltered place the women had found between two hills, and seeing a smile on her face, hope for a son again rose within him.

But when Crooked Nose came to him, Kayugh's first thoughts were of White River. "My wife?" he asked, leaving the words hanging between them.

"She is good," Crooked Nose said and squatted beside him.

Crooked Nose, one of Big Teeth's wives, was not a beautiful woman. She had been named for her nose, which was thick and bent like a puffin's bill. Her small brown eyes were set close together, and her lips were thin. But her hands were long-boned and beautiful, swift with awl or needle. Perhaps she wove spells with those hands, for often when she worked the men would gather around her, speaking to her as if she were another man, gifted with the wisdom of a man.

Crooked Nose reached out to run a finger under Red Berry's chin. "We had some trouble. White River was bleeding . . ."

"It stopped?"

"Yes."

"The child?"

Crooked Nose smiled. "A son," she said.

"A son," Kayugh repeated, and for a moment he sat still.

Crooked Nose smiled, but then glanced down at her hands. "She named him."

Kayugh was not surprised. It was a custom in White River's family; something that was to give strength in hunting.

"What did she call him?" he asked.

"She whispered the name to the baby but will not tell us until she has told you."

Kayugh nodded. "A son," he said. A bubble of laughter seemed to rise up from his spirit, and as it grew, it pulled Kayugh to his feet. He hoisted Red Berry to his shoulders, and after giving Crooked Nose a hug, he called to Big Teeth, "I have a son."

TWENTY-FOUR

The pain in her back woke Chagak. For the past three days it had grown steadily worse, and this morning it was so intense that even her jaws and teeth ached.

She pushed herself up to her hands and knees, then sat back on her haunches, one hand under her belly.

She crawled out into the ulaq and lit the oil lamps from the one that had burned through the night. She picked up the clay-lined basket that held her night wastes and climbed from the ulaq to empty the basket outside.

The wind cut cold and sharp from the beach, and clouds lay heavy enough to see even in the darkness of early morning.

"It will rain tonight," some spirit whispered and Chagak thought it was the voice of a sea otter spirit, a voice she had often heard since Man-who-kills' death.

But she did not answer as she emptied the basket a distance from the ulaq, then walked toward the beach to rinse the basket in a tidal pool.

"It will rain tonight," the otter said again. "Hard."

"Yes," said Chagak, as she squatted beside the pool. She rested her arms on the tops of her knees before washing out the basket.

"You will have your baby today," the otter said, and the spirit voice was calm as though still speaking of the rain.

Chagak closed her eyes. "Not today," she said aloud.

"Do you think you can be pregnant forever?"

"It is better than death."

"You have never feared death."

"Who will care for Shuganan if I die?"

"You will not die."

"Many women die giving birth."

"You will not die."

"The baby? Will it die?"

"How can I say?" replied the otter. "That is your choice."

"Is it boy or girl?" Chagak asked, though she had asked many times before and the otter had never answered.

"Boy," said the otter, and the suddenness of the answer seemed to bring a pain that tightened and pulled from Chagak's breastbone to her spine.

When the pain ended, Chagak said, "A boy."

"You wanted a girl."

"Yes," Chagak said. What had her mother told her? A girl carries the spirit of her mother, a boy the spirit of his father. Chagak had no husband to make her kill a girl child. She could keep a daughter if she wished, but if she had a boy, how could she keep him? How could she keep a child who might grow to hate and kill like his father? Yet she dreaded the thought of killing the baby.

"Perhaps Shuganan will kill it for you," said the otter.

"Perhaps you are wrong and I carry a daughter," said Chagak, suddenly angry with the otter spirit, as if it were the one that had chosen whether the child was boy or girl.

Another pain took her and Chagak lowered her head to her arms.

"Walk," said the otter. "You must walk. The child will come more quickly."

"I must tell Shuganan first," Chagak said. "And prepare him food."

Chagak went back to the ulaq. She climbed carefully down the climbing log, her muscles tense as she waited for the next pain. She wished she remembered more of childbirth. She had still been in her year of first bleeding when Pup was born, so she had not been allowed to help her mother in the birthing, but she had stayed at the top of the ulaq, asking questions of every woman who entered or left. Her mother had been a strong woman and even near the end of the labor had not cried out, but Chagak had heard other women in labor, crying, screaming.

The thought made Chagak shudder, and she tried to think of other things, tried to keep her thoughts to the preparation of fish and dried seal meat. She even tried to start another conversation with the otter spirit, but this time the otter said nothing, and finally, as she worked, Chagak realized that her hands were shaking, her knees trembling. She had a sudden need for her mother and, like a little child, Chagak began to cry, huge, hard sobs that pulled away her breath.

"Chagak?" Shuganan crawled from his sleeping place. "What is the matter?"

Chagak held in her tears and tried to smile, but some spirit seemed to control the corners of her mouth, to twist her face. "I am all right," she said, her voice thin. "I am all right." Then quickly, "The birth pains have started."

"Good," he said, but Chagak saw the quick widening of his eyes, a flash of fear.

"Have a son," he said. "I will teach him to hunt."

Chagak tried to smile, but the thought of a son brought her no joy. She set out a mat and layered it with fish and seal meat.

Shuganan ate, using only his right hand, his left arm still weak. It had seemed to heal well, but the arm's broken bone had attracted the spirits that stiffen joints, and both elbow and shoulder were swollen so that Shuganan could barely move the arm.

When he had finished eating, Chagak put away the remaining fish and meat.

"You must eat, too," Shuganan said.

"No," she answered. "I am not hungry. I need to be outside. It is too hot in here. It is too dark."

Shuganan watched Chagak during that long day. She paced the length of the beach, a small, dark figure, hands under her suk, supporting her large belly. As the sun neared the northwestern horizon, the rain clouds grew darker, heavier. Chagak walked more slowly, and Shuganan moved from the roof of the ulaq. He would bring her back now. He could tell by the stiffness of her steps that the pains were coming often.

She needs a woman, Shuganan thought, and in the years since his wife's death he had never felt a greater need for her wisdom.

As he approached Chagak, Shuganan saw that she was walking with her eyes closed, breathing deeply, her cheeks puffing out with each pain, like a child blowing up a seal bladder.

She stopped when she saw him and crouched on her heels in the sand.

"Come back to the ulaq," Shuganan said to her.

"The pain is not bad," she answered. "I need to be in the wind. I need to be by the sea."

Shuganan nodded and squatted beside her. They sat in silence for a time, but then Shuganan noticed that Chagak's cheeks were wet with tears.

"Why do you cry?" he asked. "Is the pain so great?"

She wiped her cheeks with the backs of her hands. "No," she said, then murmured, "I am afraid."

Shuganan did not answer, for he felt the tremors of his own fear. Many women died in childbirth, many, many women. What if something happened to Chagak? What would he do? He did not want to live without her.

Suddenly she gripped his arm. "Something has happened," she said, her eyes round. She stood and water streamed from between her legs. "What is it?" she asked. "Why do I do this?"

Shuganan watched in wonder. "I do not know," he answered.

"Perhaps there is no baby. Perhaps, only water," Chagak said, and began to laugh, and Shuganan rose in fear as her laughter became higher and higher, until it peaked like a scream.

"No, no. The water is a good thing," he said, grasping her shoulders and shaking her. "You see, it is only water, like the splash of a hunter's boat against the shore."

He helped her stand and together they walked toward the ulaq, Chagak leaving a wet trail over the rocks. Shuganan put an arm around her waist and pulled her close to his side. She leaned against him, and as they reached the ulaq, she crumpled into a heap at his feet.

He bent to help her up, but she waved his hand away. She drew her knees up inside her suk and gripped the new spring grass that covered the ulaq.

Shuganan stood beside her and watched the pain distort her face.

"Ah! Ah-h-h!" she screamed and Shuganan's eyes filled with tears. He had hoped this child would be a blessing, a boy he could teach to hunt, a boy who would bring seals for Chagak. But now he wondered how he had ever thought the child would be a blessing. Chagak had suffered so much. Pain and pain. First in the giving, now in the birth.

"Ah!" Chagak cried again, then she reached between her legs, and with a start Shuganan realized that her hands were covered with blood.

"Go!" she said to Shuganan and the strength

of her voice encouraged him. "Go! Do not curse us all."

Shuganan backed away from her, wanting to stay, wanting to help, but knowing he could not. Then he thought of Pup's carrying sling in the ulaq.

"I will bring the sling," he said, but he did not know if Chagak heard him.

The darkness of the ulaq temporarily blinded Shuganan, and he groped for the heap of furs Chagak had prepared for the baby. Finally he found Pup's sling. He draped the piece of leather over his arm and went back out to Chagak.

When he saw her, Shuganan realized that she was no longer in pain. She held her head straight and her arms rested loosely over her knees. But then Shuganan saw that something red lay beside her in the grass, and he heard a tiny, gasping cry.

Chagak looked up at him, her eyes dull, and said, "A boy."

Shuganan hurried to Chagak's side. A fine, fat baby lay in the grass at her feet. Chagak pulled a few long hairs from her head and used them to bind the pulsing cord that led from the baby's navel to somewhere under Chagak's suk. Then she leaned over and bit the cord, severing it.

But she left the child lying in the grass. His

cries grew harder, his arms and legs jerking with each breath.

"He is cold," Shuganan said and began fumbling with the sling, trying to wrap it around the infant.

"He must be washed," Chagak said.

And Shuganan, seeing she made no move to do anything, asked, "With water or oil?"

"Bring water. Do not waste our oil."

But Shuganan brought back both water and oil, a tanned hide and several soft furred skins. He picked up the baby, and his touch seemed to calm the child. He dipped a piece of tanned hide in the water, stretched the hide to soften it, then wiped away the blood on the baby's body. He smoothed the child's skin with oil. The baby was well formed, long-armed and fat-bellied.

Shuganan struggled again with the carrying strap and finally decided that the wide part must go under the child's buttocks, the strap going up the back to support the head before fastening over Chagak's shoulder. But after he had the baby in the sling, he realized that Chagak must put the strap on first, then slip the baby into it.

He held the baby in his good arm and tucked him close to his parka. "Put this on," he said to Chagak, holding out the strap. But Chagak did not move.

"Chagak," Shuganan said, his voice louder. "Your son is cold. Put on the strap."

"He is not my son," she said. "He belongs to Man-who-kills. Let the baby's father care for him."

"Chagak you need this child. He will be a hunter. He will bring meat for you. If you kill this child, who will take care of you when I die?"

"I will hunt and fish. I have done it before."

"You will be old then. It will be too much for you to do."

"Then I will die," said Chagak.

"Chagak," Shuganan said quietly, "a son does not always carry his father's spirit." He tried to meet her eyes, but she looked away. "He will be a good man. We will teach him to care about people."

Finally Chagak turned her head toward Shuganan. "He is strong?" she asked.

"Yes." Shuganan held him out to her so she could see his arms and legs, his small, round belly.

But she turned away again, then said, "I must bury the afterbirth."

"Let me bury it."

"You would be cursed. I must bury it since my mother or sister cannot."

Slowly, unsteadily, she stood. It began to rain — heavy, cold drops. The baby started to cry. "Take the child into the ulaq," Chagak said. "I will be back."

She watched as Shuganan wrapped the baby in fur seal skins and then carried him down the climbing log into the ulaq.

Chagak walked to the far edge of the beach, against the edge of the cliffs. She kept her mind blank, would not let herself think of the child. It was enough that the birth was over.

She picked up a flat piece of shale and used it to dig a hole.

In the ulaq, Shuganan began to sing to the baby, a lullaby, something his mother once sang long ago, but the words seemed to catch in his throat and the song that came from his mouth was a mourning song.

TWENTY-FIVE

White River named their son Amgigh. Blood. It was a strange name for a child, but Kayugh could think of no reason to object. Blood was life. What spirit did not respect blood?

They made a ceremony on the beach, something quick, without feasting or fire. They told the name to the winds and the sky and sea, then prepared for another day traveling.

Kayugh was packing his ikyak when Little Duck came to him. Little Duck, Big Teeth's second wife, was a small, round woman. Unlike the other women, who wore their hair loose, falling over their shoulders or tucked into their collar rims, she bound her hair back tightly with a strip of sealskin, the hair hanging down her back like a long black tail. Little Duck was shy and seldom spoke, but she was gifted in preparing and storing meat, and sometimes the spirits told her what would happen in days to come.

She said something to Kayugh, but her head was lowered and her voice soft so he could not make out her words. Fighting down his irritation at the woman's shy ways, he bent close and heard her say, "Three days, we will come to a beach. Some spirit told me. It will be a good place to live, with tidal pools and fresh-water spring." She paused, glanced up at him and then away, as if he frightened her. She pressed a hand to her mouth and said something else.

"I cannot hear you," Kayugh said, his words too loud.

"There will be cliffs there," she said without looking at him. She turned back toward the women who were packing supplies into hide-covered bundles, but as Kayugh watched, her back seemed to stiffen and she turned slowly to face him. "Your wife," Little Duck said, but then walked away as if she had said nothing.

Kayugh felt a catch of fear somewhere in his chest. What about his wife? He watched White River among the other women. She was pale, looked tired, but what woman would not be tired, working during the day to please her husband, awake at night to feed her new son? Kayugh was suddenly angry at Little Duck, but then he remembered what she had said about a beach. It was a good sign. When had Little Duck ever been wrong? Perhaps she had meant that Kayugh should insist his wife do less work, that she take more rests.

He walked over to the women. Their chatter stopped and they looked up at him. He rested his hand on the top of his wife's head, tucked his fingers into the warmth of her hair.

"Crooked Nose, my wife will have many sleepless nights with our new son," he said. "Could she go without a turn paddling the ik today?"

"That will cause no problem," Crooked Nose said. "My son is big enough to take a turn at paddling."

And looking at the boy, Kayugh saw the sudden flash of pride in his eyes. Yes, it would be a good way to prepare First Snow for the ikyak. Kayugh remembered how hard it had been for him as a boy First Snow's age to ride in the women's ik rather than have an ikyak like the men.

"Thank you," White River murmured, but when Kayugh looked at Little Duck to see if she approved his action, the woman had her head lowered, her hands busy tying a bundle of dried grass.

The next day they traveled from early morning until the sun had lowered in the sky, then stopped to spend the night on a beach covered with fist-sized round rocks. The women collected enough driftwood for a fire, but there were no small, close hills to give shelter from the wind that blew in from the sea.

They huddled in a semicircle around the

fire, backs against the wind so the fire was in the lee of their bodies. The women brought out dried meat. Little Duck sharpened green willow sticks and skewered the fish she had caught that day, then stuck the sticks in the sand around the fire.

The day of paddling had made Kayugh so hungry that he did not wait for the fish near him to be fully cooked. When the skin began to brown, he pulled the stick from the sand and ate.

When he had eaten half of the fish, he held the stick out toward White River, offering her the other half, but she shook her head.

"You must eat," Kayugh said to her.

"I will," she said and smiled, but there was a tiredness in her face, a darkness around her eyes, that worried Kayugh.

Again Little Duck's words came to him, and so during that evening Kayugh watched White River. He was relieved when she ate, and he noticed that she laughed when Big Teeth told his stories. Though she walked slowly, one hand against her belly, she helped the other women with the fire and the sleeping robes.

By the time he had lain down for the night by the fire, Kayugh had nearly forgotten his concern.

At first the sound was in Kayugh's dreams.

It was a gull screaming, then the cry of a woman giving birth, but gradually it woke him, and he realized it was the muffled cry of a baby.

He sat up, and in the twilight of early morning he saw that Little Duck and Big Teeth had also been awakened by the noise.

"Your son," Big Teeth said, and when he spoke the words, Kayugh felt the sudden nausea of fear. A baby among the First Men did not cry as long as his son had been crying. A baby was bound close to his mother's body, warm inside the suk and able to suckle whenever he wanted.

Little Duck slipped from her sleeping robes, and to Kayugh her movements seemed too slow, each step taking forever, but Kayugh himself, in trying to rise, felt as if his arms and legs were made of stone, too heavy to move. So he sat watching, as though the child crying were not his own, as though the woman Little Duck shook were not his wife.

Little Duck turned her head toward him, and when she spoke, the words were too slow, like a part of some dream. "She has been bleeding," Little Duck said. Then: "She is dead, Kayugh. Some spirit has taken her."

Kayugh could not move his head to nod, could not speak. But then Big Teeth was beside him and all the camp was awake. "Come," Big Teeth said, and his voice seemed to give

Kayugh the power he needed to move again. He threw the robe back from his legs and stood up.

"We will go to the beach," said Big Teeth. "The women will take care of White River."

"She is dead," Kayugh said, looking into Big Teeth's eyes, hoping Big Teeth would tell him, "No, she is not. Little Duck is wrong."

But Big Teeth nodded and said, "Yes, she is dead." Then, reaching out to take Kayugh's arm, Big Teeth added, "Come with me. We will check the supplies. We will . . ."

"Where is my daughter?" Kayugh asked, suddenly irritated with Big Teeth, with the carefulness of the man's words.

Then Crooked Nose was handing him Red Berry, the child rubbing her eyes, her movements stiff and jerky from being awakened. Kayugh hugged the girl to him and then turned away from them all, the men and women in a tight circle before him. But when he had taken a few steps, he turned back and said to Crooked Nose, "Give me my son."

He saw the quick look of surprise on Big Teeth's face, heard Gray Bird snort. Crooked Nose hesitated, then said, "He cries."

"Give me my son," Kayugh said again. He set Red Berry down and waited until Crooked Nose brought the infant.

The baby's legs and arms trembled in the

cold and his cries changed from a high, broken wail to a bleating sound, like a noise Kayugh sometimes heard from baby seals.

"He is cold," Crooked Nose said and asked Little Duck to bring a furred skin. The woman wrapped the baby, and the child stopped crying, as if the warmth were all he was seeking. She handed him to Kayugh and Kayugh took the child, first holding him awkwardly in both hands, then tucking him into the crook of his left arm. Kayugh picked up Red Berry and left the circle of his people.

Kayugh found a place in the lee of some rocks where the ground was dry. He sat down, settling Red Berry on one leg, and lowered his left arm to rest against his thigh. He looked at both children. Red Berry leaned against him, her eyes closed, but Amgigh's eyes were wide as if he were studying Kayugh's face.

Kayugh could cry now, with his daughter nearly sleeping and only his son to see. A son would not be ashamed to see his father cry for the death of a wife, but though Kayugh willed the tears to come, they would not, and so he watched his son, saw how beautiful the child was, with fine black brows, huge dark eyes.

His daughter, too, was beautiful, looking so much like White River. And Kayugh wondered why — with two such beautiful children

— White River's spirit had chosen to leave them. Was some other spirit already at the Dancing Lights, pulling her away from Kayugh, away from the earth? Would Red Leg do such a thing? No, in all her years as Kayugh's wife, Red Leg had always taken more thought for others than for herself.

Perhaps Kayugh had not been a good husband. Perhaps his thoughts had been too often of himself, not enough on his wives. But no, he had loved his wives. And he was a good hunter. Had they ever been without meat? Without hides to work, without sinew for sewing?

They had had a good life together. His wives were like sisters, caring for one another, and Red Berry called both women "mother."

Perhaps his wives had not chosen to die. Perhaps they were taken because Kayugh did not give enough thanks for what he had.

He had been an honored hunter of a large village. They had a good beach, enough to eat, and Kayugh, though a young man, had two good wives, a son growing within one wife, and a fine, strong daughter. Had he ever stopped to think how good his life had been? Kayugh could not remember. There were too many things to think of: hunting, repairing his ikyak, trading trips.

It had taken one night to change his life. A wave — something that happened once, twice in a lifetime, but now had happened three times in five years to his people's village.

The other times, the losses had not been as great, but this time only Kayugh's ulaq, the one on highest ground, had not been destroyed, and many people had died.

If Little Duck had not spoken of another wave, one coming again that summer, perhaps Kayugh would have stayed with the families that had decided to rebuild their village, but he had thought of his daughter and of the baby — then only a small swelling in White River's belly — and wanted a place for them that would not always bring death.

"It is not a good place to live," he had told the men. "The beach is too low, too easy for the sea to overcome. The spirits bring a wave to kill us and laugh at our stupidity. We must find a new beach for our village."

Only Big Teeth had agreed with him, and finally Gray Bird as well, a man afraid of everything, someone Kayugh would have preferred to leave behind.

Words came easily to Gray Bird. His insults were subtle, leaving barbs that stayed beneath the skin and worked into a man like nettles. But perhaps it was Gray Bird's sly way of speaking that had won him his beautiful wife, Blue Shell — Blue Shell with smooth-skinned face and white, unbroken teeth, eyes wide and quick. Even her name, which reminded Kayugh of the luminescence of a limpet's inner shell, was beautiful.

Her father had not chosen well for her. Gray Bird beat her often, even now though she would soon deliver their first child, and he traded her to any man for a night's favor with another woman. When Kayugh had first met Blue Shell, the young woman a new bride, she had often smiled, often laughed, but now she was quiet, quick to duck if Gray Bird came near with raised hand or walking stick.

But Gray Bird was a man, a hunter, and who could deny Blue Shell the chance of safety for her unborn child?

So Gray Bird and Blue Shell had come with Kayugh, Big Teeth, and their families when they left the village. Leaving seemed the best thing to do, Kayugh thought, but if I had stayed, I might still have two wives. I would be able to keep my son.

"And now I must leave you," he whispered to the baby. "For who can feed you? If I take you, you will only die and it is better if you die here with your mother. Then your spirit will not be lost. She will guide you to the Dancing Lights. But if I take you, how will you find your way if you die?"

The baby looked at Kayugh as if he understood.

"You are too wise," Kayugh said and lowered his cheek to the soft, dark hair on his son's head. And finally the tears came, as Kayugh cried for his wives and for the son he must leave. The baby, too, began to cry, and Kayugh, hearing his son, felt as if their hearts were one, their spirits joined.

Big Teeth and Gray Bird had dug a shallow grave no deeper than the length of a man's hand, and then had piled a heap of rocks at the foot of the grave. When Kayugh again saw White River, the women had washed her and laid her in the grave. Knees tucked to her chin, face marked with the red of ocher, the woman was a child again, an infant, being birthed into the world of the spirit.

The people were gathered around the grave, even First Snow, the boy standing beside Big Teeth.

Kayugh took his place in the circle. He set Red Berry down beside him, and she looked at the woman lying in the grave but said nothing. The baby was quiet, sucking at a corner of his fur wrapping. As the women began the death chant, Kayugh laid the baby into the grave, tucking the child in the space between his wife's upraised knees and her chest. The baby nuzzled against his mother, opening his mouth as he rooted against White River's suk.

Kayugh stepped back to his place in the circle and tried to join in the chant, but he could not remember the words, could not make his voice rise with the song, and finally he only stood, his eyes closed to hold back his tears.

Big Teeth came to him, pressed the first stone into Kayugh's hands. Kayugh laid it over his wife's feet, remembering how he had done the same for Red Leg. And he felt that he had buried many wives, had buried wives since he was a child. Had spent more time singing death chants than chants to bring seals, than songs to push away the loneliness of an ikyak in the sea.

He watched as each of the men and finally the women laid a stone, then Big Teeth and Gray Bird continued to lay rocks, piling them up over his wife's body.

"Mama?" Red Berry said, her voice small and almost lost in the noise of rock pressing against rock. "Mama?" the word louder, higher, almost a scream. She began to cry, and each cry tore something from Kayugh's chest, until finally he knew he could not stand and watch but must be alone, away from the people, away from his daughter, from the sight of his son, soon to be buried with stones.

He turned, meaning to walk to the beach, but then he heard the high, thin wailing of his son. His children were calling to him. He turned, scooped Red Berry into his arms and, bending toward the grave, pulled the baby from his wife and handed him to Blue Shell.

The woman stopped her chant and looked with round eyes toward her husband, but Gray Bird said nothing.

"How long until your baby comes?" Kayugh asked.

Blue Shell shook her head but finally said, "Soon."

"She will have enough milk for two?" Kayugh asked Crooked Nose.

"Most women do."

"Keep my son," he said to Blue Shell. "If you can feed him, he will belong to you and to your husband."

Then Kayugh took his daughter to the beach while the others finished burying his wife.

TWENTY-SIX

The baby was under Chagak's suk, bound to her chest with a leather sling. Chagak's breasts had grown heavier and fuller each day during her pregnancy but seemed to lose some of their tenderness as the baby suckled.

He was a strong, fat baby, his head covered with dark hair. He does not look like his father, Chagak told herself. Had she not heard the sea otter whisper that he looked like her brother Pup or even her own father? Maybe he carried their spirits or the spirit of one of the men of her village.

But perhaps he carried the spirit of Man-who-kills. Who could say?

Even if he did not, it was the duty of a son to avenge his father. To kill those who had killed the father. How would a man feel if he had to kill his mother to honor his father?

Chagak tried to make her fingers work on the basket she was weaving, a fine, tightly woven basket with split willow for the warp and rye grass for the weft, but she could not keep her thoughts from her son. Shuganan sat near an oil lamp on the other side of the ulaq,

271

smoothing an ivory carving with sandstone.

He had not said much to Chagak in the three days since the birth, though once Chagak had asked him if he thought she should take the child back to Aka, to let his spirit go to her village's mountain. He had given her no true answer, only saying that she must decide herself. It was her child, not his.

Chagak looked at the old man. He had never truly recovered from Man-who-kills' beatings. Although Shuganan never complained of the pain, he held himself carefully, favoring his left side, and his limp was more pronounced. But it seemed that, in exchange for one thing, the spirits had given another. Shuganan's carvings were better, more intricate, so detailed that Chagak could make out the individual feathers of a soapstone suk, the thin ivory hairs on an old man's head.

"Shuganan," Chagak said, trying to speak softly, but in the quiet of the ulaq her words sounded loud, and even the baby jumped when she spoke.

Shuganan looked up at her and paused in his work, but Chagak could think of nothing to say. How could she tell the old man that she just wanted him to talk, wanted words in the ulaq to pull her from her thoughts?

Finally she said, "Do you think, if the child

lives, he will have to kill us to avenge his father's death?"

Shuganan's eyes rounded, and for a long time he studied Chagak's face. "No one can know what the spirits will tell a man to do," he said, his words coming slowly, as if as he spoke he were thinking of other things. "But do not forget, a man who avenges father must also avenge grandfather. Who killed your family?

"If he kills you for his father's spirit, who will he kill for his grandfather's spirit? Perhaps the only one he should kill would be me. But I am old. I will probably die before the child is old enough to have his own ikyak."

"No," Chagak said. "If you die, then who will teach him to hunt and use the ikyak?"

"You have decided to let him live then?"

"I have made no decision. I do not know what to do. I do not know enough about the ways of the spirits to choose."

Shuganan held her eyes with his. "Do you hate him?" he asked.

The question surprised Chagak. "What has he done to me that I should hate him?" she asked. "But I hated his father."

"You loved his grandmother and grandfather. His aunts and uncles."

"Yes."

Shuganan bent over his work, did not look

up at Chagak. "I think he should live."

Chagak sucked in her breath. Something inside wanted to scream out that the child should die, that his spirit would surely carry the taint of his father's cruelty. But instead she put away her weaving and then took the baby from his carrying strap. She removed the tanned hide that was tucked between his legs and dusted his buttocks with fine white ash she had collected from cooking fires and kept in a small basket.

Then she wrapped him again and picked him up.

"I need to know what kind of man he will be," Chagak said. "His father's people are so evil. What chance does he have to be good?"

Shuganan studied Chagak's face. It was time he told her, but still he held the deep dread of losing her. Once she knew, perhaps she would leave.

But he had been alone many years, and he still had to make the journey to warn the Whale Hunters. Who could say whether he would survive that? But the thought that Chagak might leave was something horrible to him, and he realized how much he had missed people, how much he needed to talk and laugh.

But if he told her the truth, then perhaps she would decide to keep the baby, to let the child live, and then the plans he had been making might be possible, and Chagak would have her true revenge.

So he said: "There is much you do not know about me. Now is the time for me to tell you. Listen, and if you decide you cannot stay with me, I will help you and your son find another place to live, and I will stay here and tell Seesfar that you and Man-who-kills both died. He will believe me. He will see the death ulaq."

Chagak pulled the baby close to her and, when he began to cry, slipped him under her suk and into the carrying strap. She was squatting on her haunches, elbows on her upraised knees, her chin resting on her hands, and Shuganan smiled, a sadness pulling at him. She looked like a child prepared for the storyteller.

He cleared his throat and said, "I know Man-who-kills' language and his ways because those things were no secret to me even as a child." He paused, trying to see if Chagak understood, if there was any fear or hating in her eyes. But she was sitting very still and gave no sign of her thoughts.

"I was born in their tribe, of their village. My mother was a slave captured from the Walrus People; my father, or the one who claimed to be my father, was the chief of the village.

"He was not a terrible man, not cruel, but since my mother was a slave, we had little, and since I was tall, thinner and weaker than the other boys, I was not allowed to own an ikyak, nor was I instructed in hunting or using weapons. But I made my own weapons, first only pointed sticks with tips hardened in fire, but then, by watching the weapon-makers in the camp, I learned to make harpoon heads of bone and ivory and to knap flint and obsidian.

"Usually I worked in secret, for I did not know if my father would approve. But as the other boys became hunters, I decided I did not want to be called a boy forever, to never have the joys and responsibilities of being a man, so I began to make a harpoon. I worked carefully, calling on spirits of animals to help me. I spent all of a summer working on it, carving the barbed head. I carved seals and sea lions on the wooden shaft, then smoothed it until it was as soft as down.

"One day, when the sea was too rough for hunting and my father was sitting at the top of his ulaq, I gave him the harpoon, and though he said nothing, I saw the wonder in his eyes, and later that day and the next I saw him showing the weapon to other men.

"Three, perhaps four days later he began an ikyak frame and told my mother to sew a cover for it. That summer he taught me to hunt and he gave me a harpoon that had belonged to his father.

"For the first time I felt as though my father's people were my people, and I worked hard to please them. I learned to hunt and I continued to carve. My father filled our ulaq with pelts and fine weapons — things other hunters gave in exchange for my carvings.

"I had fourteen summers when I went on my first raid." Shuganan stopped, then said quickly, "I did not kill anyone. We raided, but usually only to get weapons, perhaps capture a woman for a bride, and most women came willingly.

"I brought back nothing, but there was an excitement, something I cannot even yet explain, a power in capturing what belongs to others.

"But sometime during that summer a shaman came to our village. He and my father became friends. The shaman claimed to be the son of a powerful spirit and he did signs with fire, making flames come from sand and from water. He knew chants that made men sick and medicine that made them well again. Soon everyone believed what he told them, and since his beliefs were similar to ours, it was not difficult to follow him.

" 'If a hunter gains the power of the animals

he kills,' the shaman told us, 'then will he not gain the power of the men he kills?' "

Shuganan heard Chagak suck in her breath, but he continued, "It was something that even I believed for a time."

He stopped, but Chagak remained still. Her head was lowered so Shuganan could not see her eyes.

"Our raids became killing raids," Shuganan said, his voice soft. "But I found, though it was easy to knock a man down and take his weapon or his ikyak, it was a terrible thing to kill him. And each raid was worse for me, and not only for me but others as well.

"By then I was old enough to take a wife and have a ulaq of my own, and there were a number of us who decided to find wives and leave our village — to start a new life without the killing.

"We were told we could go, but we would not be given wives. Some then decided to stay, others left, but as I was packing my ikyak, the men of the village came to me. The shaman told me I could not go. That, though I did not have to raid, I must stay with our people, and if I did not, he would make chants that would kill my mother and all the men who had been allowed to leave.

"I stayed alone in a ulaq, someone guarding, someone bringing food. My earlobe was clipped as my mother's once was. A sign that I was slave, not hunter. Each day I was told what to carve, for the shaman saw great power in my carvings. He said that a man who owned the carving of an animal would draw a small portion of the living animal's spirit and carry the power of that spirit with him always.

"It was a horrible time for me, Chagak," Shuganan said, his voice low. "I spent two years doing nothing but carving. I had always loved the feel of ivory or wood, but I grew to hate it. I wanted to escape, but if I left, who could say what the shaman would do? But one day, when my mother brought food, I saw that my pain was also her pain, and it was her grief that gave me power to do what I did.

"The shaman often came into the ulaq and watched me, though neither he nor I spoke, but one day as he was watching I showed him a whale's tooth my brother had brought me and told the shaman I had dreamed a design for it and that it would be a gift for him.

"I carved many animals over the surface of the tooth. Around the animals I carved tiny people, images of each man we had killed during our raids. And for some reason as the shaman watched me do all this, he began to trust me. He gave me more freedom in the camp, once even let me go with others seal hunting, but what he did not know was, in the night, when I was in my sleeping place, I also carved.

"I made a place in the center of the tooth for an obsidian knife I had been given in exchange for a carving. I made a plug of ivory to cover the hole and I never let the shaman hold the tooth. Finally, when I had finished, I told him I would make a ceremony of giving.

"He did as I asked and came to the edge of the beach in early morning, when no one was yet awake except a few of the women.

"I had told the shaman to bring his weapons and make a hunting chant. He brought many weapons: harpoons, spears, bolas, and spear throwers. When he began the chant, I placed the carved tooth in his hands and told him to close his eyes. Then I pulled out the knife and pushed it into his heart. He did not even call out, just opened his eyes and died.

"I stole his weapons and an ikyak and traveled many days until I found this beach, then made a ulaq and lived alone. I took seal and sea lion and learned to sew my own clothes." Shuganan rubbed his hands over his forehead and cleared his throat. "I traded with the Whale Hunters, and after three years of living alone I traded for a wife." He paused, then said, "We were happy."

Chagak looked up at him. "So you lived here alone, the two of you," she said. "And you hunted and carved."

"No, for a long time I did not carve," Shuganan said. He shook his head. "It seemed to be something evil. But there was a part of me that was crying, as if I mourned a death. And mornings when I woke, my hands were numb and aching.

"Then my wife had a dream. A woman she did not know spoke to her, told her that I should carve, that my carving could be something good. A joy to the eyes and help to the spirit. I think the woman was my mother, and I think her spirit came to us on its journey to the Dancing Lights.

"I mourned her death, but I began to carve again, and the emptiness I had felt for so many years was replaced with peace. Then I knew my carving was something good."

Shuganan stopped talking and moved closer to Chagak. "Now you know that I was part of Man-who-kills' tribe," he said. "Do you hate me?"

For a long time she said nothing, but she did not move her eyes from his face. Shuganan felt that even his heart was still, waiting for her reply. Finally she answered, "No. I do not hate you. You are like a grandfather to me."

"You can love a grandfather but not a son?" Shuganan asked quietly.

Chagak began to rock. She crossed her arms

over the child within her suk, felt the warmth of his skin next to hers. The hopelessness she had carried since she had first known she was pregnant slipped away and in its place joy grew, hard and strong and shining. "He will live," Chagak whispered.

TWENTY-SEVEN

Kayugh thrust his paddle into the sea and sent his ikyak skimming between swells. Unable to bear the sound of his son's cries, he had paddled ahead and soon outdistanced the women's ik and even the other men.

It had been six days and still they had not found the promised cove, the good beach. Little Duck, her dream proven wrong, would not raise her eyes in his presence and would not sit with the women to eat.

But the mistake in days meant little. It was not Little Duck's error that tore at Kayugh's heart.

Each night the women passed his son from one to another. Each woman had tried to coax milk from her breasts. Women who had borne many children and nursed many years could make milk easily. In Kayugh's village it had been no surprise to see a grandmother nursing her grandchild. But Little Duck had never had children, and of Crooked Nose's four children, three had been daughters, given to the wind. The fourth, a son, had been taken by the great wave that destroyed their village only months after his birth. Crooked Nose had not nursed long enough to have milk for Amgigh.

Blue Shell gave Amgigh the small amount of yellow spirit-milk she held in her breasts, and Crooked Nose fed him broth. But the baby grew thinner, his cries weaker, each day.

And so he will die and have no one to guide him to the spirit world, Kayugh thought. I should have left him with his mother. What chance does he have?

But White River had been the one to name the child and thus give him his own spirit, separate from hers. It was a custom in her family, the naming shortly after birth.

What had White River's father told Kayugh? Early naming was the reason the family always bred strong hunters. And who could argue with the man? What hunter had brought more meat and furs than any of White River's brothers and uncles?

Suddenly the anger Kayugh had directed against himself changed to anger against his wife. He had always treated her well, brought her gifts, praised her before other men. Why had she chosen to die?

Kayugh's anger built until, forgetting all he had learned of hunting and traveling the sea, he thrust his paddle into the air and screamed out his frustration. He gave no thought to the animals he frightened, to the seals that would hear.

He screamed until his throat burned with the screaming, and until he had emptied his anger into the sky.

Then Kayugh closed his eyes and in the darkness behind his eyelids saw the image of his son's face. And Kayugh thought: Amgigh does not need to go alone. I can go with him.

Who says it must be mother who guides her children to the spirit world? Crooked Nose will care for Red Berry. I have no wife who needs me.

But then he thought, Should a hunter give himself for a child, a baby that might die even if his mother had lived? Was it better to give himself for his son or to keep his life for his people?

Perhaps he chose death to avoid life, to avoid the sorrow of losing two wives, then a son, or perhaps, if he chose life, it was because he feared death. Who could say?

Kayugh turned from his thoughts and scanned the sea, then moved his ikyak south toward the dark line of land. For days they had passed nothing but narrow beaches and high cliffs, places that thrust into the sea with no sheltering coves, no protection from the wind. But now, as Kayugh moved his ikyak closer to the wall of cliffs, he saw the turn in the rock, the sudden spume of spray that often told of a cove beyond. He paddled quickly, moving forward and closer to the land. Suddenly the cliffs split; a cove, wide and with beach, sloped back into grassy hills. The beach was large enough to hold tidal pools, and kelp fanned out in a dark mass around the cliffs.

Kayugh glanced at the sun. It was near setting. By now his people, far behind, would have made camp on some small beach.

Kayugh turned his ikyak and started back. Tomorrow he would return. They would claim this good beach and build a village far into the hills, away from any waves that might come.

And so I will live another day, Kayugh told himself, another day until I bring our people here. Then I will decide for myself and my son. By then, perhaps Blue Shell will have her baby, and my son will live.

TWENTY-EIGHT

Chagak woke early. She felt her son press his mouth over her nipple, felt the tingle of her breast as it released its milk.

Today they would name the baby. They would have a small feast, she and Shuganan, then the next day prepare for a journey to the Whale Hunters.

Chagak was afraid her grandfather, Many Whales, would not remember her. How many years had it been since her grandfather visited the First Men's village? Three? Four? And even then her mother had been quick to keep her out of Many Whales' way, sending Chagak and her sister to fetch water, to look for roots, to gather sea urchins.

And even if he did remember her, he and the men of his tribe might not believe what she and Shuganan told them. Then the Short Ones would come and there would be another slaughter. Chagak shuddered but reminded herself of Shuganan's wisdom. He would know what to say to convince the Whale Hunters.

Then sea otter's voice seemed to come to her, to whisper that, even if the Whale Hunters believed Shuganan, even if they fought the Short Ones and defeated them, there was danger to her son.

Yes, Chagak thought, if they find that my son was fathered by an enemy, they will kill the child. The thought made an emptiness come into her chest, a hollow that she knew could draw evil spirits, so she said aloud, "No one will know. I will not tell and Shuganan will not tell. The child will be safe."

As though he had understood her words, the baby gave a short cry, and Chagak crawled from her sleeping place. She pulled the baby from her suk. In another moon he would be big enough to sleep in the wood-framed cradle Shuganan had made and hung in Chagak's sleeping place. But now she was glad to have him close to her in the night.

She unwrapped him and placed the soiled sealskins that covered him in the basket of sea water she kept by the climbing log. Later she would wring out the skins and hang them from the rafters. They would dry stiff and hard, but if she stretched them and worked them with her teeth and fingers, they would be soft enough to use again.

When Chagak finished with the baby, she wrapped him in fresh skins and tucked him back into her suk. Because it was the naming day, she was supposed to stay in the ulaq until

Shuganan prepared a driftwood fire on the beach. But since Man-who-kills had beaten him, Shuganan was slow to rise in the morning. Chagak, tired of the stale ulaq air and tired of waiting, climbed up the log and opened the door flap. The morning was gray but bright, and the wind carried the rich oily smell of seal.

But what man had been hunting seal? Not Shuganan. Chagak climbed from the ulaq and looked toward the sea. Her eyes widened and, wrapping both arms around the baby, she slid down the ulaq and ran to the beach.

Shuganan awoke and lay still, listening to hear if Chagak was up. Many mornings since Man-who-kills had beaten him, Shuganan's arm and leg joints ached so badly, he could not rise from his bed of grass and furs. On those days he moved only a little at first, then gradually more and more until he could get up.

But today was the naming ceremony. He could not stay in his bed. Slowly he straightened his legs. Pain brought tears and, unable to move his hands to his face, Shuganan wiped his cheeks against his shoulders.

What good am I? Shuganan thought. I cannot even get up from my own bed. How will I paddle an ikyak? How will I bring meat for Chagak and the baby? She needs a hunter.

He called for Chagak, but she did not answer. He called again, surprised that she did not come. It was the naming day. What was more sacred than the naming day? Chagak was to stay in the ulaq until he had prepared a beach fire for the ceremony.

A sudden pulse of fear numbed Shuganan's arms. He thought he had convinced Chagak to keep the baby, but perhaps not. What if she had done something to him so he could not be named, so he could not make claim to his spirit and to a place in the spirit world? Shuganan's fear sharpened to pain, and he pressed his hands against his chest, took a shuddering breath.

Surely Chagak understood the importance of the baby's life in the plan they had discussed. But perhaps she had no real need for revenge. Perhaps she wanted only to escape. She could do that more easily without an old man who could not hunt or paddle an ikyak, and without a baby.

Ignoring the pain, Shuganan pushed himself to a sitting position and called again. Still no answer.

She is only emptying night baskets, Shuganan thought, but then saw his basket in the corner of his sleeping place. Perhaps she had forgotten the naming ceremony and just went outside. But Shuganan realized the foolishness of the thought, so it brought no comfort.

Shuganan moved his shoulders and, using his good arm for leverage, pushed himself from his bed.

When he stood, the stiffness of his knees seemed to be the only thing that held him, and he moved with slow, shuffling steps.

I should have spoken more about the baby, he thought. I should have let Chagak tell me her true feelings instead of trying to make her see the child as a blessing. What made me pretend . . .

"Shuganan!"

Chagak clambered down the climbing log and nearly ran into Shuganan, but his relief was so great that he merely laughed. "I called," he said weakly, then laughed again.

Chagak danced around him, the words coming from her mouth in rhythm like a song: "Come. You must come! Wait until you see!"

She helped him up the climbing log, and when Shuganan was at the top of the ulaq and felt the warmth of the wind, he thought that Chagak merely felt the joy of a warm day, but as she helped him from the roof hole he saw the true reason for her excitement, and the strength of his wonder nearly brought him to his knees.

"Tugix did this," he whispered to her as

they stared at the thing that had been given to them. It lay stretched out on their beach, the tail still in the water.

"We will never starve," Chagak said. "We will always have oil for our lamps. And we will save the jawbones as beams for our ulaq, better than the wood beams the sea brings us."

Shuganan shook his head. A whale. Who could believe that such a gift would be given to them? Its dark skin still gleamed with wetness from the sea, and even from the ulaq Shuganan could see the white of its huge lower jaw. The long baleen fibers in its mouth would make strong, waterproof baskets, and its meat would be rich and sweet. The oil boiled from its bones would burn without smoke, and the blubber would give strength in the coldest days of winter.

"Can we still have the naming ceremony?" Chagak asked in a small voice.

Shuganan laughed. "Have you ever seen a better naming gift? What is usually given, a few sealskins, a seal stomach of oil? Meat for the feast?"

And Chagak, too, laughed.

"We will have a ceremony, but first we must claim the whale. Bring my spear and some rope. Go quickly."

Shuganan moved slowly to the animal. The

smell of sea and fish was strong in the wind, and Shuganan tried to remember when a whale had last been washed to this beach. Perhaps when he was still a young man, when he first brought his wife to this island. And for an instant his wife's face was clear in Shuganan's mind. Sorrow gripped him, as though the years had not softened the pain, and Shuganan was filled with the weariness of his great age. But then he saw Chagak bringing the rope and spear from the ulaq, her slim legs skipping over rocks and sand, the bulge of the baby under her suk. His sorrow lifted, leaving the remembrance of what he must do.

When Chagak reached his side and handed him the spear, Shuganan pushed it into the ground. He tied one end of the rope to the spear shaft, the other end around the whale's tail. Its skin had begun to dry, leaving the white of the sea salt in lines across the body. But the tail was still in the water, and when the waves washed against it, they returned to the sea carrying blue and green circles of oil washed from the whale's hide, as though the sea, in giving the gift, did not give without asking something in return.

Shuganan raised his hands to the waves. "Listen. Listen," he said, his voice singing above the wind. "A gift has been given. This Mighty One chooses to give himself to Shuganan and

Chagak in honor of son and grandson. Respect the whale's wishes. Do not take him back to the sea."

He turned four times, to each direction of the wind, then to Tugix, and lifted his face to the sun, and each time Shuganan repeated his words. Then he told Chagak, "Now it is ours." If his power was great enough, the sea would not take the whale from Shuganan's spear.

They made the naming ceremony that morning. Chagak watched as Shuganan lit the driftwood she had heaped near the back edge of the beach. The whale blocked their view of the sea, but the sky seemed to be another, more immense sea, Chagak's world circled with water, above and below, as though she and Shuganan, her son and the whale were the only things created besides the island and water.

The ceremony would be short, Shuganan had told her, and the feast would be held another day, to celebrate both the naming and the gift of the whale.

When the fire was lit, Shuganan began a chant, something Chagak did not know, the words in the tongue of Shuganan's people. It was something she had not wanted, but she had no choice. She did not know the chants her people sang for a boy's naming ceremony. In her village, only the men and the mother of the child were present at a boy's ceremony, though the whole village came for a girl's ceremony, and so Shuganan sang what he knew, the chants of his own people. For if chants were not made, harmful spirits might linger, thinking to steal the name and use it for evil before the child could claim the name's protection as his own.

Chagak remembered the stories her father had told her about the first naming ceremony. There had been only one man and one woman then and no one to name them. And without names, they had no spirits. What spirit could exist without a name?

This man and woman saw they were different from the fish, for they had no scales or fins. They were without fur and so were not seals or otters. They did not have wings or feathers like the birds. "We are something new," the man said and so began to pray and sing in a sacred way, asking for a name. He did this until names came to him and he told the woman, "I am man and you are woman." That had been the first naming, and since then names were taken with thankfulness and in a sacred way.

Chagak felt the baby move against the bare skin of her belly. He was still a part of her, his spirit still joined to her just as much as if he were still held tight within her womb. But when he was given a name, he was separate, a new person, with a new spirit.

She had made a hooded garment for him from the skins of the eider ducks she had killed the summer before, and it was her gift to the child on his naming day. Shuganan had carved a seal, something to be hung from the baby's cradle to draw favor from seal spirits.

Perhaps the whale was a naming gift from her people, Chagak thought, from those she had worked so hard to give proper burial. But why would any of her people give gifts to the son of a Short One?

Shuganan ended his chant. The fire, once leaping with the words he shouted into the wind, was now quiet, as if the flames waited to see the baby. The wood snapped and a shower of sparks puffed up into the sky, fading as they met the greater light. Shuganan held out his arms and Chagak unfastened the child from the carrying sling.

The baby was naked. His round, fat body gleamed with seal oil. Chagak thought he would cry when he felt the chill of the wind, but he kicked his small legs and crowed, his voice like the laughter of gulls.

And as Shuganan turned him to face each of the four directions of the wind, the baby held his body straight, his head without wobbling. Then, as Chagak watched, Shuganan took the child to the whale, pressed the boy's hand against the black hide.

Chagak waited as the old man walked back over the beach gravel to the fire. An uneasiness stirred her spirit. Why had Shuganan taken her son to the whale? Her people were not Whale Hunters. She had not promised to warn the Whale Hunters so that her son could be raised in their ways. A sudden fear clutched at her. What if they wanted her baby? What if her grandfather wanted to keep him? How could she refuse, she who had no husband?

But when Shuganan brought the child back to her, Chagak pushed the fears from her mind. The whale was a good sign, a sign of Aka's favor. In choosing to let her son live, she had chosen wisely.

Chagak took the baby. He slipped easily into her arms, as though she had always been his mother, as though he had always been a part of her.

"Now you must tell him his name," Shuganan said to her and began a low chant.

As mother, Chagak had the honor of naming the boy, and she bent close to the infant, her hair falling around the child like a curtain woven of fine, dark grass. "You are Samiq," she whispered, so the child was first to know his own name, so he had the name's protection before any spirit, before wind or sea knew the name. "You are Samiq," she whispered again, to be sure he had heard.

Then she held the child up to the wind and repeated the name as Shuganan had told her. "The child is Samiq," she said to the earth and to the sky, to the wind and sea, to Aka and Tugix, to the whale and to Shuganan. "Samiq. Knife. Something that can destroy or create, something that, like a man, can be for good or for evil."

For a moment Shuganan stared at her, as though he were surprised by her voice, as though he did not understand what she had said, but he placed his hand on the child's head. "Samiq," he said, then, raising his voice and turning toward Tugix, called, "Samiq."

TWENTY-NINE

Kayugh's people had spent the previous night on a narrow beach, a dangerous place backed by walls of stone that rose to high, grassless cliffs. Each man kept his ikyak packed and the women did not cover their ik. During the night the men took turns watching the sea, hoping to have time to give warning before the water rose above the line of their camp.

Kayugh was the last man to keep watch. With each wave he lifted his prayers to the spirits that controlled sea and wind.

Finally the sun had risen, pale and shielded by clouds, and the women awoke to prepare food. But still Kayugh kept his eyes to the sea. He heard a feeble cry, and the pain of his son's hunger pierced Kayugh's heart.

For a moment he watched as Crooked Nose and Blue Shell dipped their hands into fish broth and let the baby suck the drops from their fingers, but then he had to look away.

For the first three days after White River's death, the baby had cried almost continuously, and Kayugh had worried that the men would make him kill the child so his wails would not scare away animals and fish, but now the cry was so soft that it was nearly muffled in the folds of the skins that wrapped him.

Your mother waits for you, Kayugh had silently told the child's spirit. She will come for you and then you will have no more pain.

After the naming ceremony, Shuganan flung a rope over the whale and anchored it to rocks on both sides. Chagak, using the rope to pull herself up, climbed to the top of the animal and, walking from head to tail, she cut through the thick, tough hide and down through the blubber, a long cut from the spout hole to the slope of the tail.

Twice during her cutting she had slipped and slid to the beach. After the second time she removed the baby from his sling and left him in a shaded spot in the lee of the cliff.

Then she made slashes the length of a man's arm across her first line, dividing the whale-skin into ten sections. At the top of each section she made two holes, tied a rope through each and she slid down the side of the whale. She and Shuganan grabbed a rope and pulled the section of blubber away from the whale carcass, then dragged the fat and skin to the grass near the ulaq, above the reach of the waves.

In the time the whale had been dead, the

heat of decomposition, held within the skin, was enough to begin cooking the meat. As Chagak worked, the smell of it made her stomach roll in hunger. But seeing that Shuganan still pulled, even with his left hand, she continued, the rope making burns on her fingers and palms.

But when they stripped the last piece of blubber away, Shuganan said, "I will take it. You cut some meat. I am hungry."

Chagak grinned and threw him her rope, then cut away as much meat as she could carry and took it to the ulaq.

With her woman's knife she cut a portion of the meat in strips and held it, a piece at a time, above the flames of an oil lamp. Then she packed the meat in a basket and took it to Shuganan. They sat in the shadow of the whale's carcass and ate.

They used their store of driftwood to build two huge fires, one at each end of the beach. When the fires were blazing and the coals had stored enough heat, Chagak laid stones in among the wood. As the stones heated she used a digging stick fitted with a shale blade to enlarge her cooking pit.

Shuganan brought large baskets from the ulaq, put them into the cooking pit, then Chagak filled them with water and strips of blubber.

While Chagak returned to the whale and began cutting away more of the meat, Shuganan carried hot stones from the fire and dropped them into the baskets until the water boiled. He removed cooled stones with a heavy loop of bent wood and added hot stones until a thick layer of melted fat formed at the top of each basket.

We will not starve this winter, Shuganan thought and began to sing.

Kayugh's people had started in early morning. Kayugh, pushing away his sorrow with each stroke of his paddle, soon outdistanced the slower women's boat, and by noon he was even far ahead of Big Teeth and Gray Bird. As he paddled, he memorized the land, the location of cliffs and small beaches, the color of rocks and the shape of kelp beds extending from the shore.

When he saw the cliffs, the cove marked with groups of large rocks, he felt a sudden excitement. This was the beach he had found the day before and perhaps it was the beach Little Duck had meant.

He moved quickly, paddling his canoe into the shallow cove. Then he stopped, paddle above the waves. A huge whale was lying across the beach.

He blinked, laughed and opened his mouth

to begin a praise chant to the sea, but then he noticed that the whale was partially flensed. His heart made a sudden beating, and his disappointment held him motionless in the water. His people could not claim the beach; someone already had.

The weariness of Kayugh's sorrow — the nights of sleeplessness, listening to his son cry, the search for a good beach — weighed him down, and Kayugh felt as though a giant hand were pushing him into the sea.

But then he thought, Perhaps those who claimed the beach would allow his small group to stay a few nights, to rest and gather roots and sea urchins. Kayugh held his paddle vertically in the water, keeping his ikyak steady in the waves.

A beached whale was a great gift, something seldom given to a village, but for such a gift there was little activity on the beach. Two fires were burning, but usually all the women would be working over rendering pits and the men stripping away blubber and meat.

The longer he watched, the more Kayugh wondered whether the beach was home to no one. Perhaps only a few hunters had found the whale and stopped to take meat and fat. But he saw no ikyak, no sign of temporary shelters.

Suddenly an old man limped over the rise

of the beach. His shoulders were hunched and he walked with the aid of a stick. He was not a hunter. No. A shaman living alone? Perhaps. And perhaps he had called the whale to the beach. Kayugh had heard of shamans with such power. If this man was one of them, he could destroy Kayugh's people with the wave of his stick, could harm without spear or harpoon, could kill without knives.

So can I bring my people? Kayugh asked himself, and heard a voice somewhere within saying, No. It was something he could not do. Why risk all? But if he went ashore now, the shaman might kill him. Then Big Teeth and the others might come to the beach, knowing nothing. Perhaps they, too, would come ashore and be killed.

In slow, easy movements, Kayugh directed his ikyak into the trough of a wave, then stayed within the trough until he guided himself out beyond the cliffs and away from the cove.

Chagak knelt beside her cooking pit. The whale blocked her view of the sea. The black skin and thick, yellow-white blubber had been peeled away. Gulls perched at the top of the carcass, pulling at bits of dark red meat, but there were no small boys living on this beach to chase the birds away with long poles and well-aimed stones. Some of the krill that had filled the whale's belly had spilled out onto the gravel of the beach, and blood seeped into the sea.

Chagak had taken all the grass mats and curtains from the ulaq and was sewing them into storage bags. Shuganan lashed driftwood into high, many-tiered drying racks.

During the night they would take turns watching the fire and keeping hot stones ready for the cooking pit.

Tomorrow, if the sea still honored Shuganan's claim, they would strip away the rest of the meat and string it on the drying racks.

The whale had been a wonderful gift, but Chagak could not help thinking of the celebration her village would have had: the dancing, the songs, the joy of many night fires down the long beach. And though she and Shuganan had rejoiced, it was a quieter joy, a singing of the spirit. And who could say which was better? But some perversity in Chagak wanted both.

"There is a whale beached there," Kayugh said, drawing his ikyak close to Big Teeth's. But before he could say more, Big Teeth called the news to Gray Bird and the women. Kayugh stilled his ikyak and shook his head. He tried to cut into the babble of excited voices, and finally, forcing his ikyak next to the women's ik, called out, "Wait. There is a whale, yes, but there is also an old man."

"An old man," Gray Bird snorted.

"He is flensing the whale. He has built fires to render the blubber."

"What does that matter?" Gray Bird said. "What is an old man? Our women could take him."

"If the beach is his, it is his," Kayugh answered. "Perhaps he will let us stay, but there is that chance he will see our coming as a threat."

"He will see nothing if he is dead," said Gray Bird.

"And what if he is shaman?" asked Big Teeth. "What if he called the whale to his beach? Would you want to be enemy of such a man? What would he do to you if he could kill a whale?"

Gray Bird did not answer but bent over his ikyak as if he had found a small tear in a seam, and Kayugh said, "Let me go alone. Make a camp at a beach close to the cove, and if I do not return, do not come after me." To Blue Shell he said, "Do not worry about my son. If I die, I will take him with me to the spirit world." Then, looking at Crooked Nose, Kayugh said, "I give Red Berry to Big Teeth as daughter." And he saw Crooked Nose nod and pull the child to her lap.

Kayugh turned his ikyak and went swiftly, keeping to the tops of the swells, speeding his ikyak to the cove.

It was nearly night and Shuganan's legs and arms ached, but it was a good kind of pain. Chagak had brought sleeping mats and the baby's cradle to the beach. They made a camp in the grass above the tide mark, near the cooking pit. Even with the rise and fall of the waves, the whale had remained on the beach, and the tide had risen no higher than the flippers.

Now Shuganan used hand ax and knife to detach the jawbones. It was slow work, and he realized that he would not be able to cut away the entire lower jaw before the sun set.

If the sea gives us six or seven more days, he thought, we will have enough meat and fat for two winters.

It seemed as though his arms had grown stronger as he worked, and he began to hope that Chagak could make him a chigadax from the skin of the whale's tongue. He began to hope that he would hunt again, that in the fall, when the small fur seals swam by, he would use his ikyak again.

When he heard someone behind him, he thought Chagak had come to help, and he said, "Bring me a lamp."

But then he turned and saw that he spoke not to Chagak but to a young man. Shuganan's breath caught in his throat and he stood still, knife in left hand, ax in right.

The young man's eyes moved to the weapons, but he stepped forward, close enough for Shuganan to touch, and held out his hands, palms up. "I am a friend," he said. "I have no knife."

For a moment Shuganan did not move. I was not quick enough, he thought. I have not warned the Whale Hunters. But then he realized that the man spoke the language of the First Men and that he wore the full-cut bird-skin parka that all First Men hunters wore.

"I am Kayugh," the man said. "I seek a new beach for my home. The rising sea brought waves that destroyed my village."

He was tall, well built, his eyes round and clear.

He shows his soul through his eyes, Shuganan thought, and suddenly was not afraid.

"There are others with you?" Shuganan asked and moved so he could see around the man, but there was no one else on the beach.

The man hesitated, searched Shuganan's face.

"Not with me," he said. Again he paused and his eyes seemed to hold Shuganan's eyes, as if their spirits were testing one another. "They have camped for the night farther east. I saw the whale and that you were here. We do not want to claim a beach that belongs to someone else. I have come only to ask if we might spend a few days gathering sea urchins and roots."

"How many people do you have?"

"Three men, three women, three children."

Shuganan studied the man. He seemed to be a good man. Like someone he would choose as husband for Chagak, but who could say? Sometimes evil was disguised as good. Perhaps he was a spirit come to steal the whale. Perhaps he was a shaman who had been told by spirits about Shuganan's carvings. And perhaps he did have women and children, but if so, why did he not bring them with him?

Shuganan wanted to tell him to go, but then the thought came, What if this man were some good spirit? What if he were the one who had sent the whale and now wanted to see if Shuganan was a good man, a man willing to share?

"You may stay the night," Shuganan said. "We have much meat, as you can see. Eat what you want and take some back to your people."

THIRTY

Chagak took Samiq from his cradle and hugged him tightly to her chest.

Shuganan's oil lamp was like a star on the dark beach, and in its light she was sure she had seen two men. She stood and watched until she saw Shuganan. He was pulling at the jawbones. The huge arched bones were nearly separated from the whale carcass, and yes, there was another man beside him. A spirit come to take Shuganan from her? Or Sees-far returning with his people?

Chagak wondered if she should run.

She had left her woman's knife at the other beach fire and now felt a deep grief over her carelessness. Surely if she went for the knife the man would see her. She grabbed a chunk of driftwood from the ground. It was better than no weapon.

The man seemed to be helping Shuganan. Would Sees-far help? Not unless he hoped to earn a woman for the night. But why work when the one who protected Chagak was only an old man? Why not take what was wanted? How would Shuganan stop him?

But what about the baby? Some men found no joy in another man's child.

Perhaps Chagak could lay the child in the shelter, hide him under a layer of grass mats. But if he cried . . . Better to put him under her suk, then if she ran he would be with her.

"Chagak!"

Shuganan was calling her. His voice was strong, unafraid. If there were danger, he would not call, Chagak told herself. She dropped the piece of driftwood but did not stand until she had the baby beneath her suk. Then she went to the other fire, picked up her woman's knife and walked slowly toward the men. She kept her head down and crossed her arms over her breasts, trying to hide the form of the child bound against her chest.

Shuganan hurried to meet her and, grasping her arm, pulled her to the whale. The man waited for them, his hands, dark with whale's blood, stretched out in greeting.

Not Sees-far, Chagak thought, relieved. Nor any of the traders who had once come to her people's beach.

"My granddaughter," Shuganan said, and he spoke in the First Men's tongue.

The man was tall and Chagak felt like a child beside him. Her head reached only as far as his shoulder.

"Kayugh," Shuganan said and stared at Chagak until she realized he wanted her to speak. She looked up at the man and repeated his name.

It was a good name, a name that spoke of strength. Kayugh had a wide, square face, and his eyes reminded Chagak of her father's eyes, eyes that were used to scanning the sea. He smiled at her, but she saw a sadness in his smile, something that made her wonder why he was alone.

"We need help moving the jawbones above the reach of the waves," Shuganan said.

Chagak wished Shuganan had not asked for her help. She could not take a chance the baby would be injured, so now she must admit she had him under her suk. She looked at Shuganan and said slowly, "I have the baby. Let me put him in his cradle."

She saw the sudden hunger in Kayugh's eyes and a chill pulled at the muscles of her back, but Shuganan seemed to feel no dread as he said to Kayugh, "My grandson."

Chagak hurried back to the camp she had made beside the beach fires. She knew Kayugh watched her as she left.

"He will ask for you tonight," came a whisper from the sea otter, but Chagak did not reply, and she blocked from her mind all remembrance of the night she had spent with

Man-who-kills, the pain of man taking woman.

She laid the baby in the cradle, careful to turn his face away from the wind, and returned to the men. They had cut the jawbones from the dome of the skull and pulled them from the carcass. She and Shuganan gripped the bone that formed the left half of the whale's lower jaw. They pulled against the gravel, Chagak matching her steps to Shuganan's. Kayugh took the right jawbone and, pulling it alone, dragged it nearly to the ulaq while Chagak and Shuganan were still on the beach.

The bone was slippery with flesh and Chagak's hands were not strong enough to hold it for more than a few steps. Finally she held the outward curve of the bone against her chest, so the muscles of her shoulders did the work of pulling. She looked at Shuganan, saw that he had done the same. Then suddenly Kayugh was between them, pulling so hard that most of the weight was lifted.

When they reached the rise of the beach, they dropped the bone. Chagak cut a handful of grass and wiped off her hands and the front of her suk.

"Come," Shuganan said to Kayugh. "Chagak will watch the fires for a time. You are welcome in my ulaq."

Chagak returned to the fires. A part of her was glad to be alone again, glad to have an excuse to stay on the beach, but part of her wished she might hear what Kayugh had to say. Why he was here.

She knelt beside Samiq's cradle. The baby was asleep so she did not pick him up. Shuganan had made the cradle from driftwood. A fur seal skin cushioned the woven sling that hung from the deep-sided frame. Chagak had decorated the frame with puffin feathers and disk beads she had cut from mussel shells. On one corner, next to the carved seal, Shuganan had hung a small carving of a whale.

It was not the animal Chagak would have chosen, but he told her it was what they must have, something that would make the Whale Hunters believe the child was doubly of their blood, grandson of Shuganan's wife, grandson to Many Whales. And now Chagak wondered if the carving had called the whale to them.

She added some driftwood to the fires, huddled close to the brightness that seemed to keep away the spirits that came with the dark. The sky held the color of the sun; reds and pinks lit the edges of the horizon. And Chagak remembered that on her people's beach, also an east-facing beach, the hills around her village had hidden the sun colors that came with the short summer nights. But here, if she walked to the edge of the cove, there was nothing between her and the sun except the sea.

She took her wooden loops, green willow bent and tied, and pulled a rock from the fire's coal bed. She carried it to the cooking pit slowly so that, if the rock fell, she would not walk over it before she could stop herself.

She dropped the rock into the pit. The oil and water frothed and sent up a circle of bubbles. If she and Shuganan kept the fires going all night, in the morning there would be a thick layer of oil at the top of each basket. Chagak would skim it off and pour it into other baskets for cooling.

After cooling, any sand or bits of flesh that might make the oil rot in storage would be in the bottom layer. Chagak would skim off the top and put it into seal stomach containers for storage.

She would use the oil at the bottom of the basket more quickly, some for cooking but most for oiling seal belly containers, or for greasing babiche and sinew for sewing, even for waterproofing the seams of the ik and ikyak.

Chagak was returning to the fire when she saw something moving in the darkness by the ulaq.

Her first thoughts were of night spirits, and

she called softly, speaking aloud to the sea otter spirit and clasping her shaman's amulet, but then Kayugh stepped into the light.

Chagak felt a moment of relief, then a sudden dread, fear that Shuganan had agreed to let the man have her for the night. Her throat seemed to close, and she did not think she could speak.

She stood, holding her tongs between them as though they would protect her. He made no move toward her but squatted on his heels by the fire and stared into the flames. Chagak pulled another rock from the coals and carried it to the rendering pit.

When she went back to the fire, Kayugh stood. A fierce trembling started in Chagak's hands and she turned away from him, pretending to check her son.

"You have a son," Kayugh said, moving to stand beside her. He squatted down and moved back some of the sealskin blankets that covered the child. "He is healthy and fat."

"Someday he will be a good hunter," Chagak said, the usual reply of a mother receiving a compliment.

"Your husband?"

"He is dead," Chagak said, her words abrupt. She and Shuganan had decided on a story to tell the Whale Hunters. She hoped Shuganan had told the same story to this man.

"I am sorry."

"His name was Seal Stalker," Chagak said and was surprised to find tears in her eyes, for it seemed that her words truly made Seal Stalker Samiq's father. "He was a good man."

Kayugh stroked the top of Samiq's head, the man's strong square hand lingering over the baby's pulsing fontanels. "You must be proud of this son," he said, his eyes rising to meet Chagak's eyes.

But Chagak looked down, "Yes," she murmured, the dread again closing around her throat.

"I told your grandfather that I would watch the fires for a time so you could rest."

Chagak looked at him in surprise. Shuganan helped her with the whale meat because they knew the sea might soon carry the animal away. If there had been other women here, Shuganan would have helped only with the peeling of the skin, the cutting of the largest bones. Why would this hunter offer to help?

But then the sea otter seemed to say, "Perhaps he wants a share to take back to his village."

"You should sleep," Chagak said. "You have been in the ikyak today. Shuganan will come and take my place."

"He is old. He needs more sleep than either you or I."

"I will sleep for a short time, then I will

come back," Chagak said, but she stood and watched as the man used the tongs to pull a rock from the fire and drop it into the boiling pit. Then she picked up the baby and returned to the ulaq.

"He told me to come to the ulaq and sleep," Chagak said to Shuganan. She hung the baby's cradle from a rafter over her sleeping place and then returned to the central room of the ulaq. She sat down beside the old man. "Should I have stayed with him?"

"No," Shuganan said. "He wanted me to talk to you."

Chagak had been surprised to find Shuganan still awake when she entered the ulaq, but now she clasped her hands in apprehension. "He wants to share a sleeping place with me?"

Shuganan laughed. "What man would not? But no, he did not ask. He asked only about your son and your husband."

"He asked me also," Chagak said. "I told him what we decided to tell the Whale Hunters."

"Good. That is best."

"What did he want then?" But as she spoke, Chagak suddenly remembered his gentle ways with Samiq, the longing that had seemed to be in the man's eyes when he looked at the child. "He does not want Samiq?" she asked, fear making her words too loud, her voice high like a little child's.

"You have too many fears," Shuganan said, scolding her.

Chagak pressed her lips together and felt the burn of foolish tears at the corners of her eyes.

"His village was nearly destroyed by the sea. A great wave. He is chief of a small group of people. Two other men, three women, some children. They want to come to this beach, to stay here with us."

"They would build a village? Claim this place as their own?"

"Only if we say they can. Otherwise, they will come for a few days, until the women have had time to dry fish and gather grass for mats."

"And you told them to come?"

"Only for a few days. If they are a good people they can stay, if not . . ."

"If not, who will make them leave?" Chagak asked. "It would not be hard for three men to kill us and take this beach."

"And what will prevent them from doing that now?" Shuganan asked. "Kayugh will return to his people, tell them where we are. It is better for us to welcome them. Besides, we will soon leave for the Whale Hunters' village. Who knows if we will return?"

Chagak picked up a handful of loose grass from the ulaq floor and let it sift through her fingers. "If there are three men and three women, Kayugh must have a wife," she said.

"He spoke about a wife."

The thought gave some relief to Chagak, but she knew that many men were strong enough hunters to support more than one wife. "We should have told him I was your wife," she said.

"Why? Perhaps he or one of his men will want you. You need a good husband."

Chagak shook her head. "No," she said and stood up. "I have you and Samiq. I do not need a husband. I do not want a husband." She spoke loudly, almost in anger, and Samiq began to cry, his wail small and thin from the ulaq rafters.

"If Kayugh asks for me, tell him no," she said and went to her sleeping place before Shuganan could answer.

THIRTY-ONE

Kayugh directed his ikyak around the rocks that protected the small beach his people had chosen.

It was not a good place for a village; boulders thrust from the water and blocked the view of the sea. The beach, too, was piled with large rocks. But for a short camp it was good. There were cliffs and a fresh-water stream.

Beach peas and red-stemmed lovage grew among the rocks; grooved ugyuun stalks, as tall as a man, were without their large white-backed leaves, and Kayugh knew the women had stripped them. Many times he had watched Red Leg heat ugyuun leaves on green willow racks over a fire, until the leaves were dry enough to crumble into flakes that would flavor their winter's meat.

Kayugh had spent a night and morning with Shuganan and Chagak, and though Shuganan had urged him to stay another night, Kayugh was afraid Big Teeth and Gray Bird would think something had happened to him if he stayed.

Then also, always in his mind, often numbing him to the things he should notice as a hunter in his ikyak — the shifting of wind, the position of sun and clouds, the color of the sea — were thoughts of his son. Was the child still alive? Had Crooked Nose been able to get him to eat more broth since they made the camp on the beach?

Now, even if Blue Shell had not yet delivered her child, there was hope for Amgigh if Kayugh could get him to Chagak. . . .

Kayugh untied the hatch skirting of his ikyak and with a last thrust of his paddle allowed a wave to carry him to the shale of the beach. He jumped from the ikyak and picked it up, one hand on each side of the hatch opening, and carried it above the reach of the waves.

"Kayugh!" The voice was Gray Bird's. Kayugh cringed. Gray Bird was always eager to bring bad news. Perhaps Amgigh had died.

Kayugh untied his weapons and supplies from the outside of his ikyak and piled them on the beach.

Gray Bird squatted beside him. "You found the beach again?" he asked.

"Yes," Kayugh answered, pulling off his chigadax and laying it over the ikyak so he could inspect the garment for tears.

"The whale was still there, and the old man?"

"Yes," said Kayugh.

"Did you kill him?"

322

"Why would I kill him? He let me stay in his ulaq. He gave me a sealskin of whale meat to bring back to you."

"He is alone on the beach?"

Kayugh found no tears in the chigadax and so set it with his other supplies. He would oil it later, making sure there was no water trapped in its folds to cause rotting. He bent over the ikyak and ran his hands along the seams and over the tightly stretched sea lion hide covering. He was suddenly weary of Gray Bird's questions and, for some reason, reluctant to tell him of the woman, Chagak.

"The old man is a shaman," Kayugh said, then asked, "Is my son still alive?"

Gray Bird shrugged his shoulders. "The women have made no death chant."

"And Blue Shell? She has not given you a son yet?"

"No."

Good and bad, Kayugh thought, but felt the tension leave his shoulders. He flipped his ikyak to inspect the bottom. He found no tears, so took a pouch of grease from his supplies and began to coat the seams.

"Where is Big Teeth?" he asked.

"We found a cave. Farther up in the hills. The women made a shelter there. Big Teeth and I took turns watching the beach for your coming so you would not think we had left."

Kayugh finished greasing his ikyak and picked up his harpoon and chigadax. He hoisted the seal stomach of whale meat to one shoulder. "Take me to the cave," he said to Gray Bird. "I will tell you what I have found and we will decide what to do."

"I hope he does not come back," Chagak said.

"It is not good for us to be here alone, Chagak," Shuganan answered. "What if something happens to me? What would you do? You cannot hunt and care for Samiq, too."

Chagak cradled her arms around the baby under her suk and began to rock as she sat. Her movement awakened him and she felt the tug of his mouth on her breast.

"They are people from your own tribe," Shuganan said. "They speak your language."

"Yes," said Chagak, her voice small. She tried to bring up images of the many joys she had known living in her people's village, tried to tell herself this would be no different, but some spirit seemed to bring doubts to her mind. Would they expect to live in Shuganan's ulaq? Would the women tell her what to do? She was a woman now, with a baby of her own. But there were three of them and she was alone.

"What of our plans to go to the Whale

Hunters?" Chagak asked.

"We will still go. We will tell Kayugh's people about the dangers of staying here. Then it will be their choice to stay or leave."

"Perhaps, then, they will leave," Chagak said.

But Shuganan answered, "Perhaps they will choose to go with us to the Whale Hunters."

"There are only three of them," Kayugh said. "An old man and his granddaughter. She has a baby. A son."

They sat in a circle at the edge of the cave. A fire glowed at the center of the circle, and the children sat with the adults, even Kayugh's tiny son, his hands and face cold when Kayugh touched him, though Blue Shell had wrapped the baby in seal fur.

It was still day, but the shadow of the cave and the crackling fire made it seem as though it were night or perhaps a dark winter day, a time for storytelling.

"We can kill the old man and one of us take the woman for his wife," said Gray Bird.

"Why would we kill the old man?" Big Teeth asked and spat on the ground. "You are a fool, Gray Bird."

Kayugh watched the two men, Gray Bird, his lips curled back from his teeth, fists clenched, and Big Teeth, who was ignoring the smaller man, his eyes on Kayugh.

"We are not killers," Kayugh said, meeting Big Teeth's eyes, letting Big Teeth know he agreed with him. "If the old man did not want us on his beach, we would not go. But he has invited us.

"He is a shaman, I am sure, and has great power. I told you about the whale. Now let me tell you about his ulaq."

"What do we care about his ulaq?" Gray Bird asked, but Kayugh went on as though the man had not spoken.

"There are three ulas," Kayugh said. "Two are sealed like death ulas; the other, the smallest, is where the old man lives. Inside, the walls have been cut into shelves, and the shelves are crowded with tiny images of people and animals, each carved with eyes and mouth, the seams of clothing or the marks of fur or feathers.

"At first I thought that the old man was a spirit, that he had made these things to bring animals to his beach, but as we sat and talked, he worked all the time with a knife, carving and chipping at a piece of ivory until it began to look like a whale. He gave it to me."

Kayugh pulled the carving from inside his parka. He had watched as Shuganan drilled a hole in the ivory and strung a length of braided sinew through it so Kayugh could wear the carving like an amulet around his neck.

To drill the hole, Shuganan had used a piece of obsidian knapped to a narrow point on one end, bulging at the other into a knob that supported his hand. He had set a small basket filled with oil in his lap and immersed the carving, holding it steady with one hand while slowly moving the obsidian drill with the other, pressing and turning, pressing and turning.

"The oil strengthens the ivory," Shuganan had explained; "without it, the ivory chips, sometimes shatters, and the spirit of the carving escapes."

Now Kayugh bent forward, laying the carving on his hand. It was no longer than his smallest finger and glowed white in the firelight.

The women covered their mouths and even Big Teeth drew in his breath. Gray Bird reached out but did not touch it.

"This old man," Big Teeth said, "he had a whale on his beach?"

"Yes. A baleen whale. A large one."

Big Teeth shook his head. "Perhaps he called it to him with a carving."

"I do not know," Kayugh said. "But there were other carvings of whales in his ulaq and one hanging on the baby's cradle."

Crooked Nose shifted her position and moved closer to the fire. Kayugh knew it was a sign she wanted to speak. And though women did not usually speak during village meetings,

Crooked Nose always had wise questions, wise answers. The men were usually willing to listen to her. "The woman is his granddaughter or wife?" she asked.

"Granddaughter. She told me her husband was dead. She is very young and speaks as we do, in our tongue, and her grandfather is very old and speaks as though he had not always spoken our language."

"We should kill the old man and take the woman," said Gray Bird. "More women, more sons."

"We could not kill the man, even if we wanted to," said Big Teeth. "His carvings protect him."

Gray Bird's mouth curled down and his eyes narrowed. "I have known others who carved. What great gift is that? I have carved outlines of seals on my throwing board."

"Yes," said Crooked Nose. "And we know it has not helped your hunting."

Gray Bird leaped to his feet and lunged toward the woman, but Big Teeth, sitting between them, caught Gray Bird's arm and pulled him down. Then, turning to his wife, Big Teeth bellowed "Crooked Nose! Be still!"

But Kayugh, anxious to know why Crooked Nose was interested in Chagak, said, "Why do you ask about the woman, whether she is granddaughter or wife?"

Crooked Nose smiled. "If she is truly grand-daughter as the old man told you," she said, "with a son to raise, perhaps he welcomes us because he knows she needs a husband. But if she is his wife and he has lied to us, either he sets a trap to bring us there and kill us, or he has no power and is afraid that you or another man will kill him to take his wife."

"And what good will all this do us?" asked Gray Bird. "We do not know if she is wife or not. If the old man is a spirit, he will kill us. If he is only old and frightened, his beach is probably full of evil spirits that have come to torment him. What if those spirits are there when we arrive? How will we protect our wives and children?"

"It is a good beach," Kayugh said. "The cliffs protect it from the sea, and there are many tidal pools for sea urchins. There is a fresh-water stream and bird holes in the cliffs. Rye grass grows at the edge of the beach."

Kayugh paused and his son's tight, gasping cry cut into the silence. Blue Shell dipped her fingers into a skin of fat broth and dripped some into the baby's mouth. Kayugh lowered his eyes and turned away. He had done a cruel thing, prolonging his son's pain. The baby would be dead by now if he had left him with White River, and White River would have found her spirit home. She and Amgigh would be dancing in the north sky.

"The woman has a fat baby, you say?" Gray Bird asked.

Kayugh saw the malice in the man's eyes and did not answer.

"You are willing that we risk our lives so your son has a chance to live? Even if the woman agrees to nurse him, he will not live. Look at him. He is dead already; some spirit lives in him that is not his own. You hear only the cries of a gull or puffin, something to lead you astray." Gray Bird pointed to the whale pendant Kayugh still clasped in his hand. "How do we know the old man did not carve out the whale and send it here filled with some deceiving spirit to make you lead us into his trap? You will sacrifice us all for a child who should have died many days ago."

Gray Bird stood. "I say we do not go." He stalked away from the fire.

But Big Teeth said to Kayugh, "If you decide to go, I and my wives will go, too."

Kayugh met Big Teeth's eyes, saw the wisdom and strength there. Gray Bird stood without moving, his back to the fire. No one would force him to go with them, and perhaps, thought Kayugh, it would be easier for them if he did not, but Kayugh doubted that Gray Bird had the courage to stay alone.

Kayugh looked over at his son. The child

still sucked at Blue Shell's fingers.

I must decide without considering him, Kayugh thought. And so he told his spirit, Amgigh is dead. Even Chagak's milk cannot save him. And in his mind Kayugh saw his son dead, saw the small heap of stones that would cover him, and Kayugh saw himself paddling far out to sea, then slitting the bottom of his ikyak, felt the waves close up over his head. They would both be dead and together their spirits would find White River and the Dancing Lights.

So he saw himself dead, but then thought of Big Teeth struggling to hunt for all the people, Gray Bird more trouble than help.

I cannot die, Kayugh thought. I cannot leave my people. White River will come for our son. She was a good mother. Why worry that she will allow Amgigh to be lost in the spirit world?

So again Kayugh told his spirit, Amgigh is dead. If we go to Shuganan's beach, it will make no difference for my son. The decision must be what is best for all of us.

In his mind Kayugh saw the goodness that shone from Shuganan's eyes, the power of his carvings, the strength that was in his woman, Chagak. Was there any reason for fear?

He looked up, spoke to Big Teeth's strong eyes, Gray Bird's weak back. "We go," Kayugh said.

THIRTY-TWO

Shuganan stood at the top of the ulaq and looked toward the beach. Each morning when he awoke, his stomach was tight until he saw that the whale carcass still lay on the beach, that the waves still respected his claim. And each night he rejoiced. More meat stored. More oil taken.

The whale was still there, now only skeleton, bones and blood.

Shuganan straightened his shoulders and called down to Chagak. The night before, they had banked the two beach fires, for they had needed sleep more than oil.

Today Chagak would sort the bones, boiling the large ones for oil, saving the smaller pieces to flavor stews.

Chagak came up from the ulaq, her suk bulging in front where the baby lay bound against her. "Is the whale still here?" she asked, turning to look toward the beach.

"Yes."

She said nothing more, only reached out quickly to squeeze Shuganan's arm and then jumped from the ulaq and walked down to the beach.

Shuganan watched her as she dug coals from the banked fires and started the flames again with knots of dry grass and chips of driftwood. But his eyes were mostly on the sea, waiting to see if Kayugh would return. If he would bring his people with him.

Kayugh thrust his paddle into the water and his ikyak pulled ahead of Gray Bird's. He studied the cliff to his right. Yes. It was the one, the high east cliff of Shuganan's beach.

"Here!" he called, waving his paddle in a wide arc over his head, then turned the ikyak into the cove.

He saw Shuganan hurrying down the beach, and he saw the whale carcass, now only bones. Within the arch of the ribs, gulls scolded and fought for scraps of meat.

Kayugh maneuvered his ikyak around the rocks that dotted the cove, and as he neared the beach, he untied his hatch covering, jumped into the shallow water and pulled the ikyak ashore.

Shuganan was waiting for him and greeted him with palms up. Then Big Teeth was beside Kayugh. He also greeted Shuganan, and the two helped Gray Bird from his ikyak and the women and children from their ik.

Chagak stayed at the rendering pit. Kayugh wished he could take his son to her, could pull the child from Blue Shell's suk, run up the beach and ask Chagak to feed him. With each day, as the baby came closer to death, Kayugh felt his own strength leaving. The power drained from his arms and legs as if the baby's pain were changing Kayugh into an old man.

This for my selfishness, Kayugh thought as he watched Chagak work. But when he had decided to keep the child, it seemed too much to pile another sorrow upon the loss of two wives and so many of his people. The pain was already so intense that Kayugh wondered at times if something within his chest was broken and bleeding, making his arms and legs heavy, his belly refuse food.

But the slow waiting, the hoping seemed worse. And his pain was made more intense by some spirit whispering, "He is better. Do you not see that he is a little fatter? Did you see that he opened his eyes, that his cry was louder?" So Kayugh could not trust himself and knew the truth only by seeing the sorrow in Crooked Nose's eyes, the fear in Blue Shell's.

Caught within his thoughts, Kayugh did not notice that Gray Bird stood beside him until the man said, "You did not tell us she was beautiful."

"Would that have made your choice to come easier?" Kayugh asked.

"I thought you came only to save your son."

"I chose to come here because it is a good beach."

"Then you do not care if I decide to take a second wife," Gray Bird said.

Anger filled Kayugh's chest. It pushed up into his neck and pulled against the tendons of his arms so that his fists clenched. "Who will hunt to feed her?" he asked, the taunt thrust at Gray Bird like a knife.

But before Gray Bird could answer, Shuganan was suddenly between them.

The old man held his shoulders straight, and his eyes were snapping as though there were coals buried in their dark centers. "I offer you the hospitality of my ulaq and my beach, and already you argue over my granddaughter."

"She needs a husband," Gray Bird said and stepped closer to Shuganan.

"I will decide when she needs a husband," Shuganan said, his words soft but strong enough to carry to the women and children unpacking the ik.

Kayugh waited for Gray Bird to reply, but the man said nothing, and finally Big Teeth came over and shoved Gray Bird toward the ik.

"Your wife needs help," he said and Gray Bird backed slowly away.

"No one will take your granddaughter as wife unless you and she agree to the marriage,"

Kayugh said. "We will leave if you wish."

But before Shuganan could answer, Big Teeth said, "Kayugh seems to make small concession for Gray Bird's rudeness, but he offers more than you know."

Kayugh clasped Big Teeth's arm. "A man's problems are his own," he said quietly.

But Big Teeth said, "When we are old, our people will need new hunters."

"Perhaps Blue Shell carries a son," Kayugh answered.

Big Teeth smiled slowly. "Perhaps, but perhaps he will hunt like his father."

"Gray Bird hunts."

"I do not like lemming meat."

Then, turning to Shuganan, Big Teeth said, "Kayugh's wife died in childbirth and his son has no woman to nurse him. All we ask is that your granddaughter share her milk. Not that she be wife."

"It is something she must decide," Shuganan said. "But when you have finished unloading your boats, you can bring your things to my ulaq and I will ask her."

Chagak lifted another hot stone with her willow tongs and dropped it into the pit. She tried to work as though no one else were on the beach, as though she did not see Shuganan with the men and women from Kayugh's village.

But now, led by Shuganan, they were walking past her to the ulaq, the men carrying their harpoons and spears, women loaded with packs of meat, bedding and grass mats.

There were two children: a boy of perhaps eight summers with a sealskin bag thrown over one shoulder, and a girl, surely no more than three summers, dragging a grass mat.

The adults did not look at Chagak, as was the custom of politeness, but the boy stared as he passed and leaned to look into the rendering pit.

The girl lifted her hand and pointed at Chagak with one tiny finger. She stopped, as if to speak, but then stuck the finger in her mouth and hurried to catch up with the others.

Chagak stood on her toes to watch the people as they entered Shuganan's ulaq. She wished she could be there to tell them where to put their things, to see that food and bedding were properly stored, but she continued with her work.

She used a sharpened stick of green willow to pull out the kreng — brown bits of crackling left after the fat was rendered. She piled it on a sealskin to cool. Later she would cut it into strips to use for fish bait.

She was lifting the last piece of kreng from the pit when she saw Shuganan climb from the ulaq. Kayugh and the other two men were with him. Chagak dropped her head so they would not see her watching them.

She gathered the sealskin up over the mound of crackling and pushed down with the palms of her hands, moving in a circle around the skin, pushing as she moved.

She pulled the bundle close to the edge of the pit and flipped down one side of the sealskin so the oil she had forced from the kreng ran into a basket.

As she laid the sealskin out flat again, exposing the kreng to the wind to cool, she realized that Shuganan and the three men were beside her.

"My granddaughter, Chagak," Shuganan said to the men, and then to her, "You know Kayugh. These are men from his village. Big Teeth and Gray Bird."

Chagak wiped her hands on her suk and stood up.

Big Teeth was a man of long arms and legs. It seemed as if the arms of his birdskin parka were as long as the parka itself. His face skin was dark, with lighter lines running from the corners of his eyes, and his hair poked in all directions. He smiled at her, showing a row of long white teeth that protruded from between his lips even when his mouth was closed, but there was a goodness in his smile that made Chagak feel at ease.

The other man, Gray Bird, did not smile. His lips were flat against his teeth like an otter's lips when it is angry. A clump of hair dangled from his chin, hair no thicker than seal whiskers, dark and hanging to the front of his parka. It seemed that he narrowed his eyes purposely; his forehead lined and wrinkled with the effort. He was smaller than Kayugh and Big Teeth but stood with his chest thrust out as though by his own will he could increase his stature.

He was the first to speak and he spoke without polite comment on weather or Chagak's work. "We want to see your son."

Chagak wrapped her arms over the front of her suk, holding the baby close to her.

"He is asleep," she said, though she could feel the pull of his mouth against her nipple, the working of his hands against her skin.

But then Big Teeth spoke as if Gray Bird had said nothing, as if the man were not even beside them. "We have traveled many days. Our women are tired. Your grandfather has given them shelter in his ulaq. When they have rested, they will come and help you skim the fat from the boiling pit."

And though these words were also not the usual talk of meeting — polite words about weather and the sea — at least there was caring in the man's voice.

"It will be good to have help," Chagak answered.

"Kayugh has a baby son, too, Chagak," Shuganan said.

"I am happy for you," Chagak said to Kayugh, but as soon as she had spoken, she saw the pain in the man's eyes, and it reached out to pull at the sorrow Chagak had held within herself since she lost her people.

"Is the baby sick?" she asked, forgetting she should not speak until spoken to.

But Kayugh did not seem to notice. He took a step toward her and said, "My wife died after the birth, and I chose to keep the baby with me. But none of our women have milk to nurse him."

Chagak pulled her son from the warmth of her suk and held him out for Kayugh to see. The child was naked except for the tanned hide that wrapped his buttocks. His legs and arms jerked in the cold and he began to cry.

"He is a good strong son," Kayugh said.

"All babies would seem strong compared to your son," said Gray Bird, but he did not look at Kayugh as he spoke.

"Where is your son?" Chagak asked.

"In the ulaq," Kayugh said. "Blue Shell, Gray Bird's wife, carries him."

Chagak nodded, and then, as though there were no one on the beach but herself and

Kayugh, she raised her suk and cupped her left breast in her hand. She pressed her nipple, squirting milk in a thin stream for Kayugh to see. Then she slipped Samiq into his carrying strap, poked the nipple into his mouth, and prodded his cheek until she felt him suck.

Chagak lowered her suk and smoothed it over her son. "I have enough milk for two," she said to Kayugh. "I will nurse your son."

THIRTY-THREE

When Chagak entered the ulaq, it seemed as though it were a different place. Seal stomach storage containers were set in heaps at the bottom of the climbing log; new water skins hung from the rafters. Stacks of furs filled the extra sleeping place and overflowed into the main room.

But though Chagak had expected to hear the babble of the women, they were silent. For a moment she stood on the climbing log, staring at them as they stared at her.

They were sitting in the center of the ulaq, their backs to each other, faces toward the shelves that held Shuganan's carvings. One woman, her nose large and humped, held the little girl on her lap. The boy sat beside them. Another woman, round-faced and plump, sat looking at the ground, her dark hair pulled back and tied, but it was the smallest woman who held Chagak's eyes. She had a bulge under her suk.

Blue Shell, Gray Bird's wife, Chagak thought, and then heard the spirit voice of some sea otter say, "She is beautiful, that woman."

Yes, Chagak thought. Anyone would find pleasure in seeing Blue Shell's tiny nose and wide eyes, her small, full lips. Chagak touched her own face and wondered if anyone found pleasure in seeing her.

At first Chagak did not want to speak. She wanted to go quickly to her sleeping place, to close the curtain between herself and the women, but she had told Kayugh that she would nurse his son, and even now the men watched the rendering pit so she could come here.

Finally Chagak said, "Shuganan's carvings do not carry evil spirits. You do not need to fear them and soon you will be used to their eyes watching."

And it was as though Chagak's words had given the women life. The big-nosed woman spoke quietly to the others and then all three began unrolling grass mats and pulling food from storage bags.

It seemed as though the big-nosed woman led the others and so Chagak went to her and showed her the storage cache. She pulled back the curtains and tied them so the women could put their food inside.

"I am Crooked Nose," the woman said. Then she gestured toward the little girl straddling her hip. "This is Red Berry, Kayugh's daughter."

343

"I am glad you have come, Red Berry," Chagak said, but the girl hid her face against Crooked Nose's suk.

"The boy is also Kayugh's?" Chagak asked.

"No," said Crooked Nose, "First Snow is my son. But Kayugh does have a son. Blue Shell carries him. He is very sick."

Her words trailed off and Chagak said, "Kayugh told me about this son."

Blue Shell looked up from her work. "He is very weak," she said, "and I do not have any milk. My husband is not happy that I carry the child. He says it might curse our own children to weakness."

"I have milk," Chagak said, but Blue Shell's words made Chagak uneasy. Could Kayugh's son make sickness come to Samiq? But then the sea otter whispered again, "You told Kayugh you would feed the child."

Blue Shell lifted her suk and pulled the baby from his carrying sling.

At first Chagak's eyes were on Blue Shell's belly. The woman was pregnant, soon to deliver, but then Chagak saw the infant. He looked like a tiny old man, his eyes and belly too big for his shriveled arms and legs. How long had he been without food?

Blue Shell unfastened his carrying sling and unwrapped a packet she had at her side. She took out clean fur and skins to pad the strap.

Blue Shell handed the strap to Chagak. Samiq's strap was over Chagak's right shoulder, so she fastened the other strap over her left. She laid Kayugh's son in the strap and poked her left nipple into his mouth, prodding his cheek anxiously until finally she felt a small tug. The baby's eyes opened as though he were amazed that his sucking had filled his mouth, and he sucked again, holding himself to her breast with both hands.

Blue Shell went back to the center of the ulaq and sat down beside Crooked Nose. They began to talk, voices low so Chagak could not hear what they were saying. Suddenly she felt uncomfortable and alone, as though she were the one who was visiting this ulaq.

The women laughed, and even the shy one lifted her head. Chagak felt a sudden dread that they were talking about her, so she turned away from them and watched Kayugh's child nurse. He was not strong enough to suckle continuously, but sucked and then let the nipple pop from his mouth, searching with eyes closed until he found the nipple again, sucking, taking a breath, sucking.

Chagak lowered her suk, covering the tiny child. She glanced up at the women and saw that Blue Shell was looking at her. Chagak saw relief in her eyes, but it seemed that Blue Shell's relief was Chagak's burden.

The otter spirit whispered, "The child will die."

"No," Chagak said, so quickly that she had a sudden vision of the otter sliding from shore into the sea, the animal turning its back on Chagak's rudeness. And Chagak could not help but think the otter was right. The baby had not even cried when Blue Shell took him naked from her warm suk. A child without the strength to cry. Could he live?

Chagak kept her hand inside her suk, gently moving the baby's head whenever he stopped nursing, and she moved her hand now and again to Samiq, checking that his arms and legs remained fat and strong, checking that Kayugh's son did not suck the strength from her son as he was sucking milk from Chagak's breast.

She kept her head lowered, so did not see Blue Shell beside her until the young woman asked, "Does he suck?"

The question startled Chagak and her gasp of surprise made Blue Shell giggle. But Chagak could think of no reason to smile, her ulaq full of strange women, a dying baby at her breast. Why had Shuganan agreed to let these people stay?

But Blue Shell did not know her thoughts and began to babble about rendering whale blubber and storing meat.

Chagak did not want the women to work

at her rendering pit, to help her with the meat. It was her work and she had done it the way she thought best. She had made the decisions and now did not want others to change what she had done.

But then the sea otter said, "You have been away from your village too long. What woman turns down help? You are letting the men help now. Why not the women? They know more about rendering pits than men."

So Chagak tried to listen to Blue Shell with a kinder spirit, tried to smile as the woman talked, but she did not truly hear what Blue Shell said until she began to speak about Kayugh. Then, for some reason, Chagak was interested, and she asked, "Gray Bird, your husband, is Kayugh's brother?"

"No," Blue Shell answered. "Kayugh's father and mother came to our village before he was born. They were Walrus People. The father had come to our village to trade. He liked us, so brought his wife and stayed."

Chagak had heard her father tell of trading with the Walrus Men. A good people, he had said, given to laughter, a tall, light-skinned people who trained animals called dogs to pull loads and protect their camps. And Chagak could not hold back her words, a foolish question, the question of a child: "Does he have a dog?"

Blue Shell laughed. "No, but he is a great hunter, surpassing all. He would have been the next leader if he had stayed in our village. But there was no choice. The sea rises and our island grows smaller each year. Kayugh says that someday everyone will have to leave. But our journey, until we found this place, has not been a good one, especially for Kayugh."

"Yes," said Chagak. "He told me his wife died after giving birth."

"She bled after the baby was born," Blue Shell said. "She did not tell us she was bleeding so badly.

"And before that, Kayugh's first wife also died. She drowned when we were gathering limpets. Kayugh went after her, but when he brought her to the shore, she was already dead. She was old, wife to another before Kayugh, but Kayugh took her as first wife, giving her honor, although she did not honor him with a child."

Chagak felt Kayugh's son lose his grip on her breast and was filled with the sudden fear that he was dead. She glanced inside her suk, saw that milk bubbled from the baby's mouth. He was asleep. She raised her eyes to Blue Shell and said, "He sleeps. Do you want to hold him now?"

Blue Shell looked away. "No," she said. "I

have no milk. If you keep him, you can feed him more often."

Chagak thought again of the hurt in Kayugh's eyes as he had spoken about his son. No wonder Blue Shell did not want to keep the baby. Who would want to be the one holding the child when he died?

Blue Shell stood. "I must help Crooked Nose unpack our belongings," she said, but then asked, "The old man, Shuganan, is he your husband?"

Chagak lifted her head. "He is my grandfather," she said and, grasping awkwardly for words, added, "My son's father is dead." Then she busied herself with Kayugh's son, waking him so he would eat again, and she did not look up to see if Blue Shell had any more questions.

THIRTY-FOUR

Chagak sat in the ulaq, a baby at each breast. Kayugh's people had been with them for three days, and in that time the women had helped her finish slicing and hanging the whale meat and rendering the oil.

Their racks stretched the length of the beach, from one cliff to the other, each rack strung with lengths of dark whale meat, thinner than the blade of an obsidian knife, long as Chagak's forearm.

In the ulaq, Chagak had hung floor mats as sleeping curtains, even dividing most of the large rooms into sleeping quarters.

The men had begun digging a new ulaq, one big enough for Kayugh's people, and Chagak wished they would finish it quickly, for she felt out of place in the crowded, noisy confusion of Shuganan's ulaq. In her own village, building a new ulaq was a time of joy, but the building of this ulaq was marred by Gray Bird's constant complaints and his meanness to Blue Shell.

It was difficult, also, to see the other women using her supplies, her cooking stones. Earlier that day, at the cooking pit, Crooked Nose had used some of the whale oil to cook a herring she had caught. She cooked the fish on the large, flat stone that Chagak used for pounding seeds and dried berries, a stone that Chagak was careful to keep clean and without a trace of oil, so when she had finished with the berries and seeds, they were still dry and she could store them for months without worry that they would rot. But by the time Chagak noticed that Crooked Nose had heated the oil and stone, any protest was useless, the damage done.

Chagak had held her temper, thinking that she would search for a new stone after Crooked Nose and the others had moved to their own ulaq. Travelers could not carry everything, and perhaps Crooked Nose had left her cooking stone behind.

Chagak had tried to have food ready at all times, to explain how she liked to have food packed and stored, but it seemed that each woman had her own way of doing things, and the storage room was overflowing with spilled seeds and broken storage containers.

Gray Bird had found the remaining oil- and sand-stored eggs and had eaten more than half.

But most of Chagak's worry was for Kayugh's son. The child ate and slept, but she could see no change in the thin arms and legs. His cry was no stronger; he seldom opened his eyes, and when Chagak put her finger into his hand, he did not clasp it.

In the morning, as soon as Chagak was up, emptying night baskets, lighting lamps, Kayugh was beside her, his eyes tired and rimmed with red as though he had not slept. She would lift her suk, show him the babies, one fat and growing, the other like something dying. He would shake his head and the sadness in his eyes tore at Chagak.

"He eats well," Chagak would say to Kayugh, and the first time she said the words, some hope had seemed to spark into his eyes, but now each time she showed him the baby, each time she commented on his eating, Kayugh made no response.

Chagak sang to the child as she worked, songs of seal hunting and strong sons, and she prayed to Aka. She even searched among Shuganan's carvings until she found one of a father with a strong son on his shoulders, and, getting permission from Shuganan, she sewed it on the left side of her suk, just over Kayugh's son.

Chagak had worked most of the day on the beach. She had caught two brown-winged jaegers that had floundered into the rendering pit and were eating bits of kreng left in the remnants of cooled and hardened blubber. She had thrown baskets down over the birds to catch them, then had twisted their necks and laid them aside to skin and boil later.

In the late afternoon she had entered the ulaq, hoping to be alone, but Blue Shell and Little Duck were inside, each working on grass mats for their ulaq. Chagak had placed Samiq in his cradle and jostled Amgigh so he would continue sucking. Then she sat down to help the women. But even in helping she felt out of place. They talked about people she did not know, of beaches that were unfamiliar to her. Chagak spoke only to ask for things necessary for her weaving.

Finally she left the ulaq. She carried two large loosely woven storage sacks with her and walked into the hills to gather heather. She would replace the grass on the ulaq floor with the heather. She hoped it would freshen the smell of the ulaq, rank with too many people.

When she had filled the sacks, she started back toward the ulaq, but then she saw Kayugh coming toward her. For a moment she closed her eyes. She was thirsty and had hoped to have time to refill her water skin at the spring near the ulaq, time to sit and drink without listening to anything except wind and sea, but she greeted the man with a smile, reminding herself that most women would be proud to have a strong hunter like Kayugh to talk to.

She set the sacks of heather on the ground and lifted her suk. The wind chilled her belly, and she shivered. Kayugh bent toward his son and the baby loosed Chagak's nipple from his mouth. At first Chagak thought the thin cry was from Samiq, the child protesting the cold of the wind, but she saw the rounding of Amgigh's mouth, then heard Kayugh's laughter, the two sounds of crying and laughing blending to make one note, like a hunter's sealing song.

She saw the tears that were on Kayugh's cheeks, heard him whisper, "He cries." And his voice carried the pride of a father announcing his son's first seal kill.

Yes, Chagak thought, looking down at the child. He did look a little stronger, his arms and legs not quite so thin, and for the first time since she had started to nurse the infant Chagak felt a stirring of that hope he might live. But though the hope leaped within her chest like something close to joy, she also felt a thrust of pain, the knowledge that if the child did die her acceptance of the death would not be as easy.

But she smiled at Kayugh, and to her surprise he reached out and pulled down her suk. Then he picked up the bags of heather and walked with her back to the ulaq.

In the evening, after the men had been fed

and the women had eaten, Chagak sat with a woven mat in her lap. She meant to finish the edges, but she was so tired, she could hardly make her fingers move. The noise of voices pulled at her from all directions and she wished that Kayugh's ulaq was finished so that she and Shuganan could be alone again, so that she could nurse the babies in quietness, the thick ulaq walls shutting out even the sound of waves and wind.

The men had left the ulaq after eating, but soon they would be back, and Chagak would be expected to offer food and full water skins. It would not be a night that Chagak could excuse herself and go to her sleeping place early. She glanced down at the babies. Both slept.

Chagak kept a soft furred skin tucked around both children when she was in the ulaq, her suk off. Though Samiq did not need the skin, she had noticed that Kayugh's son did not nurse as well without something tucked tightly around him.

Little Duck was beside her, the girl Red Berry on her lap. Crooked Nose squatted next to them. Suddenly First Snow slid down the climbing log into the ulaq. The boy sat down beside Crooked Nose and pointed at Chagak. "Your man, Shuganan, says he will make stories tonight."

Chagak felt a quick happiness. There would be no long awkward evening, the men grumbling over too many children in a small place, Chagak trying to please everyone and feed babies, too. There would be no need for her to keep food ready for the men, lamp wicks trimmed and lighted. There would be only telling and listening. Quietness except for the storyteller's voice.

Big Teeth came in first. He sat between Crooked Nose and Little Duck. He ruffled First Snow's hair. The boy grabbed Big Teeth's hand and growled like an otter. Big Teeth exchanged glances with Crooked Nose and laughed. Chagak, seeing the look, felt like an intruder, and she dropped her head, pretending to study the weave of her apron.

Shuganan and Gray Bird climbed into the ulaq. Chagak had hoped Shuganan would sit by her, but he squatted beside Big Teeth, and the two men spoke about building the new ulaq.

Kayugh entered the ulaq last. He squatted beside Chagak and watched his son nurse. Knowing the gratitude that she would see in his eyes, Chagak found she could not look at him.

But soon Red Berry claimed her father's attention, climbing into his lap, and Chagak found herself wondering about this man, a man who cared for his daughter as much as most men cared for their sons. A man who had not been able to leave a newborn son to die.

Chagak was sitting on her heels, knees raised, each baby in his sling resting against one of her thighs as he nursed. Chagak stroked the babies' heads. They both had much hair, thick and dark. When she stroked Samiq's head, he stopped nursing and stared at her for a long time. Amgigh did not stop nursing but clung more tightly to her breast.

"Granddaughter, bring me water," Shuganan suddenly said, his voice strong enough to carry over the noise of the men and women talking.

Shuganan moved from his place beside Big Teeth and sat down on a pile of sealskins next to Kayugh. Chagak stood and untied a seal bladder water skin from a rafter and handed it to him. He drank, then set the skin down and rested his gnarled hands on his knees.

First he addressed Kayugh and spoke as if no one else listened.

"You have asked me the story of my people," Shuganan said, "how I came to this place. Now I will tell you. This is the time to remember what has been."

Chagak closed her eyes. She could relax. No one would care if the oil lamps flickered and died; no one would notice if she did not bring food.

She knew what Shuganan would tell them, mostly the truth, but also what was not true, the story they had decided to tell the Whale Hunters when they went to warn them. She knew she must remember what he said — to protect Shuganan and herself and, most of all, Samiq. But also she would give herself to the telling, allow herself to slip into the story, to feel anger and joy and wonder as Shuganan spun his words into the silence of the ulaq.

"When I was young," Shuganan began, "I was trader for my people." He stopped, and Chagak knew he waited for the murmur that would show everyone listened, everyone could hear him. Then he said, "I journeyed to the edges of the world where ice walls mark the boundaries of the earth. I traveled far into the sea, to islands few men have seen. I knew the Walrus Men and the people who hunt the brown bear. But mostly I knew the men some people called Short Ones, small, strong men who were known for their hunting skills and shrewd trading.

"In most of my journeys I traveled with Short Ones. We traded with people, bringing seal oil to the Walrus Men and walrus hides and meat back to trade for whale oil from the Whale Hunters.

"I learned to speak the Short Ones' language and even stayed in their village. But the longer

I stayed with them, the more I realized that they were a greedy people. They did not trade to provide food and clothing for themselves and bring joy to others. They traded so they could have more than they needed. It was this greed that opened the way for evil spirits to come into their tribe.

"A shaman came to them, one who knew evil, not good. He saw the many things the Short Ones had and decided he wanted everything for himself. He told the people he would make other tribes weak so the Short Ones could take without trading.

"They went to villages pretending to trade, and in the late night after a trading celebration the Short Ones rose from their beds and hid all weapons. Then they killed the people and took what they wanted.

"Finally they no longer pretended to trade but came to a village in the night, burned ulas and killed people.

"I was then, as I am now, a carver," Shuganan said, pausing as the people murmured assent. "The Short Ones put great value on my carvings. If they were going to take a village of Walrus Men, they wanted walrus carvings to tuck into their amulets. If they were going to Bear Hunters they wanted carved bears."

Shuganan lowered his voice, spoke not with

the authority of a storyteller but as a man relating a dream. "There has always been something in me, some spirit that dwells in my head and hands, that urges me to carve."

Chagak, realizing that Shuganan had departed from the story they had decided upon, opened her eyes and watched the old man. She hoped he would remember to talk with care about Samiq's father.

"When I was small," Shuganan said, "still sleeping in my mother's sleeping place, I would wake in the night with a tingling in my arms and hands, and a desire to carve something I had seen that day. The desire was so great that my head felt as though it would break open with the need to release what my eyes had stored.

"The evil shaman saw great power in my carving, and at first I was flattered by his attention. But later I realized that my work was being used to hurt others.

"Though they tried to make me stay, I left the Short Ones. I knew they would search for me, so I could not return to my own village. Instead, after many days in my ikyak, I found this beach. I made a ulaq here and, after a number of years, took a wife from the Whale Hunters. We had a son who took a wife from the First Men's village on the south side of Aka's island. They both died and after many years my wife also died, but they left me with Seal Stalker, my grandson."

Chagak, though she kept her eyes on Shuganan, knew the others were looking at her. She could feel their thoughts hovering near her. She pretended to adjust the babies' slings.

The lamp wicks had burned down to the level of the oil and so gave little light, but when Chagak looked up at Shuganan, his face glowed as if lit by many lamps.

Then she heard the sea otter say, "Has it been so long since you have seen a story told? Do you not remember the power of words; so many people thinking the same thoughts, lost in the same dreams? Have you forgotten the power of that?"

But Chagak knew Shuganan had come to the part of the story she must not miss, the part about herself and Samiq, and so she blocked the otter's whisper from her thoughts and listened to Shuganan.

"When my grandson was old enough, he took a wife from his mother's village." Shuganan looked across the ulaq at Chagak. "Now I claim her as my granddaughter, Chagak. But one day when Seal Stalker went hunting, he did not return to us. Chagak was ready to begin mourning, to call herself widow, but on the seventh day Seal Stalker returned. Our joy at his return was soon lost in sorrow, for he told of Chagak's village destroyed, all her family dead. He had spent three days burying them and making death ceremonies.

"I knew it must have been the Short Ones. And later that summer two scouts from the Short Ones came to our beach. We killed one, but the other killed Seal Stalker and escaped, leaving Chagak a widow with a son who would be born in spring.

"Before he left, the Short One told us he would be back; he would bring his people to kill us and to kill the Whale Hunters on the island to the west.

"Chagak's mother and my wife were both of the Whale Hunter people, so Chagak and I decided to make a journey to the Whale Hunters this spring, to warn them, and soon we will go.

"We do not ask that you go with us. It is not your people who have been killed and you owe no allegiance to the Whale Hunters. But we will go."

Chagak sat very still in the quietness of the ulaq. She could feel the surprise of Kayugh's people at the abrupt ending of stories. Stories usually lasted far into the night, one story's ending spawning the beginning of another.

Did they believe Shuganan? There were few

lies: only that Shuganan was not a Short One, that she was wife to his grandson, and the lie she wished was not a lie: that Seal Stalker was Samiq's father.

But when she heard Shuganan say the words, it was as though they were true, as though his telling had changed the past and made Samiq Seal Stalker's son. Her arm tightened around Samiq. What if they knew? Chagak thought. What if they found out about Man-who-kills? They would never let Samiq live. He would be considered a Short One, an enemy.

She squeezed Samiq to her chest, and the baby began to cry, his wail loud and startling in the quiet of the ulaq. Then Kayugh's son also began to cry. And it seemed to Chagak that the babies had heard some whispering of spirits, that they cried for sorrows that Chagak and Shuganan did not see.

Chagak left the story circle and went to her sleeping place. She closed the curtains behind her and wished she could stay within the ulaq forever, both babies safe in her arms.

THIRTY-FIVE

Chagak sat on the bare floor of the new ulaq, sorting through a sack of dried heather. She cut away bruised and frayed stalks, those parts of the plants that would rot quickly. The rest she would scatter over the ulaq floors to be covered by grass mats.

Crooked Nose and Little Duck worked beside her, finishing the last of the mats. The new ulaq was larger than Shuganan's. Even with the sleeping places curtained off, there was enough space for many people to work comfortably in the main room.

Crooked Nose pointed out the largest sleeping place at the back of the ulaq and said, "Big Teeth will sleep here."

Chagak frowned. "I thought Kayugh was head man of this ulaq."

"Shuganan did not tell you?" Crooked Nose replied. "Kayugh and Red Berry will stay in Shuganan's ulaq. Kayugh wants to be with his son, and since you nurse him . . ."

Chagak's stomach tightened. She and Shuganan would not be left alone as she had hoped. But she tried to hide her disappointment. Of course Kayugh would want to be with his son, she told herself, and so he would choose to stay in Shuganan's ulaq. But would the ulaq still belong to Shuganan or would Kayugh now be head man? And what about Shuganan? He would be humiliated if he were no longer head man in his own ulaq. Perhaps Chagak should offer to come to this ulaq, drawing Kayugh back to his own people. But then who would care for Shuganan?

"Your husband is dead," Crooked Nose said.

The words startled Chagak and she sat without answering, her mouth open.

But Crooked Nose did not wait for a reply. "Perhaps Kayugh seeks someone as wife," she said.

Chagak felt her face redden. She tried to listen as Crooked Nose told her about Kayugh's skills as a hunter, but fear numbed Chagak's hands and quickened her breath.

She knew her mother had been happy as a wife, and Crooked Nose, when she spoke of time spent in the sleeping place with her husband, spoke with flashing eyes and giggles, not dread, but Chagak had once known the pain of a man within her and did not want it again. She had seen how often Big Teeth visited his wives' sleeping places, even in the few days they had lived in Shuganan's ulaq, and Chagak had shuddered as she lay on her sleeping mats, remembering what Man-who-kills had done to her.

"All men are not cruel," the sea otter whispered to her, night after night. But Chagak did not want to be wife again.

Kayugh smoothed his harpoon shaft with a piece of lava rock. It was the first evening since Big Teeth and Gray Bird had moved to their own ulaq, and Kayugh was glad for the quietness in Shuganan's ulaq.

Shuganan sat next to an oil lamp, the old man leaning into the light. He carved a bit of ivory, his eyes and mouth moving as he worked, as though he spoke in silent words to the thing he was creating.

Chagak was finishing a chigadax for Shuganan. Made from the skin of the whale's tongue instead of strips of seal intestine, it had taken only a few evenings to sew. Red Berry had her head on Chagak's lap and the babies were nestled, one at each breast. Chagak was so small that Kayugh could hardly see her through the children.

It should stay like this, Kayugh thought. In peace, in quietness. He had spoken several times to Shuganan about the planned journey to the Whale Hunters. Kayugh wanted him to leave Chagak here, but Shuganan had disagreed.

"What do women know of fighting?" Kayugh had asked, but Shuganan countered, "You say you may decide to go with me. If you do, I will be glad. But what do you know of fighting? Have you ever fought against other men?"

"No," Kayugh had said. "But I can throw a spear. I have fought seals and sea lions. Men cannot be much different."

"Men think," Shuganan said, "and they hate. Animals fight only to live, perhaps at times to protect their young. Men fight for hate, for power, for owning things. It is a different kind of fighting, something that draws in evil spirits."

Kayugh fingered his amulet. The quiet of the ulaq seemed so far from fighting. He watched Chagak as she nursed the babies. His son was still thin compared to Chagak's son, but the thinness did not make Kayugh fear for the child's life.

"I do not want Chagak to go to the Whale Hunters," Kayugh suddenly said, his words loud in the ulaq's stillness.

"What is better," Shuganan said quietly, "to take her or to leave her here? The Short Ones know about this beach. They know about my carving.

"There were two scouts here, Kayugh. One was going to stay with us, to take Chagak as wife and live here for the winter. We killed him, but the other returned to his people. He will come back to this beach.

"Do you want Chagak to stay? To be the one who tells the Short Ones that her grandfather killed one of their hunters? Besides, there is Gray Bird. If we leave the women, he will want to stay. I have seen the hunger in his eyes when he looks at Chagak."

Kayugh sat in silence, then said, "You are right. But if we go, we should go soon. What if the Short Ones come to this beach and we are still here?"

"They are hunters first, warriors second," Shuganan said, his hands turning the ivory he carved, his knife working until Kayugh could see the eyes and nose of a seal peeking from between Shuganan's fingers. "They will not come until the best of the seal hunting is finished."

Kayugh nodded, but still he was uneasy. It was not good to be taking Chagak with them. And what would the Whale Hunters think of her, one of their own — a beautiful woman with son and no husband?

Chagak was making holes with her awl in a sealskin, marking the line her needle would follow on the first stitching of a waterproof seam, but now and again she lifted her head to watch Kayugh and Shuganan.

Shuganan, as always when he carved, paid little attention to the things around him, to what others said, to the noise and activity of the ulaq. Perhaps that was why he and his wife had no children, Chagak thought. Perhaps he gave so much of his spirit to his carvings, there was nothing left for his wife, nothing to begin the soul of a child.

Chagak glanced at Kayugh and quickly looked away. He was watching her. It bothered Chagak that the man was often in her thoughts, and once in the past few nights he had even come into her dreams, lying beside her, stroking the side of her face until Chagak had awakened, shaking.

To comfort herself, she had pulled Kayugh's son closer to her and wakened Samiq, sleeping in his cradle above her head. Then she had nursed both children, feeling Samiq's strong, glad nursing, and Amgigh's gentler tug. She had run her finger along Samiq's arm, smiling when he clasped the finger in his small hand, then had done the same with Kayugh's son. She expected no response; the baby seldom moved his hands from her breast. But as she stroked his hand, he, too, clasped her finger, his grip strong.

Chagak had lowered her cheek to the top of Amgigh's head, a gladness singing inside her. She had wanted him to live for Kayugh's sake. The man had suffered enough without the loss of his son. But now she knew she also wanted the child to live for herself. Before there had been a distance, something Chagak put between herself and the child. A protection. It was still too soon since she had lost Pup. She could not bear the thought of hoping and praying, of watching and telling herself the child was improving when he was only growing closer to death. Hope brought more pain.

But though she had fought it, the caring had come, had crept into her soul when she was busy with other things, and now she nursed the child not only for Kayugh but for herself.

As Chagak sewed, she thought of Samiq and Amgigh growing up together, learning to use the ikyak, learning to hunt. Then suddenly, as if the idea were not her own, but something someone else thrust into her head, Chagak thought: It would be better for Samiq to have a father.

No, he has Shuganan, Chagak told herself, but Shuganan's own words came to her: "I am old."

Chagak shook her head and thrust her needle into the awl holes. I do not need a husband, she thought, and with each thrust of her needle pushed Shuganan's words further from her mind.

It was early morning, and Chagak had just finished rinsing out the night baskets. She stood at the top of the ulaq and watched the red circle of the sun tuck itself under the clouds that filled the sky.

For the first time since Kayugh had brought her his son, she had left both babies in the ulaq, Kayugh holding Amgigh, Samiq in his cradle.

Suddenly, in the wind and the brightness of a new day, she felt like a young girl again, as though, if she shut her eyes and gave enough strength to her thoughts, she would find that she stood in her own village on her father's ulaq, watching for Seal Stalker's ikyak among the waves. But then she heard Shuganan's slow steps up the climbing log, and she again felt the heaviness of the milk in her breasts and the pressure of the grief she had carried since the death of her people.

"He asks for you as wife," Shuganan said, but he had spoken even before he pulled himself from the ulaq, and Chagak, not quite sure what he had said, squatted close to the roof hole so she could hear him more clearly.

"Kayugh," Shuganan said. "He wants you

to be his wife. He does not want you to go to the Whale Hunters without a husband."

For a long time Chagak said nothing, but she kept her eyes to the sea, finding some small escape in watching the waves. But finally she leaned toward the old man. "We should go away now," Chagak said. "We could find a new island. Start again. We could come back here and trade . . ."

The anger in Shuganan's eyes stopped Chagak.

"And what would you do with Amgigh?" he asked. "Would you leave him here without milk just when he is becoming strong? Or would you take him, leaving Kayugh without the joy of a son?"

Shuganan pulled the sleeves of his parka above his wrists and held his hands out to her, stretching the twisted fingers. His hands trembled.

"I am old, Chagak," he said. "How will I hold the spear? How will I set the snare? I cannot care for you and for Samiq. Can you be both man and woman? Hunter and mother?"

Something hard and tight pressed against the inside of Chagak's throat. "I do not want to be a wife," she said to Shuganan.

"Chagak," he said, his voice stern but quiet. "It is not something you can choose. You must have a husband and Kayugh is a good man. If you do not choose Kayugh, perhaps another man, someone weak like Gray Bird, will take you by force. Then you will have no choice."

"I am strong enough to kill Gray Bird, and I am strong enough to be alone."

Shuganan sat down on the ulaq's sod roof. "Yes," he finally said. "You are strong enough to be alone."

For a long time he did not speak, and Chagak began to hope that he agreed with her, but then he said, "For you, perhaps, it will take more strength to belong to someone."

THIRTY-SIX

"A son!" Gray Bird said to Blue Shell as she entered the birthing shelter.

Chagak, remembering her own pain during Samiq's birth, was disgusted with the man. Did he not think of his wife's pain or the fear that comes to every woman when she gives birth? Chagak almost opened her mouth to speak but, catching Shuganan's eye, she saw the warning there and did not.

"Come with me, Gray Bird," Kayugh said. "We will find driftwood to build your new son an ikyak."

Gray Bird looked toward the hastily constructed driftwood and skin birthing shelter. Crooked Nose shrugged and said, "It is her first baby. It will be a long time."

Gray Bird went with Kayugh, Shuganan trailing after them, and Chagak noticed that Kayugh dropped back to walk with the old man.

Chagak continued her work. She and Crooked Nose were preparing sea lion skins as a covering for an ikyak. They had soaked, scraped and dried the skins, then stretched them until they were pliable. Now they would cut the hides, using an old ikyak cover as a pattern for their knives.

Red Berry played nearby, and Samiq and Amgigh, wrapped against the cold of the gray day, were in their cradles at the side of the ulaq. Kayugh had told Chagak that in the winter he would start working with both boys, stretching their arms and legs with exercises so they would be agile hunters.

So young, Chagak thought, and already learning to be men. And though she was proud she had given birth to a son, she suddenly felt a great and shameful longing to have a daughter.

Crooked Nose stopped her work and squatted down beside the babies. Both boys had cradles now. Shuganan had made one like Samiq's as a gift for Kayugh's son. The rectangular driftwood frames suspended beds of sealskin strips that rocked with the babies' own movements.

"Two fine sons!" Crooked Nose said.

Chagak smiled.

The first thing that Chagak had noticed when she met Crooked Nose was the homeliness of the woman's face, the large nose, the small, close-set eyes, but now Chagak saw only the shining goodness of her, the wide smile, the laughter that made the children cling to her.

"And now your son, First Snow, is nearly a man."

"Yes," Crooked Nose said. "Already Big Teeth trains him in the ikyak. Soon he will be a hunter."

Crooked Nose smiled, but Chagak felt her sorrow. What woman found it easy to lose her son to manhood?

Crooked Nose took a hide from the pile and positioned the pattern skin over it. "I had four other children," she said, then pulled her knife through the hide with a quick, even stroke. "Our first three were daughters, but we had no husbands promised for them, and so..." She waved her hand toward the hills. "I had many tears, although Big Teeth did not see them. Then Big Teeth took Little Duck as second wife, hoping for a son.

"But I gave him a son and Little Duck has not given him any children, even in these eight years she has been wife."

Poor Little Duck, Chagak thought. No wonder she was quiet and shy. But she was fortunate that Crooked Nose was the first wife. Crooked Nose treated Little Duck like a sister.

"He was a fine son," Crooked Nose said. "After his birth Big Teeth made a feast for the village. During the feast we heard a rumbling noise, but no one thought it was more than some spirit angry in the mountains, but that night the waves came, washing into our village, killing many. The water tore the side from our ulaq and pulled it into the sea. My son was in his cradle and the waves floated him away from me."

Crooked Nose's voice broke and Chagak could think of no words to comfort her. Chagak pulled another skin from the pile and began cutting, her eyes on her work, giving Crooked Nose excuse to stop speaking if she wished, but after a moment of silence the woman continued.

"I still dream of it. I am reaching toward the cradle, but still my son floats away from me . . ."

"I am sorry," Chagak whispered.

"Yes," Crooked Nose said. "It was a terrible time. But First Snow's parents were also killed, and I took him as my son.

"We built our ulas again. In the next few years there were other waves, but they were not as strong. They took no lives. Then in this past year, when the snow changed back to rain and we knew that the fur seals would soon come past our beach, the rumbling began again.

"Kayugh took many of us into the mountains and we were safe, but not everyone would go, and when we returned to our village, we found many of our people dead. So we followed Kayugh and now we are here."

A cry from the birth shelter interrupted Crooked Nose. Little Duck called, "Crooked Nose, the baby comes soon."

Crooked Nose left the sea lion skins and went to the shelter. Chagak felt suddenly alone, and she wished that she, too, had been called.

Someone must stay with the children, she thought and smiled at her own foolishness. There were still times she wished that Crooked Nose and the others had not come to this beach. So why did she want to be included?

But then Blue Shell screamed, and Crooked Nose called, "Chagak, come quickly. We need you."

Chagak ran to the skin tent. Inside, Blue Shell lay on her back, her knees raised. Little Duck held Blue Shell's hands and Crooked Nose knelt between her legs.

Why was Blue Shell lying down? Chagak wondered. She should be squatting so the baby would come more quickly.

Chagak saw Blue Shell strain with another pain, and a tiny buttock was forced from the birth canal and then drawn back inside.

"Where is the head?" Chagak asked.

"The baby is backward," Crooked Nose explained. "Come here. Hold Blue Shell's hands."

Chagak, facing Little Duck and Crooked Nose, knelt at Blue Shell's head. She clasped both of Blue Shell's hands in her own. Crooked Nose worked her hand up the birth canal. "Try not to push," she said to Blue Shell. "Wait. Wait. Now, Blue Shell!"

Blue Shell grasped Chagak's hands and pulled, then she screamed, and suddenly the baby was lying in Crooked Nose's arms. It was a girl.

The baby made a small cry and Blue Shell tried to sit up, but Crooked Nose pushed her down, saying, "Wait." And she pressed on Blue Shell's belly until the afterbirth was expelled.

Crooked Nose handed the baby to Blue Shell, and Chagak shivered at the sudden quiet that had come into the tent.

Blue Shell clasped the baby and then closed her eyes. Tears seeped from beneath her lids as she whispered, "Gray Bird will make me kill her."

Chagak sat at the entrance of Shuganan's ulaq scraping a sealskin. Samiq and Amgigh nursed beneath her suk and Red Berry played with colored stones at the grassy edge of the beach.

Chagak thought of Blue Shell and the new baby, then folded her arms over her son and Amgigh.

Kayugh had not made his wife kill Red Berry, but perhaps Red Berry had been promised in marriage even before her birth.

Resentment rose in Chagak's chest, filling her lungs until she could not breathe. If Gray Bird had suffered as Blue Shell had, would he be so anxious to kill the child? Did any man know what it cost a woman to give birth? But then she thought of Shuganan. He had been with her during Samiq's birth, had watched over her. And the thought came, Do I know what a man goes through to bring seal oil? Do I understand the dangers of the ikyak? She shook her head, closed her eyes and began to rock the babies.

She tried to stay above her grief, to make a pattern of thoughts that floated her above the pain as kelp floats on the sea, but she could not forget Blue Shell's tears.

"I have had enough sorrow," Chagak whispered angrily, boldly directing her words across the strait toward Aka. But then she heard other voices raised in anger, and Kayugh and Gray Bird came from Big Teeth's ulaq.

Kayugh scanned the beach and then, in long, quick strides, he overtook his daughter, pulled her into his arms and held her against his chest. Red Berry clung to him, her face small and white against his parka, and she peered from her father's arms as Kayugh's

380

words lashed out at Gray Bird.

"We try to begin a new village. We have found this good place. We have found wisdom here and life for my son. You will build this place without women?"

Chagak kept her eyes on Kayugh's face and prepared to grab Red Berry from his arms if Gray Bird attacked.

"Who will bear your grandchildren? That?" Kayugh pointed to a rock. "That?" He pointed to a tangled mass of heather.

Kayugh clasped Red Berry at her waist and held her out toward Gray Bird.

Do not cry, Chagak pleaded silently with the child. Please do not cry. But Red Berry held herself stiff and still, her eyes shifting between Gray Bird and her father.

"She brings me joy," Kayugh said. Then in a voice so low that Chagak strained to catch the words, he added, "I will kill any man who tries to hurt her."

Slowly he set Red Berry down. The child stood for a moment looking at her father. Chagak held out her arms. Red Berry ran to her and snuggled into her lap.

Then Gray Bird spoke. "If Blue Shell's daughter lives, I will have to wait three, perhaps four more years for a son. Perhaps I will die before then."

Chagak looked at Kayugh. Would Gray

Bird's words soften Kayugh's resolve? But Kayugh did not speak and Gray Bird continued, his anger hard in his voice: "Each man rules his own family."

Kayugh's jaw tensed and Chagak began to creep backward, holding Red Berry against her with one arm.

"Chagak!"

Chagak jumped and rose slowly, her eyes searching Kayugh's face.

"Bring my son."

She did not want to obey. Amgigh was too small to be caught in a fight between two men. She hesitated and Kayugh called again. Chagak pulled the baby from beneath her suk and hurriedly wrapped him in the furred skin she had been scraping.

She took the child to Kayugh. Red Berry followed her, one hand clinging to the back of Chagak's suk.

Chagak handed the baby to Kayugh and he held the child toward Gray Bird, opening the fur wrapping so that Gray Bird could see the child's arms and legs.

"I claim Blue Shell's girl child for my son," Kayugh said, then he turned and held the baby toward Tugix. "I claim Blue Shell's girl child for my son."

Gray Bird's jaw clenched and he spun away toward the birth shelter.

Chagak thought that Kayugh would go after him, but he stood where he was, holding his son, the baby now crying in the chill of the wind. But soon Gray Bird returned. He held Blue Shell's baby, wrapped in a coarse grass mat. He opened the mat and flipped the child from front to back. In the coldness of the wind, the baby's skin quickly mottled and turned blue.

"Wrap her," Kayugh said. "She will be wife for Amgigh."

Gray Bird wrapped the child, moving her too quickly to his shoulder. The small head jerked against his chest.

"If you kill her, you kill my grandsons," Kayugh said, and he stood with his eyes fixed on Gray Bird until the man returned to the birth shelter. Then Kayugh gave his son back to Chagak, hoisted Red Berry to his shoulders and walked to the beach.

THIRTY-SEVEN

Shuganan was not sure how he knew. Perhaps it was the wisdom of old age. Perhaps the voices of his carvings spoke to his soul as they often seemed to do when sleep stilled his body and gave his spirit time to live without the interference of doing and making. Perhaps it was Tugix or some greater spirit. But whether by spirit or by wisdom, Shuganan knew.

He had begun carving the seal many days before. He had used a walrus tusk, old and yellowed, fine-grained but brittle with age. He had soaked it for a long time in oil, softening it so his knife could shave away the pieces necessary to reveal the spirit within.

He sharpened the point of the tusk until it was nearly as fine as the barb of a harpoon. That was the seal's nose. Then the body curved and widened into flippers. Shuganan smoothed the blunt end of the tusk into a ledge that fitted snugly against the heel of his hand.

He finished the seal, then asked Chagak for tanned skins and heather. Chagak had seemed puzzled when he laid Samiq out on a sealskin and, using long sinew strands, mea-

384

sured the boy's arms and legs, the length from his head to his fat, round toes. But she had not asked questions.

Shuganan used a woman's knife to cut the shape of a baby from the sealskin. He used the first shape as pattern for a second and sewed the two together, then stuffed them with heather.

From a wide curve of driftwood, bleached to whiteness by the sun and sea, he carved a mask, making nose and mouth and closed eyes. Then, drilling holes through the sides of the mask, he sewed it to the head of his sealskin baby.

And one evening when Chagak was busy setting out food, Shuganan had asked to hold Samiq. He had felt no threat to his manhood in this, seeing that Kayugh sat beside an oil lamp, holding his son. And when no one was watching, Shuganan cut a bit of hair from Samiq's head. Perhaps there might be some power toward reality in the hair, some strength that would turn a man's eyes to seeing what he thought he was seeing instead of what was truly there.

That night, in his sleeping place, Shuganan stitched the hair on top of his sealskin baby's head.

Now in the early morning, before the women

had risen to trim wicks and carry out night wastes, Shuganan wrapped his baby in one of the sealskins Man-who-kills had given as Chagak's bride price.

He waited on the beach, the baby within his parka, the carved tusk inside his sleeve. He waited until he saw one of the women leave Big Teeth's ulaq, then he returned to his ulaq and pretended he had gone outside only to watch the sea for signs of seal.

The next morning he also went out and the morning after that. On the fourth day he woke in the night and, feeling the urging of some spirit, again went to the beach, taking his baby and the ivory seal.

He waited during the darkest part of the night, watching the sea, listening for noise within the waves that was not animal but man.

When the sky had begun to lighten, he was sure he heard the dipping of a paddle, something that kept its own rhythm, not the rhythm of the sea.

Shuganan slipped the ivory seal down into his hand, felt the tip of the tusk, as sharp as a knife, caressed the ledge that he had carved for the heel of his hand, something to lend strength to his thrust. Then he tucked it inside his sleeve and wrapped his arms over the sealskin baby as though he were a mother carrying her husband's son.

Shuganan saw the ikyak and the hunter within. He smiled. Yes. It was Sees-far.

He watched as the man guided his ikyak through the rocks toward the shore, as he untied his hatch skirting and leaped from the craft, pulling his ikyak to the beach.

Sees-far grinned at Shuganan but made no greeting. And so Shuganan, too, gave no greeting but said only, "Man-who-kills told me you would be coming. I have waited these four mornings for you."

"I have come to teach Man-who-kills how to fight again," Sees-far said and laughed. "He has lived too easily over the winter. He must be ready to fight Whale Hunters. We go soon."

Sees-far scanned the beach. "And so where is he?" he asked. But Shuganan had made sure that the men's ikyan were not within sight, and so knew that Sees-far saw nothing but beach gravel and drying racks.

"He is in the ulaq. His wife is also in the ulaq," Shuganan said. "She has been a good wife to him. They have a son."

"A son!" Sees-far said and began to laugh. "Now that she has given Man-who-kills what he wants, maybe he will not be so reluctant to share her with me."

"I brought the baby for you to see," Shuganan said, keeping his eyes on Sees-far's face, hoping to know when the first doubt came into the man's mind, hoping to act before Sees-far knew the truth.

"So he makes you do woman's work," Sees-far said and laughed.

"I can no longer hunt," Shuganan said and held out his bent and stiffened left arm.

"And so you will show me this son?" Sees-far asked. And pointed toward the bulge under Shuganan's parka.

"There is too much wind here. We should stand against the cliff where there is shelter."

But as soon as he said the words, Shuganan saw the doubt in Sees-far's eyes, saw the man look quickly to the top of the cliff. So Shuganan said, "But Man-who-kills' son is strong, perhaps he is old enough for the wind."

The doubt faded. Shuganan reached inside his parka and pulled the sealskin baby from its place against his chest.

Sees-far smiled and leaned down to see the child. Shuganan slipped the carved tusk along the inside of his arm and worked the point to the palm of his hand.

Shuganan held the baby out toward Sees-far, then pretended to stumble. He saw the surprise in Sees-far's eyes, the quick movement of the man's hands to catch the baby. As Sees-far clasped the sealskin bundle, Shuganan dropped his right arm so the walrus tusk fell into his hand.

Shuganan had killed many seals, many sea lions. He knew the place of the heart, the sheltered place beneath the breastbone, and so he knew the best way of killing a man, the blow to the heart from the unprotected side, up from the stomach. He thrust the sharp point of his carved tusk up and into Sees-far's heart. The tusk-knife cut even as Sees-far said, "This is not a baby. . . ."

And the words, though they had begun in a strong voice, ended in a whisper.

Sees-far dropped to his knees, the sealskin baby still in his arms. Shuganan placed a hand on the man's chest. The heart had stopped, but Shuganan could still see the spirit peering from Sees-far's eyes.

Shuganan drew his flint knife from the scabbard he kept on his left arm and, grabbing Sees-far by the hair, sliced through the front of the man's neck.

A hiss of air pushed out from the man's windpipe and vomit came up from his stomach and spilled from the open neck, but Shuganan continued to cut until he had sliced through the tendons and muscles. Then he snapped the head back, cradling the thing against his thighs until he had cut between the small round bones of the neck. Then the head was loose, the spirit no longer in the eyes.

Shuganan left the corpse on the beach. He wished that waves would suddenly come, would pull the body away before the women saw, but the waves were weak, and so Shuganan slipped the sealskin baby from Sees-far's arms. He placed it in Sees-far's ikyak, then went back to the ulaq. He would wake Kayugh, ask him to help lift Sees-far into the ikyak. Together, they could cut the body apart at the joints and thus make the spirit helpless, then Kayugh could tow the ikyak out past the cliffs, where the currents would take it into the middle of the sea.

And the spirits would see the sealskin baby, the tuft of Samiq's hair on its head, and they would know that Samiq's hair had made Sees-far believe he was seeing a real baby, perhaps only for a moment, but long enough for Shuganan to thrust the knife. Yes, Shuganan thought, the spirits would understand the power of a child not yet a man, and honor Samiq, a boy who had already helped avenge the deaths of his mother's people.

But then Shuganan looked at the man's body, and he thought, Sees-far should be hunting seal and sea lion. He should be in his ulaq, waking slowly to the sounds of his wife laying out morning food; he should be repairing weapons in the light of oil lamps, watching his wife as he worked, seeing the glow the light lent to her skin, the shadows it made on her face and beneath her breasts. He should be thrusting his seed deep into the softness of his wife's body and watching through the months as her belly stretched out with the baby he had put within her. These things were what Sees-far should be doing.

Instead he had chosen to kill men. How could that joy compare to the joy of each day's living?

And so, Shuganan thought, I who am old am alive, and he who is young is dead.

Kayugh heard Shuganan in the middle room, heard the slow, shuffling steps of the old man, and wondered why Shuganan was awake, the day still too early for even Chagak to be awake. But then he heard Shuganan call to him and also heard the cry of one of the babies, heard Chagak shush the child, the cry muffled in a sudden stillness, breast against mouth.

Kayugh crawled from his sleeping place and saw with surprise that Shuganan's hands were covered with blood. Kayugh opened his mouth to speak, but Shuganan shook his head, then led the way up the climbing log.

"A seal?" Kayugh asked as soon as they were outside. He looked toward the beach, but in the dim light of early morning, the grayness of the cloudy sky, he could not see if there was an animal on the shore.

"No," Shuganan said. "Get Big Teeth and Gray Bird. We must talk."

And seeing the intensity in the man's eyes, Kayugh asked no more questions but went quickly to Big Teeth's ulaq. He called down for the men and they came out, pulling on their parkas. Big Teeth was grumbling but also made jokes between his complaints. But when Kayugh pointed toward Shuganan, Big Teeth stopped talking, his joking gone, the man suddenly silent, staring at Shuganan's bloody hands.

"A seal?" Gray Bird asked. But Shuganan did not answer as he led them down toward the beach.

When Kayugh first saw the heap beside the ikyak, he did not think it was a man, but then he saw parka and sealskin boots, then the severed head lying a short distance from the body.

"You did this?" Kayugh asked Shuganan.

"He is a Short One," Shuganan said. "One of the men who killed Chagak's husband."

And though the old man spoke with hatred in his voice, with anger, there was something in his words that also spoke to Kayugh's spirit, something that said: The old man speaks truth and untruth. There is reason for killing this Short One, but perhaps not the reason Shuganan gives.

Shuganan squatted down on his heels beside the body and began to speak, but the hissing of waves against the beach gravel blotted out his words and so Kayugh squatted beside the man, and then Big Teeth and Gray Bird also, the body in their midst, as though they were men squatting around a beach fire, staying as near as they dared for warmth.

"I have told you that Chagak and I will take Samiq and go to the Whale Hunters. We know the Short Ones' plan to attack their village. The Whale Hunters are my wife's people. I cannot let them die.

"We made this decision long ago, even before Chagak's baby was born. Now that Blue Shell can nurse Kayugh's son, we will leave. Today. This man I killed was a scout. The yellow markings on his ikyak say this to those who know. The others, the warriors, will come soon. Not to this beach. This beach is only a stopping place, a place where they thought one of their men had stayed for the winter.

"We do not ask you to come with us. You have no reason to kill Short Ones. This beach is yours now. Perhaps we will come back, perhaps not. If I am killed and Chagak is not, surely one of the Whale Hunters will take her as wife and she will not return. And if we are both killed, we will be with our people in the Dancing Lights."

Kayugh watched the old man as he spoke. If Chagak had once had a husband, where was the man's ikyak frame? Where were his weapons? Shuganan had only his own weapons and the weapons of the Short One killed the summer before. No more. But why would Shuganan lie?

He waited, hoping that Gray Bird in his ignorance or Big Teeth in his wisdom would ask a question, something that would make Shuganan speak more of the truth, but they said nothing. So Kayugh turned his thoughts to the decision he must make. Should he go with Shuganan or stay on this beach?

At the mention of a husband for Chagak, he had felt his stomach twist. If he went, he might be able to keep Chagak from becoming wife to a Whale Hunter. But if he told Shuganan he would go, Big Teeth would follow. Then who would care for the women? Had they come this far to leave Gray Bird as hunter for three women, to have Little Duck, Crooked Nose and Blue Shell die of starvation during a long winter?

But if he went with Shuganan to the Whale Hunters, he would be promising to kill men. How did a man hunt other men?

I would be like a boy on his first seal hunt, Kayugh thought. I would know little and endanger others by my ignorance.

And what would the killing do to his spirit? Would he become evil like the Short Ones?

But men who killed people should be killed. How else was the evil stopped? Would men who killed men listen to reason? Could words make them stop? Would trading? Why trade when, by killing, they could take everything and give nothing in exchange?

Kayugh looked at Shuganan. The old man sat with head bowed, hands, dark with dried blood, between his knees. His bones, beneath his lined and ancient skin, were fragile. And Kayugh saw that death would come easily to Shuganan, that his spirit was close to those spirits who called from the Dancing Lights. The old man had finished his young years — the years of taking — and was nearly through the old years, when the soul releases what it has clasped, when the threads that hold it to life are broken, one by one. And now there was only Chagak, holding him. Chagak without a husband.

And Kayugh saw her with a Whale Hunter husband, someone who took her only for the work she would do and the sons she could give. Or what if a Short One took her to be his wife? How would she serve someone who would teach Samiq to kill men?

He saw Shuganan's knife still jutting from the Short One's body and was not surprised that the handle was the seal Shuganan had spent many evenings carving. Kayugh thrust his own knife into the body and withdrew Shuganan's tusk-knife, then gave it back to Shuganan.

"I will go with you," he said. And as quickly as he spoke, Big Teeth also thrust his knife into the man and withdrew Kayugh's knife.

"I will go also."

Gray Bird scowled. "We cannot leave the women," he said.

But Big Teeth said, "My women will come with me."

Again Gray Bird scowled, but he thrust his knife into the body and withdrew Big Teeth's, handing it to the man. "I will go," Gray Bird said. "And my woman."

THIRTY-EIGHT

What difference will it make? Chagak thought as she thrust her paddle into the water.

Why should she care whether she lived or died? Why should she be afraid of death? If, in fighting the Short Ones, she were killed, then she would be with her own people. With Seal Stalker.

But the thought of death made her uneasy. Who truly knew what happened after death? Perhaps there were evil spirits against which she had no protection. And how would she find her way to the Dancing Lights? Would traveling north be enough?

Chagak and Crooked Nose were paddling the ik. Chagak sat in the front of the ik, Crooked Nose, doing the more difficult paddling, in the back. Little Duck and Blue Shell sat in the center of the boat with Red Berry, First Snow and the babies.

Blue Shell was thin and white, and though she was gentle with her girl baby, she seldom looked at the child, even when caring for her. Since the birth, Chagak noticed that Blue Shell often had bruises on her chest and belly.

Gray Bird, Chagak thought, and was glad she had no husband.

Gulls circled and called, occasionally dipping close to the ik, and twice as the ik neared kelp beds sea otters had come out to swim beside the craft. The otters turned on their backs and swam with their bellies up, and the women had begun to laugh, even Blue Shell.

Chagak watched the mists lift from the beaches and pull away from the land, and she tried to remember each thing, the sea, the birds, the otters, for she was afraid she would not see them again.

Then as she paddled she began a song her grandmother had taught her, a simple song of basket weaving, and in singing she was reminded of her people. Of the revenge she would take for their deaths. But when she tried to picture Seal Stalker's face, she saw Kayugh's instead. In place of Pup she saw Samiq and Amgigh, the boys growing up together, one tall and long-armed like Kayugh, able to throw the spear long distances, the other short and heavily muscled, gifted with the strength necessary for long hunting trips in the ikyak. And the pictures she saw called her to stay in the world.

So Chagak told herself, It is important to fight the Short Ones. The spirits of my people will not rest until I have made an attempt at revenge. I am the only one left to do this, just as I was the only one left to bury them.

Then Chagak heard the sea otter spirit speaking in a quiet voice. "It is your duty to be a woman, to continue the blood of your village. To bear children, to make sons who hunt and daughters who bear more sons, so old ways will not be forgotten."

"No," Chagak whispered. "I can give them nothing else. I cannot be both woman and warrior. If they needed both, they should have let Seal Stalker live. Then Samiq would carry his blood and not the blood of Man-who-kills."

"Perhaps it is not the blood of Man-who-kills that is important," the sea otter said. "Perhaps, through Samiq, the good that is in the Short Ones will live on, their strength and fearlessness, perhaps even Shuganan's ability to find animals hidden in bone and ivory."

Chagak did not answer but the sea otter said, "And you bring others with you, men who owe no revenge."

It is their choice, Chagak thought. If they do not kill the Short Ones, perhaps they, too, will be killed. As my people were killed.

"And that is why Kayugh comes with you? He has no other reason?"

But Chagak pulled hard against her paddle until her effort blocked out sea otter's voice, and when her shoulders began to ache, Chagak was glad for the pain. Then she could think of sleep rather than life or death.

They spent the night on a small beach, a place that reminded Chagak of the beach where she had stayed the previous summer, before she found Shuganan's beach. And with the memories came the pain of her loss, so sudden and tearing that it pulled the breath from her body. She did not listen whenever she thought she heard sea otter's whispery voice and stayed close to the other women, trying to join in their conversations. But their talk was about the Whale Hunters, and Chagak could hear the fear in their voices as they spoke, and she felt, though no one said anything, that they were facing danger because of her.

Finally she sat beside the coals of the beach fire and began to nurse the babies. But when Chagak looked up, Kayugh was walking toward her. He squatted beside her and stirred the fire with a long piece of driftwood.

At first he said nothing, merely grunting when Chagak lifted her suk to show him his son, but then he said, "I do not know if Shuganan has told you, but I have spoken to him of my need for a wife."

Chagak did not look at him, and though

she opened her mouth to speak, the rapid pounding of her heart seemed to close off her throat and she said nothing.

"If we are still alive after all this," Kayugh continued, "I would like you to be my wife. Shuganan has given his consent."

He waited for a while, then stood, and Chagak finally said, "You would be a good husband for any woman, but I still mourn my husband's death."

"The Whale Hunters will want you," Kayugh said. "Do not choose one of them above me."

And, shuddering, Chagak answered, "I will not."

Then Kayugh leaned over her and Chagak felt the weight of something at her neck. Looking down, she saw that he had slipped a necklace of bear claws over her head, a gift fine and rare, something that he must have taken in trade from the tribes far to the east who hunted the brown bear. She lifted the necklace, let it lie smooth and heavy against her hands. Each yellow claw had been polished, and between the claws were circles of shell beads. It was something a wife might hope to receive after giving her husband many sons.

"For saving my son," Kayugh said, and for a moment pressed his hands against her shoulders, then he walked down the beach to join the other men.

★ ★ ★

They came to the Whale Hunters' cove the next day. It was as her mother had described it: a wide sand beach with a large pool in the center where even now ducks were swimming.

There were women on the beach and ikyan on racks near the pool. Children played at the edge of the beach. Meat racks were full, hung with dark red meat, and Chagak called back to Crooked Nose, "They have already taken a whale."

I should have come here when my village was first destroyed, Chagak thought, and thrust her paddle against a rock to turn the ik toward shore. But then the sea otter whispered, "You know you could not. Pup was dying. And besides, if you had come here first, would Amgigh be alive? Would you have Samiq? And could you offer what you offer now? Shuganan's wisdom, Kayugh's strength, a grandson for your grandfather?"

But Shuganan's plan might not work, Chagak thought, then pushed that fear from her mind. Why hold any doubt? Why strengthen the Short Ones with her questioning?

Five ulas were set in the highest corner of the beach, where the waves could not reach but a man sitting at the top of a ulaq could watch the sea.

Several of the women who had been on the

402

beach had run to the central ulaq when Kayugh and the other men began pulling their ikyan ashore.

"The central ulaq belongs to my grandfather, Many Whales," Chagak said. "If he still lives."

"You have not been here for many years?" Blue Shell asked.

"I have never been here," Chagak answered. "But my mother spoke often of the village and my father visited each summer."

Kayugh waded out to their ik and Chagak laid her paddle in the bottom of the boat. She hiked up her suk and thrust her legs over the side.

"Stay in," Kayugh said. "You have the babies. I will pull you."

But Chagak jumped into the icy water, clamping her teeth together so they would not clatter. She grabbed the edge of the ik and pulled with Kayugh. "I should be the first to see my grandfather. Perhaps he has heard about my village. Perhaps he thinks I am dead. Then he will not believe Shuganan and will not listen to his plan to protect this village."

Kayugh shrugged, but Chagak saw irritation in the set of his jaw, the snapping of his eyes. Was it so important that he pull her ashore, that she keep her suk dry? But some part of her wished she had done as he asked. And when they had dragged the ik ashore, she straightened her suk, wrung the water from the bottom edges, then adjusted the bear claw necklace over her breast.

Looking down at the necklace, she began to tell Kayugh how beautiful it was, but when Chagak looked up, he had gone to help Big Teeth and Gray Bird pull their ikyan up the beach.

"At least the Whale Hunters will think you have a husband," the sea otter whispered. "What woman, unmarried, has such a fine necklace?"

But the words were no comfort. For the first time Chagak thought of herself among so many men, granddaughter of their chief, unmarried. A shiver of fear moved over her.

"What would be wrong with a husband from your mother's people?" sea otter asked.

"I do not want a husband."

"What would be wrong with Kayugh for husband?" sea otter asked.

Then, speaking loudly, Chagak answered, "Do not talk to me about husbands." But then she turned and saw that Crooked Nose stood beside her. Chagak blushed, but Crooked Nose only smiled, then said, "Shuganan calls us," and pointed toward the others gathered beside the ikyan.

Some of the Whale Hunters were speaking

to them. One, Hard Rock, Chagak recognized. He was not much older than Chagak, strong, and strong-willed. A good hunter. He had come several times to her people's village when her grandfather visited.

"Hard Rock," Chagak called out to him, ignoring the startled looks from Big Teeth and Gray Bird. Who knew these people? They or she? Should she wait, giving no sign? Was she granddaughter to their chief only so the men could give the first greetings? "It is Chagak."

Hard Rock turned and the others with him. He gripped his amulet and held it toward her. "Chagak?" he called and Chagak heard the quivering in his voice.

"I have come bringing friends."

"We saw your village. We thought you were dead."

"I was in the hills gathering heather when the village was destroyed. I alone am alive. I have come to see my grandfather. To bring a warning to this village."

For a moment Hard Rock stared at her, then he whispered to one of the men beside him. The man ran to her grandfather's ulaq and Chagak waited, hoping her grandfather would come to meet them on the beach, but the man returned alone.

"You are to go to your grandfather's ulaq," he said to Chagak. "The others must wait here. Our women will bring food and water."

Chagak and Shuganan had planned what they would say, even before Kayugh and his people had come. And now she wondered if she would say the right things. What if she said what Shuganan had told her not to say? And he would not be there to correct her, to smooth over her mistakes.

But Shuganan smiled at her and she felt some of the strength of his spirit flow into her. She wrapped her arms over the babies she carried within her suk and followed Hard Rock to her grandfather's ulaq.

The ulaq was higher and longer than the ulas of her own people. Instead of carved soapstone oil lamps, there were boulder lamps. The boulders were as high as Chagak's waist and each had a hollow at the top that held oil and a circle of moss wicks.

Many Whales, Chagak's grandfather, sat on a mat in the center of the ulaq. He wore an otter skin parka decorated with fur and feathers along each seam. He also wore his whaler hat. The hat was cone-shaped, pointed at the top and sweeping to a wide edge that kept rain and sea spray from funneling down the neck of his parka.

When Chagak was a child, she had been fascinated by whaler hats and sometimes set a basket upside down on her head and pretended she was a Whale Hunter.

But Chagak's mother had explained that women did not hunt whales, though they were the ones who made the glorious whaler hats; that someday she would teach Chagak how to make such a hat, to split thin slices from the curve of a driftwood log, to steam the wood and bend it into shape, then smooth and oil the hat until the wood gleamed like the inside of a yoldia shell.

Many Whales' hat, with long sea lion whiskers protruding from the back and feathers and shells hanging from the curved edge, marked him as chief hunter.

Fat Wife sat beside Many Whales. Fat Wife was not Chagak's true grandmother but a second wife taken after Chagak's grandmother had died. She was a short, fat woman and she wore her hair pulled tightly back from her round face and bound with an otter tail at the nape of her neck.

Many Whales held his amulet in both hands, and as Chagak took a step toward him, he lifted the charm and said to her, "I saw your village. How did you live?"

The straightness of the old man's shoulders, the singing way of his words, reminded Chagak of her mother. Any apprehension she had felt, the fear he would not remember her, lifted as though her mother's spirit were beside her, and she said, "I was in the hills picking heather. I stayed almost until dark, and when I came back to the village, the ulas were on fire."

Many Whales motioned for Chagak to sit down on the mats spread in front of him. Chagak sat cross-legged in the manner of her grandfather. She glanced quickly inside her suk and adjusted Samiq's carrying strap. She noticed her grandfather's interest but said nothing about the babies.

"And of all your people you were the only one who lived?" Many Whales asked.

"No," Chagak said. "My brother Pup also lived for a short time. I buried the people. Made ceremonies and sealed each ulaq. It took me many days. Then I took food, an ik and Pup and started toward your village, but I came to Shuganan's beach first."

"Shuganan?" said Fat Wife. "Who is Shuganan?"

But Many Whales said, "I know Shuganan. Many years ago he took a wife from our village. He lives on a small beach a day's journey from here. He harms no one, but men who have stopped at his beach say there is some magic in him. He carves stone and ivory into animals. They say the carvings hold great power."

Chagak slipped the carving of woman, husband and baby from her neck and handed it to Fat Wife.

"The statue has the power of giving sons," Chagak said, then lifted her suk. She held her smile inside her cheeks as first Fat Wife then Many Whales opened their mouths to speak but said nothing, both staring at the babies strapped to Chagak's chest.

"Boys," Chagak said and lowered her suk. "Shuganan is a good man. He could not save Pup, but for loss of a brother I have two sons."

"Shuganan is your husband?" Many Whales finally asked.

And Chagak, remembering what Shuganan had told her to say, thought for a moment and then met her grandfather's eyes. "Shuganan's grandson was my husband," she said. "He was a good hunter, bringing many seals. A strong man. His name was Seal Stalker and he was killed last summer by one of the men who raided my village."

Many Whales nodded and seemed about to speak when Fat Wife handed Chagak the carving and said, "You say your village was raided. You are sure it was men and not spirits?"

The question was not one that Shuganan and Chagak had discussed. Chagak clasped her hands in her lap and tried to decide what Shuganan would want her to say.

"Shuganan was once a trader," she began. "For a time he lived with a people called Short Ones. He told me their men were strong and good hunters, but they hunted men as well as animals. They destroyed villages and killed the people."

"Why would they do this?" Many Whales asked.

"Shuganan said they believe that, for each man killed, the killer's power is increased."

Many Whales shook his head, and the sea lion whiskers at the back of his whalers hat bobbed as he said, "A hunter may gain some power when he kills an animal, if he carries respect and uses the right weapons. But a man . . . a man's spirit has too much power. It draws evil."

"You should have come to us sooner," Fat Wife said to Chagak and leaned so far forward that her large breasts pressed against her knees. "We have hunters here. You say your husband is dead. You can choose a husband here. The finest hunter."

But before Chagak could answer, Many Whales said, "Who are the men and women with you?"

"They came from a beach to the east. They are from a village of the First Men, but a village my father did not know. A wave killed many of their people and destroyed their ulakidaq, so they have sought a new place to live. Shuganan has asked them to stay on his beach. They have built a ulaq there."

Again Chagak lifted her suk. "This child is my son," she said, laying a hand on Samiq's head. "This child belongs to Kayugh, the leader of those people. The mother is dead, so I nurse him."

Fat Wife reached out toward the babies, but Many Whales grasped her thick wrist with his bony hand and drew back her arm.

"So you have come to bring my grandson to stay with us," Many Whales said.

Chagak lowered her suk, smoothing it down over the babies. She lifted her head and looked into her grandfather's eyes. "No," she said. "Samiq also belongs to Shuganan. When Samiq is older, perhaps you will teach him to hunt whales, but for now he will stay with me and with Shuganan.

"I have come to warn you of the Short Ones. Two of their warriors came to our beach. My husband killed one; Shuganan killed the other. They were scouts, sent to learn about your village. They will destroy your village unless you defeat them."

Many Whales began to laugh. "Our village. Who has power to take a man who hunts the whale? If an old man like Shuganan could kill one of their warriors, how can the Short Ones have enough power to stand against my hunters?"

"I cannot tell you how they gain their power," Chagak said. "But I know how they come and how they kill. We have come to tell you. To help you prepare."

Again Many Whales laughed, and Chagak wondered how her small, gentle mother had come from such a loud and boasting people, a people who laughed too much and complained too much, who made noise and argument for each task.

Finally she said, "You will take a chance of losing a grandson to the ones who killed your daughter and her children? There is power in the knowledge of something. What will it hurt to listen? If you do nothing and the Short Ones come, you could lose everything. If you prepare for them and they do not come, what have you lost? A day's hunting."

For a long time Many Whales did not answer her, but then he murmured, "For a child, you are wise."

Turning to Fat Wife, he said, "Tell the women to make a feast. We will listen to Shuganan and make him and his people welcome. Tell Many Babies I want her to make my granddaughter a necklace of beads. It will be a gift, and if it is beautiful, I will give Many Babies two otter skins."

THIRTY-NINE

The Whale Hunter women made a feast and the people of the village, men and women, even the children, crowded into Many Whales' ulaq to eat.

Fat Wife laid out two lines of mats at the center of the ulaq, and the women layered them with sliced dried whale meat, dried fish, freshly cooked herring and piles of dried chitons. Bitterroot bulbs, their sour taste good to cut the tallow of the meat, were heaped in shallow wooden bowls.

Chagak was given a special place of honor among the women. No one allowed her to carry food to the men or to help with oil lamps. She held her babies wrapped in sealskin on her lap and smiled, saying little when Whale Hunter women bent over her to look at them.

The Whale Hunter women wore only their aprons in the crowded ulaq. And even Chagak, after a time, took off her suk and sat on it, and she noticed that Crooked Nose had done the same.

The Whale Hunter women's aprons were short, ending above the knee where dark tattoos marked their legs. Chagak's mother had told her that the tattoos were a sign of beauty. She had told Chagak how upon her first time of bleeding she had stood the long hours of pain, night after night, sitting while her own mother drew a needle with sooted thread through the skin of her thighs to make a design of squares and triangles.

But unlike Chagak's mother, most Whale Hunter women were big, and seemed to admire strength in themselves as much as in their men. Twice Chagak saw men summon their wives, only to have the women ignore them. One woman even laughed when her young husband called to her. And Fat Wife said to Many Whales, "Get your own food. I must eat, too."

And though at first Chagak was surprised, finally she began to laugh. The laughter shook her so hard that she bent low over the babies to hide her face, but when she finally lifted her head to draw a breath, she saw that Kayugh was watching her, a sternness in his face. Then a man sitting beside Kayugh called to his wife, and as she leaned toward him to give him food, he said something else, and with a quick blow of her fist his wife pounded the man's whaler hat down over his eyes.

Then Kayugh, also, began to laugh. He looked at Chagak, and his laughter seemed to flow into her, bringing joy. Chagak, puzzled by the feeling, looked away from Kayugh and pretended to adjust the babies' wrappings.

Then Many Whales stood. He shouted until he was heard above the clamor. "There are fires on the beach if you want to dance."

The men began to leave the ulaq, and Chagak, watching them, noticed that many turned to look at her as they left.

They want me to sleep with them, Chagak thought. They will ask Shuganan, and she began to search for Shuganan in the crowd of men, hoping to catch him, to tell him she wanted no man in her bed. But when she finally saw him, he was at the top of the notched log, slowly making his climb from the ulaq, other men behind him.

Then Many Babies came to Chagak and slipped a long necklace of disk beads cut from shells over Chagak's head. "From your grandfather," she said, then called Blue Shell over to them and directed both women into a curtained room at the side of the ulaq.

"Leave your babies here," she said. She pointed to a wide cradle box filled with furs. "The three will fit. One of you can come back from time to time and be sure they do not cry."

Blue Shell looked at Chagak, then laid her daughter in the box.

"A beautiful baby," Many Babies said. "Son or daughter?"

"Daughter," Blue Shell said softly.

"Husbands want boys," Many Babies said.

"She is promised to Amgigh," said Chagak, laying Amgigh beside Blue Shell's baby. "So you see she is my daughter, too."

Many Babies said nothing more, and as Chagak laid Samiq into the box, she smiled at Blue Shell, but then Chagak realized she had claimed Amgigh as son, and she was glad that Shuganan had not heard.

On the beach the men and women had formed two circles around the fire, the men in the inner circle, the women in the outer.

Crooked Nose and Little Duck were sitting on a large rock, watching. Chagak and Blue Shell sat down beside them. The wind from the sea was cold. Chagak tucked her hands up inside the sleeves of her suk and pushed her chin deep into the collar rim.

The Whale Hunter men wore only their aprons and danced in a slow sidewise step, but Kayugh, Big Teeth and Gray Bird jumped and kicked, bending their arms and legs in a sharpness that reminded Chagak of the flames that rose from the driftwood fire. Each man made a noise in his mouth, holding his lips pressed together and mumbling words deep in his throat, and the old men, Shuganan among them, kept the rhythm of their feet with the pounding of sticks.

The Whale Hunter women stayed in one place in the women's circle, shuffling their feet and swaying to the rhythm of the dance. Blue Shell and Little Duck joined the women, and soon Crooked Nose pulled Chagak to her feet and they also entered the circle.

Chagak watched for a time, but soon the pounding of sticks seemed to match the beating of her heart and she began to sway. She closed her eyes and the noise of the dance seemed to sink into her bones, loosening her muscles and warming her skin. But when she opened her eyes, she saw that Kayugh had stopped dancing and was watching her. His eyes held her for a moment so she felt the intensity of his desire, and she left the women's circle, sat down on the rock and pulled her knees up inside her suk.

Kayugh began to dance again, but every time Chagak looked at him, he was watching her. And she noticed that many of the Whale Hunter men also watched her, and Gray Bird, too, his eyes narrowed, the tip of his tongue curled to touch his upper lip.

When Crooked Nose came back from the dancing to sit with her, Chagak laughed and said, "I have too much milk. I am going to my grandfather's ulaq. Tell Blue Shell, if she would like to stay and dance, I will also feed her baby."

Crooked Nose, watching the dancers, nodded but did not look at Chagak, and when Chagak was nearly to the ulaq, she thought she heard the woman calling her, but Chagak did not look back.

The thick ulaq walls shut out most of the noise of the dance. Only two lamps were lit, one on each side of the main room, and the light had a softness unlike the flames of the beach fire. Chagak went into the curtained sleeping place where the cradle was hung. She pulled it from the rafters, holding it steady so the babies would not awaken. She set the cradle on the floor and squatted beside it.

They are beautiful babies, Chagak thought. Amgigh was still thin, but beside Blue Shell's daughter he looked large. Samiq was the largest of the three, and in his sleep he sucked on his fist. Chagak took Amgigh from the cradle. She moved carefully, not wanting to wake the other babies.

"You need to eat," she whispered to Amgigh as she fastened his carrying strap over her left shoulder and slipped the baby into her suk. He did not seem to awaken until she pressed her nipple close to his mouth, then he grasped her breast and began to suck.

After he had nursed for a time, milk began to trickle from her other breast, and Chagak picked up Blue Shell's daughter. She was a pretty baby, round-faced and delicate like Blue Shell. Gray Bird had refused to claim her life from the spirits by naming her, but Blue Shell called her Little One, not a true name but something to hold against spirits meaning harm.

"Little One," Chagak whispered, "perhaps this milk is not as good as your mother's, but it is better than having nothing." Chagak fastened a strap over her other shoulder, leaned up against the side of the ulaq, and pressed the baby to her breast.

Chagak was nearly asleep, the babies warm against her belly, when she heard people coming into the ulaq. At first she thought it was Blue Shell coming to get her baby, and Chagak pulled the infant from her breast and laid her back into the cradle beside Samiq, but then she heard voices and knew that Many Whales and Shuganan had come to the ulaq.

Chagak covered Blue Shell's baby with the furred skins that lined the cradle, then picked up Samiq. He gave a short cry and rooted against her breast until Chagak guided the nipple into his mouth.

Again, she leaned back against the ulaq wall and closed her eyes, but the men's voices kept tangling into the threads of her dreams and she could not sleep.

"And so you are sure," Chagak heard Many Whales say.

"He told me before I killed him," Shuganan said, and Chagak knew he must be speaking about Sees-far, and she thought again of the trickery Shuganan had used to kill the man, and the honor Samiq was to receive from Sees-far's death. Samiq is too young, Chagak thought. What does he know of killing men? And suddenly she wanted Samiq to stay a baby. Always to nurse at her breast. How could she protect him when she could no longer hold him, could no longer comfort him with her milk?

But Many Whales' words interrupted her thoughts. "Soon then?" he asked.

"Yes."

For a long time no one spoke, then Chagak heard another voice. "Is there a place in the hills the women can hide?" It was Kayugh.

"Many places, I am sure," Many Whales said.

"Nothing on the beaches," Shuganan said. Again, a pause.

"They come in the night, when there is still light, but not enough to see well," Shuganan said. "That way the village hunters are confused and sometimes, in the fighting, even kill men from their own village.

"The Short Ones kill everyone, even babies and children. They set the top of a ulaq on fire, and as the people come out through the roof hole, they kill them. One at a time."

"We cannot be in our ulas then," Many Whales said. "What if they come tonight? There is not time to hide our women."

"They will not come with the beach fire," said Shuganan. "There is too much chance hunters will be on the beach and so their coming would not be secret."

"Then I will set watchers, and we will keep the fire going, and the dancing," said Many Whales.

"You have five large ulas," Shuganan said. "How many hunters?"

"Eighteen," Many Whales said. "And three old men who still have some strength. Four boys, nearly men, one my son. They stay in the watcher's hut on the ridge above the village. They watch for whales. They are old enough to fight."

"Send the old men to protect the women in the hills. Perhaps some of the Short Ones will try to find the women. Three old men and the women against one or two warriors should be sufficient. Let the boys stay on the ridge as watchers to tell us when the Short Ones come."

"And the rest of the men?" asked Many Whales.

"Some should be hidden on the ridges that surround the village. The others, ten of your best warriors, should be hidden inside the ulas, two in each. Then when the Short Ones wait at the top, our hunters will come out, spears ready, and when everyone is fighting, our men will come down from the ridges and attack."

"How many warriors do the Short Ones have?" Chagak heard Kayugh ask.

"When I lived with them," Shuganan said, "perhaps twenty men."

"And so they will put four men on each ulaq?"

"Two, perhaps three," Shuganan said. "The rest wait between the ulas for those few who escape."

"So if we put two men in each ulaq, we will be fighting only two or three, at least at first."

"Yes," Shuganan said.

There was silence for a moment and Chagak thought perhaps the men would say no more, each content with his own thoughts, but then she heard Kayugh say, "I will be one who waits inside a ulaq."

And at his words Chagak felt a sobbing begin within her breast, as though sea otter were crying. She suddenly seemed to smell the smoke, to hear the cries of the people of her own village. And she wished Kayugh were old like Shuganan and could come with the women and children.

FORTY

The women and children went to the caves at the center of the island. The old men left with them, except for Shuganan, and the boys were set as watchers atop the ridge that lay behind the village.

Before leaving, the women had replaced much of the thatching on the ulaq roofs with green grass, then carried baskets of water to soak the grass so it would not catch fire easily. They also rolled up the mats and heather that covered the ulaq floors, leaving bare dirt, and moved all baskets and curtains into storage places farthest from the roof hole. Then the fire of a torch thrown into the ulaq would not spread.

The men enlarged each roof hole so another climbing log could be set into place. Then two men could climb up and emerge from the ulaq at the same time. It had been Blue Shell's idea. Kayugh, lying in the sleeping place next to hers, had heard Blue Shell suggest it softly in the night to Gray Bird, who told the men as though he himself had thought of it. But Kayugh said nothing when Gray Bird claimed credit. The idea might save lives. That was enough.

Kayugh had watched as the women, following White Face, an old man, left the village. Kayugh had spent time the night before making an amulet for his son. Inside the tanned skin pouch he placed one of his small bird dart points, a piece of whalebone he had kept from the whale on Shuganan's beach and a lock of his own hair. Then he braided a cord of babiche to tie the bag at the top and hang it around the baby's neck.

The evening before the women left, Kayugh had asked Chagak for his son. And though there were questions in her eyes, Chagak said nothing as she took Amgigh from her breast and handed the child to Kayugh.

He took the boy outside to the lee side of the ulaq where the wind would not pull the baby's breath from his mouth. Then he spoke to the child, telling him about his mother, about his grandfather and great-grandfather. He spoke of hunting and of taking a wife — all the things Kayugh would have told him gradually through the years — and as Kayugh spoke, Amgigh kept his dark eyes on Kayugh's face, as though he knew he must remember his father.

Before Kayugh took the baby back to Chagak, he said, "Amgigh, if I am killed,

Chagak will be your mother. She will choose a husband, and he will be your father. You must make them proud of you."

Then he took Amgigh back inside the ulaq and asked if he might also hold Samiq. And Chagak, though she looked surprised, had given him the child.

Kayugh took Samiq outside and spoke to him as he had spoken to Amgigh, of hunting and the honor of a man, of choosing a wife and building an ikyak. And Samiq, too, appeared to be listening, to hold what Kayugh said.

Then Kayugh had taken Samiq back to his mother, and as the woman took the child, Kayugh said, "I would be proud to claim him as son, but if I do not return, take Amgigh as your son. Choose a husband who will be a good father to both boys."

Chagak opened her mouth as if she would say something, and Kayugh waited, hoping that she would give him some reason to believe that if he returned safely she would become his wife, some hope that would strengthen his arms and give true aim to his spear in the fighting. But she looked away and said nothing.

Then in the morning, as the women filed from the village, Chagak had turned back, first to Shuganan, giving him an amulet, something that looked like a shaman's pouch, and then to Kayugh, pressing against him briefly to slip something into his hand and whisper, "It gave me strength once." Then she ran back to join the women. Kayugh opened his hand and saw that she had given him a dark eider duck feather, and though he did not know how the feather had helped Chagak, he tucked it into his amulet.

Shuganan told Kayugh the story later, and the old man smiled as he explained how Chagak learned to use the bola. Now as Kayugh paused for a moment in his work, hauling one of the ikyan up to the top of the cliff, he thought about the woman who had lost everyone and now might lose all again. He remembered how many times after his wives' deaths he had considered death for himself and his son, and he wondered if Chagak had felt the same hopelessness.

He set the ikyak he was carrying beside the others they had hidden. They had left a few ikyan on the beach, but most were on the cliffs. When the Short Ones came, they would see those that were left and think there were few hunters in the village. Shuganan said that the Short Ones' scouts had probably watched the village for several days the summer before and knew how many men were in the ulas, but if the ikyan were gone, the warriors would probably think the men were away hunting.

Kayugh returned to the beach and helped Big Teeth notch driftwood logs, second climbing poles for each ulaq. Both men used stone axes hafted to strong driftwood handles.

"When do you think they will come?" Big Teeth asked Kayugh.

But Gray Bird joined them and answered Big Teeth's question before Kayugh could speak. "Shuganan is a fool. They will not come. Who would attack the Whale Hunters? They are strong enough to kill whales; they have eaten whale meat since they were small boys. Who can stand against that power?"

Kayugh, angry at Gray Bird's answer, said, "Shuganan lived with the Short Ones. He knows how they think and why they fight. We do not."

Gray Bird shrugged and squatted on the beach. "If they come, I will fight," he said. "But I do not think they will come."

But Kayugh saw the muscles of Gray Bird's jaw twitch and he sensed a nervousness in the man. Perhaps he talked only to relieve his own fears. Why argue with him?

Kayugh finished the last notch at his end of the log and waited while Big Teeth finished his. Then, without speaking, they hoisted the log to their shoulders and carried it to Many Whales' ulaq.

When she was a child, Chagak sometimes

428

wished she had been born a boy. Her father had a pride in her brothers that she knew he did not feel for her. But when she had become a woman, able to bear children, she no longer wanted to be a man.

Now, as she and the other women waited, she again wished she had been born a boy, wished she could do more against the Short Ones than sit and weave baskets and pray.

Occasionally Fat Wife, who had proclaimed herself leader among the women, sent one of the older girls up to the ridge where the boys kept watch for sign of ikyan. But each time the girl had returned shaking her head. There was no one. Only the men of the village waiting.

Two days passed slowly. Chagak listened to the Whale Hunter women tell of coming to the cave in other summers, for other reasons. They talked about the salt marshes, less than a morning's walk away; how they were filled with scaup and with bowitcher nests, and that the green-brown eggs — sometimes even ten in a nest — were good fried in whale oil or boiled in seawater. And near those same marshes, cranberries grew thick on their glossy-leaved stems and a woman could find mossberry roots, something that made good medicine for the eyes.

As she listened, Chagak wove baskets, but

her fingers seemed slow, as if the waiting had aged her; and the baskets were misshapen, so that the Whale Hunter women looked at them slyly from the corners of their eyes, and Chagak was ashamed of her clumsiness.

Their cave was wide and shallow. It cut into the back side of the ridge so anyone coming from the village would see only the ridge and not the cave. It was deep enough to be a shelter from the wind, but it dripped water from its high vaulted roof, and hard, spiny deposits had built up on the floor.

The first day the women had chipped at the deposits with hand axes and smoothed out the floor as much as they could. Crooked Nose, Blue Shell, Little Duck and Chagak chose a section for themselves near the back of the cave. A short distance from the ridge, Crooked Nose had found several stunted willows and, using the supple branches as supports, had hung sea lion skins over their sleeping area so water would not drip on them in the night. Shuganan had given Chagak one of his hunter's lamps. It held only three or four wicks and a puddle of oil, but it was enough to light their small corner and give some heat.

They had laid grass mats over the floor, one layer over another, and had spread sealskins over them, so their bedding stretched over the entire area. And Chagak had laughed, telling the others that she had never worked while in bed, weaving and sewing as she squatted in her sleeping place.

But now, at the end of the second day, Chagak wanted only to know how the men were, to see Shuganan, Kayugh and Big Teeth and even Gray Bird. And she wished she were a man so she could fight beside them.

Many Whales' son came as they had told him, quietly, creeping into the village like a shadow, crawling into Many Whales' ulaq. Shuganan, Many Whales and Kayugh squatted near an oil lamp, each man working on his weapons, and they jumped when the boy spoke.

"They come," he said. And Kayugh heard fear in the words.

"How many?" Many Whales asked.

"Twenty ikyan, maybe more," the boy said, his tongue darting out to lick his lips.

"Do the men on the ridges know?" Many Whales asked.

"The ones on this side."

"And those in the other ulas?" Shuganan asked.

"No. I came to you first."

"As you should," Many Whales said.

"But you must warn the others."

Kayugh looked at the boy, at the fine otter fur of his parka, at the new spear in his hands.

His thoughts went briefly to Amgigh, and a sudden fear pressed into his chest that he would not see Amgigh grown to this age, the age of boy almost a man.

"You go to the west cliff and tell them," Kayugh said. "I will go to the other ulas."

They left together, and Shuganan called after Kayugh, "Be careful. Do not let them see you."

The boy skirted the back of the village, and Kayugh crawled to the top of the first ulaq. He slipped in through the roof hole, calling out his name before entering.

When he had warned the men in the village, he returned to Many Whales' ulaq. He called down that he would stay at the top of the roof hole and watch the beach.

For a time there was nothing. The fog had moved in from the sea, softening the edges of rocks and dimming the late light of the sun. Wisps settled between the ulas, and the whiteness crept up toward Kayugh. Finally he saw movement on the beach — men dragging ikyan ashore.

Though fog always carries sound well, Kayugh heard no voices and, watching the men through the haze, it seemed they moved more slowly than they should, carefully, quietly, so that Kayugh began to wonder if he was in some dream.

But he climbed back into the ulaq and called to the others, "They are on the beach."

Shuganan pushed himself to his feet and picked up his harpoon.

One more time Kayugh tried to talk to the old man. "We need you to pray for us," Kayugh said. "Let me take you to the cliffs. You can pray there as well as here."

"If I go to the cliffs," Shuganan said, tightening his crooked fingers around the shaft of his weapon, "I will not be able to come down with the men and fight. Here, I will be ready to help. I am old, but I still hunt."

"Be careful, Grandfather," Kayugh said, honoring the man with the title. "Chagak needs you."

Shuganan smiled. "No," he said. "She needs you."

It seemed they had been waiting for days, avoiding conversation so they could hear the approach of the Short Ones. But they had heard nothing, and still they waited. Kayugh was on the climbing log, watching out the roof hole. He had decided not to wear his parka for fear it would hinder his movements in the fight, and so had oiled his chest and shoulders to hold in his body heat and make his skin less vulnerable to injury in the fighting.

The wind was cool, and Kayugh knew the

nights would soon bring frosts that would rime the grass and darken the scrub willows that grew in the hills.

Shuganan murmured prayers. He spoke to his ancestors, men who were of the Short Ones but who would have found no honor in killing other men. He spoke to Tugix and to spirits in sea and sky.

He asked if they would let evil men kill everyone, if they would never stop the killing, and as he pleaded, Shuganan sometimes felt his spirit expand in anger. Why had the killing continued for so long? Did spirits have no control over choices made by men?

Shuganan had his eyes closed, an amulet in each hand, when Kayugh slid quickly to the floor. "They are coming toward the ulas," he said. "They look like ghosts in the fog."

"They are not ghosts," Shuganan answered. "They are men with no special powers, no great gift but their daring. We will match them."

Kayugh straightened his shoulders and lifted his head. His fingers sought the whale carving that hung at his neck. Shuganan had carved a whale pendant for each of the men in the ulas. He had done those whales quickly, without much detail, but Kayugh's whale was the one Shuganan had given him before they came to the Whale Hunters' village, and the carving was beautiful.

They waited, Kayugh at the bottom of the notched log, Many Whales beside him. Shuganan strained to hear sounds that were not wind or sea. He heard nothing.

Nothing, but then suddenly a torch was thrown through the roof hole, the thing blazing. It burned harmlessly against the packed earth floor.

Kayugh bent to smother the smoking fire with a partially tanned hide, but Shuganan caught the young man's arm.

"No," Shuganan said. "They must think it has caught the floor mats. They must think we do not know who threw it."

He pulled a dividing curtain from the wall and put it in the middle of the dirt floor. Then, using the torch, he lit several of the oil lamps around the room and also the curtain.

"If it smokes too much we will smother it," Shuganan said. "But first we must scream." He smiled at Many Whales. "Pretend we are women."

He pitched his voice into a high scream and Kayugh and Many Whales did the same. And between the screams, he was sure he heard laughter coming from the top of the ulaq.

Kayugh looked over his shoulder at Many Whales, and when Many Whales nodded, both men ran up the climbing logs. They went up, backs toward each other, spears thrust ahead of them.

When Kayugh was halfway up, he saw the two men who waited for them, one man at each side of the roof hole.

The men carried short spears, much more easily maneuvered than the long-shafted spears Kayugh and Many Whales carried. The man whom Many Whales faced had a spear and torch, and from the corner of his eye Kayugh saw the man feint with the torch, then throw it into the ulaq thatching. But in the wet thatching it only sputtered and smoked.

Kayugh thrust his spear at the other man, backing him toward the edge of the ulaq where the slope would make the Short One's footing precarious. The longer spear was more difficult to control, but Kayugh realized that with the long shaft he could keep the Short One far enough away so he could not use his short spear except by throwing.

The man raised his spear, swinging it toward Kayugh like a club but exposing a wide section of his chest. Kayugh lunged forward and thrust his spear toward the man's belly, but the Short One sidestepped and the thrust left Kayugh off balance. He stumbled into range of the Short One's spear and felt the sharp edge of the point cut into his left arm, skin slicing from skin, the sudden heat from his own blood.

The Short One thrust again, jabbing the spear point into Kayugh's shoulder. Waves of pain pressed against him, forcing him back until he slipped down the side of the ulaq.

Kayugh landed on his feet and raised his spear with his good arm. If the Short One slid down the ulaq to continue the fight, the man would be vulnerable until he gained his footing on the ground.

The Short One cocked his spear as if to throw, then suddenly turned and attacked Many Whales from behind.

Kayugh sucked in his breath, expecting to see a spear thrust into Many Whales' back. But Many Whales took two quick steps sideways and jumped from the top of the ulaq. He ran to Kayugh's side and Kayugh saw that blood was dripping from a shallow wound across Many Whales' cheek.

"How bad?" Many Whales asked, gesturing toward Kayugh's arm.

"It is not broken," Kayugh answered but he kept his eyes on the Short Ones at the top of the ulaq, two dim figures in the fog. "They will throw their spears at us," Kayugh said.

"No," said Many Whales. "If they do, they will have no weapons but knives. Besides, they can barely see us in this fog."

Using the edge of his spear, Many Whales cut a strip from his woven apron and bound it over Kayugh's wound. The pressure sent pain through Kayugh's body, and a hard knot of nausea settled into his stomach.

"It will stop the bleeding," Many Whales said.

But Kayugh, fighting down his need to retch, could not answer.

Pain seemed to muffle his hearing and darken his vision. He felt himself sway and from a distance heard Many Whales say, "You have lost too much blood." Kayugh's body ached to sink into the rye grass at the side of the ulaq. But then he thought of Amgigh and of Chagak, of Chagak's son, Samiq.

How could he take the chance that they might be killed or taken back as sons and wife of the Short Ones? Kayugh filled his chest with air and stood straight, willing his body to be strong.

"We must go back up," he said to Many Whales.

"No," Many Whales said. "They are in the ulaq."

"Shuganan . . ."

Many Whales shook his head. "He is old, but he is a hunter. We cannot help him; they would kill us as we climbed inside. There are others who need our help."

Yes, there were others. Kayugh could hear the groans, the sounds of weapon against weapon. On each ulaq men were fighting. But where were the men from the ridges? Why had they not joined the fight? Had someone changed the plan?

His thoughts were interrupted by a sudden scream. Someone wounded, or killed.

"Shell Digger," he heard Many Whales mutter. "One of our best hunters."

Kayugh held his left arm against his body and tried not to think of the pain that had caused that scream. His own wound seemed to drain the strength from his body and the hope from his mind.

What chance did they have against these hunters of men? And this village was not taken in surprise as most villages were. But where were the men who were to attack from the ridge? Were they cowards who would wait until the Short Ones left before returning to the ulas?

The darkness of his pain again pulled at Kayugh and he leaned heavily against the ulaq. Many Whales crouched beside him, and Kayugh, his anger rising at his own weakness and at the men who did not come to fight, asked, "Where are your men? They were to attack from the ridges."

"They cannot see us, cannot hear us," Many

439

Whales said. "How will they know the fight-ing has begun? If we call to them, the Short Ones will be warned of their attack."

Yes, Kayugh thought, annoyed that his pain seemed to dull his thinking. What would they see in the thickening fog? None of the ulas were on fire. The noise of fighting had been an occasional grunt, the sound of bare feet on sod roofs, only Shell Digger's scream would have carried to the ridges where the other Whale Hunters waited.

Kayugh clutched Many Whales' arm. "Scream," Kayugh said. "We must scream. They will know we are fighting if they hear screams. Any man can scream in battle."

He raised his voice in a high shriek. Once, twice. Then, as if the Whale Hunters suddenly knew Kayugh's plan, other screams began to rise from the ulas.

Many Whales laughed. "Yes, they will come," he said. "Now they will come."

FORTY-ONE

Inside Many Whales' ulaq, Shuganan waited, following the fighting on the roof by the sifting of dirt from the rafters. Many Whales had arranged a circle of Shuganan's carvings on the floor. A strong animal for each of the five ulas, he had said. But Shuganan ignored the carvings. He held his amulet in one hand, the shaman's amulet Chagak had given him in the other, and he prayed. The fighting at the top of the ulaq seemed to stop, and Shuganan held his breath. Then he heard men at the roof hole.

His arms trembled. Kayugh and Many Whales would not come inside unless they were too badly wounded to fight. Shuganan grasped the spear that lay at his side and pushed himself to his feet. He crept into the darkness behind the climbing logs and waited, all the while his mind giving reasons why Kayugh or Many Whales would come inside: a strip of hide to cover a wound, a weapon to replace one that had broken. But when Shuganan saw the feet on the climbing log, toes, soles and tops painted black, he knew.

A bleakness filled his chest, squeezed into his throat and nearly choked him.

Many Whales had lived a long life, but Kayugh . . . And what of Chagak? Who would take care of her?

The Short Ones jumped down the last notches of the climbing log. One man kicked at the unlit torch lying on the floor.

"It did not burn," he said. He was large, his head a thatch of black hair smeared with grease and mud.

"Someone was here to put it out," said the other man, and he pointed to the door openings at the far end of the ulaq.

Shuganan watched as they crept toward the sleeping places. I should have attacked when the men were climbing into the ulaq, Shuganan thought. I could not have killed both, but perhaps I could have taken one. When they find nothing in the sleeping places, they will search the main room, and what chance do I have, an old man facing two young warriors?

But then both men stopped at the circle of carved animals.

"Shuganan," one of them said.

So Man-who-kills had not lied, Shuganan thought. The Short Ones still believed in the power of his carvings.

And if there is power, he thought, it is mine.

He slipped from the shadows behind the climbing logs. He took two quick steps and, ignoring the pain of old joints and muscles, threw his spear.

It entered the big man's back with a hard, thick sound, like the ripping of roots from wet earth. Then the man fell forward, slowly, and just as slowly his companion looked back at Shuganan.

Shuganan glanced at the climbing logs, but he knew his legs were too old to take him up quickly, and so he drew his knife from the sheath on his arm and said to the warrior still standing, "I am Shuganan."

"You are dead," said the warrior.

"Perhaps."

"You are dead," said the man again, his voice rising to a peak, "and I will have all your power because I will be the one who kills you."

"No," said Shuganan, moving to give himself an advantage, to stay in the shadow and keep the young man in the light. "True power is earned, not taken."

But the warrior laughed. "Spear against knife," he said.

"Throw it," Shuganan said.

Again the man laughed.

Shuganan shifted the knife in his hand, grasped it by the tip and lifted his arm to throw. The warrior lifted his spear.

The tip of the knife left Shuganan's fingers, then he felt the sudden weight of the spear in his side, and at first no pain, only a thrust that knocked him down, but at the same time he saw the young man clutch at his chest, saw the hilt of his knife protruding from the warrior's breast. And, watching from the floor, Shuganan saw him fall.

Another Short One appeared out of the fog and Kayugh, ignoring the pain in his left shoulder, gripped his spear and stepped forward, but Many Whales pulled him back and met the Short One's attack. They were fighting between the ulas, where the haze of the fog was thickest.

Kayugh watched, both men thrusting with spear in one hand, knife in the other, Many Whales using the spear shaft to ward off blows. Kayugh strained to see in the fog, to intercept others before they could help the Short One. Then Kayugh realized that Many Whales was maneuvering the Short One toward him, the warrior's back now only a few steps from where Kayugh crouched.

Kayugh waited until the man was close, then gripped his spear in both hands and took a running step. Many Whales quickly moved back, and for a moment the Short One stopped and stared. Then Kayugh's spear hit. He rammed it with all his strength, thrusting it up under the man's rib cage and out the front of his chest.

The man turned, his mouth open, and looked at Kayugh, then his knees doubled and he fell.

Kayugh grasped his spear shaft below the point and pulled, careful that the blood did not make his hand slide into the sharp barbed end.

But then there was a sudden rushing of wind, the clatter of spear against spear. A man fell against Kayugh and knocked him to the ground. Lying on his belly, Kayugh tried to roll away from the man but felt the edge of a knife slice across the top of his hand. A shallow wound but a painful one.

Kayugh flipped to his back. Many Whales came at the man, but the Short One suddenly lurched and fell. A spear was in his back.

Many Whales stepped forward and, bracing his foot against the dead man's back, withdrew the spear. He studied the spearhead, then laughed and shouted, "Where are you?"

"I'm here," came a voice from the top of the ulaq.

Kayugh looked up, saw a man standing at the sloped edge of the ulaq roof.

"Hard Rock," Many Whales shouted. "Come

get your spear or do I throw it back to you?"
He laughed again, then turned to Kayugh.
"They heard us from the ridges. They have
come!"

In the ulaq, Shuganan lay with eyes closed,
his hand pressed against the wound in his side.
He felt little pain, only a deep weariness, a heaviness that seemed to hold him down so even the
smallest movement took all of his strength.

Then, again, he heard someone at the roof
hole. He sat up, and the movement made another flow of blood gush from his wound.
Then there were feet on the climbing log; the
soles were not painted black; a Whale Hunter,
perhaps.

Shuganan pressed his hands against his side
to stop the blood. When he looked up, he
saw Gray Bird standing at the base of the
climbing log.

"The fighting is over?" Shuganan asked, the
words hissing out between breaths.

"No," Gray Bird said. "They still fight.
Some have been killed."

"Kayugh?"

"I do not know."

"Why are you here?"

"I am wounded." Gray Bird limped toward
Shuganan, pointed toward a gash on the calf
of his leg.

446

For a moment Shuganan closed his eyes, fought against the pain of his own wound, then, shaking his head at the man, said, "Your wound . . . is nothing. Fight . . . go fight."

The whites of Gray Bird's eyes glimmered and the man knelt beside Shuganan. "You have stayed here inside this ulaq," he said, and Shuganan heard the anger in his voice. "Who are you to tell me to fight?" Then, as though he saw them for the first time, Gray Bird looked at the two Short Ones lying on the ulaq floor.

"Those men?" Gray Bird said. "You killed them?"

Shuganan closed his eyes and lowered his head. Why answer? What need did he have to boast to Gray Bird? Let the man think what he wanted.

Then Gray Bird was bending over him, easing him onto a padding of skins, pressing a water-soaked rag against his wound.

Shuganan let his body relax against the softness of the furs.

"You are dying," Gray Bird said. "I will stay here with you."

"Go . . . help the others," Shuganan said. "Leave me."

Gray Bird laughed. "You are dying," he said again. "Yes, you will be dead, but I will be honored. Did I not kill two Short Ones to try to save you? Was I not wounded protecting you? Chagak will come to me in gratitude as wife and you will not be able to stop her."

Shuganan looked up at the man, at the narrow, hard eyes. He tried to speak, but words would not come. His eyes closed, and when he finally opened them again, he saw Gray Bird's face and another face, like the mist that comes before a rain, the face of some spirit, crouched beside Gray Bird.

The spirit-face shifted and gathered, like smoke, to form eyes, nose, mouth. It was Man-who-kills, his spirit.

I was not strong enough, Shuganan thought. Now he is here, waiting for me to die. Then he heard a voice: "You thought you could destroy me, old man." Laughter.

Shuganan looked at Gray Bird, but Gray Bird did not seem to hear the voice, see the spirit.

I dream, Shuganan thought. In my dying, I dream.

"You think you have power," Man-who-kills said. "You think you can destroy me." Again he laughed. "Your circle of animals, they protect you?" He kicked at several of the carvings, but the ivory animals did not move.

So Man-who-kills still has power, Shuganan thought, but not enough to touch my animals.

Can he harm Chagak, Samiq?

Pain. Suddenly it surrounded Shuganan, squeezed him tight, pulled his thoughts into thin, broken threads.

"I have watched you," Man-who-kills said. "All these months. You and Chagak. I know I have a son."

"Man-who-kills, do not hurt Chagak," Shuganan whispered. "Do not hurt the baby. Samiq is one of your people, a Short One. Do not kill him."

Man-who-kills laughed, and then his face began to fade. Shuganan's pain eased. Then the one who bent over him was not Man-who-kills but Gray Bird. And it was Gray Bird who was laughing.

"So you speak to the spirits, old man," Gray Bird said. "Did you forget that you speak also to me? Now I, too, know that you and Chagak lied. And Chagak, what will she give me for her son's life?"

How many men? Kayugh asked himself. How many more? What had Shuganan said? Twenty? Thirty? He, Many Whales and Hard Rock worked as a team, taking on new men as they came. Kayugh hid in the darkness between the ulas, ready to thrust his spear when an enemy's back was toward him. They had killed three men this way and yet others still came. The pain of his exhaustion was nearly as great as the pain from the wound in his shoulder.

A dark form lurched out of the fog toward Kayugh and Kayugh raised his knife, but the man called out, "I am Round Belly," and Kayugh remembered the man as one of the Whale Hunters — a short, fat man who laughed often and always carried three long-bladed knives sheathed on his legs. Now he held two of those knives, one in each fist, and his face was smeared with blood and dirt.

"There are no more coming to the far ulaq." His voice told of his weariness.

Kayugh pulled him to the side of the ulaq and the man let his body sag against the wall. During the fighting the sun had set, but now the sky was lightening again, blacks becoming purples and grays.

"Perhaps they quit fighting because it is morning," Round Belly said.

"Perhaps they quit fighting because they are dead," Many Whales said.

"No," said Kayugh. "The first two who came to us went inside the ulaq."

"I saw them," Many Whales answered. "They did not come out."

"Shuganan is dead," Kayugh said, but the words seemed empty, and he could feel nothing, only the horror of the killing, and anger at the foolishness of men fighting men.

"Perhaps Shuganan killed them."

"He is an old man," Kayugh said, and was surprised when a sob caught in his last word.

"He is old, but he has great power. Power is greater than strength."

For a moment Kayugh leaned his head back against the ulaq. He wished he could close his eyes, but did not. Who could say what would happen in the brief darkness of closed eyes? The sounds of fighting had ceased, and in the quietness his mind was no longer filled with thoughts of the next warrior, the next fight. His shoulder began to hurt. The throbbing of it pulsed into his head and down the side of his body. But he thought of Shuganan, the old man probably dead, and he thought of Chagak's sorrow.

What great evil had she done to deserve the pain the spirits had allowed in her life? She was not a woman of the Short Ones, one who would welcome home a husband who had killed many. She would not take necklaces torn from dead women and wear them as her own. She had not hated her people, nor eaten more than her share. She was not lazy.

Kayugh looked at the wound in his shoulder, saw that it had crusted over and no longer seeped blood. He pushed himself from the side of the ulaq and clambered up to the top. If the Short Ones were inside waiting, they would know he was coming. The weight of his body would make dust fall from the roof, but he could not wait, wondering.

Kayugh took several steps down the climbing log, expecting the slash of a spear at each step. Finally he spun and jumped from the log, landing so he faced the large main room. A whale oil lamp glowed and sputtered, its circle of wicks nearly extinguished in the oil. Shuganan lay on a pile of furs; Gray Bird sat beside him.

Two Short Ones were crumpled, lying in their own blood on the floor before him.

"Shuganan killed them?" Kayugh asked, speaking to Gray Bird.

Gray Bird smiled crookedly. "Believe what you like," he said, then, leaning toward Shuganan, added, "I tried to protect him from them. But . . ." His voice trailed away and he whispered, "He is badly wounded."

Kayugh frowned. He saw the bloody rag at Shuganan's side, the wound on Gray Bird's leg. Gray Bird would not have tried to protect Shuganan, only himself. Kayugh squatted beside Shuganan, gently laid his hand on Shuganan's forehead.

The old man opened his eyes, blinked. "Kayugh," he said. "You are alive."

"They are beaten, Shuganan," Kayugh said.

"They will not be back."

Shuganan closed his eyes. Nodded. "Then you must get Chagak. I must speak to her."

"I will get her. Sleep if you can. I will bring her to you."

Gray Bird took Kayugh's arm, pulled him away from Shuganan. "You are tired. I have rested. I will go and get Chagak."

"No — "

"He is dying, Kayugh, and you are wounded and tired. You will not reach her in time. Shuganan will die before you can bring her back."

Kayugh looked into Gray Bird's eyes, saw that he told the truth. "Go then," he said. "Hurry."

It was morning, still early, and all the other women slept, but Chagak had slept fitfully and now a restlessness filled her. The babies were in their cradles, and so she did not disturb them as she rolled from her sleeping mat and slipped from the cave.

Outside, the heather was wet with dew and a fog spread out in the valley below but did not reach the cave. The sun was hidden under high gray clouds but in the west Chagak could see bits of blue sky. At the broad flat entrance of the cave she squatted on her heels and rested her arms on her upraised knees.

Though she knew she was too far from the village to hear shouts of men or clash of fighting, it had seemed that the night carried strange sounds, something above the noise of the wind. During the evening the other women had been quiet, as if they, too, heard the difference. The voice of sea otter had not spoken to Chagak, had offered no wry comments on Fat Wife's behavior, no gentle responses to Chagak's fear each time she thought of the Short Ones.

Chagak had tried to speak to the otter. She whispered about the parka she would make Shuganan when they returned to their island, about the sealskin boots she would make for Kayugh, but still sea otter did not answer her, and now in the new morning fear rose up into Chagak's throat and she clamped her teeth together until her jaws ached.

"Chagak," she heard someone call, and realized that the voice came from the valley. A man emerged from the fog.

It was Gray Bird and for a moment joy banished Chagak's fear, but then she saw the tiredness of his face, the dirt and blood smeared across his cheeks, signs of battle, and she wondered if perhaps Gray Bird had fled the fighting.

Questions jumbled together in her mind, but when Gray Bird stood before her, she could do nothing but stare at his torn parka, the slash wound on his right ankle, a blood-stained strip of grass matting wrapped around his left hand.

"They came," he said, for once his voice low and tired, not raised in a boast. The string of hair that grew from his chin trembled. "Some of the Whale Hunters were killed in the fighting, but all of the Short Ones are dead." He wiped a sleeve across his face, then said, "Even the few who tried to get away are dead. Some of the boys who had stood watch crept down during the fighting and cut the bottoms of their ikyan. The Short Ones who tried to get away drowned."

Gray Bird groaned and, jerking his parka above his knees, sat down cross-legged on Chagak's mat. Chagak saw that the slash on Gray Bird's ankle extended up the calf of his leg. The wound gaped open over the bulge of the muscle and Gray Bird pressed the sides together with his hands.

"It does not bleed much, but it needs to be stitched," Chagak said.

Gray Bird curled back his lips in a scowl and said, "Tell Blue Shell to bring me food and water."

It angered Chagak that Gray Bird had not mentioned Shuganan or Kayugh or even Big Teeth, and as a woman it was not her place to ask, but the questions pounded so hard in her head that she turned before entering the cave and said, "And Shuganan? He was not hurt?"

"Better you ask about Big Teeth," Gray Bird said. "He killed four and has only a scratch on one thumb to show for his fighting."

Chagak's throat tightened. All the fear and dread she had been holding flooded up into her mouth and forced out her words. "You are telling me that Shuganan and Kayugh are dead?" she asked.

"I did not say that," Gray Bird answered. "But by what right do you ask? I am a hunter and you are only a woman."

"I ask by right of caring," Chagak said, anger replacing some of her dread. "And if you want food you will answer me."

"You will keep food from me?" Gray Bird asked.

And suddenly a voice behind Chagak answered, "We all will keep food from you."

Chagak turned. It was Fat Wife. She stood in the entrance of the cave. She was wearing only her apron, her arms crossed over her pendulous breasts, her feet splayed in the stance of a hunter.

"You were sent here to warn us or to bring us back to the village," she said. "But you

456

sit and threaten us. Is my husband dead or alive?"

"Your husband is alive, not injured," Gray Bird said. "But he did not send me. Shuganan sent me."

Joy leaped into Chagak's chest. Shuganan was alive. But then Gray Bird said, "He is badly wounded. Dying. He wants to talk to Chagak."

The hope that had been with her through the days in the cave vanished and Chagak felt empty, like a water skin, drained and flattened.

And then she thought, Why did Shuganan send Gray Bird and not Kayugh? Surely he would know that Gray Bird would cause problems.

"And Kayugh?" Chagak whispered, the words thick in her throat.

"He is wounded, too," Gray Bird said, glancing back quickly at Fat Wife.

"Dying?"

Gray Bird shrugged. "I do not know. Too weak to come and get you."

Chagak pressed her lips together, holding her grief within. "I will go now," she said to Fat Wife, but Fat Wife did not seem to hear her.

"My son?" Fat Wife asked.

"He was one who slit the bottoms of the

Short Ones' ikyan," Gray Bird said, and Chagak heard the woman's low chuckle. "The Short Ones killed him before they left to drown."

Fat Wife's laughter rolled up into a high scream and she began the wail of mourning. She dropped to her knees and Chagak started toward her but already women were pouring from the cave, all singing the mourning cry, even before being told what had happened, who had died.

"The Short Ones are dead," Gray Bird shouted. "All of them are dead." But as the song of mourning rose, Chagak could no longer hear what he said, and she, too, began the cry, mourning for Shuganan and Fat Wife's son and men she did not know.

FORTY-TWO

Chagak made her way through the crowd of women and entered the cave. Both her babies were crying. Something inside her chest also wanted to cry and to scream, as if anger and sorrow could bring Shuganan back to her. She began to gather the few belongings she had brought, but her hands were cold and clumsy and slow.

"Be still," she heard the sea otter whisper. "There is no need to rush. Gray Bird will not go back before he has eaten."

I will go without him, Chagak thought. I know the way. But sea otter said again, "Be still."

And Chagak bowed her head and laid her hands in her lap, willed the rapid beating of her heart to slow. She felt the heat of tears on her cheeks.

"He is an old man," the sea otter said. "He has lived a long life."

"I do not care," Chagak answered. "I do not want him to die. I need him."

"Perhaps he is ready to rest. Perhaps he wants to meet his wife at the Dancing Lights.

His body is old and he is tired. You have others who care for you: Kayugh and his people. Your grandfather Many Whales."

"Yes," Chagak said, "but Gray Bird said Kayugh was wounded. What if he dies?"

"Then you will raise his son."

Chagak followed Gray Bird back to the village. She carried the babies in their slings and a basket of her belongings on her back. Gray Bird had not offered to carry anything, but Chagak did not expect him to.

The man favored his injured leg and used a stick to pick his way slowly over the path. At first Chagak wanted to hurry ahead, and she felt her impatience gathering into a hard, full lump inside her chest, but as they walked, the fear that she would find both Shuganan and Kayugh dead grew, and her feet seemed to become heavy and clumsy, so finally, plodding behind Gray Bird, Chagak lowered her head and watched the path, thinking of nothing but the next step she would take.

When Gray Bird suddenly stopped, Chagak nearly ran into him. She looked up, blinked. "What?" she asked. "Why do you stop?"

"We are near the village," he said. "There is something you must know before we arrive."

Chagak lifted her head, met his eyes. She

saw hate in his eyes, hate that spread out from his body like heat spreading from a fire. The muscles in her arms and legs tightened, but she held herself still. She would not tremble before a man like Gray Bird. She clasped her hands over the babies and Gray Bird smiled.

"One son belongs to Kayugh," he said. "He will be a hunter. But the other son . . ." Gray Bird's lips stretched wide over his teeth. "Man-who-kills — "

Chagak gasped and Gray Bird laughed.

"Shuganan, in his dying, speaks to spirits," Gray Bird said.

Chagak straightened, took a long breath. "It is not unusual that he would speak to spirits," she said.

"No, not unusual," Gray Bird replied. "But perhaps strange that Samiq's father is a Short One."

"No," Chagak said. "Samiq's father is Shuganan's son."

Gray Bird took a step toward her and clasped her arms. "You lie. Anyone can see that you lie. And I will tell them the truth. They will kill your Samiq before he can grow into a warrior, a killer like his father."

Chagak jerked her arms away and pushed past Gray Bird.

"I will tell them," Gray Bird called after her, "unless you decide to be my wife. Then perhaps I might find it good to have such a son, a killer like his father."

Chagak did not look back at him. She kept walking, her heart beating like something wild within her ribs. Tears pushed at the backs of her eyes. She prayed to Tugix, to Aka, prayed they would save her son from Gray Bird; prayed they would let Shuganan live.

But only the otter's voice came to her, whispering, "Shuganan must be dying if he has spoken to Man-who-kills' spirit. But Shuganan will defeat Man-who-kills, in the spirit world, when he goes to the Dancing Lights. You, you are the one who must defeat Gray Bird."

Chagak kept walking, eyes straight ahead, toward the village. Gray Bird caught up to her, walked beside her, but she did not look at him.

They came to the crest of a hill, together, Chagak on the left, Gray Bird on the right, and in that moment Chagak's heart seemed to lodge itself in the base of her throat.

A Short One stood at the bottom of the hill, the man's clothing torn, his hair matted with blood. He was taller than Man-who-kills, his shoulders square, wide. He raised his spear.

Gray Bird gasped and stepped behind Chagak.

The Short One laughed.

Chagak could not think, could feel nothing

but the throb of her heart. But then Samiq moved under her suk and a sudden need to protect her son seemed to clear her thoughts.

"Your people are defeated," Chagak called to the man.

He called something back to her, in the language of the Short Ones, but she did not know what he said.

"Where is your spear?" she said in a low voice to Gray Bird, but he did not answer her. From under her suk, Chagak felt Samiq move, heard the thin beginning of his cry. Dropping the basket from her back, she reached inside for her bola. The stones were small, made for killing birds.

"What good will they do against a man?" some spirit whispered to her. And Chagak felt doubt numb her hands. But Samiq, then Amgigh, moved under her suk, and Chagak heard the otter say, "Who is stronger, a man who kills other men or a woman with two sons? Who has more strength? Who has more power for good?"

Chagak grasped the braided bola handle and swung the stones above her head. The man at the bottom of the hill lowered his spear, began to laugh, laughed until his eyes were squeezed tight with his laughter.

Then Chagak let the bola fly, watched as the stones spun in wide jerking circles, watched as the Short One opened his eyes, then flung his arms up to cover his head.

The ropes wrapped around his arms and head, the stones hitting his mouth and neck. He dropped his spear and roared, blood rushing from broken teeth.

Chagak stooped to pull her knife from her basket, then ran to where the man stood. She slashed his belly, and he kicked her, kicked so she could not reach him. But then, in his kicking, he fell, and Chagak, seeing his short spear in the grass at the side of the path, grabbed it and before he could turn away plunged it into his heart. Again the Short One roared and Chagak leaned all her weight on the spear. The man shuddered, but Chagak did not loose her hold on the spear until he lay still.

Then Gray Bird was beside her; he pulled the knife from Chagak's hand and slashed the Short One's throat.

Chagak looked at Gray Bird, saw the narrowing of the man's eyes. She spat into the grasses beside the Short One. "You, the child who hides behind a woman," she said to Gray Bird, "who did you say was Samiq's father?"

Gray Bird curled his lips and would not look at her. Finally he said, "Shuganan's son."

"Yes," said Chagak, "Seal Stalker, Shuganan's son."

★ ★ ★

Chagak had expected to see burned ulas and bloated bodies, but the only evidence of fighting was the number of ikyan on the beach and a litter of broken weapons in the narrow valleys between the ulas.

"Where are the bodies?" Chagak asked Gray Bird, the first she had spoken to the man since they had left the Short One. Gray Bird pointed to a group of men on the beach. They were gathered around an ik filled with what looked like meat and skin. But then Chagak realized she was seeing the bodies of many men, arms and legs cut at the joints to sever the power of the spirits.

"They will pull the ik out to sea and sink it," Gray Bird said. "I will tell them of the man we killed."

"I killed him," Chagak said. "I and my sons."

Gray Bird straightened, looked into Chagak's eyes, but then looked away as he said, "Women do not kill men."

"I saw how you kill men," Chagak said. "But that is something only you and I know."

For a moment Gray Bird stared at her, then he pointed to Many Whales' ulaq. "Shuganan is inside."

Chagak nodded, then set her basket down and climbed up the side of the ulaq. At the top she turned her eyes in the direction of Aka. She could not see the mountain, but she whispered her words into the wind. "Let him live," she begged. "Let Shuganan live, and Kayugh. I have given a Short One's spirit to you. Give me their spirits for the one I gave."

She took a shuddering breath and climbed down the notched log into the ulaq. Many Whales sat at the center of the ulaq; Kayugh was hunched over Shuganan in the far corner.

"You are welcome to stay here and raise your son among us," Many Whales said as Chagak stood at the base of the climbing log. "I will teach him to hunt the whale."

There was a softness in the man's voice and Chagak saw the black of ashes on his cheeks, sign of mourning. "I am sorry about your son," she said.

"He died a brave death," Many Whales answered.

"Yes," Chagak murmured, then said, "whether I choose to live here or to go back to Shuganan's beach, you will always have a grandson. Either way, he will know you and you will know him."

Many Whales nodded and Chagak walked back to stand beside Kayugh. He looked up at her and she saw the pain in his eyes.

"Gray Bird said you were wounded," Chagak whispered, and reached out toward him, but she stopped her hand before she touched his face.

But Kayugh took her hand in his. "The wound is in my shoulder," he said. "Only in the flesh of the muscle."

Chagak pulled her hand away and pressed her fingers lightly against his neck and forehead. His skin was cool; no evil spirits had entered the wound.

Kayugh grasped her hand again, but Chagak's eyes were drawn to Shuganan, still and white on the mats beside Kayugh.

"He is dead?" she asked, choking with the words.

But then Shuganan slowly opened his eyes. "I would not go until I said goodbye to you," he said, his voice soft and broken by frequent breaths. "There is another, too, who is looking for you . . . an enemy . . ."

Shuganan tried to raise his head, winced and closed his eyes. Chagak dropped to her knees beside him. "Do not worry, Grandfather," she said. "Gray Bird will not harm us. He is afraid. Of you and of me."

She placed her hands over his, felt his fingers relax.

"Your grandfather killed two Short Ones," Kayugh said.

But Chagak did not hear him. She leaned close to Shuganan. Suddenly she did not feel brave, did not feel strong. "Grandfather," she whispered, "Grandfather, what will I do if you leave me? Whose food will I cook? Whose parka will I repair? Tell the spirits you need to get well. Tell them you have a daughter who needs you."

"No, Chagak, no. I am old. It is my time to go." He paused, opened his eyes and smiled at her. "You brought joy to me, and a part of me wants to stay with you, but I must go.

"You have a son to raise. He needs a father. Your husband Seal Stalker would want his son to have a father. Kayugh will be a good father to Samiq."

"No," Chagak said. "Do not ask me to be wife. How would I bear the sorrow if my husband dies? I have mourned too many deaths."

"Is the sorrow of my death greater than the joys we shared in living?" Shuganan asked. "When you remember your father and mother, Seal Stalker and Pup, do you remember their deaths or what you shared in life?"

And as though the power of Shuganan's spirit drew the answer from her, Chagak whispered, "I remember our lives together."

Shuganan smiled and closed his eyes. In the silence of the ulaq Chagak watched the rise and fall of his breathing, the breaths growing shorter and shallower, but then the old man opened his eyes again. "Before, when I closed my eyes, there was either darkness or dreams," he said. "Now there is light. Hold to life, Chagak, but do not fear death."

Then his eyes were suddenly dim, without the light of his spirit, and Chagak fought against her tears. For a moment she wished she could go with Shuganan, could know the freedom of death. But then she felt Samiq move under her suk, and sea otter whispered, "You have many who need you here. Would you choose to leave Samiq and Amgigh, even Kayugh?"

And Chagak, hoping Shuganan's spirit still hovered near, said to Kayugh, "If you will raise Samiq as your own son, I will be your wife."

They stayed with the Whale Hunters through the burials and ceremonies of death, through the days of mourning. Many Whales gave Shuganan an honored place in the death ulaq, but Kayugh watched the man carefully, saw the desire in his eyes when he held Chagak's son.

There were many Whale Hunters anxious to have Chagak as wife. Kayugh heard two men ask Many Whales the bride price, and Kayugh's heart thudded hard in his chest. After months of travel, what did he have to offer Many Whales for his granddaughter? He had no sealskins, no whale oil. A Whale Hunter could give the bride price and Many Whales would have his grandson raised in his own village, perhaps even in his own ulaq. What hope did Kayugh have?

But several days after the burials he went to Many Whales, interrupted the man's mourning. Fat Wife sat in a dark corner of the ulaq. She seemed smaller, quieter since her son's death, and though Kayugh spoke a greeting, he could not bring his eyes to Fat Wife's face.

Many Whales had marked his body with charcoal and at his side lay a boy's spear, a man's harpoon. "They are my son's," he said to Kayugh. "Someday they will belong to my grandson."

Kayugh was pulled into the pain dark within Many Whales' eyes, and for a moment he could not speak, but finally he said, "I have come to ask the bride price of your grand-daughter, Chagak."

For a long time Many Whales did not answer. And the thought came to Kayugh: What right do I have to ask? What right to take a grandson and granddaughter?

"Others have asked for her," said Many Whales.

"I am a strong hunter," Kayugh said, but the words came out like a boast rather than an assurance of Chagak's happiness.

But Many Whales continued as though Kayugh had not spoken. "Others have asked," he said again. "I had no answer for them. But for you I have a price. Something that is fair." He sighed and looked at Kayugh for a long time. "A whale."

Kayugh sucked in his breath, felt the pain of disappointment tense the muscles in his wounded arm.

Many Whales pointed to the whale pendant lying against Kayugh's chest. "The whale Shuganan carved for you."

Kayugh opened his mouth but could think of nothing to say.

"Would it be fair for me to ask for more?" Many Whales said. "Chagak belongs with you. Just promise me I will see my grandson."

"Yes," Kayugh said. "You will see your grandson."

Kayugh's shoulder ached, but the wound was healing. He would hunt again, would throw the harpoon. The pain was nothing.

He dipped his paddle into the water and looked back at the women's ik. Chagak sat in the bow, Crooked Nose in the stern.

Kayugh still had questions about Chagak's first husband and the manner of his death. Gray Bird avoided Chagak, but if she left

Samiq with Kayugh, Gray Bird would squat beside Kayugh, talking about hunting or ikyan or the man he had killed when he was bringing Chagak back to the village. And though he spoke of other things, Gray Bird's eyes were always on Samiq, studying the boy's face, his hands and feet.

But Chagak's sorrow — something that seemed a part of her, the shadow cast by the light of her spirit — kept Kayugh from mentioning Gray Bird's interest in Samiq, and kept Kayugh from asking her his own questions.

Though Chagak had said she would be his wife, Kayugh had been careful to give her the choice of coming with him or staying with the Whale Hunters. She had chosen to come, and for now that choice was enough.

Knowing they would reach Shuganan's beach before night, that she would come to his sleeping place that evening, Kayugh felt a pulsing of joy in his heart and a rush of blood to his loins.

Big Teeth had been telling jokes all that day. He would run his ikyak close to Kayugh's, make a remark about marriage and taking wives, then quickly push his ikyak away, the man's laughter rolling back over the sea swells.

But the last time Big Teeth came near, Kayugh, laughing, had called, "You are only jealous because I will have two sons."

"Yes," Big Teeth had answered, still smiling. "But you would have neither if it were not for Chagak. Be a good husband to her."

"Yes, I will be a good husband," Kayugh had told him, and during the rest of that day Big Teeth had made no more jokes.

FORTY-THREE

Chagak arched her shoulders against the soreness of her muscles. When they arrived at Shuganan's beach, the women had unloaded the ik and now were cleaning their ulas.

Chagak had wiped the dust from Shuganan's many carvings, and again wished they had brought his body back with them, to lie in the death ulaq beside the bones of his wife. As she worked, Chagak began to cry but quickly wiped away her tears. "You have cried enough," she said out loud. "Finish your mourning and care for your children."

She nursed the babies and put them in their cradles over her sleeping place, then she sat down beside an oil lamp and pulled out her sewing basket. Knotting a heavy thread of sinew to the end of her needle, she tried to work on the sealskin boots she was making for Kayugh, but her needle caught in the awl holes and the sinew slipped from the end of the needle until finally Chagak folded her hands in her lap and only sat.

Even her worry about Gray Bird, the knowing he held in his small black eyes when he looked at Samiq, was only at the edges of her thoughts. She knew Kayugh would come soon, and her fingers moved to clasp the necklace he had given her. There was a part of her that could not pull her eyes away when he sat with parka off, muscles shining in the glow of lamplight, a part of her that laughed at Crooked Nose's jokes about husbands and wives, but she remembered her night with Man-who-kills, the pain.

Then Chagak heard someone on the ulaq roof and she wrapped up her sewing and slipped it into the basket.

"At least he will bring Red Berry," the sea otter whispered, and Chagak nodded, thinking with relief that the child would give them something to talk about, something to distract from the time of becoming husband and wife.

But when Kayugh climbed into the ulaq he was alone. "Crooked Nose has taken Red Berry for the night," Kayugh said and smiled at Chagak, and Chagak also tried to smile.

"Your sons sleep," she said.

Amgigh was strong now, always eating, clinging to her breast even when asleep, milk bubbling from the corners of his mouth. Chagak felt a great pride in his strength. She had not been able to save Pup, but perhaps in her sorrow, in her struggles with Man-who-kills, she had grown stronger, able to help others, to save a baby too weak to live.

"Amgigh's cradle hangs in there, over my sleeping place," she said.

But Kayugh merely nodded and made no attempt to check on his son. He removed his parka and stood before Chagak wearing only his apron.

Chagak, feeling the need to remain covered, had left her suk on, but her empty hands felt awkward in her lap and she wished she had not put away her sewing.

"Are you hungry? I can prepare food," Chagak said.

But Kayugh shook his head and spoke the beginning words of the marriage ceremony: "Someone says you will be my wife."

"Yes," Chagak answered carefully, following the custom Crooked Nose had explained to her, the few words the people of Kayugh's village used before a marriage. "Someone has said that."

Kayugh squatted beside her. "Someone has said your husband, father of Samiq, is dead."

Chagak looked anxiously toward her sleeping place. Why had she fed the babies so well? They could be awake now, crying to be fed, giving her more time to settle her spirit before becoming wife.

"Chagak?"

Then remembering that she was to answer,

Chagak said, "Yes, he is dead." And for a moment her mind was not on Man-who-kills or Kayugh but on Seal Stalker, the one who was to have been her husband, and she felt a great sadness rise up within her. Then, looking at Kayugh, she saw there were questions in his eyes.

"Do you want to belong to someone else?" he asked quietly, without anger. "To a Whale Hunter or to Big Teeth or Gray Bird?"

"No," Chagak said quickly and then dropped her eyes in embarrassment.

"I will keep this ulaq filled with meat. I will bring seal oil and teach our sons to hunt."

Chagak felt tears form in her eyes, and she could not answer him. She covered her face with her hands. What would he think now that he had seen the foolishness of her weeping?

"You do not want me," Kayugh said, his voice hard and flat.

Chagak wiped the tears from her cheeks. She sat quietly for a moment, steadying her voice. "I am afraid," she said finally.

Kayugh's face changed again to softness, and he smiled. "You have had a husband before, Chagak. Why are you afraid?"

"I am foolish," she said and tried to smile.

He sat down beside her then, as a man sits in an ikyak, legs straight, flat against the floor, and he pulled her to his lap, holding her against his chest and stroking the back of her suk — the same way she comforted Samiq or Amgigh when they cried.

She held herself very still. Why be afraid? This was Kayugh, a gentle man, a good man. She had not been true wife to Man-who-kills. She had been slave. His way was not the way of men with their wives.

Chagak pressed herself closer to Kayugh, and he slipped his hands under her suk, stroking the bare skin of her back. But then suddenly in Chagak's mind was the image of Man-who-kills holding a knife, slicing into the curve of her breasts, and she remembered the painful thrusting of Man-who-kills' body, the fish smell of his breath, his weight crushing her chest until she could do nothing but stay above the pain.

But no, Chagak told herself. This is Kayugh. This is Kayugh. His body smelled warm, rich like seal oil. She touched the pink shining scar where he had been wounded, and felt a keen gladness that the shoulder healed so well.

Should she tell him about Man-who-kills? No, why take the chance that everyone would know? Why take the chance that Samiq might face scorn, perhaps even death. But still, Kayugh must be given some explanation. Some part of the truth.

Chagak leaned away from Kayugh's chest and looked up into his eyes. "Samiq's father hurt me," she said softly, and she saw the surprise in his face, then the anger.

"He should be glad he is dead," Kayugh said, then he pulled off her suk and laid it beside them. He put his hand under Chagak's chin and raised her face to his. "I will not hurt you, Chagak," he said. He pressed her to his chest, the warmth of his skin hot against Chagak's breasts.

Chagak put her arms around his neck, felt the joy of his closeness. Kayugh stood and picked her up, then carried her to his sleeping place.

He laid her on the furs there and sat down beside her. "I will be a good husband to you, Chagak," Kayugh whispered. "I will never hurt you." He slid his hands down Chagak's arms, felt her fingers close over his.

There was a shivering inside of Chagak, something pulling her to him, but the fear was still there, and in the darkness Chagak reached out to touch his face, as if to assure herself that it was Kayugh who was with her, Kayugh who touched her.

He stroked her arms and legs, then moved his hands to her belly, touching her in the same places Man-who-kills had touched her, but with gentleness, fingers moving slowly.

It is what Shuganan wanted me to understand, Chagak thought. That there would be another beginning. Another and another. For each ending a beginning. For every death, new life.

And when Kayugh finally moved over her, lying his full length upon her, Chagak was not afraid.

GLOSSARY OF NATIVE WORDS

AKA:
(Aleut) Up; straight out there.

AMGIGH:
(Aleut — pronounced with undefined vowel syllable between "m" and "g" and unvoiced ending) Blood.

BABICHE:
Lacing made from rawhide. Probably from the Cree word "assababish," a diminutive of "assabab," thread.

CHAGAK:
(Aleut — also; chagagh) Obsidian. (In the Aleut Atkan dialect, red cedar.)

CHIGADAX:
(Aleut — ending unvoiced) A waterproof parka made of sea lion or bear intestines, esophagus of seal or sea lion, or the tongue skin of a whale. The hood had a drawstring and the sleeves were tied at the wrist for sea travel. These knee-length garments were often decorated with feathers and pieces of colored esophagus.

IK:
(Aleut) Open-topped skin boat.

IKYAK, pl. IKYAN:
(Aleut — also, iqyax, pl. iqyas) A canoe-shaped boat made of skins stretched around a wooden frame with an opening in the top for the occupant; a kayak.

KAYUGH:
(Aleut — also, kayux) Strength of muscle; power.

SAMIQ:
(Aleut) Stone dagger or knife.

SHUGANAN:
(Origin and exact meaning obscure) Relating to an ancient people.

SUK:
(Aleut — also, sugh; ending unvoiced) A hoodless parka with a standing collar. These garments were often made of birdskins and could be worn inside out (with the feathers on the inside) for warmth.

TUGIX:
(Aleut) Aorta, large blood vessel.

ULAKIDAQ:
(Aleut) A multitude of dwellings; a group of houses.

ULAQ, pl. ULAS:
(Aleut — also, ulax) A dwelling dug into the side of a hill, raftered with driftwood and/or whale jawbones and thatched with sod and grass.

The native words listed here are defined according to their use in *Mother Earth, Father Sky*. As with many native languages that were recorded by Europeans, there are multiple spellings of almost every word as well as dialectal differences.

AUTHOR'S ACKNOWLEDGMENTS

Mother Earth, Father Sky is not only my book. It belongs to all those who helped me through their encouragement and by sharing their knowledge, special skills and abilities. Though I have done my best to ensure the accuracy of *Mother Earth, Father Sky*, any errors are not the fault of those listed below, but the result of my own interpretation of the information given to me.

My appreciation and my thanks go first of all to my husband, Neil Harrison, who is my partner and closest friend. Without his encouragement I would not have had the courage to continue to believe in myself and my work. Also, my heartfelt appreciation to our children, Neil and Krystal, for their pride in my work and their tolerance of late suppers and a mother who, though sitting beside them, was often nine thousand years away.

My thanks to my parents, Bob and Pat McHaney, who gave many helpful suggestions about the manuscript and taught me to love books and wildlife. To my grandfather, Bob McHaney, Sr., who was my inspiration for Shuganan, my love and thanks.

My sincere gratitude to Dr. William S.

Laughlin, author of *Aleuts: Survivors of the Bering Land Bridge*, whose dig site on Anangula Island was the basis for the fictional village site in my novel, for his graciousness in sending me information and answering my questions concerning his work and his discoveries.

Also my thanks to Mark McDonald, who was an exploration geologist for Tenneco Oil and is now with Scripps Institution of Oceanography. Mark spent many hours answering my questions about geology, topography and climate.

To others who gave time and interest to my project, my thanks and highest regards:

- Dr. David Knowles for his help explaining topographical maps;
- Joan Harrison Morton and Linda McHaney Shelby, both nurses, who answered medical questions;
- Jack McDonald, who took my husband and me on an excursion to collect flint;
- Ruth Neveu, who spent much time finding and ordering research materials through the Lake Superior State University Library;
- Artist Cynthia W. Hook, who drew a map for the novel;
- Tom Harrison, my brother-in-law, a master carver;
- Linda Hudson, also a writer, for her sug-

gestions on the manuscript and her encouragement;

- Gary Kiracofe, scrimshander, for sharing his knowledge about his craft, his collection and his books;
- Forbes McDonald, Dick and Carol Beemer, Dick and Jan Johnson, Richard Hook, Patricia Walker, James Moody, Dennis and Jody Harrison and Jaynce and Gerri Leach who lent me resource materials;
- The writers and staff of the Bay de Noc writers' conferences.

Finally, my most sincere admiration and appreciation to my agent, Rhoda Weyr, and my Doubleday editor, Loretta Barrett. Without them, *Mother Earth, Father Sky* would still be stuck in a desk drawer, a small embarrassment to the author, a book that was rejected numerous times by many people. Everyone has days that are very special to them and are remembered each year. This past year I have added two such days to my calendar, January 16, the day that Rhoda called to tell me she would take me as a client, and April 26, the day that Loretta acquired *Mother Earth, Father Sky* for Doubleday.

OKAVANGO ADVENTURE

OKAVANGO ADVENTURE

In Search of Animals in Southern Africa

JEREMY MALLINSON

Foreword by Gerald Durrell

W · W · NORTON & COMPANY · INC ·

NEW YORK

© Jeremy Mallinson 1973

Library of Congress Cataloging in Publication Data
Mallinson, Jeremy.
    Okavango adventure.

    1. Wild animal collecting—Africa, Southern.
2. Zoology—Africa, Southern. 3. Okavango River.
I. Title.
QL337.S66M34   591'.075   73–16012
ISBN 0–393–08687–9

Printed in the United States of America
1 2 3 4 5 6 7 8 9 0

In fondest memory
of
Tissi and Gub

Contents

Illustrations

ILLUSTRATIONS

Botswana, the territory of *Okavango Adventure*

Foreword

In case anyone should think differently, let me put it on record that I had the greatest difficulty in persuading the author of the book to allow me to write this introduction, so modest is he of his achievement.

This is really a most refreshing and enchanting book. It is that very rare species, a travel-animal book that makes you laugh, for never for a moment does the author take himself too seriously and he has avoided all the pomposity that besets nearly everyone when they start to write up their 'experiences'.

Jeremy Mallinson spikes the story of his adventures with some most endearing self-mockery, but at the same time his obvious concern for and love of animal life shine from his prose. This is the story of a great achievement, for the author, being, as he admits, as green as a baby asparagus when it came to animal collecting, nevertheless organised his trip himself (in itself no mean feat, as I know) and then after many adventures and mistakes – and how *nice* to read a book with the mistakes enumerated and not glossed over – he triumphantly returned with a lovely collection of animals.

Everyone yearning for an animal-collecting career (and if my mail is anything to go by, this includes the entire population of Great Britain) should read, digest and learn from this book. For one can learn from it – everything from the difficulties of force-feeding a kingfisher to attending to the internal wants of a constipated lion. This last, of course, is invaluable information for, as Jeremy Mallinson sagely points out, 'it is not as easy as you might think to give a male lion an enema'.

It will be obvious from this book that all animal life has a staunch, honest and loyal friend in Jeremy Mallinson. I wish there were a few more people like him in the world.

GERALD DURRELL

Animal Flirtation

O N a cold October afternoon I sailed from Tilbury; and began the considerable adventure of an animal-gathering tour of Africa.

Nowadays, of course, a tour of this kind is rather less adventurous than it would have been in the great days of nineteenth-century exploration. But my grandmother, a child of the Victorian age, seemed to think that Africa had changed little since the days of Dr Livingstone: she wrote in great anxiety, warning me against tropical diseases and urging me to take plenty of disinfectants. Her fears were exaggerated: even so, the voyage very nearly did begin with disaster. I had been in touch with the zoo at Pretoria, and had agreed to take them out a pair of European red foxes. The dog fox gave no trouble: I collected him from the Jersey Zoo, where he had outgrown his quarters. But I had to advertise for a vixen, and eventually bought one from some people in Pembrokeshire: she was sent by train, and arrived at Euston so very late that I nearly missed the boat train for Tilbury.

Exhilarated by this hair's breadth escape, I stood on deck as the Union Castle liner pulled away from the dockside and moved off down the Thames estuary, round into the Channel, and on towards the east coast of Africa and eventually to Capetown.

I had an impressive collection of baggage with me. There were collapsible wire cages, and traps, and nets; there was a Red Cross box for emergencies; there were trunks and suitcases, overdue for retirement but sentimentally cherished; there was a typewriter and a tape-recorder. I disposed things as well as I could, lodging my two foxes on the aft upper deck, where a smell like that of a foxes' earth soon began to prevail: this distressed the domestic canines that were also lodged there, but it had the advantage of keeping nosey people at a distance. I soon found that I had to look after my two foxes myself. In theory a member of the crew – curiously called the 'lamp-trimmer' – was supposed to feed all the livestock on board; but he was not allowed to take the foxes out, and he was too timid to clean the kennels out properly when they were occupied. His answer to this problem was to deep-litter them so lavishly that they could hardly stand up. But I had very little trouble. The dog fox was a little aloof and unapproachable; but the vixen, whom I named Pufelli, was very tame and wagged her tail whenever I came near.

Soon we put in at Gibraltar, our first port of call. I went ashore and visited Prince Ferdinand's Battery on the rock to see the famous apes: there are about thirty-five of them. Barbary apes, and apart from *homo sapiens*, they are the only primates to be found in Europe. I found them an entertaining sight: peering about them from under the heavy prominent brows that protect their eyes from the fierce winds of the Rock, they reminded me of so many sea captains, scanning nautical horizons from under peaked caps. The greyish-brown adults would pester visitors for food, while the black-furred infants developed the arts of mischief to a high degree of perfection.

I went back to the town and astonished the shopkeepers with a problem rather unusual among souvenir-hunting tourists: I needed some wood-wool. This aroused a good deal of curiosity, and I explained that I needed it to provide extra bedding for my foxes on the *Warwick Castle*, since they had suffered a rough time in the Bay of Biscay. The fourth shop that I tried was able to oblige, and I returned to the ship with a huge sack of the stuff on my shoulder, looking rather as though I had been buying tax-free luxury goods in quantity.

We resumed our voyage, and as we cruised through the

Lions: (*above*) Timmy, the dwarf lion; (*below*) Chinky, 'What is that photographer's name?'

(*above*) 'Chinky, you are a messy drinker, don't deny it!' (*below*) Self, Chinky, my father. My only picture of Chinky showing her great size. My father happened to be 'in town'.

Mediterranean, I persuaded the First Officer to let me exercise Pufelli along the passenger deck. He was intrigued. 'First time I've seen one of those damned animals so close,' he said, 'usually they're all torn to shreds by the time I catch up with the hounds.' Pufelli flattened her ears and curled her lips in a snarl, as if recognising an enemy of her species. 'Beautiful animals, really, when you get a close look at them,' the First Officer went on; and added defensively, 'You've got to remember that if they weren't preserved for hunting, there wouldn't *be* any foxes – they'd all be shot or poisoned by the farmers.' Pufelli was plainly in no mood to accept this familiar argument: she showed her fangs and growled until the enemy moved away, and then wagged her tail in relief.

At Port Said I had the chance of varying the foxes' somewhat monotonous diet. There, in the ship's lounge, a magnificent conjuring show was staged by the famous gully-gully men; and it was astonishing to see how they could produce day-old chicks from a man's beard or a young lady's blouse or the middle of a pack of cards. The show was excellent, but the chicks were in a bad way; so I approached one of the men afterwards, and asked him to quote me a price for them. Presumably he thought that I wanted to eat them myself, and he assured me that there was no meat on them, none at all. He had a much better commodity on offer: 'You buy postcards?' he asked hopefully, ferreting in a leather bag and bringing out some extremely unladylike specimens. But eventually after some argument I convinced him that I did want the chicks, and we agreed on a price of 1s 6d for each stringy and breathless little bird.

In view of their supper that night my foxes may have come to think of Port Said as a gourmet's paradise.

Each day the orange glow of the dawn would appear slowly on the horizon of the Gulf of Aden, and soon afterwards the flying fish would appear, dancing tirelessly in the ship's wake The temperature rose rapidly and almost unendurably, until the top deck – cooled by the wind of the ship's movement – was the only comfortable place to be. So on we ploughed, through the gulf, round and down towards Mombasa, passing the arid coast of Somaliland, where the blinding whiteness of the sandy shore contrasted splendidly with the sapphire blue of the sea.

During these carefree days I had time to reflect on how I had spent the seven or so years since leaving school, and on the reason why I wanted to gather together a collection of animals during my forthcoming travels in Africa.

Two years in the Rhodesia and Nyasaland Staff Corps had convinced me that I was not cut out for a military career; but during this period I had travelled widely – in the Congo, in Northern and Southern Rhodesia, in Nyasaland, and in the Union of South Africa. In those countries I came to love the African continent, with its countless and fascinating species of mammals and birds; and I started to worry about the dangers which threatened many of these species as 'civilisation' intruded upon their ancient territories.

On my return to my home in Jersey I had been rather bewildered by the number of careers open to me and it was difficult to make a sensible choice between the various options. A family wine and spirit business, the Hong Kong Police, and tea planting in Assam would have all given me financial security, but there was something undefinably wrong with all of them. Considering this question seriously, examining the depths of my own mind and heart, I soon found out what was the matter: none of those admirable careers offered any scope for what I really wanted to do, for the greatest satisfaction that I had so far discovered in life. Somehow, on whatever terms, I needed to be working with animals. They could be wild or they could be domesticated; but in one way or another there had to be animals at the centre of my life.

So my destiny had crystallised. For me, those two years in Africa had been like a party which you attend in vague sociability, and there find yourself gazing into a new pair of eyes, and realise afterwards that life is never going to be the same again. But always, after some first moment of vision and vocation, one finds oneself brought down to earth with a bump. In the British Isles, I decided, livestock farming represented the obvious way of being involved with animals, and, although I found this interesting, and seventy-six cows kept me actively engaged for eight healthy months, I decided that it was not quite what I was looking for.

A three-month course in kennel management in the heart of Surrey was much more to my liking, and when the course came to an end, I felt that my vocation was now clear. I would return to Jersey and establish my own kennels there: I would breed dogs of every kind for the connoisseur, while keeping some of them to be my lifelong friends. My search for a suitable property was handicapped by the failure to get the necessary planning permission to build. Frustrated, I decided to take a temporary job until I could get this matter sorted out.

As often in people's lives, a casually taken temporary job turned out to be a major and decisive turning point in my life. I signed on for nothing more than brief summer employment at the newly created Jersey Zoological Park, the embryo of what later became Gerald Durrell's Jersey Wildlife Preservation Trust. I knew nothing about wild animals or the life of the zoo keeper, but I thought that in this environment I could become more widely acquainted with the animal kingdom, and especially with the possibilities of genuine relationships between man and beast.

I was soon to come under the spell of Gerald Durrell, and became totally captivated with the whole idea of breeding and the study of animals in captivity. I therefore put aside my ambition to work with dogs, and served for some two and a half years on the zoo staff; first working with tropical birds, and then with mammals.

Throughout the whole of this time my knowledge of the animal kingdom developed rapidly, and I accumulated a fairsized library, over which I spent many hours of my free time. There was so much to learn, and I began to regret the time that I had wasted in Africa. There I had been, in one of the world's great reservoirs of wildlife, and I had missed practically all my opportunities for learning about it.

Gradually, but on an increasing scale, thoughts of this kind began to haunt my mind. Anybody who has been there will tell you that Africa has a way of getting into the bloodstream and obsessing the mind; now it started to pull me. Fortunately these sentiments coincided with a small legacy, not a fortune, but enough to finance an animal-collecting expedition of my own. I had a lot of friends in southern Africa who could be counted upon to help me in such an enterprise. I was single, twenty-four years old, without ties. What was to hold me back? Thanks to the long-sighted kindness of Gerald Durrell, I was given every encouragement, as well as leave of absence, with the assurance that when I returned, my job would still be available if I wanted it.

At Mombasa I left the ship as I wanted to see something of the East African game reserves before going south to start my animal collection. The foxes were supposed to stay on board until Durban; but they were both feeling the heat rather badly, so I took them ashore with me and sent them off to Pretoria by air.

Soon I was installed in The Moorings, a small hotel in Mombasa. It had been raining almost continuously for three weeks, and the air was full of the intoxicating warm earthy smell of the African wet season. Parts of Kenya, in fact, were in a state of emergency: the rains had caused the River Tana to overflow, isolating a number of tribes, destroying crops extensively, and cutting communications by road and rail.

But none of this came home to me as I sat at breakfast enjoying my first contacts with the birds and animals of Africa, thinking already of capture. There were African pied crows, a dazzle of black and white as they quarrelled over worms and the crusts and crumbs of my breakfast; there were countless lizards, utterly motionless and then flicking across the polished floor of the verandah when the hotel's terrier came after them. On my second evening a cream-faced African hedgehog climbed into my bedroom and on to my mosquito net, digging its quills in as though it sought my intimate company. I soon felt that a month in this hotel would bring me all I wanted, and might even pay for my trip; but I had larger plans than that.

I walked under the palm trees, the red soil dyeing my shoes; I passed bare-footed Africans, smiling in the warm torrents of rain; frogs were chorusing from the overflowing storm gutters: I felt a love of Africa, a feeling that I belonged there. The colour and history of the place were all about me. There was Fort Jesus, built by the Portuguese and the scene of many bloody battles in the past, later used as a prison by the British, now a museum; ancient cannons were still mounted as though to command the old harbour; picturesque dhows brought in their cargoes of dates, raw salt, spices; the streets were crowded and jostling with Indians, Africans, Europeans; and the Mombasa Club still stood there, a monument to colonialism, with its polished floors, its silently moving servants, and its fine array of English sporting periodicals all set out on a long polished table beneath a revolving fan. Many worlds met here.

But I had to move on, and I took a night train to Nairobi. There I met the sad news that the Nairobi National Park was closed because of the floods. This was a blow. It had been my main intention to collect animals in what was then called Southern Rhodesia; but before that I had hoped to see the major national parks in East Africa, proceeding south from Nairobi, in the first instance, by the road to Arusha. This road was now closed; so I decided to wait until conditions improved, and in the meantime, to accept the kindly offered hospitality of a coffee farmer who lived at Ruiru, near Nairobi.

Even here conditions were damp and difficult. A nearby river was in spate, and its muddy waters rampaged through the vegetation: weaver birds found their beautifully woven nests destroyed and their eggs lost, and they flew about in agitation and grief.

Wandering near this farm I saw a tubular roll of bark suspended from the lower branches of a blue gum tree; and in my curiosity I prodded it with a stick. This rash action was rewarded at once by the emergence of several very angry squadrons of wild bees, which zoomed after me at full power in the best traditions of Fighter Command. I managed to get away; and later I discovered that tubular beehives of this kind were a speciality that originated with the Wakambo tribe. Seasoned bark would be rolled up, rather like a brandy snap, packed with leaves of a kind that the bees found alluring, and then hung up from some tree to attract useful tenants: I would have been more careful if I had known about this, and about the fact that while these wild bees always hate to be disturbed, they are particularly touchy during the rainy season. This was not the only occasion on which I picked on the hardest way of learning some fairly simple lesson.

Here I was, then, on a large spacious farm: a farmhouse, and a thousand acres of planted coffee around it. Even so, there was an atmosphere of siege, a hangover from Mau Mau days: the windows were barred like those of a top-security jail, there was a locked armoury built into a wall, the dogs were trained to let no African on to the premises apart from the permanent house staff, and even they had to be outside when the nightly ritual of locking and checking took place. But during the day things were easier: I saw the coffee beans drying in the sun, spread out along strips of matting, line after line of them, while groups of Africans worked industriously and contentedly, grading and packing the beans. So far this area had not been affected by the activities of the land-freedom army.

I brooded over the troubles that men make for one another, and for the animal world as well. Nature may be red in tooth and claw, but at least she is innocent of racial, religious, and political hatreds: the wild animals of Africa have no worries apart from the task of feeding themselves in the coolness of the early morning and then again in the evening, with the heat of the day spent in shady relaxation. In Nairobi I visited an exhibition that had been promoted by the East African Wildlife Society: they had taken over a big shop window and were displaying a collection of animal snares that had been confiscated from Africans and were forbidden by the very humane game laws. The idea was to educate people – to make them see how cruel and barbaric these snares were. But it worked out rather differently. A great many Africans came to see the exhibition, some of them from remote places; but it was found that they were returning to their villages and compounds with drawings of the various snares on display, being very glad of this chance to improve their own snaring techniques. The exhibition was hastily closed.

I spent a fortnight at the coffee farm; and then, since the road to Arusha in the south was still inaccessible because of the continuing torrential rains, I decided to change my plans. Kisumu, to the north-west of Nairobi, is on the shore of Lake Victoria : if I went there by train, I should be able to continue southwards by water. From Kisumu the MV *Victoria* took me around the north of the lake and then southwards on the Ugandan side to Mwanza (Tanzania) : it was here, just over a hundred years previously – in the early morning of 3 August, 1858 – that John Henning Speke became the first white man to set eyes on the immense stretch of inland water, later naming it after his sovereign.

To get to Southern Rhodesia (Rhodesia) I travelled by train, bus and lorry by way of Tabora, Itigi and Mbeya, then over the border into Northern Rhodesia (Zambia) and by way of Ndola to Lusaka. I had been there before, during the emergency of 1956, when I was attached to the Northern Rhodesia Regiment. So I revisited the barracks opposite Government House, and after having renewed my acquaintance with the regiment's mascots, two Kavirondo crane, I went to see the adjutant in the hope that he had some type of vehicle travelling south to Salisbury. My luck was in, a seven-ton Army Bedford was leaving that very evening, and as an ex-regular myself, I was given permission to travel in it.

A light easterly breeze cooled the cab of the Bedford as we descended to the one-span suspension bridge at Chirundu which spans the Zambezi between Northern and Southern Rhodesia – now, between Zambia and Rhodesia. Frogs piped us on board the bridge : nightjars flew up in our faces as though from underground. The world-famous mosquitoes at Chirundu could not get at us while the truck still moved. But they got their

chance when we stopped on the bridge beneath its great structure to gaze upon the river and the light bush of the escarp-
ment: I have seldom been so extensively eaten.

Then, with the two NCOs, we motored on southwards
through the night, while I learnt a first-hand account of the
sad story of the Central African Federation, and the rather
gloomy prospects for the people of those lands, white and
black alike. I was dropped in the heart of Salisbury at Old
Meikles Hotel, where I shaved, breakfasted, and feeling suitably
invigorated I hired a vehicle to take me out to the Mazoe/
Glendale area of Southern Rhodesia where I had been invited
to set up my base.

CHAPTER 2

The First Quarry

DOUET Farm sprawled across the top of a small kopje: a long building roofed with thatch of varying antiquity, with a brick chimney at each end, tilting and precarious.

I was greeted by Major Robin Falla, my host, a tall hefty man with deep-set eyes and a jovial sort of face. As he strode around, his broad shoulders aggressively braced, he put me in mind of a gorilla: at any moment (it seemed) he might start to beat his chest in a fine display of threat and challenge. In point of fact Robin was much more likely to offer you his kingdom than to exclude you from it. He was an old soldier, an officer successively in three different armies – the Jersey Militia, the British Army and the Indian Army. With this last career cut short by Indian independence, he came with his family to settle here in Rhodesia and to wage war upon the bush. Already this campaign was succeeding, a profitable tobacco and dairy farm emerging from the raw countryside.

Immediately, before I was even allowed to enter the house, Robin led me to see his three large tobacco barns, home built with home-baked bricks. They were tall buildings, faintly ecclesiastical, cathedral like: in two of them I saw a maze of horizontal blue gum poles above my head, with tobacco leaves draped over them, extending upwards like a thatch as far as I could see. Heat rose from flues below – ultimately, from a coal furnace outside – and caressed these leaves until they attained the pallid jaundice-like yellow colour that showed them to be fully cured.

All this was interesting enough; but for me, the third barn was the important one. Here the flues had been removed: the place was empty, and Robin was offering it to me as temporary accommodation for whatever animals I might catch. He only stipulated that any lions brought in should be kept away from his cattle.

This was great kindness on his part and a most practical suggestion. The height of the building was not really essential for my purpose, but its spaciousness was exactly what I needed. At once I started to divide it up mentally into runs and cages, daydreaming of wonderful success, of countless extraordinary animals filling this place and needing eventually to be transferred into travelling cages, and then shipped home, and then... My mind went racing ahead, but I pulled it up sharply, reminding myself that I had no experience and no certainty at all of catching anything. The whole expedition might still be a failure, with no animal smells coming to challenge the tobacco smells of this splendid barn.

Then we went to the farmhouse, and I was introduced to the family, to Robin's wife Pris, and their two children Roselle and James. There was the nicest kind of welcome, and then we all sat outside on the *stoep* or verandah, enjoying the fresh air and the evening breeze, protected by screens from the countless insects which were attracted by the light but had to whine frustratedly outside.

Whisky was brought, and they drank a toast to the magnificent collection that I was to assemble. Just then a kitten ran out from under the sofa, leapt into the air, pounced upon a disembowelled slipper that was lying beside me, and started to savage it murderously. Ordinary kittenish behaviour, you might think; but this was no ordinary kitten, it was a young serval which they had found on the farm a month or so earlier, orphaned and alone. Soon she dropped the slipper to consider me: her long ears flicked with curiosity, and she watched every movement I made, narrowly and suspiciously. I held out my hand invitingly, but she ignored it and returned to finish off the slipper: a lovely creature, her yellow-golden coat

28

marked with irregular brown to black spots, her short tail swishing.

'Well, and what's going to be your first victim?' asked Robin, in the smart regimental manner of a senior officer at an order-group. Dismayed, cornered, I gulped at my whisky. What could I say? I cudgelled my brain. Should I confess that... well, that I'd been wholly absorbed by the business of travel during these last few weeks, and that my *precise* itinerary and plan were – well, a shade imperfect in detail, and that perhaps...? I could hardly answer truthfully, and say that I intended to catch anything that came along and proved catchable: the build up had been too colourful for that, I was typed already as the intrepid hunter with some masterful plan of conquest. There was a danger of anticlimax and disillusionment.

Possibly Robin thought that I was hesitating because my plans were too grand and complex to be explained easily. Or possibly not. At any rate, he came to my rescue with a list of suggestions: 'Serval cat, caracal, jackal, hunting dogs, civets, genets, mongoose, porcupines, wild pig – there's lots of that kind of stuff around the farm, you could pick them up pretty easily.' He spoke apologetically, as though I had bigger stuff in mind and would hardly be bothered by these rats and mice and such small deer. But I cheered up: if these animals were so easy to find, I was not going to be embarrassed by an empty tobacco barn.

Our glasses were refuelled and clinked together. The serval kitten, tired of that slipper, decided to attack my feet instead: first she tore at my laces, then she lay back and fought my socks, kicking and scratching furiously. It was agony: I forced myself to remember that I was a great lover of animals, and used the whisky as an anaesthetic.

The evening proceeded. At sundown Roselle and James were put to bed: three hours later Pris followed them; but Robin and I stayed up, with the drinks that were nominally 'sundowners' continuing to flow. My arrival, Robin explained, made this a special occasion: I was to find that every evening at Douet Farm was, on one pretext or another, a special occa-

sion. Eventually, by way of a climax to the evening, Robin
stood up formally by the fire in his shorts and shirt and told
an African house boy to bring in the farm's mascot. I cringed
in instinctive terror: my head was swimming, and my legs
and feet were suffering horribly from the serval kitten's attentions. What kind of animal would be inflicted upon me now?
I looked around for an escape route; but at that moment the
door crashed open, and 170 lb of African bush pig rocketed
into the room. This was Porky, a formidable mascot indeed:
bulky, covered with coarse wiry red-brown bristles, white
bristled on his face, his ears tufted. He stood downwind of me;
backed a little, as though to break cover before charging; and
then trotted forward in all gentleness to sniff my hand, his
eyes bright and friendly, his grin and grunt most charming.

I breathed again.

So Robin and I drank some more toasts, naming countless
animals that must be included in the collection; and then he
took his lamp – there was no electricity – and led me down a
whitewashed corridor to bed. We left Porky snoring under
the table in a rather pig-like manner, but the serval kitten
followed me, fighting my shoe-laces to the last. I felt that I
was taking part in some dream or pantomime of Africa: my
host bade me goodnight, the lamp went out with a hiss that
terrified the serval out of her wits, and I collapsed into a
series of dreams, each one ending with the escape of some
animal from my keen pursuit.

The morning came, and with it the secretary of the local
farming club. There were two ideas in his mind. For one thing,
some porcupines had been making a mess of his front lawn;
and since there was a well-known professional hunter staying
in the district, perhaps I wouldn't mind catching them? Then,
would I give a talk to the monthly meeting of the local farmers
at the country club? I accepted the first of these invitations at
once: it sounded as if it might be good sport to dig out crested
porcupines and net them – or try to net them – when they
made a run for it. But to lecture a crowd of Rhodesian
farmers... this was quite a different matter. I had only spoken

in public once, as best man at my brother's wedding: once was enough, and in any case I could hardly speak with authority on the catching of wild animals when I had never caught one in my life. I drew breath to explain this, when Robin interposed to say that this was an *excellent* idea, and that he would have some members round for drinks afterwards. The matter was out of my hands, it seemed.

The farmers' secretary said that he'd come back after lunch and take me to where these porcupines had dug themselves in, so that I could mount my assault upon them. Meanwhile, Robin and I took the Land-Rover and went off to the compound in search of an African who could be my assistant.

It was an unpromising search. The track swung sharply round a clump of blue gum trees, and there in front of us was a scattering of small mud hovels. African women leant against their doorposts with folded arms: listless children tumbled everywhere among the dogs and hens that scratched and scuffled in the dust. The boss boy, Moses by name, raised a mud-encrusted bush hat, spat violently, bellowed out to his fellows, and assembled a group of them for my approval and choice.

I knew what sort of man I wanted, and by no stretch of the imagination could any of these be regarded as filling the bill. I asked Robin whether there were any alternative prospects, but he wasn't hopeful: it was almost impossible to get reliable labour without patiently sifting through an enormous number of candidates. So, on his advice, I settled for John Carpenter, from Mozambique and mission educated, whose self-chosen surname indicated his qualifications and skill. He would, he said, be able to make all the cages I needed. (In my experience, such claims need to be taken with a big pinch of salt. Cut them down by fifty per cent, and you get something like the real picture.)

With that problem solved for the time being at least, I continued my conducted tour of Robin's farm. Its border on the west was a small tributary of the Mazoe River, and we drove by this stream, its red muddy waters running deep in this sixth week of the rainy season. A hammerheaded stork – locally called a hammerkop – was standing in the shallows: disturbed by the noise of the car, it flew up into its big ramshackle nest of twigs. On we drove, needing to use four-wheel drive on some of the lower tracks: I was shown the pump house, from which large galvanised tanks of water were taken daily to the farm buildings by tractor and trailer, and eventually we came back to the house.

We had seldom been out of sight of it: together with the tobacco barns, it stood on the highest point for some distance around, commanding wide views not only of the farm but of the uncultivated bush around it. Because of this strong position, it had been chosen by the local security forces to be a rallying point for all the women and children of the neighbourhood in the event of any dangerous emergency. I was shown two ten-foot numbers made up of bricks that had been sunk into the earth and whitewashed: it was their function to make the farm easily identifiable from the air. Under heavy penalties each farmer had the legal duty of marking his farm with such numbers, and of keeping them weeded and whitewashed for easy visibility.

After lunch I felt a sense of occasion. A big moment was coming. So far it had all been travel and preparation: now I was to start the actual job, the actual collecting of real animals.

I left Douet Farm with the farmers' secretary and also with John Carpenter: we had four nets, two spades, and a pickaxe. The car twisted and bumped along the strip roads, the country dotted with rocks and little clumps of vegetation in between the rich tobacco lands of the European farmers.

I felt a shade nervous. Nobody can say that I wasn't well educated: even so, I had never qualified in porcupine catching. The nearest thing in England would be the badger, which lives in a very similar sort of earth: but the nature walks of my schooldays had not led up to even an ordinary level certificate in badger trapping. I would have to rely upon whatever hunting instincts I had inherited from my prehistoric ancestors.

I was shown the big hole that was (presumably) the porcupines' front door: it was guarded by a cloud of midges. In this kind of situation the great thing is to appear to know what you're doing. So I rapped out a business-like command, and told John to fetch me a long flexible stick, which he immediately did, at the cost of heavy damage to some cultivated shrubs nearby; and then I flung myself down and prodded far into the dark dirty hole.

Vaguely in my mind was a notion that every such earth had two holes, a front door and a back door. The task was easy: you just had to light a fire at one hole and wait with your nets at the other. The trouble was that there *was* no second hole. So I improvised a different plan, thereby displaying the initiative and attack that has always marked the British officer in his country's hour of need: we would dig a series of shafts down into successive stretches of the tunnel, using my long stick as a kind of range-finder or target indicator. Spades were fetched, and two of the 'boys' from this farm got cheerfully to work. I had staked my nets over the hole: the midges flew through it freely, but a porcupine (I calculated) would not.

I seemed to have underestimated the whole business. It took nearly an hour of sweating and grunting before this first shaft was completed: it had to be a big shaft if I was to reach down into it with my sapling and feel out the direction of the tunnel's next stretch, and there were a lot of tough tangled roots to be dug through. And so far, we had only moved eight feet along the winding tunnel, or a mere five feet as measured directly.

Somewhat daunted, I marked the spot for the second shaft and netted the first. The pickaxe was now brought into action to help the spades, and the steady pounding of metal into hard earth was accompanied by the increasingly loud grunts of the African diggers, as they drew breath after every stroke. To them it was an entirely pointless exercise.

The second shaft was only a little deeper than the first, but it took nearly twice as long to dig. Like a good officer I was ready to share in the men's hardships, so I took my turn at the digging: this showed that I had the right attitude but it wasn't impressive otherwise. However, we were making progress: at any rate the tunnel was getting narrower and the midges were getting more and more interested, which presumably meant something. The light was fading, however: should we finish three shafts and then call it a day? My farmer friend thought not: he would bring lanterns if it got too dark.

I felt uncertain. Were there really porcupines down this tunnel? There was certainly a pungent smell of dung and decay: if nothing was living there now, something had been living there recently. So I rallied my troops to further exertions, in spite of their increasing gloom. The smell got worse, and my hopes revived. Suddenly, when the third shaft was nearly finished, we heard a loud furious hissing sound, as though compressed air or steam was escaping through a leaky valve. Everybody turned enquiringly to the expert: unfortunately I had never heard the noise made by a porcupine, but I felt sure that it wasn't like this. So the two Africans climbed out of the shaft and I climbed in: the bottom gave way at once, and my feet plunged into the tunnel, narrowly missing something that clawed and spat at me savagely and then dashed along the tunnel, past the second shaft and the first, to end up tangled and fighting in the net that we had staked over the original hole.

It was a small African wild cat, a creature not unlike the wild cat of Scotland, with tabby markings on a light orange-yellow coat and black rings round the legs and the rather short tail. There was total fury upon its black-striped face: if it had been able to wriggle past the net! But there it was, tangled and trapped. I wrapped another net round it for extra safety, and told the boys that they would get a good *bonseller* for the day's work. As a campaign against porcupines it had failed, but I was satisfied with the result.

I carried my bundle carefully into the farmhouse to show it to the farmer secretary, sending for the one crate that I had at the ready. I shut the doors and windows carefully to prevent any escape bid, and then, alone with John, I cautiously began work on the struggling bundle. John backed nervously against the door: the cat was twisting and striking in all directions at (*above*) An armful of orangs; (*right*) Clio, my Chacma Baboon.

With N'Pongo, a lowland gorilla: (*above*) 'I believe there is some pâté de maison inside this.' (*centre*) 'Well, give me some!'; (*below*) '*That* was worth while!'

once; it was in a mood for real trouble, and I felt nervous myself. But I managed to keep the initiative, manipulating the net so that the brute never quite got its balance: I bellowed to John to face the music, and together we managed to get it crated without bloodshed.

The farmer came in to see what we'd achieved, and rashly put his face rather close to the wire mesh which provided ventilation for the crate: he must have been surprised to find himself very nearly being mauled by a wild cat where he had expected to see a porcupine. I started to apologise for my failure, but he insisted on congratulating me: he had lost a lot of poultry recently, and I had caught the killer. So I felt free to join in the general excitement. John was anxious to go off and tell the other 'boys' about his courageous single-handed achievement; I gave him some beer money to share around, and told him to be back in half an hour.

An hour later there was still no sign of him, and the farmer and I started back to Douet without him. 'What was the first animal you ever caught?' I was asked as we drove along. I could hardly explain that it was the very animal that was now with us in the car: so I laughed the question off with the suggestion of a juvenile mousetrap, and was glad to find that the farmer wasn't going to take the matter further. It's never kind to disillusion people.

The next morning, just after sunrise, I sauntered down to the tobacco barns at Douet to have another look at the founder member of my collection. There by the barns sat John, looking extremely sheepish and red about the eyes: he probably expected to get the sack. I took a firm line and explained that as he plainly couldn't carry his liquor, he wasn't to touch it – except on his days off – while he was in my employ. He had paid for his orgy with an exhaustingly long walk.

Twelve hours in the crate had not brought the cat to any state of resignation: it lunged at me through the wires. But when Robin appeared, with his loud booming voice, it crouched back in terror.

'Ah,' said Robin, 'you'll have to find it a mate. What sex is

37

this one?' I agreed that it was important to ascertain its sex and then to find a mate, though I couldn't see how either task could be done. So I deferred this problem diplomatically. This crate was too small to be used except for a very short time: I had better go into Salisbury with John to buy some materials to make proper travelling cages to house a general collection. This cat's love life could wait.

I had bought a Vanguard ¾-ton pick-up, and John and I went bouncing along the strip roads until we reached a proper tarmac surface on the outskirts of Salisbury. I bought a good deal of two-by-two timber, many sheets of plywood, some wire mesh, and packets of screws, hinges, nails, catches, and locks. Then I called in at the Salisbury Museum and met Mr Reay Smithers, who was the director of Rhodesian museums, and also his deputy, Dr Brain. Mr Smithers told me that he had a good collection of waterfowl at his home, which I was welcome to inspect before I left the country; Dr Brain had a collection of live vervet monkeys and was studying them. Altogether they were most helpful: they even offered me a pair of black-backed jackals, on condition that I removed them at once.

Things were certainly moving: it was only the second day of my task, and already I had two jackals and a wild cat. I began to believe in my assumed character of an expert trapper.

So John and I loaded the pick-up with all the materials and the crated jackals. To judge by the noise they made they didn't recognise salvation when it came: they had been brought in by a farmer for the museum, and if I hadn't come at that precise moment they would very soon have been stuffed.

I drove back to Douet with a powerful feeling of success, half expecting various wild animals to leap aboard the pick-up and demand to be caged. On the way, just as we were approaching a small African settlement of mushroom shaped huts, a hen came charging across the road and collided heavily with the Vanguard. The impact proving fatal, we were immediately surrounded by a crowd of aggrieved Africans, loud in their claim for compensation. There were the makings of an ugly scene; so I leant back and slapped the sides of the jackals' box, from which a fearsome noise came at once. The villagers backed away nervously, expecting a pack of mad dogs to be set upon them: even John, safe in the cab, wound up the window. Having thus re-established my mastery over things, I pressed ten shillings into the hand of a wizened old lady by way of compensation for the deceased hen, and drove on.

Back at Douet Farm I made it my first task to get the jackals out of their crate and into a spacious run. So we got to work in the tobacco barn, and managed to wire off one corner with six-foot wire, fixing the top of this to the lowest of the blue gum poles that were meant to carry drying tobacco. Then, after unloading our timber and other materials into the barn, we brought the crate across and introduced the jackals to their new home. They seemed to prefer the security of the crate, which was hardly surprising, since my wild cat expressed her dislike of them in a very threatening way.

Robin was deeply impressed with what I'd achieved. 'Dammit, man, just a couple of days, and you've got half the animal kingdom already!' We sat long over our drinks, and he told me many stories of his tiger-shooting adventures and escapades in India – small stuff, as he confessed, when compared to my own heroic work.

The early morning is the best time for hunting and trapping, and I decided that I would have to cut down on these over-lubricated late nights, deeply enjoyable though they were. So I turned to the deployment of the traps that I had brought from England, and for the next few days I made a point of rising early to see what treasure they held for me.

They were big wire traps, tunnel shaped, with a hook in the middle from which some appetising bait could be suspended. Beneath this hook was a treacherous platform, which, when trodden upon, would release a spring mechanism so that doors were instantly clicked and locked shut at each end of the tunnel. I set these traps each night, varying the bait from eggs to raw meat to fruit to seeds: each morning I would approach them breathlessly on tiptoe, which was a bit pointless – if

I'd caught anything, no amount of noise would frighten it away. But I never had caught anything: there was the trap each time, untouched, the bait still there.

Robin came to my rescue. 'I don't want to teach my grandmother to suck eggs; but you could do what the Indians do – smear the traps with animal dung. Sorry, I'm being silly: you've probably got some good reason for wanting the traps to have a human smell.' 'Yes, of course I know about that technique,' I said hastily: 'but before doing that, I thought I might experiment a bit with – well, I shan't bother you with the details now, it's rather technical.' 'Sorry,' said Robin, 'you know best.'

The next time, therefore, I did that rather unpleasant smearing; the traps stank all right afterwards, and not of humankind. I also sprinkled their floors with earth, so as to conceal the difference between the trip-platforms and the rest; and I camouflaged the tops and sides. I did all this, including the arrangement of the bait, with gloved hands. Nobody could say I didn't know my job.

I set the traps now in a part of the farm where there were a good many boulders; and I noticed among them some very brightly coloured lizards, which basked peacefully in the sun until I came near, but then flashed away into crevices in these rocks. Presumably they hadn't met an animal trapper before, but they were taking no chances and always got away. I was intrigued by this challenge and by the lizards themselves, and after setting my traps, I went back to the farm to make a kind of butterfly-net which might defeat them.

I made a big one, and returned to my hunting ground in the afternoon with my mind wholly upon lizards. I had almost forgotten my traps until a sudden noise from one of them caught my attention. I ran up and saw a slender weasel-like animal inside, with a brown body and a long tail tipped with black: on seeing me it panicked, running up and down the trap in a frenzy. I picked the trap up carefully, making sure that my hands were safe from angry teeth, and walked the half mile back to the barn.

There I found John engaged in some low-speed carpentry: he grinned guiltily when he saw me. I put the trap down – the jackals were deeply interested in this strong-smelling new arrival – told John what kind of cage I wanted now, and went off to the farmhouse in search of *Mammals of Central Africa*, by Asterly Maberly. This useful book made it clear that my guest was a mongoose – the slender mongoose, to judge by its shape in the picture. I had never seen one before, so I took the book back to confirm this identification.

It took us two hours to complete a cage for the mongoose. John wanted to nail everything, which was easier, but I insisted on screws. He certainly looked the part of a carpenter, with a pencil behind his ear, a piece of paper with lines and numbers in one hand, a hammer or screwdriver in the other. But his actual performance was less impressive; and when the mongoose cage was finished, complete with its front of machine-made wire mesh, it was necessary to put plugs of wood into the gaps between the wire and the frame. Otherwise the animal could have simply walked out. But John was very pleased with himself: to sober him up I said that if the mongoose got away he would have to recapture it himself.

The cage was now ready, but the mongoose decided to stay in the trap. I coaxed, I pleaded, I tilted the trap: I even put a couple of eggs into the cage as an inducement. But he sat fast, glaring at me. This time my problem was solved for me by one of the jackals: it sprang at the wire of its enclosure, and the noise caused the mongoose to leap forward in panic and into the cage, where I had the door shut upon him in an instant.

Now there were four animals in the barn. I saw that I would soon need more cages, and I begged John to apply himself more seriously to the art of carpentry. I didn't want to have my collection escaping: I envisaged having a lot of them before long, varied and valuable. But now luck seemed to turn against me. However carefully I baited and camouflaged my traps, however richly aromatic the dung with which I anointed them, they remained obstinately empty. As for the lizards ... their agility, so pleasing to behold, proved to be a trapper's utter frustration. I would creep up upon them clutching my butterfly-net and admiring the red and blue and yellow and orange of their spots and stripes: they sat immobile on the scorching rock in their trendy gear, apparently asleep or unaware, and it looked too easy, but their radar was in perfect order, and they always flicked away at precisely the last micro-second. Soon I gave up, and returned to the animals I already had. Who *wants* lizards, anyway?

I would rise at 6.30 each morning and go down to see my collection. The jackals and the mongoose ate well and seemed to accept their destiny, but the wild cat refused to touch food or to accept my friendship, spitting with incurable hatred instead. In theory John helped me with the task of cleaning out the cages and watering and feeding the animals: in practice he seemed so frightened of all animals that I had to do nearly all the work, while he just passed plates and shovels and so forth to me from a very safe distance, grinning nervously. But by breakfast-time each day the job was done, leaving the rest of the day free for other activities.

For John there was the simple task of cage building. But as well as persevering with my traps, I had to look ahead: if I was to export animals from the Federation, there would be permits to get and arrangements to make. So I made a trip to Salisbury for those purposes; I had to see the Game Depart-ment, the Veterinary Department, and the people at the airline office. Everybody was very helpful, but the airline's freight manager was baffled by the vagueness of my plans. He wanted to know the exact weights and dimensions of every crate: but although I had been fairly successful so far, I had no means of estimating the scale on which I would eventually be flying my private menagerie out of the country. It might be huge, it might be very small. These details would have to wait.

Meanwhile, rumour seemed to be telling all Salisbury about my activities, and I found myself confronted by an anxious and quick-talking young reporter who – in the intervals of covering the tobacco auctions – wanted to know about myself and my background, and how I had first achieved the success which made me now a well-known professional trapper. Embarrassed once again, I changed the subject, and told him that I had once been a regular soldier in the Rhodesian and Nyasaland Staff Corps. He scented a story at once: EX-RHODESIAN SOLDIER TURNS BIG GAME HUNTER, 'BRING 'EM BACK ALIVE,' SAYS EX-RHODESIAN REGULAR, and such other headlines were plainly in his mind as his pencil flew. I tried to get him interested also in the study of wild animals, their care and breeding in captivity, the importance of conservation, and such subjects; but his mind was already back in the tobacco auction rooms, and he gulped down his beer, shook my hand, and was off at high speed.

On my way back to Glendale I called in upon Mike and Winky Smoelke, who were friends of Robin and Pris partly because they had similar pets. (Even in England, I have noticed that people often become specially friendly with those who have the same unusual breed of dog.) We had afternoon tea on the verandah while the three cats of the household chased around in a suitably crazy cat-like fashion. Two of them were serval cats, well domesticated by now, while the third can only be described in contradictory terms: it was a tame wild cat. All three, however, were tame only in respect of their owners: they would not allow anybody else to touch them, and I was careful not to try. But they were lovely to watch, with their agile leapings and their mad games; and I could easily imagine how they could kill small antelopes – duikers, for example – with those powerful legs and teeth. I studied the wild cat with particular interest, not having seen one in the adult state before: I hoped that my own kitten would exhaust its present ferocity and become as friendly as this one.

Then one of the farm boys brought in a 'legervarn' or rock monitor. Mike took this reptile out of a sack and handed it across the table to me, perhaps not with the actual intention of upsetting me: he held it behind the head, steadying its body with his other hand, while its pointed tail trailed into the strawberry jam. This must be the correct way of handling such brutes; so I gulped and grinned and swallowed and grabbed it, making brave noises of admiration. 'Well, if you like it so much, you can have it,' said Mike. I accepted gratefully, and dropped my first reptile into its sack with some relief.

The very appearance of a monitor would justify every observer in regarding these rapacious lizards, as the prototype of all dragons in fairy tales. It was a slender reptile with a strikingly long neck, elongated jaws, well developed legs with long sharp claws and a whip-like tail. Like all other monitors, it was covered with a very strong, rough skin, which the fangs of the smaller venomous snake cannot penetrate. I soon found out nearly to my cost, that when it became excited it would inflate itself, give a warning salvo of hisses, then open its mouth and attempt to strike the intruder with powerful and well aimed blows of its tail. When picked up during further encounters, it would attempt to bite, and scratch, particularly with the claws on the back legs which lashed out with its tail.

That evening I borrowed one of Robin's horses for a ride over the farmlands. But it was six years or so since I had ridden, and I was horribly out of practice: my knee-grip had gone, I could only rise in the saddle very uncertainly, and the expected gallop became a walk. Slowly, therefore, I rode down the winding muddy track to the banks of the Mazoe. There, between the rows of tobacco, I saw four long-legged bustards: they strolled about and nodded to each other, like four elderly clergymen at a theological conference. Perhaps because I was mounted they seemed to have no fear of me.

The sun was just beginning to set. Two brace of helmeted guinea-fowl took to flight, protesting noisily at being disturbed; warned by them, a ram reedbuck sped past on my left. The sun sank deeper, an orange glow like barley sugar spreading over the farmlands: a pair of grey touracos uttered their call from across the river, a nasal 'go away, go away', while a tropical yellow bishop bird flew up into the towering blue gum trees by the river side, looking much refreshed by its evening bathe.

And so, in the peace of the evening, I turned back towards the farm. My mount scented home, however, and his walk accelerated into an uncontrolled canter, tending towards a gallop when I tried to pull him up with the snaffle. So I abandoned myself to fate and concentrated on the single problem of staying aboard: we sped in steeplechase fashion, and most dangerously, among the ant-hills and potholes, and we made it. For him, the stable; for me, drinks and dinner in good company.

CHAPTER 3

Monkeys and Tranquillisers

BEFORE long I was able to feel that my base at Douet Farm was soundly and agreeably established. John had managed to make some cages in the tobacco barn, and some travelling-boxes too; he had even mastered the art of feeding the animals and cleaning out their cages without damage to himself, and was very proud of this new skill. I had made a somewhat random start to my collection, and I felt that the time was now ripe for me to go away and do some planned trapping of specifically chosen animals. Later on the larger collection would need my continual presence; but for the time being I could leave it in John's hands, with Robin and Pris keeping a supervisory eye upon him.

Tucked away in the Vumba Mountain-Mellsetter area, in the south-eastern part of Southern Rhodesia, lived a sub-species of the white-throated guenon, otherwise known as the Stair's or Mozambique monkey, or (among zoologists) as *Cercopithecus albogularis erythrarchus*. This kind of monkey was very seldom seen in captivity; if I managed to catch four or five of them I would have the nucleus of a breeding group, which the Jersey Zoo would be very pleased to have.

So I loaded up the truck with five travelling-boxes, two wire traps, and my nets, together with my personal effects – excluding, however, my grandmother's tin of disinfectant, which I left behind at Douet. And so I set forth. Since the rear suspension of the pick-up lacked the refinement of shock-absorbers,

I had a somewhat rough ride, bumping down the 280 miles to Umtali grimly rather than enjoyably, and with frequent halts: every so often the radiator would boil, sending clouds of steam up through the floor to cloud the windscreen. I then waited until things cooled off: the disease seemed incurable.

Reay Smithers had advised me to call at the small museum at Umtali, since he knew that they had the odd Stair's monkey in their live collection behind the building. The curator – a Captain Boathby – was only too glad to let me see this animal, also some vervet monkeys and a spotted hyena that was supposed to be tame.

The Stair's monkey and I looked into each other's eyes almost like a pair of lovers. She had interesting markings: the dorsal pelage was a speckled light grey with a tendency to olive green, her legs pale grey, her forearms and hands and feet black, her bright eyes ringed with light brown, her ears well camouflaged by yellowish-white tufts. In sharp contrast with the rest of her colouring, and especially with her black tail, she had a collar and underparts of dazzling white.

I was distracted from the study of this monkey beauty by Captain Boathby, who wanted to show me just how tame his hyena was. He called an African, who at once put on a heavy army greatcoat and – with no show of reluctance – unlatched the animal's cage and went in.

The spotted hyena had been asleep in a patch of sun; now he got up, looked narrowly at the intruder, and charged.

'He's a great one for a game!' said the Captain, admiringly. It looked to me like the kind of game that the Romans watched in their amphitheatres, the lions sporting playfully with the Christians. The hyena had got his teeth into the sleeve, held on like a wolf, and was leaping and pulling with furious malevolence. It went on and on, with the African grimacing with terror: I very much hoped that this was put on as a stage-effect for my benefit, but soon he looked genuinely punch drunk and in danger of being really hurt. At this point the Captain intervened, broke off the engagement, thanked the African, and told me proudly that to the best of his knowledge this was the only tame hyena in Africa. It wasn't quite my idea of tameness.

I now made him an offer for the Stair's monkey, but this was turned down since it had been at the museum for two years and had become quite a pet. The Captain thought that I would have no trouble in securing what I wanted in the Vumba Mountains. 'You can shoot a mother and then catch the young ones,' he said, 'or if you don't want to do that, you can always net your specimens by hiding tranquillisers in fruit. They get drowsy, and you can catch them before they get away.'

He gave me an introduction to a vet in Umtali, who – after questioning me carefully – wrote me out a prescription for some nembutal capsules. Suspicions of suicide were plainly in the chemist's mind when I came in and asked for an enormous quantity of sleeping pills. But when I told him my purpose, and stressed the cruelty of the only alternative method, he gave me what I wanted and wished me luck. The dose needed to be kept in proportion to the body weight of the animal, which was 30 to 38lbs in the case of an adult Stair's monkey: I would have to spead my drugged bananas over quite an area, to reduce the risk of a single monkey getting a big overdose and thus leaving this cruel world in the Hollywood fashion.

And so I left Umtali, down colourful avenues lined with flamboyant and mimosa trees, down plain tarmac roads which soon became dirt roads, and so on up into the Vumba Mountains. As I climbed, a thick mist or *guti* came rolling down from above, reducing visibility to ten yards or so: thick vegetation flanked the road, sometimes closing in overhead to form a tunnel, and then parting suddenly to reveal precipitous valleys, falling away on one side of the road or even on both sides. Thus, with the mist and the winding road and the danger of a fall, I had to proceed in bottom gear: this meant that, despite the cool moist air, the engine overheated even more often than usual.

I was heading for the famous Leopard's Rock Hotel, which had been built by Italian prisoners of war during the last war;

but, being very much preoccupied with the dangers of the drive, I missed two turnings and found myself at the end of a cul-de-sac. There was a house there: I left the engine to cool off once again, and went to ask for directions to the hotel. There I met a Lt-Col H. G. Sewerd, who drew a map for me and pressed a drink into my hand.

'Stair's monkeys!' he exclaimed. 'Damned things. They come down here from up by the summit, and they go through my orchards stealing everything. I shoot them when I can. But they're getting wise to me, much harder to bag.'

So I asked him about my chances of catching some of them alive. 'Nothing easier,' he said. 'Just shoot a mother and pick the youngster off her back. That's the only way.'

No, I explained; I never shot anything. That would be contrary to the philosophy of my whole expedition.

The Colonel raised his eyebrows, and to show what I was missing by reason of this eccentricity he brought out the skins of two specimens that he had shot. He had meant them to be used as rugs or spread over chairs; but the skins had not been cured properly and let off a pungent smell; his wife therefore insisted on relegating them to the attic.

Before I left England Dr Osman Hill had told me that he would be very glad to have any material relevant to the primates of Africa: he was writing an immense monograph, and needed more data for his sixth volume. I mentioned this to the Sewerds, and thus triggered off a domestic disagreement. To Mrs Sewerd this was a fine pretext for getting those smelly skins out of the house; but to the Colonel they were his own trophies, shot and mounted (however imperfectly) by himself, and he didn't want to part with them. The battle raged to and fro, ending with a compromise: I took one skin, and the Colonel kept the other. So I took my leave before he could change his mind, and made my way on to the Leopard's Rock Hotel.

It was almost empty: this was not the tourist season for the Vumba Mountains. The building was turreted, and stood out against a mountainside that was swathed in mist: I might have been visiting a castle in Argyllshire. I ate alone in a vast dining room, feeling very self-conscious because of the numerous staff of liveried Africans, who stood there in shy silence, observing every mouthful that I took. I was glad to reach the solitude of my spacious bedroom.

I rose at 6.15 next morning, put a groundsheet cape around my shoulders, left the hotel by a back door, and set off through the thick vegetation on the mountainside. Some African pied crows squawked their astonishment at seeing me emerge from their private thickets: one of them followed me in deep curiosity, while a number of small red squirrels – later identified as the Swynnerton's red squirrel – dashed nervously around in the upper branches of the trees, their tails flickering.

I climbed higher. By the time the mists began to clear my feet and legs were saturated from the wet vegetation. Below me I could just see the tops of the hotel turrets, and, on the other side of the valley, the sun-drenched peaks of the mountains emerged from a sea of mist. Some black-faced vervet monkeys passed me to the left, leaping from one flexible branch to another, shaking the leaves and scattering showers as they went: some of them scampered down the heavy limbs of a baobab tree, crashed through the thin twigs in a manner that looked suicidal, caught their handhold further down, and continued along at unbroken pace. Birds were everywhere, pure-voiced choristers, singing their matins of gratitude for the light of daybreak.

The point was that this mountainside – according to the hotel manager – ought to have been thickly populated with Stair's monkeys. But I was unlucky: I stared every way with my powerful binoculars and found none. After an hour of searching I slithered down to the hotel, fortified myself with a good breakfast – invigilated, as before, by many shy attentive waiters – and ordered a packed lunch. I told the manager about my disappointment, and he lent me two of his men to show me the way to Castle Beacon. There, he explained, the Stair's monkey was *sure* to be seen.

So I drove as far as I could with these two Africans, and

with my traps and nets and my packet of tranquillisers: then we left the pick-up, shared the burdens around, and walked in single file towards the beacon. Above this, a long strip of forest had been cleared for the erection of telephone wires between the mountains and Umtali, and to serve also as a fire-break: this meant that if any monkey came down the mountainside, he would have to come down from the trees and make a dash through the grass, on the surface, before regaining the forest cover further below. I examined the grass and soon found their crossing place, with the grass trampled here and tunnelled there.

So I found an ant-hill, and used its soft soil to wipe my traps: they still smelt slightly of mongoose. Disguising this smell (I hoped) successfully, I then set traps carefully in two widely separated monkey tunnels in the long grass, being careful not to disturb anything.

Then I started on my doping operation. I took out a good supply of bananas, and chose about one out of every five for the treatment: I made a V-shaped slit, raised the flap, scooped out the soft contents, broke open a nembutal capsule and packed the white powder into the banana, and then pressed the flap down so neatly as to deceive and tempt even the most suspicious of monkeys.

I then scattered these bananas around in fives, each little pile consisting of four innocent and one doped. And in each of those tunnels or monkey runs through the grass I put a doped banana, but beyond the trap, to serve the purpose of a long-stop or second string. I took great care to disturb the grass as little as possible. There remained the question of what to do with my rather obvious nets. I spread them over some bushes beyond the traps and tunnels and the doped bananas, in the hope that some bemused monkey might take his slumber in them, or at least, conveniently close to them.

When all these preparations were completed, we retired to a vantage point high up on the summit side of the clearing, downwind from the traps and fruit; and we awaited developments.

By now it was almost midday. We waited. My hands began

to ache with the weight of my binoculars, and they kept on getting out of focus. Still we waited. Surely this generous distribution of fruit would attract monkeys in quantity! But after two hours there was still no sign of any kind of animal life. My two helpers became restless: they did not fully understand what I was doing, or why we had to be so quiet. Eventually, at four in the afternoon, I let them go back to the vehicle where they could talk without disturbing any potential captures. Left alone, I tried to concentrate, lifting those heavy binoculars to my tired eyes. But only the birds came near me; and soon after six I realised that the night was closing in and that the entire monkey kingdom would now be settling down for the night. So I staggered wearily down the valley and rejoined my sleeping aides, and back we went to the hotel.

One of the directors of the hotel, Mr Seymour-Smith, now displayed the great interest and also the optimism which characterised so many people where the capture of wild animals was concerned – especially thieving animals like monkeys. 'You just want to appear at the back door of this hotel with a banana in your hand,' he suggested; 'you'll soon get any number of Stair's monkeys around you.' I brushed aside this crudely amateurish approach and told him of my own more professional arrangements, also of my early morning climb and my disappointment. 'Well, then,' he said, 'in that case you want to get up at first light and go along to your traps then. The monkeys seem to come down from the summit in the morning and go back in the afternoon. Go in the morning, and you'll probably find them fighting to get into your traps and eat your drugged bananas.'

Cheered by his confidence, I gazed once again, and longingly, at the picture of a Stair's monkey in my reference book – also at my odorous monkey skin: then I sank into an anxious sleep.

I was out of bed at first light, as the director had recommended, and in the damp cold mists of early morning I drove up to my hunting ground, driving at a snail's pace up the (above) With Paula, a cheetah: 'Let's go for a run.' (centre) 'Whoa, not so fast!' (below) With Paula and my Bassett Hound asking: 'How do you run like that?'

Paula plays rugger: (*above*) 'You're offside'; (*below*) but the 'ref' has not noticed.

twisting and badly graded road that led to my parking place near the beacon. As the light improved I was able to retrace my tracks of the previous evening: water dripped off my hair down my face, and my feet soon became soaked inside my canvas boots as I completed the journey on foot. The mists dispersed, the rising sun shone down the mountain to my level, then down to the telegraph posts and the forest beyond: the animal kingdom began to wake up, and the birds repeated their morning anthems.

At about 6.30 I heard a snapping of twigs from above me, and froze at once into total immobility. The faint crackling sound grew nearer and then turned off to my right, towards the monkey trails and the traps. In high excitement but very cautiously I raised my binoculars: branches were swaying, and here and there I caught glimpses of the back or the long tail of some monkey – of the common vervet or of the Stair's monkey, I couldn't say which. Either way, I trembled with excitement: success appeared to be in sight at last.

Soon, to my delight, I was able to distinguish a small troop of Stair's monkeys. They were feasting upon the fruits of a wild fig tree, and were still on the uphill side of the clearing. This was frustrating: I wanted them to be still hungry when they reached my bananas. After a few minutes, which seemed like hours, they started to come down from the trees and into the tall grass, their heads occasionally lifting and breaking cover in the style of the patas monkey, which lives habitually in long grass. Then, in ecstasy, I heard a noise of wire against metal: a monkey was dashing to and fro in one of my traps! But I controlled my excitement and kept still since I wanted the rest of the troop to stay around and eat those bananas.

There I was disappointed: all too soon I saw them in the trees below the clearing, chattering and climbing away in the most active and wideawake fashion, not looking the least bit dopey. Never mind: at least I had caught one in my trap. So I stumbled and slid down, forgetting the cramp of my long vigil and the wetness of my feet, hurrying in some fear that the monkey might get away : I could hear the wire platform rattling up and down on the steel base, and too much activity might possibly loosen the locking device.

I parted the grass and looked down; and there, safely inside my trap, I saw not the longed-for Stair's monkey but a blotched genet : it snarled in rage and hatred, and snapped at my fingers when I touched the trap.

Crestfallen, I looked up at the monkeys in the trees, and they looked down at me with deep suspicion, all fully alert, not one displaying any sign of the drug-taker's lethargy. So I studied my bananas, which were rather black by now : they were all untouched. The smaller of the two traps had been sprung, but there was no sort of animal inside : my nets, spread below the clearing, glistened with sunlit dew but were empty. I cursed the genet for upsetting all my careful plans, and went to have a closer look at it.

Blotched genets were not on my list of required specimens. On the other hand, I actually had one; I had caught it myself, and it certainly could be fitted into my collection. I sat down on a cushion of wet grass to work the matter out. I was not a commercial trapper, anxious to catch anything that could be sold. But then again, I was trying to build up a collection of African wild animals. But then once again, I had a con- science in the matter of conservation. I pondered all aspects of the question for some time, but in the end this last con- sideration proved decisive. Some vervet monkeys frolicked in the trees overhead, and some glossy starlings flew across the forest gap, their violet-blue plumage brilliant in the sun : the beauty and sacredness of wild nature came home to me sharply, and before I could change my mind, I ran to the trap and released the catch. My genet bounded off to freedom.

I hunted out my drugged bananas, feeling rather like a sapper clearing landmines from neutral territory, and then I dug a hole and buried them by an old ant-hill, not wanting them to be unsuspectingly and uselessly eaten by some human or other animal. Then, with great difficulty, I disentangled my nets from the bushes and made two arduous journeys down to the pick-up with all my gear. It had been an unproductive morning from the point of view of my collection, but it had been a worthwhile and memorable experience – a refutation, too, of Captain Boathby's assurance that drugged bananas were an infallible way of catching monkeys.

I spent the next few days there, high in the Vumba Mountains, without adding anything to my collection. My mind was constantly on the Stair's monkey, and all the more so because my book told me that they make excellent pets; I dreamed up many splendid ways of catching them, but never even saw them in the flesh. Then I remembered that they were said to come to the back door of the hotel in search of food. So I tied a long string to the door of an outbuilding, so that I could shut it quickly by remote control, and then laid a long trail of nuts across the yard and into that door, with a big heap of nuts inside to provide the principal bait.

Then I settled down again to the familiar routine of waiting for the Stair's monkey. Eventually, one of them actually turned up, ate the nuts and followed the trail, exactly as I had planned; but when he came to the door of the shed he pushed it, and this tightened the string, over which he immediately tripped and then took fright, making off at once, and abandoning all thought of the alluring nuts within.

From that point on, it was as though the local Stair's monkeys were keeping me under strict surveillance, checking me in and out of the hotel, following my movements just as though I was a potential kidnapper and they were the French police.

And so I went, bumping down the pot-holed road that led for twenty miles, through lush forest and then over undulating green hills, back down to Umtali. I felt a definite respect for my conquerors, and I hoped that the Stair's monkeys felt a corresponding respect for me.

At the Umtali post office I posted that smelly monkey skin off to London, labelling it as 'scientific material'. As I passed the museum, I accelerated and looked the other way:

I did not want to talk about my failure, nor to tease my frustrated self with their captive specimen.

When I arrived back at Douet John was at work on another mongoose cage, stapling on the wire front. He seemed delighted to have me back. The animals appeared to be in good working order: the jackals were snoozing on their bed of freshly cut reeds, and the wild cat had lost none of its dislike for me. I walked over the farmhouse and found Porky blocking the front door, sleeping in the shade: I tickled his ear and he erupted like a volcano, springing up, twitching his tail, snorting angrily. I apologised politely, and he trotted off to settle down again under a flamboyant tree, scratching himself a cool resting place in the dust. Inside the serval cat was passing the time of day by catching the flies on the wire screens. She took no notice of my arrival. The farmhouse was deserted.

At the far end of the verandah I saw an old-fashioned meat safe which had not been there before: it sounded as though there were birds inside. So I came and peered in, and there – perched on a branch near the top of the meat safe – I saw two fledgelings. Of what species could they be? With their downy plumage, their hooked beaks, their yellow legs and feet, they looked rather as though they had been invented by Walt Disney. I thought that they must be some kind of falcon, so I went back to the pick-up and collected my luggage and dug out my copy of Austin Roberts's *Birds of South Africa* and started to leaf through it. But while the book described the fledgelings of various species, the illustrations were all of adult birds. I brooded over various combinations of colour and form, in respect of beaks and legs and plumage and eyes and the rest, and still was no wiser: these little birds might have belonged to any one of a variety of different species.

How little I really knew about natural history! I could recognise any creature of a species that we had in the Jersey Zoo, and many others that I had seen elsewhere. But when suddenly confronted with young birds to identify, I was wholly at a loss, even though a first-class reference book was in my hands.

I was having a bath when the Fallas came back together, and I had to shout through the closed door and the steam to tell them about my recent disappointment. It was a blow for them too: they had been very enthusiastic about my Vumba Mountain trip, and shared my interest in the Stair's monkey.

' "And I too, my lord, have not been idle",' quoted Robin. 'We've got a couple of hawks for you. We can't tell whether they're a pair or not, but you'll know all about that.'

I finished my bath and came out to join them on the verandah, pretending that I hadn't already had a look.

'Mike Smoelke tells us that they're goshawks,' continued Robin. 'What do you think?' Evasively I told him that there were two species of goshawk in that part of Africa, and that we'd be able to identify these two specimens in about a year's time. He then told me that they had got a leveret for me, a young specimen of the Rhodesian bush hare: I didn't really want this for my collection, but I accepted it so as not to dampen their enthusiasm.

It turned out that during my absence the wild-cat kitten had taken a fancy to Roselle, would come up to the front of the cage when she approached and allow itself to be scratched on the back of its head. This was another instance of something that I have noticed elsewhere: young animals will often respond to young people, while still distrusting the adults of our species.

During the evening of the following day I heard music in the distance, a tribal sounding beat of drums and singing across the river. Here, I thought, was the ideal opportunity for me to record some authentic African music. I had brought out from England a very heavy tape-recorder: I now loaded this on to the pick-up and drove down the dirt track to the pumphouse. Here I had to leave the vehicle and proceed silently across a single-plank bridge: I wanted to approach and make my recording without being noticed. If my presence and my intention were to be detected, the performance would either come to an end or else become self-conscious and therefore falsified.

That rhythmical wailing continued, to the accompaniment of massed choirs of frogs and crickets. I pressed on, wishing the tape-recorder wasn't quite so heavy, and wondering why my steady progress seemed to bring me no closer to the music. Here and there the bush had been burned, and black charred roots caught my canvas boots at almost every step. I still pressed on, and the drumming and the chanting never seemed to falter, but continued steadily, with a single voice occasionally calling out some sentence and then being answered by the rest.

Eventually I breasted a small rise and saw the glow and smoke of a fire among some native huts. So I turned off from the path and hid behind a shrub that had survived the fire, attached my microphone and tested the recorder. Its 'magic eye' lit up with interest, visibly responding to the sounds that were being received: I sat back and let the machine do its work.

After twenty minutes or so the tape came to an end and I switched the machine off. It was now time for me to steal away as silently as I had come. But perhaps I was in too much of a hurry: I happened to brush against one of the branches of the shrub that was hiding me and thus dislodged some roosting poultry. At once they clucked and chattered in noisy alarm, left the shrub and ran off to the huts. The drumming and chanting stopped abruptly. I froze in the sudden silence, feeling rather like a schoolboy discovered out of bounds. What could I say to them, how could I explain my presence? Would they think I was a police spy? My heart seemed to be beating as loudly as those now silenced drums, and I felt sure that they would hear it and so find me: I even saw a torch being flashed in my direction. But then I heard some relaxed laughter, and soon a single drum started up again, beating steadily to recall the others to the continuation of the programme.

I stayed behind that shrub for another twenty minutes, so as to be sure of making no further disturbance: then, at a moment when clouds cut off the revealing moonlight, I stole away, back to the path and down to the river and my pick-up. In some relief, and with a great sense of achievement and acquisition, I drove back to the farmhouse. Nightjars would rocket up before the headlights as I drove, always waiting until the last possible moment before taking off.

'Hullo,' said Robin as I came across the stoep, tripping over the solid form of Porky as I did so; 'You've just missed a phone call from Que Que. A farmer wanted to know whether you would be interested in buying a female cape hunting dog from him. He wants you to phone him back in the morning.'

This raised, in urgent form, a question which had been bothering me for some time. The animal collection that was being formed and accommodated in the tobacco barn was growing steadily, and with little effort on my part: it seemed that I only needed to spread the word around, letting people know what species I wanted, and most of them would be offered. But this method of working, added to the task of looking after the growing collection, meant that I had to be on the spot almost continuously. In a way I welcomed this: it was good to be in close contact with animals again, learning the art of looking after them, settling them down in captivity, persuading them to take nourishment.

But all this imposed strict limits upon my movements; and I had plans to travel more widely. For one thing, Gerald Durrell had given me an introduction to Robert and June Kay, who lived with a varied collection of domestic and wild animals in the Okavango swamps of north-western Botswana, then called Bechuanaland. I had corresponded with the Kays, and they had asked me to join them at their camp if Southern Rhodesia failed to give me everything I wanted. This idea appealed to me: I thought that life in those swamps would gratify my urge to get away from twentieth-century civilisation for a time, while also giving me the chance to see plenty of wild life.

So I made up my mind accordingly. I would spend two more months at Douet Farm, collecting 'bush orphans' and small mammals in the Glendale area, and then I would send the whole collection from Salisbury to London by air before travelling on to wilder parts where I could study the wild life, and consider the problems of its conservation, in its natural environment. So I wrote to the Kays and accepted their invitation.

This decision meant that I could collect freely in the meantime, with no fear of being encumbered in my later travels. I knew that the Edinburgh Zoo wanted a pair of hunting dogs; so in the morning I phoned the Que Que number and told the farmer that I would pay him ten pounds for the one he had, and would drive down to collect it on the following Saturday.

I had met these dogs before, when I was soldiering in Northern Rhodesia. They had been aroused by the sound of rifle fire, and I saw their characteristic sharp ears and powder-puff tails above the grass. As we drew nearer they started to prance up and down in excitement, as though they were glad to see us, thus revealing the black and white markings – different in each animal – which varied the basic mustard colour of their coats.

On that occasion they almost seemed to be welcoming us in the manner of domestic dogs. But this appearance of friendliness was deceptive: the cape hunting dog does not like human beings at all, and has great contempt for all domestic dogs, which he hunts down on sight. A fierce species: their hunting tactics are well known in this part of Africa. They gather in large packs and run down the largest game, even old lions, maintaining the pressure steadily: when the lead dogs get tired their place is taken by others, which have saved their strength by cutting corners during the long pursuit. Thus the quarry gets no relief, and will be finally dealt with by specialist killer dogs which always go for the throat. Such a pack will not be deterred by any number of casualties in its ranks: the dead or wounded will be left behind, and the pack will press on remorselessly.

A captive of this breed would need careful top-security accommodation. And so, with John's help, I wired off another stretch of the tobacco barn with some heavy-gauge pig-wire, separating this new enclosure from the jackals' cage by a narrow passage way. The wild cat, the rock monitor, the slender mongoose, the hare and the jackals all watched with deep interest, no doubt wondering what their new companion would be like. I was concerned about John's reaction: he did not recognise the picture of a cape hunting dog that I showed him, but he'd been badly scratched by the wild-cat kitten that morning, and if he got an idea of what was coming he might walk out or demand danger money.

I did not ask John to make a travelling-crate for the hunting dog: instead, I took the jackals' one. My nominal reason for this was my own uncertainty about the size a specially made crate should be: my real reason was the unreliability of any crate made by John, if it was to be used for carrying a beast that could be dangerous. The farmer would have the dog caged already, and we would just have to drive it across into the jackals' crate.

And so on the Saturday we loaded up at first light and set forth, so as to complete the round trip in one day. One diversion, which had aroused my curiosity, was planned. I had told Mike and Winky Smoelke that I was driving to the Que Que area; and they insisted that I should call at the farm of Winky's parents for an early lunch. There (they explained) I would be able to meet Sir Roy. Would this be Sir Roy Welensky, of Central Africa Federation fame? Apparently not. Then who? They wouldn't tell me; and so, frantic to find out, I found myself driving down the two hundred miles to the Fletchers' farm. It was a good tarmac road, and a good vehicle would have appreciated it: my poor old pick-up staggered and panted along so hopelessly that I sometimes thought we'd never get there – never find out about the mysterious Sir Roy, never secure that hunting dog.

But we did arrive. 'Persil,' said Mr Fletcher when we had introduced ourselves, 'go and fetch Sir Roy.' There was a long silence, followed by a kind of squawking sound, and then the gallant knight came bustling into the room. He had a long, curved, and powerful beak, surrounded by red wattling, and his plumage was black: I saw at once that he was a hornbill, and Mrs Fletcher told me, more precisely, that he represented the southern variety of the African ground horn-bill. 'We have had him since he was a chick, and he is trained to the gun.' This seemed a surprising claim; but before I could query it, Mr Fletcher demonstrated by picking up a .303 rifle and walking outside. Sir Roy followed him closely, in obvious excitement. 'Now if I were to shoot a pigeon,' said Mr Fletcher, 'Sir Roy would retrieve it for me as effici-ently as any labrador retriever.'

This remarkable gun bird was completely tame as far as those people to whom he had been formally introduced were concerned. But he would sometimes attack strangers. The day before I came, an African who had drunk too much *scakian* (a native beer) came staggering through the farm's backyard, was set upon by Sir Roy, lost his balance, fell, and received two nasty thrusts from the hornbill's beak. Mrs Fletcher pulled the bird off and rushed the boy down to the Que Que hospital, and they were now awaiting news of the patient, hoping that their faithful but fierce pet would not have to be put down. If this did have to happen, they said, I could have the remains for my collection.

After lunch I left their farm, and drove for an hour along bumpy, dirt roads and through thin bush to the farm where my hunting dog was waiting for me. At one place I saw an old silver mine, last worked in the 1920s – in a very different Rhodesia – and now deserted. Elsewhere along the road I noticed the strict etiquette among Africans who were on the move: the man always walked in front, carrying a stout stick, while his wife followed some ten yards behind like a true beast of burden, some large load balanced magnificently on her head, a *pikinine* strapped securely to her back, her hands free for balancing purposes.

The Afrikaans farmer greeted me kindly when I arrived, gave me a beer, and told me about the extent of the damage done by hunting dogs in his area. Last year they had accounted for nearly a hundred head of his cattle. I had never guessed that they were the farmer's enemy to this degree: no wonder that they were reckoned as vermin in all cattle ranching areas. But they can be judged less harshly if wider considerations are taken into account: in the wild, such predators serve an ecological purpose by killing off the weaker specimens of their victim species, thus maintaining the quality of the stock.

Why was the farmer keeping this particular hunting dog in captivity? She was useful (he told me) as bait. Each time she came into season she was manhandled into a small wire cage, which was hoisted into the higher branches of a strong tree. A cow would then be sacrificed and the carcase, well laced with arsenic, would be left at the foot of the tree. Left alone, the bitch would soon recover from the fright of being manhandled and would then recommence her mournful high-pitched wailing. This would summon the males of her species from everywhere within a ten-mile radius. Assembled together and unable to reach the bitch, all these dogs would then console themselves by feasting on the poisoned carcase, and would then die wretchedly. Thus the farmer could rid the neighbourhood of these vermin and make a small profit as well, since the Agricultural Division of the Territorial Government gave a bounty of one pound for every tail received.

This bounty could be increased by anybody clever enough to take advantage of the dogs' breeding habits. The bitches, when about to whelp, would separate from the main pack and take refuge in the communal maternity homes maintained by the pack. These were established in disused aardvark workings or porcupine earths, and within them the puppies would be born and would lead a subterranean existence until old enough to join the pack. These nurseries were so carefully chosen that they were hard to discover, but if you did find one, you would receive ten pounds for the nursery as well as another pound for every tail. This farmer told me – with obvious satisfaction – that he had once found one of these earths in use, and had blocked up all the entrances but one with old petrol cans, and had then run a rubber hose from the exhaust of his tractor into the remaining entrance. The occupants, young and mothers alike, were thus gassed with carbon monoxide; and when they dug out the workings to count the numbers they were able to claim bounty on no fewer than thirty tails. It must have been a gruesome sight.

Warned by this somewhat unsavoury story, I followed the farmer to where he kept his captive specimen. She was in a pit-like run, covered over with old netting and some barbed wire: old bones and bits of skin were scattered over the ground, while mounds of faeces in each corner swarmed with flies and bluebottles. It was strange and sad to think of any creature surviving in such surroundings. I looked at her: her bat-like ears twitched as I spoke, and she kept crouching, then running up to the far end of her enclosure, crouching there, then returning again. Perhaps she thought that she was in for another spell of imprisonment in the wire cage. This was clearly visible on top of the wire, and there were blood-stains and patches of hair upon it which told their own story of those nights in the treetop.

The animal's keeper was nowhere to be found, though the farmer sent off messengers to find him: it was Saturday, and he was probably off on one of the popular weekend beer sessions of his people. I asked the farmer if there was any-body else who knew how to handle the bitch. He shook his head. 'But I see you've got some nets on your truck: why don't you net her?'

My heart sank at this prospect; but I didn't want to return to Glendale empty handed and have to make this journey a second time. Rather against my will I had agreed to pay ten pounds for this unfortunate creature, and I was determined to take her away from this living hell, and now.

So I plucked up my courage, wishing that I were less well informed about the habits of this species, and their inbred dislike for people. Putting that unhelpful knowledge out of my mind, I folded and tied my net so as to make a sort of long tunnel or bag, closed at one end, so that if only the animal could be persuaded inside, I could tie up the open end and transfer the lot to my crate.

The farmer seemed unimpressed by my courage and resourcefulness: he watched indifferently while an African unbound some wire fastenings and then folded back part of the roof of the bitch's enclosure, so that I could get in. I waited until she was up at the far end before dropping through on to the earthen floor: net in hand, I stood there in some terror. The bitch glared at me from inflamed eyes, watching every movement I made, crouching in her dark corner. The farmer yawned.

Previously, whenever I had needed to catch an animal in a confined space, I had always made a practice of talking steadily and gently throughout. This bolstered up my own confidence at least; and perhaps the animal concerned did get some idea of being sensible and not attacking me. And so, appealing steadily to the bitch's commonsense and logic, I slowly worked my way along the narrow pit: the mouth of my net was held open by a stick, but even so, it kept catching on litter and roots as I advanced.

The bitch backed as far as she could go; then, choosing her moment, she sprang. I swung the net, but unsuccessfully: she got entangled for a short moment but broke away at once, and ran to the other end of the enclosure – the end I had just come from. I must have panicked a little at the crucial moment: it ought to have been possible to lure her into the net, but at such moments, self-preservation is often the dominant instinct, over-riding the immediate purpose.

There we were, she and I together: the African had prudently fastened the wire ceiling back again. What was going to happen? She could have grabbed a leg or arm of mine, but luckily she had refrained, being perhaps too scared and unconfident. Unless I restored her confidence by repeated and unsuccessful attempts to catch her I might be safe from attack. But I wanted more than mere safety; so I sorted out my net and confronted her once again. She faced me, red tongue hanging out, teeth gleaming. I kept the bottom of the net close to the ground, and tried to extend the sides to fill the whole width of the enclosure so that she would have no way out; but my hands were shaking, and I had to keep swallowing. There was not only hostility upon her face: there was *contempt* as well. Then she came for me; and more in blind self-protection than in good judgement, I flung myself aside and pulled the mouth of the net into the line of her attack, very much in a matador's style. She went past me, just brushing my legs, straight into the net; and as my fall continued, I must have twisted up the mouth of the net without meaning to, but quite effectively. There she was, caught; I twisted the net more tightly round and round, and there wasn't a thing she could do about it. It was a memorable moment.

The African grinned broadly as he helped me out of the pit; even the farmer seemed to have enjoyed the performance, and he opened up the door of the jackals' crate for me. But before putting her inside I thought that this would be a good moment to remove the tight leather collar that had bitten deep into the skin around her neck; so I did this, using an evil looking butcher's knife that I borrowed from the African, and sliding a piece of wood under the collar so as not to cut the skin. This tightened the collar even closer so that the poor beast was nearly choked: when the collar was finally off, she lay back and looked up at me with mournful eyes but doing nothing at all, as though she fully expected to receive the coup de grâce.

There was a nasty sore where the collar had been: if it had been left in place it would have grown tighter as she grew and would probably thus have ended by strangling her. I told the African to fetch a box from the pick-up, and I sprayed the sore with a chloromycetin antibiotic spray and packed sulphanilamide powder into the wound. Then I up-ended the travelling crate with the door open and hung the net inside it, let it unwind, and finally cut the binding: the bitch slipped out and was safely in the crate.

I thanked the farmer and the African for their help, paid my ten pounds, and started off on the drive back to Glendale, feeling flushed with success. On the way I stopped for a sundowner with the Fletchers, and heard that Sir Roy had been granted a reprieve and that therefore the African ground hornbill would not be added to my collection.

It was late when I came back to Douet Farm, and I decided to leave my hunting dog in her cage until the morning. So I topped up her water trough and went over to the farmhouse. Robin was waiting up for me, glass in hand, full of curiosity about my day. So I embarked upon the epic story of my struggles in the pit; but I was so tired that I fell asleep, in one of Robin's warm enveloping armchairs, in the middle of the conversation.

CHAPTER 4

To England with Love

I COULD not free my mind of the fate that lay in store for me: within a week I was due to deliver my talk to the local farming community. With this serious distraction, thanks to not keeping my mind on what I was doing, I very nearly let the jackals escape. Too preoccupied to learn from this I then – within an hour or two – actually did give the rock monitor a chance to escape, which he promptly seized. I wanted to clean out his cage, so I tied him up in a hessian sack, not realising the strength of his jaws: when I turned to release him I was too late. There was a large hole in the side of the sack, and no monitor. I looked suspiciously at the jackals and the cape hunting dog, but saw no monitor tail protruding from those greedy mouths, nor any look of satisfied repletion. He was gone.

This piece of carelessness made me feel guilty and foolish; and to restore my confidence I searched among the large boulders that were scattered behind the farmhouse, and succeeded in catching three more specimens of the slender mongoose. These, lodged in the tobacco barn, further increased a carnivorous smell that was already too powerful and was upsetting my bush hare, causing it to twitch its nose in continual worry. So I removed all four mongooses to a toolshed nearby.

Saturday came, and the sun set with dark sombre haste: when zero hour arrived, I launched myself into the talk as a cabaret artist into an act. At times I found myself getting out of my depth and had to change the subject hurriedly, and in

How we lived and travelled: (*above*) base camp on the west bank of the Thamalakane River, Okavango; (*below*) the Kays' DUKW, Okavango Swamps.

Vultures: (*above*) my 'first'; (*below*) releasing one too many.

general, I did flit from one subject to another: the economic use of ungulate fauna outside game reserves; the social life of marmosets in captivity; the futility of game slaughter as a means of tsetse-fly control. But what with one thing and another, I managed to keep going.

Question time came, and I was let off lightly. There was one middle-aged school-teacher, well versed in the ways of birds and bees, who commented upon the fact that I was sending home a female cape hunting dog with no mate. 'How do you expect it to breed?' No offer of a male hunting dog was then forthcoming, but a slim weatherbeaten farmer in the second row said: 'Would you be interested in a pair of serval cats?' I gulped. 'More than words can express!' What a question! It was like asking a ship-wrecked sailor if he'd be interested in a flaxen-haired beauty.

I went home to Douet with this offer in mind, after the evening had ended in general sociability. Now that it was safely over, my ordeal did not seem so very terrible: back at the farm, I was able to relax over those refreshments and drinks, enjoying my company and the sense of being an admired and successful lecturer.

In the morning I went over to the tobacco barn and found John shuffling around as usual. He grinned cheerfully, but ceased to grin when I told him about the newly expected arrivals – two bigger versions of Romeo, I explained, pointing at the wild cat to which I had given that name. John swallowed in dismay. It was rather petty of me, perhaps, to tease him about the fierceness of our animals; on the other hand, I had heard from the boss boy of the farm that he often boasted to the other Africans about the perilous deeds of his daily routine. He might welcome any alarming talk that helped to foster this image.

Soon I was off. A winding strip of road took me through some attractive hilly bushland; it was strewn with kopjes, and these were studded with gigantic boulders which looked as smooth as facecream. My destination was Combe Farm, which was fifteen miles to the north-west of the small farming centre of Banket: I could hardly get there quickly enough, in my anxiety to get hold of those serval cats before the offer was withdrawn.

Mr Shattock invited me into his farmhouse with the usual Rhodesian hospitality, and over a cup of china tea he told me how these two serval cats had been found on his farm, orphaned, during the previous year. He and his wife had brought them up indoors until they had become so boisterous that they could no longer be trusted with the children.

They were being kept in an overgrown tennis court, which could hardly have been played on for some years since within the wired enclosure shrubs and undergrowth were growing freely. The farmer told me that there would be no need for a net this time: he would be able to pick up the male, and his wife would be able to pick up the female. 'They are very tame,' he explained, 'I once tried releasing them to fend for themselves, with the idea that they might possibly do an Elsa on us, but they were too trusting, and I nearly lost Tammy – that's the female – to some Kaffir dogs. The male is called Teja, which means "beware" in the Biyla language of Northern Rhodesia.'

I took my station by the entrance of this overgrown tennis court, with my travelling-crates held ready: I was glad not to have to use the nets again, since it is sad to see elegant wild animals entangled and helpless, with all their pride destroyed. The Shattocks went inside and called for their respective pets. 'Teja mern, come here, Teja mern!' called Mr Shattock in true native tones, while his wife chanted, 'Tammy, Tammy, Tammy!': it was as though they were competing for a prize. But five minutes went by, and still neither cat had put in an appearance. Perhaps they knew what was in store. 'I know what,' said Mr Shattock, 'I'll go and shoot a pigeon.' He was back very quickly: some pigeon must have been standing by in self-sacrificing readiness. Teja must have scented blood: he broke cover, and surprised me by being the largest serval cat I had ever seen. He had a shoulder height of some twenty inches.

He walked confidently over to his master, who picked him up and tossed the dead pigeon into one of the travelling boxes and then put Teja by the door. He fell for it, and walked in at once, so that I was able to close the door gently behind him.

74

Tammy was not going to be fooled so easily. She also had scented blood and emerged from the undergrowth, standing straight upon her long legs, her short tail twitching, her large bright eyes gazing upon her mistress inquisitively. But when Mrs Shattock bent down to stroke her and then pick her up, she sprang aside: she had probably heard her husband spitting and cursing in his box, and in a moment she was off into the deep jungle of the tennis court. But another shot was fired and another pigeon brought down, and Tammy reappeared as though that bang was the dinner gong: when the second bird was put into the second box, she too sprang upon it and was secured.

I stowed the boxes on the back of the pick-up, made my farewells, and went. I could not help feeling a certain guilty compassion. These wild and noble beasts were going to live in pampered and secure circumstances, more comfortably (in most senses) than they could ever hope to live in the wild. Even so, the prospect immediately before them was a totally incomprehensible experience of imprisonment and travel: they were going to suffer – for a time – very much as a young conscript suffers during his first bewildering days in the army.

There were now ten days to go before this collection was due to be shipped to England; and the housing of these cats presented a problem. Servals are great climbers, and an open enclosure would not do: furthermore, I did not want them to fight the jackals or the hunting dog through the wire. Fortunately the Smoelkes came to my rescue: at their farm, some twenty minutes' drive from Douet, they had a large clean outbuilding, with a big window and – half-way up the wall – a concrete ledge. They put this accommodation at my cats' disposal: I arranged for some long grass to be cut as a floor covering, and I brought the two crates inside.

It would be a welcoming gesture, I thought, and a help to their happy establishment in this new temporary home, if I shot them a pigeon each. So out I went with a borrowed .22 rifle, and spent half an hour trying to do what Mr Shattock had done in a moment. The trouble was that I am not a very good shot: in my army days, I had never done well on the rifle-range. I also knew that it was considered unsporting to shoot a sitting bird. So I found some sitting pigeons and shouted at them, and when they flew away I followed them with the rifle-sights and fired. By this means I brought down just one feather. So I reminded myself that nature is cruel anyway, put aside my sporting instincts, crept upon sitting birds and shot them successfully. As I carried the two carcases to the servals I apologised to them, explaining that it was in the good cause of kindness to fellow creatures.

Even with a good meal offered I found that the servals refused to come out of their crates in my presence. I left them there in the shed, thanked the Smoelkes, and went back to Douet, to find John looking scared out of his wits and one of the jackals crouching in the corner of the barn. Apparently he had been giving them some fresh water and went into their enclosure without fastening the wire door properly: the jackal had not attacked him but had started to run around in alarm and had thus escaped into the open barn. John had managed to get between it and the barn door, but when he tried to drive it back into its pen, it had just bared its teeth and uttered a low-pitched growl. This was quite enough for John: he stayed by the door in mounting terror until I came. Seeing itself outnumbered, the jackal then slunk back into its pen and John could get away to safety.

I was up early the next morning, anxious to drive over before breakfast and see whether the serval cats had settled down sufficiently to eat the pigeons. I peered in through the grimy glass of the shed window, and there was the male, sitting on the concrete ledge and hissing at me angrily. Tammy, I thought, must still be in one of the crates; but when I went into the shed – very carefully – she was nowhere to be seen. I couldn't believe it: I had locked the door, she hadn't escaped as I came in, the window did not open, there was no other exit. I ran up to the farmhouse to ask the Smoelkes if they had needed to take Tammy out for some reason: no, they hadn't. We went back to the shed and examined it again more carefully; and this time, we found a wooden panel at the back, under the concrete ledge, which would open if pushed at top or bottom.

So Tammy had escaped. I wondered what I would say to the Shattocks: they would despise my incompetence and feel sympathy for poor widowed Teja. But Mike Smoelke was encouraging: he thought that Tammy wouldn't have gone far from the mate to whom she had been married so long and so happily.

So for the next few hours I crashed about in the shrubbery and bush around the shed and then further afield, often tripping over, but never seeing anything in the least like a serval's spoor. So I took the Smoelkes' advice: having kept servals themselves, they knew their ways. They thought that Tammy would come back to Teja under cover of darkness, and probably at dawn the next day: we would organise a search then, but in the meantime they would watch out for her during the day. So I went back to Douet with a promise to return at half past five next morning, half expecting to find further escapes from the tobacco barn, relieved therefore when all its occupants were safely at home and apparently in good spirits.

In the morning, I was met in the Smoelkes' drive by two Africans and a number of thin disreputable looking dogs. Mike then came out with his pedigree dalmatian, which looked upon its canine company in aristocratic disdain, and we all went round behind the farmhouse to the shed. The two Africans and their dogs went round to the left and we went round to the right: the idea was to join forces behind the shed and to cut off two lines of retreat if Tammy happened to be lurking in the undergrowth.

The daylight was just peeping through the blue gum trees, and a thin layer of ground mist enveloped the dogs. As we came round we heard them barking excitedly as though in hot pursuit of something: we could see their tails waving about the mist, and we followed eagerly, hoping that they had not merely flushed a rabbit or something similar. They closed in on one of the blue gum trees and clustered around it, barking and leaping: I looked up the tall trunk and there was Tammy, clinging for all she was worth.

I quickly told the two Africans to take their dogs away: if Tammy had fallen among them – and she seemed about to fall – they would be almost certain to attack her. Then I spread out my net, which I had wisely brought with me, and Mike and I held it out under the tree, just as though we were firemen under a burning building. The dalmatian was told to sit down and did so, downwind of the net, from which there came a rich bouquet of varied animal smells which plainly intrigued him. Then Tammy's hind legs started to lose their grip, thus increasing the load upon her front claws: her lynx-like tail, some thirty feet above us, twitched, and she started to slip and fall, sliding and scratching, but very soon ending up in our net.

There she was easy to manage, being exhausted by the chase and the climb: we lifted her gently and took her back to the shed. Teja growled and hissed and spat by way of welcome, and indeed took angry steps towards us: we put Tammy on the ground and left them. Then, through the window, we saw Teja go up to his mate and start to lick her face gently, occasionally glaring up at us. Tammy was still panting, and a small trickle of blood came from her mouth: she must have hurt herself slightly while falling or in the net. Teja tended this small wound, fussing over her like a devoted and attentive husband, and soon Tammy rolled over, stood up shakily, and went across to lap slowly at the water dish.

I felt wonderfully relieved: it was like unexpectedly good fortune in love. I wanted to thank everybody. I patted the dalmatian gratefully, and gave the Africans beer money on an exaggerated scale – it was more like vintage port money – begging them to give their helpful dogs some extra rations, though without much hope that this would actually happen.

The bonds between animals are often stronger and more binding than the bonds of friendship and matrimony between humans. It was only because of the close bond between

Tammy and Teja that they were now together again. I hoped that when they had settled down in England, this same bond would make their marriage fruitful as well as happy, and that kittens would be born which would not have to suffer this very damaging kind of dislocation in early life.

Robin was delighted with my news, and suggested that since in the event Tammy had come to no harm, there was no need to tell the Shattocks about the episode. I agreed. It is extremely disappointing if you entrust a pet to somebody and then learn that it has been allowed to escape. I remember once, at the dog kennels in Surrey, greeting two people who were going to leave their pekinese for a fortnight's stay. While they were explaining their pet to me, and telling me that he needed to have chicken and rabbit on alternate days, we were interrupted by shouts from one of the kennel-maids: an alsatian had escaped from the exercise paddock. 'Back in a minute,' I shouted, and ran off in pursuit. I was back twenty minutes later, leading that ungrateful dog by my tie, but the pekinese and its owners had gone without even leaving a note or message. This was rude but understandable: how could they trust an establishment from which pets were able to get away?

By this later stage of my stay in Rhodesia the news had penetrated to the more distant parts of the locality that I would purchase any kind of animal that anybody was able to catch and offer. In actual fact I wasn't quite so undiscriminating in my requirements, and I was somewhat disconcerted at the variety of the birds and small mammals that were brought to the farm, with even the occasional reptile. So I tried to make it clear all round that I was only interested in certain species. But I didn't want the rejected offerings to be cooked and eaten, so I released them among the boulders behind the farmhouse – possibly repopulating the farmland thereby with species that it had not seen for many a long year.

One wizened old Mdala, who looked as though he had been journeying for a week or so to meet me, came and produced a small green snake from a cigarette box. Casually, without thinking, I touched the snake. It had been one of those really hot days, and for the last three hours I had been tiring myself in another attempt to catch some of those rainbow-coloured lizards: the only thought in my mind was that the collection would – after all – acquire some kind of reptile that day.

The old man had come a long way so I caused his face to light up with a generous payment. Then, for want of a safer place, I put the cigarette box in the glove compartment of my pick-up, and went into the house to consult my reference books. I didn't want to lose face with John by ignorance of what kind of snake it was. After careful consideration, I identified it – to my considerable alarm – as a striped skaap-steker, which is the Afrikaans for 'sheep-killer': a poisonous species, or semi-poisonous at least. I had broken an elementary rule. The wise man never handles a snake without finding out what species it is.

I went over to the tobacco barn to collect one of the small plywood boxes which I had originally intended for frogs. John offered to help, but hastily withdrew the offer when I told him that I was going to collect a poisonous snake.

I went back to the pick-up, opened the door very carefully, and looked inside the glove compartment. The box was there, open, but with no snake to be seen. I threw myself out of the cab hurriedly, as though there was a hand grenade inside: then, feeling rather like a timid woman in the reptile house at the zoo, I peered in through the windscreen and the side windows, searching every corner in sight, but finding no sign of any sheep-killer. So I opened the door nervously and lifted the seat-cushion, but there was only some odd bits of rubbish beneath it. I poked at this with a stick: still no snake. I felt even so that it was probably somewhere in the cab, since the windows had been closed; this made me reluctant to drive the pick-up, so I left it with both doors open and borrowed Robin's Land-Rover for my evening visit to the servals. If the snake was still around perhaps it would take the hint and go.

Reay Smithers managed to find me a mate for the female cape hunting dog, since a museum had just offered him one for five pounds. This was a stroke of luck for me and (I thought) for the female too: she had wagged her tail and tried to play when one of the farm dogs had come up close to the pig-wire of her run, and I felt sure that she would be glad to have a companion of her own kind. On this basis I replanned the travelling arrangements, asking John to make a large crate in which these two could travel together.

Then I went to the museum to collect the male. He looked very frightened, and when I pressed my face to the wire door to get a better look he cringed back into the corner of his box, his large ears flattened down. I took him back to the tobacco barn, intending to put him in with his new girl friend, so that they could get used to each other before they started on their long journey to Edinburgh. But when I manoeuvred the crate into the wire enclosure I was sorry to find the female growling at the new arrival from her corner, and not showing any of the signs of friendship that she had shown to the farm dog. I opened up the crate and had to tip it up to get the dog out: the female flew at him at once and there was a short scuffle which ended with his abject submission, his lady love standing over him victoriously. This fight made the jackals very excited, and they ran around their enclosure yelping, their dorsal hairs standing almost on end; by contrast, the young hare went almost frantic with anxiety, his eyes glazing over; so I took his cage away from the commotion.

One of my wire traps, baited with the usual selection of mixed foods – raw egg, meat, grain, fruit – now caught another rock monitor. At first I thought he was the one which got away, but when I looked closer I saw that this one had quite a different facial expression: he also responded very differently to my friendly overtures. I was careful not to put him in a hessian sack, and he became quite tame before long, developing a passion for duck eggs.

The serval cats were eating well by now, though they stuck to pigeons and refused to touch the raw meat I offered them daily. My shooting therefore had to improve, and did: in front of Mike Smoelke I actually shot a bird in flight. I had difficulties, however, in keeping the shed clean: if I came in unprotected, Teja would attack me at once, and the only thing he respected was a net, which I therefore held in front of me, matador-style, whenever I entered the hut. This drove both cats up on to the concrete shelf, from which they would spit and hiss at me while I cleaned up the previous day's leavings of meat, replenished the water, and changed the soiled grass.

Time was now running out, and I needed to think about packing and transport. On a previous visit to Salisbury I had gone around the confectionary shops asking for large tins of the sort used to package biscuits or sweets. I explained that I wanted them to keep a collection of frogs and toads in: I would line them with moss and other vegetation, and thus they would remain damp enough for those amphibians to live in. Now I went back to collect my tins, and those shop-keepers had certainly taken trouble on my behalf: there were ten times as many as I could use, but I didn't like to refuse any of them. So when I drove back down Jameson Avenue to Mazoe Road, it was in a pick-up loaded high with brightly coloured tins, rattling horribly; and when I came to the rough strip roads I had to slow down to a walking pace unless I was to lose both my hearing and my sanity.

I returned to Douet, to find an unexpected addition to the collection: one of my traps, set in hopes of a slender mongoose, had caught a female cape pouched mouse instead. I had not thought of having any sort of mouse, but then, I'd never met this kind before. She was unbelievably tame. I picked her out of the trap by the end of her pink stubby tail, set her down in my hand, and stroked her mottled grey-black coat: her nose twitched in appreciation of this new sensation, and she was soon nibbling at some bread. I took her into the farmhouse to show the children, who were charmed: the goshawks, in their cage on the stoep, were charmed as well, but in a different way – they looked at the little mouse hungrily. I found Mrs Tittlemouse a home in one of the smaller sweet-tins, having first punctured the lid for air and given her some wood shavings for bedding.

On the last evening but one before the collection was to depart, I packed some of the larger tins with cotton wool and moss, making sure that it was thoroughly damp. Then I took John with me and drove down to a flooded area of the Mazoe River, where each night the noise of the amphibians was almost deafening. Wearing some outsize wellington boots that I had borrowed from Robin, with a canvas bag attached to my army belt and a powerful torch in my hand, I splashed about in the moonlight, grabbing at frogs and toads with varying degrees of success, and putting the ones that I did catch into the canvas bag. John watched in silence, with the air of a man who's just had final proof of something that he's suspected for a long time: crazy or not, I kept at it, transferring my captives to the moist and mossy tins whenever the canvas bag started to get full. Some slithered out of my hands, or leapt from the tin before I could get the lid on, but I persevered until I had some fifty specimens. There were a mixed bunch, and I had no notion what species were included: there would be time later for classifying them.

The last days of any collection are hectic: there is so much that cannot be done before the last moment, since animals must stay in their travelling-crates for the shortest possible time. Cages have to be made absolutely secure, water containers have to be devised so as not to spill in transit, and food has to be provided to last the animal for a period of twice the anticipated time of travelling.

Tammy was the first animal to be crated. I put a pigeon into one of the crates, and being either hungrier or bolder than Teja, she went straight in and was secured. At six in the morning on the day of departure I went in to catch Teja also, and had to use a subtler trick: I held the net in front of me and advanced towards the shelf, under which he was crouching, pushing the crate forwards with my foot as I came. He could thus see my foot *through* the cage, and he sprang upon it, thus landing inside the cage, which was immediately closed upon him. Even a double lock upon the door was not quite enough to reassure John as we drove back to Douet.

During the previous evening I had put the jackals' and the hunting dogs' crates into their respective cages, in the hope that they would get used to them overnight: I might even find them already inside. But now, unfortunately, I saw that the opposite had happened: all four animals were sitting as far as possible from their crates, looking very suspicious, and all the more so when I began my preparations. I went into the hunting dogs' enclosure, making sure that John fastened the door behind me, and carrying a net for protection: as with Teja, I then tried to manoeuvre the heavy crate across the floor with my foot, towards the two animals which were now crouching angrily. The female leapt, but on top of the crate, not into it: I talked to them both very soothingly, begging them to go quietly, pointing out that there were big steaks of horse-meat inside. And so, slowly, I got within striking distance of the male, pushed the box forward sharply, trapped him inside, up-ended the box and fastened it securely.

The trouble was that the female was supposed to travel in that same box: I would have to catch her in another crate and then transfer her. I tried this, using the original jackal box, but it soon became clear that she didn't intend to be caught as easily as her husband. At this point Robin came in, and gave me another of his pearls of wisdom. 'Chase the damn thing with the monitor,' he said, 'she'll soon get into the crate to get away from it.' I wasn't at all anxious to handle the rock monitor, but time was getting short, and I had to leave for Salisbury soon. So Robin grabbed the monitor out of his box as casually as if he had been handling reptiles all his life, and passed it over the netting to me. The female hunting dog looked alarmed at the introduction of this new and unfair weapon, and when I advanced upon her, holding the monitor in front of me like a gun, she backed nervously into the box, just as Robin had expected. She wasn't the only nervous one: the monitor had been wriggling in my hand and scratching my arm with its sharp hind claws, and I was glad when I could put it safely away.

All this had been too much for John, and he had gone.

84

Robin and I managed to decant the female into the travelling-crate with her mate easily enough, but with a certain amount of noise, which brought a gathering of inquisitively grinning Africans around the door of the tobacco barn. They scattered, however, when we suggested that one of the hunting dogs was still loose.

The trickiest part of the operation was now over. The jackals gave no trouble: they must have been watching the hunting dog episode carefully and anxiously, since when I merely showed the monitor to them – from outside their enclosure – they took the point at once and got into the safety of their crate.

Romeo – the African wild-cat kitten – was already in his travelling cage, and the four slender mongooses, the chameleons, the hare and the pouched mouse were already in theirs. I checked everything carefully, and made some more air-holes in the tins of the frogs and toads. My last task was that of crating the two young goshawks: I decided to line the wire walls of their travelling-cage with hessian so that they could not catch their feathers in the wire. When I started to remove the two birds from the safety of their cage for transfer, the farm's pet serval cat went almost wild with excitement, thinking her great moment had come. We had to shut her up until the job was done.

We now stacked all these cages on the pick-up, with the heavier ones at the bottom and the whole lot just about managing to balance safely. Roselle said a tearful goodbye to Romeo, and indeed Romeo looked genuinely upset at having to become estranged from his admirer: Porky, less well mannered, ran off in terror at the barking of the hunting dogs, and took refuge on the familiar verandah. Robin banged on the roof of the cab by way of farewell to my collection, Pris and James waved from the shade of the farmhouse, the jackals wailed like bagpipes, and we were off.

In Salisbury John and I had to wait for the veterinary office to open before we could get the necessary health certificates. While we waited an inquisitive crowd gathered, and we had a hard task to stop them from pulling back the hessian from the cages and even climbing on top of the load. The more noise the animals made, the bigger the crowd grew, and I was glad when an African policeman arrived to turn them back.

Eventually the office opened, and a veterinary surgeon came out to give the animals a close inspection. Romeo just missed his fingers when the hessian was lifted up, and one of the servals also tried to attack him: he decided to call it a day, and issued a comprehensive health certificate forthwith.

Then I had to get an export permit from the Game Department; this was quickly done, and then we could drive out to the airport. Here I found that the customs forms had not been completed, as the airline authorities had promised: this meant another hour of filling in forms, in the middle of which I was interrupted by a journalist who wanted a full account of the collection. Then each crate had to be weighed and loaded into the aircraft under my anxious eyes, with careful stipulations about which crates were to be put together and which were not; and the airline's animal attendant had to be briefed about the individual needs of every animal.

I knew they would be all right: I had cabled the time of their arrival at Heathrow to the zoo representative in England, and I knew that they would be looked after on arrival by the RSPCA hostel at the airport. Even so, it was not easy to part. I went from crate to crate, growing more and more miserable as I said so many successive farewells; and when I finally took my leave of the attendant I did so most reluctantly. He was my last link with the collection into which I had put so much of my time and energy and devotion.

And so, sadly, John and I left the airport alone. These last two months had been a remarkable experience for me: I had learned an enormous amount about the animal kingdom, and the difficulties that animals meet when their wild native habitat is turned into farmland. In a sense man and beast are always at war, but the war intensifies when economic issues are involved, and many animals are then destroyed, often in ignorance, often quite pointlessly. Conservation is most necessary: this fact is shown by the vast stretches of Rhodesian bush through which I travelled without seeing any signs of wildlife.

Fortunately, the Rhodesian Game Department is progressively minded and does much towards creating animal sanctuaries and other conservationist measures, such as the Wankie Game Reserve and the newly created Lake McIlwaine Park. But such measures are of little value unless they are backed up by an awareness among the people generally of the importance of conservation; and this is chiefly a matter of education, since people seldom give serious thought to a problem that does not confront them personally in daily life.

Education is indeed the main thing, but money comes into the picture too. As we drove away from the airport, I thought of how useful it would be if Porky – the very endearing bush pig of Douet Farm – were to be employed as a flag seller in the streets, pestering people to buy his little flags, raising money for the cause of wildlife conservation. He'd raise a lot.

CHAPTER 5

Lions, Hens and Spaniels

IT was now time for me to leave Southern Rhodesia for the next stage of my expedition, which was to take me into the country now called Botswana, then the British Protectorate of Bechuanaland. John and I left Salisbury in the pick-up, heading for Francistown in that country.

On the way I stopped to spend a weekend in Bulawayo and make good any deficiencies in my kit, with a view to the new problems which would be created by life in the swamps. This city had hardly changed at all since my Rhodesian Army days, when I had spent some five months in the Llewellyn Barracks at nearby Heany. It is a more mellow city than Salisbury, its architecture much less modernised; its heavily cambered highways, originally laid out so that a U-turn could be made within their width by a waggon and its four oxen, still retain the same width, giving the city a spacious uncongested character. Wandering in those broad streets among those old houses, I could easily imagine what the life there must have been like for the early settlers at the turn of the century.

I sat back to read my Sunday newspaper, and was very disconcerted to find myself and my activities made into a major news item. There was a bold headline: THIS WEEK A FLYING ZOO TOOK OFF FROM SALISBURY. Then the article followed: 'Mr Mallinson should right now be somewhere out in the wilds of the Okavango Swamp region of Bechuanaland Protectorate: lean, bronzed, going after his quarry with the (*left*) With a Collared Peccary at Jersey Zoo;

(*right*) trade both ways – Pufelli's (my European red fox) first view of Africa from the *Warwick Castle*.

A vulture tucked underneath my arm.

age-old excitement of the hunter out in the open, but with the added zest of knowing that what he is doing is infinitely worthwhile.' The writer couldn't leave it at that: 'How many Rhodesians,' he went on, 'must envy these fortunate characters who come out to Africa on assignments to film our wildlife or collect specimens for Zoos, and disappear on safari for months. He may of course be swatting mosquitoes as I write this, and wishing to high heaven that he, too, was somewhere in a city within reasonable distance of a long cool one with ice chinking in the glass. But for all that, I'd still like to be with him, and I am aware of no small degree of envy. Good luck to you, Mr Mallinson, as yours is the kind of "hunting" that warrants a salute.'

This is the kind of thing that happens when you get into the clutches of the press. Feeling an urgent need to get away and out into the wilds, I drove rather fast down the last stretch of Rhodesian tarmac to the border town of Plumtree, and then over the bumpy earthen roads of Bechuanaland to Francistown.

We arrived there in baking heat, the temperature being well up in the nineties. I parked the exhausted pick-up in the shade of a fig tree so that it could cool off a little, gave John half a crown with instructions to be back in two hours, and set out to explore the place. The dusty pavement was mostly overshadowed by the corrugated iron verandahs of the shops and houses: I picked my way among them and eventually found an eating place which gave me an uninspired sort of lunch, which needed to be washed down with plenty of iced beer. As seen from this shanty-town hotel, in this midday silence and under this intense heat, Francistown looked like the ideal setting for a Western: I half expected that cowboys would come riding wildly into town with a blaze of six-guns in all directions.

A big man like a mastiff sat beside me at the lunch table, shovelling his food down greedily; so I asked him the best way of getting to Maun, my next destination, which lies on the edge of the Okavango Basin. 'What's yer got?' he asked between mouthfuls. I told him about the pick-up, admitting its limitations, but explaining that it always seemed to get there in the end. He stopped eating and looked at me in amazement. 'If I was in yer shoes, mate,' he said, 'I wouldn't even bother to start.'

This was hardly encouraging. I paid for my lunch and set out to get a second opinion from a garage. But the only garage was shut until three; so I went back to the pick-up, waited twenty minutes until John came, drove back to the garage, and waited endlessly until it opened.

Around mid-afternoon a European mechanic turned up. 'Do you see any reason why I shouldn't drive this to Maun?' I asked. He looked casually at the pick-up and told me that I had to be joking. 'The police wouldn't even allow you to point a thing like that in the direction of Maun. If you're thinking of driving it there, you can just forget it.'

Reluctantly I accepted this expert opinion and arranged to leave the pick-up at the garage until my return from the swamps. Very fortunately I was not immobilised by this decision: I was told that Riley's Transport trucks ran twice a week to Maun, and that one was leaving that very evening.

I went to see what I was in for. It turned out to be a big diesel truck, its back covered by a canvas awning: the bonnet was open and the engine was steaming, and a fair-sized crowd of Africans was gathered around the back. Among them was a character touting tickets, so I bought two for myself and for John and our luggage: the ticket made it clear that I travelled entirely at my own risk. Then I had the task of stowing on board my three cases, my two wire traps and my tape-recorder; this was not easy, since the truck was already piled high with cargo of every kind, from galvanised dustbins to bags of onions, with less than four feet of clearance between all this stuff and the canvas roof. I got in and crawled around and eventually stowed my luggage, and even managed to level out a flat six feet of space on top of some packing-cases, on which I could lay out my sleeping-bag. I can sleep anywhere, provided that I can stretch out fully; so now, with two hours to go, I tried to catch up on the sleep that I had lost during the journey down from Bulawayo.

I woke up, slightly refreshed and rather disconcerted by the quantity of people and equipment that still had to be found travelling space. There were many Africans, with John very much established by now as one of their crowd, and they all seemed to have bundles of clothing, pots and pans, grimy blankets, angry chickens, commodities of every kind. Somehow the miracle took place, and everything and everybody was stowed, though I forfeited some of the space which I had enjoyed earlier: there were grins all round and a general atmosphere of goodwill.

Twenty minutes later the truck's diesel engine roared into vibratory life: the truck shuddered, the dustbins rattled, the bruised onions gave forth their savour. We moved off, and everything shook and settled down: soon I found myself wedged between two big piles of canned beer in crates, and when I eased myself clear I found that my sleeping-bag kept sliding down into the cracks between the various items of loose cargo. After some experiment I discovered a more or less stable position: it depended upon my keeping my knees wedged against one of the tubular steel supports of the roof.

So, congestedly, we moved on. According to the map, this was a 'secondary' road: when I peered out from under the green tarpaulin, it looked to me more like a rough track of sand and stone, and it was certainly rough. We were shaken up and rearranged incessantly. Even so, John and his African friends managed to sleep in the most remarkable and constantly changing positions: legs tucked beneath them, hands clutching the steel framework of the roof, bodies twisted. I began to suffer from cramp: human pressure around my feet prevented any comfortable stretching. I began to think nostalgically about my bus journey down through Tanganyika and Northern Rhodesia: this seemed rough at the time, but now in retrospect it seemed like luxury.

There were many stops on the way; and just before the sun

disappeared over the dusty dry horizon of the northern Kalahari, we made our eleventh and major stop. The engine was switched off for a well-earned rest, and all the passengers sorted themselves out, extracted their limbs from each other and from the cargo, and jumped out on to the ground, taking their cooking pots with them. Soon small fires were burning beside the sandy track, newspaper parcels were opened and mealie-meal taken out, tea was brewed. I was offered some of the mealie-meal, but declined politely: instead, I wandered down to an empty river, which had just a few stagnant pools where – at the right season – there would be a torrent. The rains had broken already, but it would be months before a river of this seasonal sort became more than pools and a trickle.

Ploughing on through the night and through the loose sand, leaving a trail of swirling sand behind us: the sun rose eventually, rosy in the east, and before eight it was already quite hot. One of the cockerels in the truck kept up a steady crow of complaint.

Before long we were travelling through a more thickly vegetated country, and soon we arrived at the Thamalakane River, which is the eastern border of the Okavango swamps: its crystal-clear waters and the lush greenery of the riverside were lovely to behold, and I reflected upon the ecstasy that they must have given to such early explorers as Selous, arriving here after crossing the dry lands of the Kalahari.

There was a crude bridge over the Thamalakane: vertical stakes and cross-poles, all boarded in and filled with rubble, with just a few square gaps through which the water could pass. There was no barrier, nothing to save a vehicle which wandered off its very narrow track: when our heavy truck drove across, the whole thing creaked.

Seven miles further on, we arrived at Maun, a tribal and administrative centre and my destination. There was nobody to meet me, and I was glad of this: I must have looked more like a dilapidated gipsy than like a keen young British naturalist. John looked comparatively fresh: he was used to this sort of travel and could take it in his stride. He collected my luggage and I went to the small hotel for a shave and a shower. It was a very primitive shower. I thought nostalgically of the motoring trip through the Swiss Alps which I had enjoyed some eight months earlier, and I tried not to think about the fact that, sooner or later, I would have to go back to Francistown under the same awful conditions.

Robert and June Kay were encamped some way down the river, and we were driven out there by a member of the Veterinary Department. The track ran along the cool riverside, winding its way among fallen trees and patches of boggy ground. Soon I saw a copse of impressive fig trees on our right, and three spaniels and a white bull terrier came out to meet us, barking and wagging their tails. 'You've come to a proper menagerie here,' said the veterinary officer, and before I could think of a reply the Kays were welcoming us. They called off their overwhelmingly friendly dogs, and we moved off into the cool shade of the fig trees and made mutual introductions.

I looked around with interest. Among the trees I saw the bulky form of a DUKW, or amphibious vehicle, adapted by the Kays for their travels in the swamp-lands. Nearby, in the open centre of the copse, stood their living tent, its canvas verandah serving as a dining room: freshly cut water reeds covered the ground so as to keep the dust down, the chairs were covered with animal skins, and a Basuto drum added to the bush atmosphere. To the left of the living quarters was a small bathroom tent, with a canvas hip-bath hanging on a nearby tree. Twelve respectable looking brown hens scraped and foraged around among the cut reeds and in the earth close by, perpetually harassed by one of the dogs, which insisted on taking over any comfortable looking dust bath which a hen had made for herself.

John organised my luggage and was then introduced to the Kays' boss boy, Kisi, who took him away to show him his quarters. Then Robert turned to me. 'I expect you're dying to see Chinky and Timmy,' he said, and took me off to see their two pet lions.

Timmy was tied to a tree by a long chain. He was a dwarf lion which they had reared from a cub, having taken pity on him and bought him when they first met him in a circus that visited Bulawayo. When he stood up, his short front legs suggested a bow-legged and plump bishop in tight gaiters. From this first moment my relationship with him was uneasy. There was obvious friendliness in his eyes when he played with Robert or June, but he had no affection to spare for me: he tended, rather, to fasten aggressively on to my ankles.

It was very different with Chinky. I fell for her at once, and I felt that the sentiment was reciprocated. She was housed in the back of an old vehicle, since the chief men of the local Batawana tribe had insisted that she should be caged when in their vicinity. She was the largest lioness I had ever seen, and, although she was two and a half years old, she still carried on her flanks some trace of the spot-markings of cubhood. Her hazel-coloured eyes were large but somewhat slit-like, somewhat oriental: her muzzle was fawn, and her chin was forcefully shaped and snowy white. Part of the side of the truck had been cut away for cleaning purposes, and she would reach her paws out through this narrow slot to play, patting at one's hand or arm as a kitten pats at a reel of cotton, with her claws always retracted. When I went inside to make her closer acquaintance she licked first my hand, then my arm, then my cheek: her tongue was as rough as the surface of a pineapple, but our friendship was now sealed.

Robert cooked a superb curry, and after dinner we talked. He and June, I learned, had fallen in love with the natural beauty of these swamp-lands and had dedicated themselves to the protection of the unspoilt wildlife of this isolated inland delta. Robert had served in the British Army, then in the Palestine Police, then – during World War II – in the Royal Air Force, being stationed in Southern Rhodesia: here in the swamps with June he was wonderfully contented and cheerful, subject only to fits of irritation when the subject of conversation turned to the ways of modern youth. June was artistic, vivacious and petite: whenever possible, even in the heat of the day, she would sit down to her typewriter and work steadily away – at some further article on game conservation in N'gamiland, perhaps, or at another chapter of her second book, *Wild Eden*.

It was certainly a lovely and Eden-like place. We sat and talked in the dusk under the canvas of the verandah: through a gap in the trees we could see before us, until the light failed, a wide panorama of river and swamp-land. The hens roosted in the safe trees of the camp, and the dogs sprawled asleep on the rug by the tent door – all but one of them, Gilly-Anne, who had decided to be my favourite animal against all competition and therefore kept her head pressed against my legs and her eyes fixed sentimentally upon mine.

A peaceful moment – until Robert dropped his bombshell. Casually, as though asking for a glass of water, he said: 'When you go back to Jersey, would you take Chinky with you?'

'Take Chinky?' I gasped in amazement; and then, playing for time and frightened of commitment, I stammered: 'Wh – *what in*?'

'Oh, I've thought of that. I've arranged for a firm in Bulawayo to make a travelling-cage for her, and Riley's Transport ought to be bringing it here before the month is out.'

'Yes, but ... but why?'

'Well, a fortnight ago the authorities here told us that we had to have Chinky taken out of N'gamiland. We couldn't go with her: we've made this place our home. So we were at our wits' end; but then June had the brilliant idea of cabling your zoo. They said that they would be delighted to have her, provided that you were willing to travel with her. And I knew there wouldn't be any question about that ... '

I recognised the hand of fate: I was stuck with a lioness as travelling-companion. And when I came to think of it, I decided that if I was to have one animal, I might as well have

97

a collection. Robert and June were very willing to help, and it was decided that when the travelling-cage had arrived and when I had received the permissions that were needed if I was to collect animals, we would move camp to the Kwaai or Machaba River in the northern regions of the swamps, where there should be any amount of game to see and capture.

Things were taking shape. The Kays were very much relieved to have Chinky's future settled; I had made a good start on what I hoped would prove an affectionate and sympathetic relationship with her; there was interesting work ahead; meanwhile, I was very nicely accommodated in the DUKW – more comfortably, I reflected, than the soldiers were accommodated when this same amphibious vehicle took them to the Normandy beaches. So I fell asleep in high satisfaction.

N'gamiland was then a native reserve area administered by the Colonial Office. Geographically it is like a large inland delta, with waters flowing from the Angola highlands in the north, through the Caprivi strip, and then spreading out into the Okavango swamps; these drain into the shallow lake of N'gami, then peter out into the northern Kalahari in Lake Dow and the M'kuri-M'kuri salt flats.

The swamps were very isolated since the nearest railhead was some three hundred miles away across arid desert, with few good roads and poor communications generally. Moreover, most of the area was occupied by the tsetse fly. For these reasons, the wildlife was pretty well intact. But now it was in danger. Because of the political upheavals in East Africa the big safari firms were looking elsewhere for places where they could bring their rich clients; they had their eye on the Okavango, and were sending representatives to survey the prospects.

This commercialism could do a lot of damage, and the Kays saw it as a challenge: they wanted to get at least some part of the swamp-land recognised as a non-hunting area, and they also wanted to set up a N'gamiland Fauna Preservation Society, an official body with teeth that could be in operation before the safari firms could move in. I was very much in

sympathy with them; for my part, I wanted to see as much
as possible of the wildlife of the region, and this would help
them indirectly, since when I returned to England I would be
able to report to influential bodies such as the World Wildlife
Fund and the Fauna Preservation Society. Meanwhile, I looked
forward to seeing the concentrations of wildlife in the
Okavango; my only anxiety was that this purpose might be
hampered if I burdened myself with too large a collection
too quickly.

Before I could start collecting there were a great many
regulations which needed to be complied with. But first of all
I had to ask and receive the permission of Mahumahati
Moremi, Queen Regent of the Batawana: this was a native
reserve area, within which no European could own property
and within which the Africans had the last say in all matters.

This meant a formal call. The Queen Regent lived in a
pair of whitewashed buildings, which were somewhat out of
place – rather suburban – among the more natural-looking
mud huts that surrounded them. Robin dressed for the
occasion, immaculate in white shirt, white shorts, and white
stockings: the best I could muster was a clean bush-jacket,
which was perhaps suitable for my role as a keen naturalist.
I had never met a Queen Regent before, and I approached
in some nervousness, feeling rather like an ambassador about
to present his credentials.

Mahumahati Moremi turned out to be a small plump lady,
dressed in European style. She was sitting behind a desk
when we came in: Robin started to tell her what I wanted
to do, emphasising that my chief motive was conservation,
and she listened attentively, as did two tall Africans who stood
behind her. All three looked at me with obvious interest, and
I felt embarrassed: it is difficult to know what to do when
three people are looking you up and down while another
speaks on your behalf. What was the correct protocol?
Should I smile at them? Should I try to look like a keen
high-powered scientist whom they ought to respect, or like a
vague naturalist whom they could safely indulge? I decided

that until I received the Queen Regent's permission, a look of serious anxiety would be the best thing.

After an endless five minutes of uncertainty she agreed to my request, but (I gathered) without entirely believing my story: she seemed to suspect that what I really wanted to do was to collect some wild animals and breed them for meat, as with domestic livestock. Before we went, one of the two Africans in attendance told me that I would have to pay a nominal fee to the tribal treasury, as their law stipulated that a fee should be paid whenever animals were exported from N'gamiland: he therefore wanted to see the collection before it left the country so that he could assess the amount of tax that would be due. This struck me as instant law-making: I knew perfectly well that the question had never arisen before, since I was the first person to collect live specimens in this part of Africa. But I had no intention of disputing the point, and I bowed, shook the graciously extended royal hand, and thanked the Queen wholeheartedly for her co-operation. To mark our gratitude Robert gave her two guinea fowls which he had shot that morning.

My next step was to go and see the District Commissioner, and get the blessing of the European administration and a typed permit. The DC seemed pleased to see a new face: he told me that he had been at school with Peter Scott and was naturally interested in wildfowl and in all kinds of wildlife. He proved to be extremely helpful, and passed me on to the Veterinary Department. Here I was given permission to move animals within the boundaries of N'gamiland, but not to export them to Francistown: that would need separate authorisation when the time came.

As I left the administrative centre the DC came running after me to say that there was one bird which he did *not* authorise me to take away, namely, a fish eagle which was in the habit of perching on a dead tree opposite his house. This bird has the distinctive habit of throwing back its head and uttering a clear six-bar call which is one of the finest sounds of Africa: the DC didn't want to lose his own local performer.

I managed to buy a number of old wooden boxes and two rolls of wire netting from a local trading store: I took these back to camp, and started John on the task of dismantling the boxes and rebuilding them as general-purpose cages. We also made a number of wooden frames, covered with wire netting, which could be lined with hessian and fixed together to serve as cages for any larger birds that I might secure. I was working in the dark, of course, since I had no idea of what species I might capture, or in what quantity: the only thing I could do was to make several cages of different sizes and supplement these when required. I also ordered half a dozen reed baskets to be made, of a type that I had seen locally, but to my specification: these would also make good cages for birds or – if I caught no birds – good presents when I came home.

By extreme good fortune a young pair of black spur-winged geese came into my possession, constituting – together with Chinky – the first members of my N'gamiland collection. A man called Dave Calver, who lived at Maun, had bought them from an African and intended to fatten them up for food: when I heard of this, through Robert, I drove into Maun at once and offered to buy them, if he would keep them for another six weeks at my expense. Fortunately he agreed, and took me behind the house to see them. The spur-winged goose is an odd-looking creature, especially at this early stage of its life. The plumage of these two was just changing to a greenish-black on the back and the neck; they were white underneath, and their beaks and legs were pinkish-red. I went to pick up the young gander, and he tried to strike at me with his right wing: I clearly saw the carpal spur from which this species is named, and I could well imagine how painfully effective this would be if one were attacked by an adult specimen.

Next came a very welcome invitation. A coloured man and five Africans, all connected with the local administration, were planning a weekend in the Chuchubegha region, some forty-five miles to the west of Maun; and they suggested that

June and Robert and I might like to come along with them. We would see a big concentration of game, including buffalo. This invitation was not entirely disinterested: the Batawana tribe were in the habit of shooting for the pot, with no close season, and if this weekend party succeeded in shooting a buffalo, they would be glad of a second vehicle to help bring the meat back.

June knew how much I would value the experience, and she nobly volunteered to stay behind and look after the animals. John and I set forth with the party. It was rather a featureless journey: the track to Chuchubegha looked like any other sandy track, and the mopane bushes looked like any other mopane bushes. The destructive grazing of goats was much in evidence during the first fifteen to twenty miles of our journey. At one point a goat jumped out and ran along in front of us, sticking to the centre of the track in its panic, slowing us down considerably, refusing to turn aside even though Robert kept his hand on the horn. Eventually it tripped and stumbled angrily off to one side.

Along that track we drove, sometimes over hard-packed sand and sometimes through soft drifts which needed to be taken at speed, until we reached another tsetse-fly control-post. We were not expected and there was nobody on duty: we blew the horn but nobody came. So we drove on. By now there was no definable track, and the driver of the leading vehicle had to thread his way through the light bush, between small copses and thickets, across tracts of parched yellow grassland, then through the mopane once more, and so onwards, with the spoor of both vehicles stretching behind.

We came to a small graceful herd of impala. They stopped grazing as the trucks approached, and the nearest buck sniffed the air, trying to catch our scent. Then, to my amazement, the sound of a rifle shot came from the Africans' truck in front: I actually heard the smack of the bullet as it tore into flesh, and saw the buck stagger sideways from the force of the impact, then pull himself together and run, some way behind his harem of five or six does. The leading truck drove straight on, making no attempt to follow up the wounded animal: left to itself it was certain to die a slow and painful death. So Robert swung aside, drove in search, located the buck within five minutes, and put it out of its misery. Then the other truck retraced its tracks to find us and perhaps to share in the kill; and Robert had some very pointed remarks to make to the trigger-happy African who had fired that casual and pointless shot. It is one thing to shoot for the pot: this is inevitable, in fact, in regions where the tsetse fly prevents any keeping of domestic animals and makes protein food hard to come by. But it is quite another thing to use small game for casual target practice; and Robert told the guilty man exactly what he thought of him.

The episode left a nasty taste in our mouths, but we were consoled by the spectacular and rewarding drive during the next hour. Three reticulated giraffes towered above the long grass, browsing from the tops of stunted trees until they saw the trucks, then cantering away in their ungainly fashion; eight warthogs, disturbed from wallowing in some damp cotton-soil, ran in disorder for the nearest cover; a herd of the shaggy tsessabe, some twelve in number, crashed through the high reeds by a small stream. Their white-ringed behinds made ideal targets as they vanished, but nobody was going to risk Robert's anger for a second time that afternoon.

Around every corner, it seemed, we would come across zebra, or wildebeest (brindled gnu), and each one would snort and swish its tail in indignation at our noise and intrusion. The coloured man in the leading truck, Benjamin by name, stopped to tell Robert that he had orders to shoot one wildebeest as well as a buffalo; and then, within moments, we heard another shot and saw a wildebeest stumbling helplessly to the ground. I felt a desperate desire to intervene and defend and save it, though of course it was too late: I still thought in terms of innocent life and the brutality of sudden killing, and I could not come to terms with the economic necessity of such behaviour. And it was such a noble beast, suggesting a heraldic unicorn to me, though without the frontal horn. Benjamin chopped off its tail and threw it to me as a souvenir; I accepted it reluctantly, and I still possess it, the relic of an undeserved martyrdom.

Benjamin and his Batawana friends now set about carving the animal up like professional butchers, loading the legs and the other best cuts on to their trucks. Then we moved on, leaving most of the carcase behind for the carrion lovers, the marabou storks and the vultures. They had started to gather round as soon as the shot was fired – almost before the animal hit the ground – and the marabous had prodded the ground with impatience while the butchery went on, while the vultures perched on the trees around, hunched up, looking really devilish with their hooked beaks and their evil glittering eyes. As soon as we moved away they all closed in, and we left them to it, as they tore at the steaming flesh and quarrelled and pushed to get at the choicest morsels.

We drove on, with Henry – the male cocker spaniel – lying sprawled across my lap with his head out of the window, ecstatically inhaling the odour of fresh meat from the truck in front. Robert had brought him along to get him used to life without his mate, Gilly-Anne, and he obviously thought that there was a feast in store that would amply compensate him for this temporary divorce. He was right. Benjamin halted his truck by a small copse, flanked on the west by a stream and surrounded on the other sides by grassland, and here we pitched camp, lit a fire, and arranged our camp beds. The meal was a simple one – boiled rice with grilled wildebeeste steak – and the surroundings were not those of a luxurious restaurant; but the most fastidious gourmet would have found that meat succulent beyond compare, and all of us, eight men and one dog, retired for the night in the contentment of repletion.

The night was cloudless, and as I lay on my camp-bed and looked up into the huge African night, with the sounds of the bush all round me, I felt a wonderful sense of universal peace. One of the Africans nursed the fire, keeping up a good blaze throughout the night: Henry lay in the shadows, sleeping off his banquet of wildebeest. Every so often the high-pitched cry of a leopard would be heard, and Henry would take little notice, merely blinking in its direction. It was the same when we heard the roaring of two lions somewhere upwind of us. But when we heard the short cackle of a hyena, Henry sprang up and barked and then seemed to regret it, looking at us for reassurance, and sitting down vigilantly between our beds and the fire. It is not always wise (he was thinking) to betray one's presence to a possible predator.

We had breakfasted and struck camp by seven next morning, and I learned with mixed feelings that the buffalo shooting came next. Well, at least we were going to feed the Batawana: it was not a case of rich men looking for trophies, or business men exporting the animal wealth of N'gamiland for profit. And, as things turned out, the next few hours were among the most exciting of my life.

We spotted a herd of buffalo in a small clearing, but they moved off before a shot could be fired, into vegetation too thick and dense for the truck to follow. So we went after them on foot, Benjamin leading, his .375 rifle carried at the trail. For some five minutes we pressed on through the trees and bushes: my heavy binoculars kept getting caught on branches or banging against my chest, so that I had to carry them. I could see nothing whatever of the signs our guide was following: I felt bothered and lost.

Then Benjamin stopped and studied some hoof-marks. They were plainly those of a buffalo, but how old were they? He considered the question, moved off experimentally down two alternative trails, came back, and beckoned us to follow. On we moved, speaking only in whispers, and after about half an hour we found confirmation that we were on the right track — buffalo manure, and so fresh that the animals must be close at hand.

As we moved cautiously through the dense vegetation, aware that a clumsy step on a twig or a rotten branch would put the game to flight, I felt that this was the real art and craft of the hunter – a very different thing from the easy slaughter, so cheaply done in open country with telescopic rifles, which is flatteringly called 'big-game hunting'.

Now we came upon some manure that was still steaming, and the horsey smell of buffalo was all about us. The herd was upwind: they might hear us but would not smell us as we approached. Benjamin held up a hand and we stopped in our tracks: then he advanced in total silence and crouched down beneath a low-hanging branch. We waited tensely.

The silence shattered: we heard the bang of his rifle and then the fleshy smack of a hit, and at once the herd was snorting and thundering through the undergrowth in our direction, emerging from cover, seeing us, then swerving away at the last minute. The wounded beast had apparently remained behind and was hiding somewhere.

We were now in a tense situation. The African buffalo is considered by some big-game hunters to be the most dangerous of all African game to go after: he is extremely cunning when wounded, and can survive many bullets. We heard a distant crackling from the vanishing herd, but in front of us there was an ominous silence. Robert unslung the rifle he had brought along for self-protection, and we watched as Benjamin crept forward with every sense alert. He must have been almost upon the wounded buffalo when it broke cover and came charging at him with head lowered. The coolness of his nerve was amazing: unhurriedly, he dropped to one knee and fired. The buffalo hit the ground like a ton of rocks, shot through the heart: a few feet further, and he would have killed his killer.

I congratulated Benjamin warmly, and was rather surprised to find myself doing so: I am not normally enthusiastic about the deaths of animals. But in this case the odds were about as even as they could possibly be, and one could not fail to admire the tracker's skill and the marksman's composure at a moment of extreme danger.

We left the two Africans by the carcase, and went back by a shorter route to the trucks. Henry greeted us in high

Going home: (*above left*) Chinky looking apprehensive; (*above right*) how we packed them in; (*below*) full house.

Ostrich from N'Gamiland – 'D'you know you're taller than me?'

hysteria: he had been safely shut up in the cab in Robert's truck, but had obviously felt terrified at being alone in such wild country. Then we drove back and helped with the butchering of the steaming carcase, cutting branches and loading the meat upon them, and so dragging it to the trucks, which were soon filled almost to capacity. Africa's varied sanitary squad, from vultures to dung beetles, started to gather in readiness for the tidying-up operation.

Henry was in a great state of alarm, and would not even sample the meat: he refused to get back into the cab until it became clear that we were coming too. (He was only a brave dog when Gilly-Anne was around to be impressed.) But eventually we were loaded up and started off for Maun, stopping at various African villages on the way to distribute shares of the meat, which was very much welcomed.

And so we arrived back home at the base camp, and feasted upon the strongly flavoured buffalo meat: there were large bones for the lions and the dogs had their share too, though Henry was still off his food and feeling very sorry for himself after the terrible experience of being alone in the truck. The only thing wrong with the meat was that there was so much of it: we seemed to live on nothing else for the next week, with buffalo liver or kidneys for breakfast, buffalo steak for lunch, and buffalo curry in the evening. It was rather like those occasions when you prepare a mountain of food for a party but none of it gets eaten, so that you have to work your way through it for days afterwards.

I now intended to explore the region more thoroughly. But first, I had to recover from an unpleasant encounter with some maggot flies. I had washed one of my shirts and spread it out to dry in the sun, and the flies must then have laid their eggs in it: when I put it back on, the eggs had hatched, and the larvae dug their way into my back, causing the most awful irritation, which got worse as they dug deeper. June came to my rescue: I sat on a stool and bent forward, and she smothered the entry tunnels with Germolene. This meant that they had to break surface in order to breathe, and could then be plucked forth: after a few days of this treatment I was free of them, and could start my explorations.

I used a small aluminium dinghy with an outboard motor: Robert kept it as a tender for the DUKW, and on this suitable craft I cruised around the swampy and watery regions of the Thamalakane. The bird life was entrancing. There were pied kingfishers everywhere, hovering in the air, perfectly still, then diving upon their prey with remarkable speed and accuracy. There were brightly coloured pygmy geese – the drakes with breasts and flanks of chestnut, bills of bright orange, and heads adorned with arresting green patches on either side. There were African jacanas or lily-trotters, picking their way over the plate-like leaves of the water lilies with huge feet that were perfectly adapted to that medium of travel. Above me, in the branches of dead trees, frequently I saw a white-breasted cormorant: he would perch up there and survey the clear waters, and then dive down to pick up a fish in his long beak. High above the water, I would often see also the majestic white front of the fish eagle.

I could well understand how Robert and June, having intended to travel the length of Africa from south to north, should have stopped on the way and settled down in this Okavango paradise.

Back at the camp, I found bad news: poor Timmy was badly constipated. This was a problem I had not met before but might very well meet again, so I took careful note of the treatment and the patient's progress. First of all we tried the simple device of pouring human-type laxatives liberally on to his food. He wouldn't touch it: there was nothing for it, we decided, but an enema, and we borrowed an enema set from the small hospital at Maun.

It is not as easy as you might think to give a male lion an enema. For one thing Timmy disliked having his hind-quarters touched: in fact, being off-colour, he preferred to be left entirely alone. We tried blandishments, with Robert tickling Timmy's chin and stroking his neck, while June stood by with the enema tube at the ready and I held the bottle of soapy water. But Timmy wasn't to be fooled: he became rather angry, and demanded to be left alone.

It was plainly a case for anaesthesia. We mixed seven and a half grains of nembutal with some milk, and managed to pour it down his throat: then, for the next two hours, we stood around and waited for him to turn drowsy. But he didn't, and we began to be seriously worried: he might have an intestinal obstruction, which could only be resolved by surgery. He hadn't had anything to eat for four days.

So Robert went back to the hospital and managed to charm some chloroform out of the people there: two of them came along to help. The method used was crude but effective: we took a sack, and put at the bottom of it a good-sized wad of cottonwool, freely soaked with chloroform, and then Robert closed in and dragged the sack over Timmy's head, while the rest of us secured his legs. June held the enema tube, John held the bottle; Robert kept the cottonwool over Timmy's nose until he felt him relax. Then, triumphantly, June managed to get some olive oil and several pints of soapy water successfully into him; and we left poor outraged Timmy alone so that nature could take its course. He looked much better the next day, and ate some minced steak: we followed up the treatment with a couple of intra-muscular shots of terramycin, and soon it became obvious that the constipation was lavishly cured.

So far I had not started any serious collecting in this region. But I couldn't help leaving a baited wire trap at the back of the camp, just to see what happened. At first I made the mistake of putting it too near the camp, and thus caught several of Robert's brown hens, to their extreme indignation. When I put it further away, I caught a most endearing little rodent, the bulbous-eyed Bechuanaland gerbil: the first mammal of this collection, and I took it happily back to the camp and lodged it in a spacious wooden box.

As I moved around our encampment I could never pass Chinky without stopping to have a word with her. When I approached she would stand up and look at me appealingly, then lower her snow-white chin and utter a gently welcoming 'wow': she was irresistible.

One of my tasks was cleaning out her home in the Dodge truck: I would run it down to the riverside, and then use a long hoe to scrape out the soiled reeds and her water dish. She took all this to be a game, and made things much harder by patting incessantly at the hoe with her large paws, and also by whisking her water dish back to the farthest corner of the truck just when I had managed to coax it within my reach. But I always won in the end; I would swill down the inside of the truck with buckets of water from the river, clean and refill the water dish, and then poke in a new floor-covering of the fresh reeds which John had already cut for me.

It was now time to prepare for our journey up to the northern regions of the swamps, and Robert decided to give the engine of the DUKW a thorough testing. It was an amphibious vehicle or craft, with six-wheel drive and with no fewer than ten forward as well as four reverse gears. I tried the controls: I felt unconquerable, as though I was driving an immense tank. Then Robert took it into the river, and tried out its aquatic capabilities by a short trip downstream and up again: every so often the wheels would touch bottom and it would function momentarily as a land vehicle instead of a boat. A versatile craft: it served as our power-station as well as our transport, since Robert had installed a small generator on board, which – if run for an hour each morning – would charge the batteries so as to give us all the current we needed in the evening. But it was a noisy hour, and if one desired to talk without bellowing, one needed to be away from camp while the generator was running.

All was now ready for our northerly expedition: I could hardly wait to start, the collector's itch being powerfully on me. Restlessly I looked around at the camp vicinity. Every day I had seen squirrels in the fig trees above and heard their click-click noises, and I knew that they were in the habit of making early-morning raids on our food-store. So I got to work on the spot, strapping the smaller of my two wire traps on to a broad branch that was much in use as a squirrels' highway. It was Henry who drew my attention to the result: there he was next morning, sitting below and barking, appearing to think that he had effected the capture. I took the cage down and opened it, and found inside a small green tree squirrel which – from the black speckles on its back – I could identify as a specimen of *Peraxerus cepapi maunensis*. It seemed too bulky a name for so small an animal, and since the textbook gave it no English name, I decided that it was to be simply a Maun squirrel. It was quite exceptionally nervous and seemed likely to damage its head against the walls of the trap; so I decided to release it, and to catch further specimens in the same way at a later date, so that they could live in a padded box and have only a short time of captivity and travel.

John had made a supply of collapsible cages and wire frames, somewhat oddly proportioned but capable of being erected quickly; my bird baskets had also come, and I had paid a ridiculously low price for them; my permits were all in order.

And so I embarked upon this second stage of my collection, feeling slightly more confident now, more plausibly a real trapper of real animals, by reason of my first experience in Rhodesia.

CHAPTER 6

Flamingoes, Wattled Cranes and Aardvarks

Now, as we were ready to set forth, another difficulty arose. Chinky's travelling-cage had not arrived from Bulawayo. I did not need it immediately; on the other hand, I did not want to set out for the northern swamps until I was completely sure that it would be there at Maun when I came back, so that Chinky could be transferred to it at once, and embark upon the journey back to the Channel Islands with the rest of the collection that I hoped to gather. At that stage, with a possibly large number of animals cramped into travelling-cages, delay would be most undesirable.

In order to keep us usefully occupied while we waited for the cage, Robert suggested that we should go for a week to Lake N'gami to see the large collection of birds that abounded there, and perhaps to net some. June was busy writing yet another article for the South African press – a condemnation of the growing trade in cheetah, leopard, and serval skins – and she was rather glad to have us out of the way, so that she could enjoy the peace and quiet that every writer needs. Robert and I took with us Kisi the cook boy and John, and we loaded the truck with some baskets and cage-frames, plus a week's supply of food. Henry also came along with us: he jumped into the cab under the impression that we were only driving into Maun to collect the lions' meat, and we decided not to make an issue of it.

Our drive took us forty-eight miles to the south-west, to the small trading post of Sehitwa. The track ran, at one point, through a forest of ghost trees; they had been drowned by severe flooding two years before, and there was not a scrap of greenery upon any of them. They looked like something found on a lunar landscape, bare and dead: it was hard to see them as trees, hard also to imagine floods in a district that was now so parched and arid.

We drove on, and encountered a family of ostrich. When they saw the truck they split up; the brownish hen bird made off with her brood of five chicks, while the black-bodied male walked slowly away in the opposite direction, feigning injury and spreading his wings, gallantly trying to draw away from his family, and upon himself, any danger that there might be. Robert noticed that one of the chicks had parted from its mother and was stumbling back along the track towards us, unseen by either parent; so he stopped the truck and got out, taking care not to be seen by the devoted father, and through the driver's mirror I then saw him run back along the track and perform a kind of rugger tackle upon the chick, securing it and then gently gathering it up. He brought it into the cab, and we started off again; but after twenty yards the truck stopped without warning. At the same moment the ostrich chick, which was on my lap, relieved itself lavishly and liquidly all over my trousers.

We responded to this twofold crisis like true Englishmen. In a moment Robert had the bonnet open and was tinkering with the engine, while I emerged from the cab, shook myself clean as far as this was possible, and set about helping him. The father ostrich had apparently lost interest and had made off to join his family; thus, to leave my hands free, I tied a piece of raffia to the chick's left leg and tethered him to a nearby mopane. (My bird baskets were inconveniently hard to get at in emergency: they were packed under our week's supply of provisions.) So I got to work alongside Robert, and was soon covered in diesel oil, and found myself wondering whether mechanical work was dirtier than animal work; but then, all at once, back came the angry father ostrich. We hastily took refuge in the cab, and Henry looked up at us in mild surprise, having no idea of the great events that were taking place outside: we looked out in amazement as the father ostrich carefully pecked away at the raffia until his chick was free. It was pleasant to see them reunited: I wanted to have a pair of ostrich, but this one was not destined for my collection.

At Sehitwa we visited a small store owned by a Greek trader who lived with an African wife and a retinue of chocolate coloured children. When he learned that I had come to N'gamiland to collect animals he asked me to follow him round to the back of the store and there showed me an ostrich and an impala too, both of them living in his hen-run. 'They are yours for ten rand each,' he said, rather implying that I was certain to buy whatever he offered. I told him that I wouldn't be able to take the impala, but would be interested in the ostrich if he could hold on to it for me for another six weeks. She was a fine bird, almost four feet high, and when I looked her over appraisingly she simpered bashfully, like a young beauty in the slave market. Her pale neck was striped with delicate broken lines in pastel shades, her large eyes were overshadowed by long flirtatious lashes, and her flight-less wings sat on her body like powder puffs on either side. The Greek had been keeping her for five months. At night it was her custom to join the impala and the hens under a thatched lean-to, and the hens would roost all over her body as she crouched down, possibly taking her for one of them-selves. The warmth so provided had saved her life. In the natural state ostrich chicks take refuge under their mother's wings, and so maintain a daytime temperature in the cold night: they cannot survive without such help.

This part of N'gamiland had little or no tsetse fly, and it was the major cattle-rearing area of the region. Most of the Africans were of the Damara tribe, which had fled from German South-West Africa at the beginning of the century: they were subject to the indigenous Batawana, though the latter were fewer in number and poorer in cattle.

As we drove on to Lake N'gami, twelve miles to the south,

we could see that we were indeed in cow country. Four Africans passed us on the track and waved cheerfully; they were wearing cowboy-type hats and riding fine horses, and they were engaged in herding some three hundred head of beef cattle away from the lake to spend the night in some vast kraal or corrall. Behind the herd a great cloud of dust arose, making it hard for Robert to see where we were going and to avoid the many obstacles. But eventually we emerged from the dust and the scrub-trees and into open flat country like a steppe: then, like a mirage, the lake itself appeared on the horizon. We were surrounded, as we came closer, by an increasingly deafening tumult of abundant bird life.

The sun was sinking fast, and we stopped to set up camp for the night, lighting a fire and setting up our camp-beds in the open. John and Kisi preferred to sleep in the back of the truck. Then, as always during our stay by the shores of Lake N'gami, we were privileged to see a sunset of the most breathtaking kind. The whole horizon became a vast red-hot furnace, into which the sun sank like a fireball. Thereafter the night became cool, which we found refreshing after the hot motoring of the day. We dined agreeably off steak and rice with some rather warm canned beer, and then, with Henry lying between our camp-beds, we soon fell asleep under a ceiling of radiant stars.

Lake N'gami covers an area of some forty-five square miles. It was discovered by Livingstone in the mid-nineteenth century, and possesses in all probability one of the richest concentrations of bird life to be found anywhere in the world. There are even pelicans: in Livingstone's time they used the lake as a breeding place, but now – owing to the encroachments of domestic cattle – they merely congregate there. Most of the lake is only a few feet deep; it is rich in plankton, and has a matted forest of oxygen-producing plants growing from its muddy bottom. It is because of these water plants, and also because of the saltiness of the water that comes from evaporation, that the place is attractive to so many kinds of bird.

Next morning we drove along by the lakeside, going as close to the edge as the firmness of the ground would permit. We passed groups of marabou storks which would preen beneath their wings, then shake their shaggy necks, then return to their endless preening. The small sacred ibis, black of neck and head, would prod around in the weeds, looking for insect delicacies: the African avocet too, with its up-turned beak. Ducks, terns and plovers flew busily here and there: some large wood ibis bunched together about two hundred yards from the shore, standing as though on red stilts in order to keep their plumage dry. In the distance, near the middle of the lake, we saw the pastel shades of the greater and lesser flamingo; also those pelicans, ill-proportioned birds perhaps, with their outsize beaks and bloated throats. And all these different birds kept up their varied and continual cries, unremittingly.

We continued our drive along the east bank of the lake, with the sun's heat battering down upon every inch of the wide country. On the southern shore we chose a dry grassy stretch of ground for our base and stopped there. We needed shade badly, and so we fixed a big piece of canvas by two corners to the top of the truck, and supported the other two corners on poles which we sank into the ground: under this canopy we could sit in some comfort. Then we offloaded our provisions and my own equipment: baskets chiefly to serve as bird cages, and also four aluminium rods which could be fixed together to make a pair of twelve-foot poles. These had been specially made for me according to the specification of Reay Smithers in Salisbury, who knew Bechuanaland well and the conditions there: the idea was that I would be able to hang my almost invisible and therefore bird-catching mist-nets between them in any sort of country, without relying upon trees.

We lunched off some refreshing water melons which we had bought from the Greek trader; then, wearing only shorts and bush hats, we started to wade into the lake and among waterweeds that tickled our legs. John carried the two aluminium poles, no doubt wondering what I was going to do with them. Henry took a couple of steps into the lake, just far enough in to get muddy, and then returned to dry land and started to bark a loud protest. Robert spoke to him rather sharply: he was disturbing the birds. So Henry went back to the truck feeling misunderstood and martyred; we discovered later that he had jumped on to his master's camp-bed to sleep there, covering it with the lake mud that had clung to his person.

We did not go very far into the lake. When using a mist-net of this sort, one of the great rules is that you must always stay nearby, so that a netted specimen does not have too much time to entangle itself and thus get hurt, as well as damaging the net. We would be able to see the net easily enough, and to see when it had caught a bird, wherever it was; but we would not be able to move quickly through those weedy shallows, so the net had to be close at hand. We dug the sharpened end of one of the rods into the mud, and then, before attaching the other half, I took a brand-new mist-net out of its plastic package and attached it to the top of the pole, then hoisted it into position. Some thirty feet away we erected the other pole in the same way, taking care not to get the mist-net wet. The top of the net now stood some 9ft above the water; and there were four tension cords running through the $1\frac{1}{2}$in mesh, thus forming three shelf-like pockets, within which any bird that flew into the net would be caught. (Without such an arrangement, it would simply bounce off the net and continue its flight.)

Now we had to trust to luck. For one thing, if a flamingo or a wood ibis flew into the net, it would be the net that suffered, and disastrously. Then, how could we know that any birds would happen to fly in the right direction? I had read how ornithologists use these nets when working along some small stream or river: they stretch the net across, from one side to the other, and since the birds commonly fly up and down the river, their chances of catching them are good. But the open surface of a large lake is a different matter. We had to place our trust in the near-invisibility of the net, and hope that some of the smaller water fowl would happen to fly between the poles: with luck, a scared ibis or two.

So we waded back to the shore and to that very welcome shade. I sat on my camp-bed and watched the bird life through my binoculars: I felt like a football fan, waiting passionately for the moment when the ball would come flying between the posts and into the net. But as there was nobody trying to kick the ball through, I felt that my chances were more like those of the people who go in for football pools.

Then about an hour after we came back from the lake I saw something bulging and struggling in one of the pockets on the net. I shot up from the camp-bed and bounded into the lake, stumbling in my excitement and getting my shorts covered with mud and weeds, startling Henry into a frenzy of barking. When I reached the net and identified the bird that was struggling into a deeper and deeper entanglement. I saw in some disappointment that it was an avocet – not a species I wanted. I had a fearful task to get it loose without damaging the net. A bird in this situation will get the thin nylon twisted round its neck, over its wings, round and between its legs, and as you free one part, another becomes further entangled. In the end I had to enlist both Robert and John to hold each part of the avocet securely as it was disentangled in its turn, thus preventing re-entanglement. And so we got it free.

The net survived this adventure; and later on in the day, it survived a heavier threat. We were just going to take it down for the night, when I was appalled to see a number of assorted cattle wading in the lake in its direction. They were between me and the net: if I ran out, I would drive them into it. I considered a flanking movement, but this was out of the question. I had to trust to luck. Apparently the African cowboys whom we had met before had chosen this stretch of water for the watering of their cattle in order to gratify their own curiosity about our presence and purposes by the lakeside. I crossed my fingers and held my breath while the cattle splashed along by my precious net, and in the end no harm was done, though one of the beasts did stumble against one of the guy-ropes that supported the nearer pole.

Our next concern was with the flamingoes and pelicans. These larger birds tended to stick to the middle of the lake, and it took us a good forty-five minutes of wading to get within reasonable distance of them; as we drew nearer we had to shout louder and louder if we wanted to communicate, so deafening was their clamour.

The pelicans were the most suspicious; they would launch themselves into the air if we came anywhere near them, flying off then to the northern part of the lake. The flamingoes were more trusting: when we came within eighty or a hundred yards of them they would start to move away, in groups of about twenty, but only taking to the air if we closed in on them too quickly.

They used to take a regular evening flight, all together, and it was wonderful to behold. Just before sunset they would take off in one immense flight, with their long necks and crooked black beaks held out before them: their pink bodies would fill the western sky, contrasting beautifully with the fiery shades of the declining sun. Then they would come spiralling gracefully back to alight close to the lakeshore where they would pass the night.

I wanted to capture some, but my first attempt ended in muddy failure. Robert and I decided that we would approach them at night-time; we thought that as they slept – each bird balancing on one leg, with its head tucked under one wing – we would be able to creep up undetected and close in and rugger-tackle them. Clouds would help to darken the night and conceal our advance; a light wind would help also, by carrying our scent away and the noise of our approach too. Unfortunately this particular night was both cloudless and windless.

Slowly we advanced upon the sleeping birds, our bare feet sinking into the soft weeds and mud. We could see the flamingoes plainly before us, some fifteen of them, looking very much like the imitation flamingoes that one can sometimes see in an ornamental pond. But their immobility didn't last. As we approached, one small head came out from under a wing and one small warning noise was uttered, and at once they all started to move off. We were within ten yards of them, and we both thought that swift action was called for, and we leapt forward as one man and dived for the legs of the nearest flamingo. The splash was tremendous; and we emerged hopefully, each hoping to see a bird captive in the other's arms. In fact we saw each other birdless and smothered in slime. We laughed uncontrollably, while the fifteen birds walked away with dignity and unharmed.

The exercise had taught us one thing at least that when approached in this fashion, flamingoes would walk away rather than fly away. This meant that on some later occasion we should be able to drive them into a net.

Next day I reaped a rich harvest from the mist-net, and had my first encounter with the black and white blacksmith plover. This species seemed collectively determined to join my collection, not in ones and twos but in flocks. For the rest of our stay by Lake N'gami they would come streaming into the mist-net, and it would take the three of us – John included – a long time to disentangle them. A painful operation too: their small carpal spurs would prick our hands as they struggled madly against their own liberation. Actually we liberated too many. Two months later, when I was back in England, I was told by John Yealland – the curator of birds at the London Zoo – that he would have been very glad of a few specimens. For us, on the spot, these plovers were just a nuisance; quite apart from the work they made by filling up the net and struggling in its folds, they made other birds suspicious of it, so that they avoided it. We therefore had to keep moving it from one place to another.

In between these onslaughts from the blacksmith plover, I managed to catch two species of teal in the net: the red-billed teal, and the smaller hottentot teal. I was particularly interested in this latter species, as its distribution is confined to this southern half of Africa, and it is not seen as often as the red-billed kind. So I felt that our visit to the lake was beginning to bear fruit, even though John did go through a phase of allowing birds to fly away when I had released them from the net and passed them to him to hold. This was not good for my temper, and once, when he had let a hottentot teal escape, I furiously told him to run after it and catch it. He began to do exactly that, but I called him back. He probably thought I was crazy; but then, the whole of my activities must have seemed rather crazy by African standards.

My baskets now had their first occupants, and I stretched canopies of hessian across their tops, under the lids, so that the birds would not damage themselves by jumping and struggling. I also kept the hessian damp, so that these waterfowl would not dry out and lose the natural oil of their bodies.

By the end of the week the baskets held a small collection: two pairs of the red-billed teal, and three pairs of the hottentot variety. They provided me with a feeding problem. The difficulty was not to know what to give them, since a mixture of corn millet and mealie-meal was certainly right: the difficulty was to get them to eat at all. In captivity they just crouched at the bottom of their baskets and refused to touch anything, regarding themselves as doomed. So I had to coax them, holding the head gently, dabbing the beak into the food. This usually worked. When it failed I had to make little pellets out of the food and work these into the obstinate bird's beak at the side, then close the beak and point it upwards and stroke the neck until the pellet went down.

And so we passed five days by the lakeside, and then took our canopy down and packed up and drove northwards along the western side of the lake. As we went, we saw no fewer than eleven specimens of the majestic wattled crane, foraging along the shore with their mincing dancer-like tread. A tantalising sight: wattled cranes are very seldom seen in zoological parks, and if I could capture a pair, the scope and value of my collection would be wonderfully enhanced. But how *could* I capture them? They are active birds, and in that flat countryside they would be able to see us coming from miles way. I started to dream of a vast net, a mile or so long, to be launched into the air by rockets. . . But then I came down to earth, and remembered that I had just one mist-net, just thirty feet long, holed already by a small duck.

But the frustration became unbearable; I told Robert to stop the truck, and we left John and the cook boy to look after everything and keep the ducks fed, while we went off crane hunting. We stretched out long leg-nooses on the ground, and then we moved slowly around selected cranes, trying to drive them in the right direction. It was a bookies' day, the odds were against us, but we found the suspense exciting. One crane actually did get its feet caught in a noose: our hopes soared but immediately fell, since the bird just danced a little jig and then continued on its way. The sun was merciless, and Robert lost his sun glasses, so that we had to retrace our steps with our eyes on the ground: altogether it was a disappointing day.

We camped a little further on, and decided that before we finally left the lake, we would have another and last shot at flamingo catching. So we used some of the wood and wire frames and made a trap, a big thing like a barn, and fixed this in the lake about half a mile offshore. Then we erected two mist-nets in the shape of a broad V, with the trap at the point: the idea was that we could drive them into the V and thus down into the trap, or at least, into some position where they would be at our mercy.

We waited once again for the cover of night-time, and – but without success – for the further cover of clouds. Then we set forth, stumbling as quietly as possible through the familiar slime and tickle of the lake, alerting the birds but cautiously, not wanting them to panic. It seemed to be working; they started moving off, and in the right direction.

This was getting exciting. Steadily the gap between the

Just back: (*above*) Helen of Troy's Paris — Eared or Lappet-faced vulture; (*below*) Chinky's arrival at Jersey Zoo.

(*above*) Martial Eagle at Jersey Zoo; (*below*) a brace of immature white-headed vultures.

birds and the net work narrowed, and if some flamingo decided to change course, we could easily outflank it and turn it back. We weren't helped by the moonlight and starlight, which showed up the net and the trap with what seemed to us great clarity; but there was no sign that the flamingoes noticed them. On we plodded, sinking and quelching through the weed entangled shallows. We counted eleven specimens, and it seemed that our technique was going to work.

The birds kept up their quiet murmur and their steady progress; but then, as they came within the open jaws of the funnel of net, they suddenly fell into complete disorder and broke ranks noisily. Robert and I reckoned that it was important to force them against the nets, and so we splashed forwards shouting, driving the birds on to those fragile mist-nets and indeed through them. The confusion was frightful: when it was all over Robert and I found ourselves sitting once again on the lake's muddy bottom, alone and birdless.

Next morning, sobered and saddened, we went out to dismantle the trap. There were four blacksmith plovers entrapped in the tattered mist-nets, as though in a last determined effort to join the teal in captivity; and our defeat of the previous night was underlined by the presence there of several pastel-pink feathers. It was obvious that the mist-nets could not be used again: we cut them down from the poles, liberated the plovers, collected the frames, and returned to shore. At least I was learning by experience that some methods of trapping were *not* practical.

So we left Lake N'gami, after a whole week on its shores. I don't think Henry had enjoyed one moment of that week. He didn't like the muddy and weedy waters of the lake; he had continually been shouted at for going too close to the duck-baskets; he had missed Gilly-Anne; his meat ration had been atrocious. Now, as the baskets were loaded up on the back of the truck, it dawned upon him that we were actually going home: he wagged his small copper-coloured tail forgivingly, leapt to his seat in the cab, and sat there bolt upright, his eyes longingly on the north.

At Sehitwa we called again at the Greek's store, and fin-alised my arrangements for collecting the ostrich. The Greek came out of the store and peered curiously into the back of the truck, probably expecting to see any number of flamingoes and cranes. I had to explain rather sheepishly that these particular birds had somehow avoided capture, chiefly because of the time factor: this showed my trapping ability in a rather poor light, especially in view of the huge quantities of bird life that crowded there by the lake, begging to be captured.

We drove back to Maun and on to Robert's base camp on the Thamalakane, stopping three times on the way so that I could check up on the teal and keep their baskets damp and their food topped up. Soon we were home. June, the lions, the spaniels and the hens all seemed glad to have us back, and Henry was in heaven. I had a word with Chinky, and then went to see how my Bechuanaland gerbil was getting on. I looked into the cage and there it was, sitting in front of a mound of grain that was nearly as big as itself, and may have looked much bigger, what with the magnifying curve of its bulbous eyes. It was applying itself in a dedicated sort of way to the problem of eating right through this mound of grain: I decided to make its paradise complete by catching it a mate.

The next journey that we had in mind would take us up to the northern region of the swamps, and as two Africans would stay behind at the base camp, I decided that the teal could also remain in their care. So John and I set about building an aviary. We chose a pool by the riverside, with a steady flow of water to keep it fresh, and we fenced this in, sinking the wire deeply into the mud for security, and roofing the enclosure with more wire, supporting this from the con-venient branch of a fig tree. We scattered reeds over the wire roof so as to provide shade, and threaded some more reeds through the bottom part of the wire walls, so as to camouflage them and discourage the birds from damaging themselves in fruitless attempts to escape. I put the hottentot teal in first:

they panicked a little, but soon settled down to bathe in the pool. The red-billed teal were also upset at first, but before long the water and the weeds calmed them down and gave them something to do.

We drove into Maun every day to collect provisions for the camp and meat for the lions. On one such trip we saw in front of the truck the long hosepipe shape of a python. Robert asked me if I wanted it. 'Well, yes,' I answered without much enthusiasm, 'I suppose it would be a nice thing to have.' Robert jumped out at once, and with all the agility of a mongoose he grabbed the writhing serpent by the nape of its neck. It was about five feet long, and not at all pleased by this treatment. We hadn't got any kind of box on the truck to put it in, so I hurriedly suggested to Robert that he should hold on to the python while I went back to the camp and fetched one. He took the view that he ought to ride back with us, so he climbed into the cab, python and all. Henry jumped out in terror and refused to come in again: I had to stow him in the back. And so we drove back to camp, with the python winding itself like a creeper around Robert's leg, and darting out its forked tongue in hostility towards everybody and everything.

Back at the camp we disentangled it from Robert and put it in a large box, taking care to keep it out of sight of the gerbil, which would be upset by a meeting. I found that I very much disliked handling this reptile, and I wondered why: after all, I had managed to handle the rock monitor often enough in Rhodesia, and it could have hurt me a good deal more than this python. I decided that this revulsion was a matter of ignorance on my part, and that the snake was probably as nervous of me as I was of him; so inwardly shuddering a little, I set to work on the task of winning his friendship.

My Bechuanaland collection was now beginning to grow and take shape: I had a python, a gerbil, two species of teal, and the prospect of having two spur-winged geese and an ostrich. I also had Chinky, and she was a joy, and would play with me, or with Robert or June, in the most agreeably kittenish manner. John looked upon this phenomenon with never-ending astonishment: for him, a lion was simply a predator, and a danger to be avoided. Even so, he seemed to be taking an interest in this new aspect of the matter, which would be socially useful for him when he returned to his own village at Mazoe. I could see him dining out on this experience for years to come, astounding his cronies with tales of his long fearless involvement with a terrible lioness.

I now heard rumours of another animal, the clawless otter. About a mile upstream from our camp, at the confluence of the small Boro river with the Thamalakane, there were two large posts. I had already seen how these were used by the Batawana tribesmen; they would work their way up to the poles in their dugout canoes, and fix a string gill-net between them, and then go away. When they came back soon afterwards, there would be a few fish in the net. I thought that I could modify this technique and so secure one or two of the clawless otters which (I was now told) abounded thereabouts. Out came my strong nylon animal nets, which had cost me a good deal of money, having been made specially for me at Bridport in Dorset; and I went out during the night in the little aluminum dinghy and fixed these nets between the poles. Then I manoeuvred the dinghy into the cover of a nearby reed bed and settled down to keep watch and see what happened.

It was not an altogether lonely vigil: all around me there was the high-pitched sound of frogs and the french-horn-like belchings of toads. A few mosquitoes alighted on me, but were driven off by my own supremely effective technique of repelling insects, the essence of which is the steady chewing of garlic.

The night moved slowly on: the reeds swayed in the gentle breeze, and the water rippled slightly where the top of my nets broke the surface. I relished the novelty of my situation, sitting there in a dinghy in the middle of a reed bed, with countless frogs and toads for noisy company and with the slowly wheeling stars for illumination. But soon the novelty wore off, and I found it hard to concentrate on my vigil. The seat was uncomfortable and I started to get cramp; when I moved to ease this, the boat scraped against the reeds beneath it, the noise causing the frogs and toads to fall totally silent for a few moments, then resuming their chorus when it became apparent that there was no danger. I yawned and rubbed my eyes, which were becoming dazed by the effort of concentrating in that dim light upon the small patch of disturbed water above the nets. I made great efforts to hold my heavy head upright, but with diminishing success. At about three in the morning I decided fuzzily that I would be more comfortable if I lay down in the dinghy, on the duck-boards between the seats, and there continued my vigil, keeping very carefully awake. . .

The next thing I knew was that my name was being shouted at me from the far bank downstream; also, that the sun was high and already hot. I sprang to my feet, almost capsizing the dinghy, and called out weakly to show where I was. No evasions, no excuses were possible: the sentry had fallen asleep at his post. I slid the dinghy out from the reed bed and over to the nets, sheepishly admitting to Robert that I wouldn't be able to hold down a job as a night watchman. He was standing there on the opposite bank, with his guns and his dogs, and if it hadn't been for the big bush hat he was wearing, the whole picture would have suggested an English squire going out on a duck shoot and coming across the lair of a guilty poacher.

I had caused them some worry. By the time the sun had been up for two hours without any sign of my return, they had begun to think that the dinghy had capsized or that I had otherwise contrived to drown myself. I explained, lamely, that I had stayed awake until three o'clock at least. But when we had a look at the nets, it became obvious that my shameful weakness had caused me to miss a real chance. There were a few dead fish in the nets, and also two large and expensive holes. While I was sleeping so peacefully two otters must have come for the fish and become entangled in the nets, but then had had all the time in the world to bite themselves free with their razor-sharp teeth. I was grieved: Robert laughed. Then we went back to camp empty-handed, and on the way we saw the dinosaur-like form of a big water monitor as it slid from the bank into the security of the reeds. It was a good five feet long. Water monitors are larger than their land-loving cousins, the rock monitors, and can grow to as much as ten feet, three-fifths of which, are accounted for by the tail. On dry land they can move well but not very rapidly, and although they have no webbing between their toes, they are excellent swimmers, using their long powerful tails: I felt rather glad that it had not decided to climb into the dinghy while I slept.

One might have expected that after this failure – which was not my first – my reputation as a trapper of wild animals would be somewhat diminished. But no, almost at once I was enlisted to help in a serious crisis. I visited the Calvers to have another look at my spur-winged geese, and Dave Calver told me that for the last four nights they had been troubled by an aardvark which had come into the garden, chosen the best of the flower beds, and had dug into it most destructively. Each morning they repaired the damage as best they could and even fenced off that flower bed with branches and wire; but each night the aardvark came back and did it again. On the fourth night Dave stationed one of his Africans to keep an all-night vigil; 'But would you believe it,' he told me, 'the fellow fell asleep on the job!'

'Shocking,' I replied, 'outrageous.'

'So you're the right man to help.'

I seemed to be stuck with the job, and I pondered over its difficulties. How on earth *do* you catch an aardvark which has buried itself in a flower bed? I had read that this animal, with its powerful claws, can dig itself into soft earth quicker than men with spades can follow. Could I grab hold of it above ground-level? I had been told of an African who had tried this and had been pulled down the aardvark's burrow up to his waist even though two men were holding his legs: if he hadn't let go he would have been pulled right down into the animal's network of underground tunnels.

I returned to camp and asked for Robert's and June's advice. June suggested, not too seriously, that we should use Chinky, who would be glad of some aardvark meat. Dogs might be more practical; but I knew that Henry would be off like a shot if confronted with any such grotesque creature as this. It would have to be human cleverness once again, deployed quickly: I had promised the Calvers to solve their problem on the next day.

Robert's suggestion was a pit-trap: they had made one a few years ago in order to catch some lion cubs, which they had photographed and then released. He drew me a diagram: it was an elaborate affair, a large pit with a collapsible roof, covered over with earth, triggered off by a pull on a rope. But this wasn't the easiest sort of answer. For one thing, it would be a major operation, quite destroying the flower bed that the Calvers wanted to preserve. Then, we would have to line the pit very strongly: otherwise the animal, when trapped, would simply dig down and be as inaccessible as ever. And what would we do with the aardvark when we had caught it? I didn't want it for my collection, and in any case, I had no cage strong enough to hold such a powerful digger.

Even so we decided that this was the only workable answer. So next morning we set off for the Calvers, with John and another African well armed with digging implements.

Dave greeted us jubilantly. 'I've saved you a little bit of trouble,' he said. 'I shot the thing from the verandah in the early hours of this morning, so my wife's flower bed will soon be back to normal.'

My first reaction to this news was one of pure relief; then, when I was shown the aardvark's body, I felt sorry for it. I had never seen one before, and I studied it with interest: the hunched massive body, with its long head and snout, and the round blunt pig-like muzzle with its big round nostrils; the tubular ears, that move independently and can be folded down to exclude dirt while the animal is burrowing; the tapering tongue and the similarly tapering tail; the short stocky legs with their power-ful claws. I could well understand the animal's effectiveness as an excavator. The name aardvark means, literally, 'earth-pig'; but this creature, with its dull yellowish-grey body, looked more alien and remote than any pig in my experience.

Relieved of that task, we went back to camp and relaxed. Just below the bridge over the Thamalakane, there was a stretch of river where the east bank was clear of weeds, where we could therefore dive and swim in the crystal-clear waters without any danger of being ambushed by lurking crocodiles. We used to visit this swimming place daily, going there some-times by truck, sometimes by dinghy. It was my own pleasure to take the inner tube of a tyre and lie cradled in it, floating gently upon the water, staring at the sky, and watching a pied kingfisher that haunted the spot. It seemed almost tame; it was quite undeterred by our presence, and in fact seemed to delay its hunting until we arrived. Our swimming and splash-ing would disturb the fish and drive them out to the nearby shallows, where the kingfisher could get at them more easily. It would hover there above the water, then suddenly flash down like an arrow, coming up a moment later with a fish: I felt rather glad that there wasn't any bird big enough to play the same game with my inner tube and my defenceless person.

Eventually Chinky's travelling-cage arrived, delivered at the camp by Riley's Transport. It was a heavy metal cage, need-ing two men to carry it, and perhaps six (I thought) when Chinky was inside. Robert examined it carefully and studied the workings of the sliding door at the end; and then he told me that it could be loaded on to the back of the DUKW. The point was that until I was ready to leave the district with Chinky, this cage would serve as a trap: we could take it with us, and possibly catch a number of larger animals, when we set forth on the journey to the northern regions that was going to be the next stage in my adventures.

CHAPTER 7

Lions, Lions and More Lions

IT took us two days to pack all that we would need during our stay in the northern regions of the Okavango swamps. We had three vehicles. Robert was to drive the DUKW, loaded up with all my boxes and cages and frames and nets, and carrying Timmy as a cabin-passenger; June was to drive the diesel truck, with Kisi and two other Africans as her passengers, and with the twelve brown hens crated and stowed in the back; I was to drive the old Dodge truck, with John as my passenger and with Chinky in the back. To complete the procession, there was a well-seasoned grey horse, which Robert had just bought and which a local Batawana guide had agreed – in a rash moment – to ride.

My collection – apart from Chinky – was to be left in the care of the African who was staying behind to look after the camp. Now, and for about the hundredth time, I ran over his instructions for the proper care of the teal, the python, and the gerbil, and promised him a good *bonseller* if everything was all right when I came back. A member of the local veterinary department agreed to call in from time to time and make sure that all the animals were all right: this eased my anxieties a good deal.

And so we formed up and set forth, with Robert giving the starting signal from the cockpit of the DUKW: I felt a sense of excitement and occasion as our parade moved in order out of camp, the grey horse first, then Robert, then June, and myself in the rear. It was a noisy parade; the

DUKW, in particular, made a terrible racket, scattering the wildlife, with fleeing wildebeest and zebra visible from time to time. We kept a good distance between the vehicles, since the ground was often sandy and needed to be negotiated at a good speed, by the trucks at least. The DUKW could look after itself: it had a low-geared six-wheel drive that could negotiate any sort of country, and it also had a winch at the back. Provided that there was something to attach the cable to, it could winch itself out of any sticky spot.

For the first part of the journey we stuck to the well-established track which led in a north-easterly direction towards the village of Mababe. On this track we could maintain a steady ten miles an hour. But after four hours we left it and took a more northerly course into a more isolated and uninhabited region. Here the going was tougher. At times we had to stop and cut back some of the branches of the mopane trees so that the DUKW could get through. When things got really difficult, our mounted guide would go ahead and find the best route for us to take.

We were travelling across country, not following the winding courses of the waterways, and through a rather featureless landscape, in which it would be easy to get lost. As a precaution we made a practice of blazing trees as we went by, thus making it easier to retrace our steps if necessary.

It was in this kind of country that we halted for our first night out, setting up camp by a small water-hole that was covered with a carpet of weed. The spaniels insisted on drinking thirstily from this stagnant looking pond, although they had already been given some safer water. We fed the lions, we fed the brown hens, and then we fed ourselves, with Kisi doing the cooking over a campfire.

To any African who might have come upon us unexpectedly, our camp would have presented a strange and unnerving sight: the trucks, the tank-like bulk of the DUKW, the people and the lions among them. In the event we were ignored by man and beast, with just two exceptions. The numerous tsetse fly were extremely glad to see us, and gave us a welcome which could not be controlled by the use of the fly-swat or by my own chewing of garlic. This was our bad luck. The whole of this area to the north of Maun is considered to be a tsetse-fly area, but they do not occupy the whole of it: they appear to concentrate upon certain stretches of bush, which cannot be identified in advance. Only experience could tell us whether we had chanced to pitch our camp in one of these occupied areas or not. On this first night, we had.

Then there were lions in the region; and of course we had a very charming lady lion with us. After her dinner, perhaps realising that she was back in the wilds, Chinky started her full-throated roaring: four deep drawn-out bellows, and then three shorter descending notes, and then all over again. At first Timmy replied, with a rather pathetic flat howl, but Chinky ignored him and he soon shut up. We went to bed; but in the early hours of the morning I was woken up by further loud roaring from Chinky, and then heard in the distance the deep answering reply of a wild male. This would not do: when sleeping out in the open, you don't want an untamed and amorous lion prowling around your camp. So I went over to the truck and had a few quiet soothing words with Chinky, begging her to keep a maidenly silence. Fortunately she agreed, and together we listened in silence to the receding roars of the disappointed suitor.

Next day we set out again through more of that mopane shrubland and then over open veldt until we arrived at the Machabe River, sometimes called the Kwaai. Chinky was very much on the alert now, and took a deep interest in her new surroundings: for her sake I was pleased at this, but I was less pleased when in her excitement she started to swing her heavy person from side to side in the truck, thus altering its balance and causing it to swerve rather dangerously. This added to John's nervousness: he kept looking back through the small cab window to see where Chinky was, fearing that some extra violent swerve or jolt might throw her forward into the cab and on top of him.

We travelled along the south bank of the river, keeping

carefully to the firm ground, well away from the tall reed beds: it was rather like driving through a lonely region of the Norfolk Broads. Robert was looking for a crossing-place; eventually we found one where, by laying branches and reeds in the tracks made by the DUKW, we could provide a surface across which the lighter trucks could cross without getting stuck. So we crossed the river and went on, and arrived at what Robert and June called Fig Tree Camp. It was a beautiful place, with two fig trees standing alone in the middle of some dry veldt, a most pleasant change from the scruffy disorder of the mopane shrubland. We set up camp under the fig trees, with the veldt sloping down before us to the reed beds and the crystalline waters of the river. It was as though we were in a country mansion, looking out at the park and the lake, well stocked with ornamental waterfowl.

Here the tsetse fly were few and far between: even the nocturnal mosquitoes were as considerate as was their nature to be. A flock of spur-winged geese flew past along the line of the river, their long black necks and bodies thrusting through the air like jet fighters, their formation a perfect V, up to the highest standards of an RAF ceremonial fly-past.

Robert lifted Timmy down from the DUKW and exercised him, using a collar and a long chain, afterwards tethering him with a strong metal peg in the shade of the nearby shrub. I was tempted to give Chinky also some measure of freedom, since her accommodation in the truck was cramped; but the danger was too great. She was all too likely to go off on a honeymoon with one of the local lads, and thus miss her appointment to travel to Jersey with me. I explained this to her as best I could, while engaged in cleaning her out and covering the floor of the truck with fresh reeds. This confinement was temporary, I told her, and so was her celibacy: she was in fact betrothed to a very good-looking lion which had been at the Jersey Zoo for the last three years and would doubtlessly prove to have all the charm and blarney of the Irish, since he had been born in the Dublin Zoo. She licked the back of my hand with her rough tongue when she heard this, just as if she understood everything and would be faithful and save herself for marriage.

Alas! Good resolutions often go down before the stormy forces of nature. On our third night at Fig Tree Camp she came into season, forgot the voice of conscience, and set about making quite sure that every male lion in the Okavango knew of her presence and loneliness. June at once put the tape-recorder into action, so that we would have an audible souvenir of this trip. I found the noise rather romantic at first: it was certainly a great experience to be sleeping out there in the wilds of Africa, with a real live lion roaring its head off a few yards away. But the old problem recurred, sweeping aside all such sentimentality: we heard a male lion answering Chinky's call, and much closer at hand than the one we had heard before. She continued with her calling, in a voice less plaintive, more compelling and urgent; and then, from another direction, we heard the reply of another male.

Robert came up and spoke to her sharply, rebuking her provocative behaviour and showing her his rifle. No, he wasn't threatening her with death: the point was that she found the deafening report of a gun an unnerving and sobering experience, and therefore respected even the sight of one. The formula worked for a time: she became calmer, and settled down on to her bed of reeds. We relaxed and went back to bed ourselves. But soon we heard the perplexed calls of those two lions once again, and much nearer. Chinky rose to her feet, and before Robert could show her his rifle again, she gave forth the most beseeching roar I have ever heard.

Things were getting out of hand. We put the three apprehensive spaniels into the safety of the DUKW – the bold Henry was quaking in terror, so that I could hardly hold him – and prepared for action. June came out of the cabin of her truck with a Verey pistol at the ready, and climbed up and stood on top looking around. It was a fine clear night; we had a good view over the veldt and down to the river. We awaited developments.

Soon we heard a startled wail from Timmy, who was about fifteen paces behind the DUKW, and when we looked we caught a quick glimpse of the eyes of a lion on a game-trail in the bush behind him. They disappeared at once into the shadows of the mopane: the wild lion had been expecting to find a female, and his encounter with Timmy must have been equally unexpected on both sides. But we couldn't take risks: we decided to bring Timmy right into the middle of the camp as quickly as possible. June switched on the small 80-watt light that was mounted on top of the DUKW and started to sweep the surrounding bush with its beam: Robert persuaded two of the Africans to climb down from their place of safety and rekindle the fire into a blaze. Chinky gave a few faint sounds, but was silenced utterly when Robert fired his rifle into the air. Now, perhaps, Timmy could be fetched in. Robert walked in his direction, while June and I kept him covered with searchlight and rifle respectively: he was approaching the point where the wild lion had been seen. Then we heard Timmy's welcoming noise and he came bounding back into the light of the camp fire, with Robert holding the chain.

Chinky was on her feet again, swaying from side to side, her eyes fixed on the direction from which Timmy had just been fetched. In the distance we heard the call of a hyena, which obviously thought that the lions must have made a kill and was hunting for the carcase. We needed to strengthen our position; so we tethered Timmy and the grey horse at opposite ends of the DUKW and arranged all three vehicles so as to make a sort of triangular stockade, with the camp fire in the middle. But Chinky resumed her amorous roaring, despite some hard words from us and another deafening rifle shot from Robert. The wild lions seemed unlikely to go away.

It was not easy to decide what to do. Chinky herself was in no danger, imprisoned within the strongly-built Dodge truck; but if the lions came for her, Timmy and the horse would be in danger of being attacked. Our own position was not altogether safe.

For a while there was silence. Then it was broken by the simultaneous roar of two lions, very close at hand; Chinky answered, and was answered in her turn from an even shorter distance. Then, in the beam of the searchlight, we saw the emerald gleam of four eyes. Robert fired a warning shot over their heads, and they disappeared at once into the mopane on our left. There was silence again, and then the barking of some baboons not far away, disturbed by the noise of the rifle. I could hear branches snapping in the bush, telling us where the lions had gone: Chinky was straining her eyes in that direction, and soon – yet again – she had started up on her anthems of love.

There was nothing we could do except keep guard all night. June continued to sweep our surroundings with the searchlight, and Robert and I sat vigilant, rifles across our knees, looking (I suppose) rather like the sheriff's posse in some doubtful Western. Our Africans certainly looked as though they had just survived one attack from the Comanches and could expect another at any moment. Time ticked by: Chinky kept up her lovesong, but with less and less conviction and with no further result, until – just as the first touches of dawn lit up the sky – she gave it up, sank down, and went to sleep.

We didn't want another night of that kind, but while Chinky remained in her present loving mood, there wasn't much that we could do. The main thing was to shift the locality of our camp, removing it to more open ground, so that any courting male lion – or any predator, for that matter – would have to cross a good area of open veldt before reaching us. So, while Chinky slept peacefully and enviably, we set about packing our recently unloaded gear and moving. By lunchtime we had found the right place: it was still close to the Kwaai River, but with no bush or other real cover within a quarter of a mile. We arranged the three vehicles in the same defensive triangle, and then set about surrounding the camp with branches, thus erecting a barrier which any lion would need to jump before reaching us. But as we had chosen the site for its remoteness from cover, this meant that the branches had to be dragged a quarter of a mile before being put in place. The operation almost brought us to our knees: dinner, that night, was served to a very exhausted camp.

We made a point of giving Chinky a really enormous meal. Then (we hoped) she would fall into the deep sleep of repletion: alternatively, the pains of indigestion might divert her thoughts from love. And in fact she did behave rather better that night, with just a few enticing roars, these being halfheartedly answered from afar. No doubt the wild lions felt they had seen through her: she was plainly a decoy, set up to draw them into some kind of human devilry. But we couldn't rely on this: they might come back. So Robert and I decided to take it in turns to watch over the camp, with two Africans taking it in turns to keep the fire blazing, while the rest caught up on their sleep – on top of the DUKW in the case of the Africans, though Robert and I slept on the ground.

This exhausting routine went on for four days, sapping our energies and making it impossible for us to make a start on my collection. It was really tiresome of Chinky, and we did feel exasperated with her, but never for very long: her charm could soothe away anybody's resentments and irritations, and she never lost her temper. We forgave her. But I found myself reflecting upon what the novelists and the poets have told us about the disruptive and shattering effect of love upon the female: seldom (I felt) can there have been a more painful example.

Eventually we started to move around. We had brought the aluminium dinghy with us, strapped to the top of the diesel truck: we fitted the outboard motor to this, and so we were able to explore up and down the Kwaai. The rainy season had started, but the water level was still very low indeed. The bird life was much the same as I had seen on the Thamalakane, but without the multi-coloured pygmy geese: it seemed also that the cormorants had been replaced, here, by the goliath heron, large birds that went about in pairs, not in flocks as the

Under the discerning eyes of the Hon Director of the Jersey Wildlife Preservation Trust or learning about seriemas from Gerald Durrell.

Beauty and the beast.

cormorants had done. On one occasion I saw a saddle-billed stork standing alone, the yellow saddle on its beak suggesting the squadron badge on the nose of a fighter aircraft. It took off and flew away purposefully, as though to a defined target.

My first capture – I should rather call it my first find, since no pursuit or trapping was involved – was a Bell's hinged tortoise. I carried it back to our camp and showed it to Chinky, who begged me to give it to her to play with. Henry rushed up and barked at it: Gilly-Anne was close behind him, and he needed to seem tough and aggressive, he therefore plucked up enough courage to sniff at it timidly, growling at the same time, as though to warn it not to start any tricks.

I selected the lushest area of grass within our camp area and made a wire enclosure. This was useless: I hadn't realised how well tortoises could climb. This one, with its horny legs, functioned like a small climbing tank, and it was up and across those eighteen inches of wire in no time, so that I had to find closer accommodation for it. In this species, the bottom shell or plastron is hinged in front like the bows of a landing-craft, and closes up to protect the head in any emergency. Examining my specimen, I found that the surface of the plastron was distinctly concave. In tortoises this is a mark of maleness: the plastron is concave so as to accommodate the top shell or carapace of the female during copulation. I thus had a male tortoise on my hands, and I decided to call him Albert after my grandfather, and to find him a mate if possible.

Robert now came forward with a somewhat hair-raising suggestion. 'You have often told us about that crocodile in the Jersey Zoo,' he said, 'how it likes having its neck scratched. Well, how about catching a companion for it? How about this evening?'

This prospect shook me a little: Robert was a bit too keen on any scheme that promised entertainment. It is one thing to scratch a crocodile with a stick through a slit in a glass door: it is quite another thing to venture out into the swamps at night and fling your arms about an unknown saurian and carry it away, despite all protest. But Robert swept aside my misgivings and started off on explanations and arrangements. The main thing, he told me, was to pick up a young one and not an adult: the thing to note was the distance between the reptile's eyes. In the dark, this would give you a clue to its size.

Crocodiles, like alligators and gharials, belong to a very old family which can trace its ancestry right back to Jurassic times, some 140 or 170 million years ago. They are all amphibious and egg-laying and they feed mainly on fish, but they do catch mammals as well, and sometimes man. The Nile crocodile, which is the species found in the Okavango swamps, can reach a length of sixteen feet; it is the baby of the family, since the Mississippi alligator is known to reach nineteen feet and two inches, and the Orinoco crocodile has been recorded at over twenty-three. I was glad that we were not going out after these larger reptiles.

That night turned out to be unusually dark, which was useful, as it would enable us to come right up close to the crocodiles before being seen. We pushed the dinghy out into the river and droned away, the noise of the outboard motor silencing the music of the frogs: I attended to the motor, Kisi sat amidships, and Robert knelt in the bows to guide us. He had a powerful torch fixed to the front of his bush hat: this left his hands free to gather up crocodiles. The beam from the torch swept the dark surface of the water as we went, and Robert kept his eyes ahead, alert to catch the reflection of the light in a crocodile's eyes.

He had to watch out for something else as well: at any moment we might see the mountainous form of a hippopotamus, browsing in the reed beds at night. If it were alarmed it would probably come crashing back into the safety of the deeper water, which would not be healthy for our frail dinghy: and if we met it head on in some narrow channel, we would have to turn about very sharply, since these big creatures will not reverse. Altogether, I hoped that we would not meet a hippopotamus that night. But I was grieved to hear that they were becoming scarcer and disappearing from their old haunts. This had practical disadvantages. When the hippo was plentiful people did not fully realise that by bulldozing his way through the reed beds and following the water in the dry season, he provided a free dredging and irrigation service. Where he has disappeared many of the lesser waterways have become silted up and good pasture lands have thus been deprived of water.

A refreshing breeze prevented the ubiquitous mosquitoes from settling on our skin. We puttered on, and in the moving beam of the torch we saw a continuous diving display, given by frogs and toads of every shape and size as they leapt off the water-lily leaves on our approach. Robert gesticulated like a French policeman, guiding us in what he hoped was the right direction; and, sure enough, we soon sensed an extra excitement in his movements. When I turned the boat to port, as indicated, I saw two reptilian eyes reflecting the beam of the torch. I now had to bring the dinghy up close, so that Robert could grab hold of the crocodile as we went by : fortunately it seemed to be hypnotised by the torchlight, and there was a pounce and a splash and a spraying of water from the flailing tail as Robert swung the creature over and dropped it neatly into the awaiting box.

'Your turn now,' he said, and we carefully changed places. In the dark I saw a white flash of teeth : Kisi was grinning sympathetically, doubtlessly glad that it was not he who had to make the attempt. I strapped the torch to my jungle hat, feeling rather like a coalminer about to descend a flooded pit to rescue a comrade : I tried to build up my morale by thinking of the loneliness of that crocodile back at home in Jersey, but I didn't care very much at this time. But I pointed ahead bravely, as a signal to Robert to proceed, and tried to remember my instructions. If the eyes are far apart, leave it alone : it's a big specimen. If they're close together it will be a small one and easy to manage, as we had just seen. But what if there were two big ones side by side, their inner eyes close together? And in any case, how can you assess the distance between the eyes when you don't know (because of the dark) how far away the creature is? Two reassuringly close eyes could widen alarmingly on a closer approach, and it might be too late by then. 'Oh well,' I said to myself in resigned fashion, as the motor puttered away behind me and my torch played over these dangerous waters, 'perhaps I'll get away cheaply and just lose my fingers.' That would mean an end to my piano-playing – a sad thing for me, but possibly in the public interest.

It was altogether too much of a gamble, too much like Russian roulette. What a fool I had been to consent to this rash game! But being now committed, I could hardly back out. Henry was always trying to appear heroic in Gilly-Anne's eyes, and here was I trying to appear heroic in Robert's eyes: for dog or for man, the fear of appearing cowardly can over-rule all other fears.

Forests of reeds slid by on either side, and there was that steady plunging and plopping of amphibians in the torchlight. I started to relax, thinking joyfully that the riparian version of a bush telegraph must have told all the crocodiles that there were kidnappers abroad, so that they had gone into hiding. But then, suddenly and with mixed feelings, I saw two icy eyes straight ahead.

I flapped my hands wildly, like a learner driver making a hand-signal, and kept the spotlight upon the animal's head. Robert must have seen it too: he brought the boat alongside with effortless precision. Did I try to assess the distance between the eyes? I can't remember, but presumably Robert would have warned me if I were trying to haul a twelve-footer aboard. I just remember plunging my hand into the cool water, aiming at a point about two inches behind the eyes and allowing for refraction: my hand made contact with the cold slimy shoulders, and my fingers closed over them tightly. At once the crocodile took fright and started to flail around: I clung and wrestled, and managed to swing it up and over the gunwale of the dinghy in the nick of time. As it came over it wriggled out of my grip and fell into the bottom of the boat, where it created a certain amount of chaos: Kisi very nearly abandoned ship, but remembered in time that there would be other crocodiles in the water. In the dark I could not see where my captive had got to: I wrenched the torch off my hat to see, and Robert went into efficient action and cornered the angry beast under the duck-boards by his seat. I opened the box that already held one specimen and Robert firmly put the second inside, then closed the box firmly. We breathed again, and I felt a certain sense of achievement. I was to blame for stupidly dropping my crocodile, but at least I had managed to catch it, and it hadn't got away.

Like the hippopotamus the crocodile is now becoming somewhat rare, and is hard to find outside such isolated places as these Okavango swamps: too many of them have been shot or trapped so that the skin from the belly can be made into such luxury articles as ladies' handbags, wallets, and shoes. In this age of synthetics it is quite inexcusable to bring a wild animal close to extinction for the pleasure of having its beautiful skin. A good plastic substitute can be made easily enough. Failing this, if the human race insists on authenticity, then breeding colonies could be maintained for the purpose, so that the wild stock can remain unmolested and undiminished. We have done this with the chinchilla, the mink, the coypu, and some others: we should do it with the crocodile as well — an interesting and archaic animal which will soon be nothing but a memory, if the present rate of killing continues.

The moon now slid out from behind a blanket of rain clouds, and we turned back for camp by its light, speeding past those diving frogs at full throttle, the propeller churning up the water like a kitchen mixer. On three separate occasions we had to stop and tip up the outboard motor to clear the propeller of weeds: then, with a pull on the cord, we would be on our way again, down the winding river, until we arrived back at our camp just after midnight. The crocodiles were quite motionless in their box as Kisi and I carried them ashore, and even when we showed them to Henry, who barked at them terribly, they remained as though frozen.

At first light the following morning, I put John on to

making a holding cage for the two now, very stern looking crocodiles. I designed the cage in such a way that the cage's bottom and ends were made of wire, so that when it was placed amongst the cool of the reeds, and angled correctly, the crocodiles had the choice of either being partially submerged in water, or being able to remain on dry land. They would also be able to take advantage of eating any fish or amphibian life that came their way. Both the specimens were between 2 and 3 feet long, and as young crocodiles develop rapidly during their early years, they were probably both still under five years old. Although I knew that it was comparatively easy to sex crocodilians, by simply feeling within the anus as to whether a penis is present or not, I decided not to trust my luck too far, after dropping the specimen I had handled during the capturing operation.

I now turned my attention to carrion-eating birds. There were plenty of these: I had left some meat around to attract their attention, and through my binoculars I had seen three species of vulture, one tawny eagle, many parsonical-looking marabou storks, and also (to vary the theme) a black-backed jackal. I therefore decided that a representative collection of carrion-eaters – of birds especially – would add to my collection on very interesting lines. This is an aspect of African wildlife which everybody has seen in films and read about in books. Whenever an animal dies, a kind of natural public health and sanitation department goes into action at once: the jackals, the hyenas, the vultures, the marabou storks all play their part in disposing of the flesh and the bones, while the dung beetles and other insects clear up the excreta. Soon there is only a rather trampled patch of ground to show where some animal has recently died.

And so, after our night with the crocodiles, we sat and discussed the matter over a good breakfast. Our twelve brown hens were well established in the camp and provided us with plenty of large brown eggs. We ate some of these, drank coffee made from Nescafé and evaporated milk, and considered the capture of carrion-eaters. Our kit included a reel of strong fishing gut, too thin for a bird to see easily, and from this we planned to make a number of loops or nooses. These could be attached to tins or cans, filled with earth and therefore very heavy, and arranged in a big circle around the place where we proposed to put out some meat as bait. The plan depended upon the birds' habits. They would land some thirty or forty feet away from the carrion and then approach it with their customary and very ungainly prancing motion. Thus, we hoped, they would get their feet caught in these nooses; and if they tried to take off and fly away, they would be held down by the heavy tins. I would then be able to break cover, sprint a hundred yards, and clasp the captives to my bosom.

It was an obviously sound plan, and we set to work. We decided to bury the cans which anchored our nooses, so as to make them less conspicuous and more secure: Robert helped me in this work, but the spaniels were not helpful at all, since they insisted on digging up each can as soon as we had buried it. We had to imprison them in camp for the duration. Chinky seemed anxious to take part in the adventure, but had to be refused; perhaps for the same reason Timmy ran out to grab me by the ankle – just in play, Robert told me – but was fortunately restrained by his chain. Robert gave me a big wildebeeste haunch that came from an animal shot for food, and we placed this in the centre of our circle and retreated into a small copse – alive with tsetse fly – to await developments.

Soon through my binoculars, I saw the first vultures approaching and circling, their great wings flapping slowly. When the first of them landed, I saw that they were immature specimens of the white-headed vulture. It all went as we expected, but only for a time: they pranced along the ground towards the meat and became duly entangled in my gut snares, but then, after a moment's flap and panic, they shook them off easily and flew away. We decided to repeat the experiment, and rearranged the whole trap and the bait on another site. Their suspicions had now been aroused, and it was quite a long time before they came. They were plainly on the look-out for the thin gut; and when one of them touched it with its talon, it gave the alarm and they all flew away. We could lure them to our trap, but not catch them.

I gathered up my useless equipment and went dejectedly back to camp with my African helpers, who had been watching my methods with some incredulity. Then our Batawana guide came up and broke the silence which he had maintained so far: if we liked, he told us, he would demonstrate the method which he would use in such a case.

He cut a sapling and stuck it into the ground. About eighteen inches away from its base he stuck into the ground a staple-shaped piece of wood, surrounding this with small twigs arranged in a circle. He then made twine from long grass, tied one end of it to the top of the sapling, and divided the other end. One part of it became a noose, held in place by that circle of twigs; the other part was attached to a short stick to serve as a trip or catch. Then he bent the spring sapling down, fixing it with a forked twig under the wooden staple. The bait was to be attached to this twig: when the greedy bird tugged at it, the sapling would be released and would straighten upwards, thus drawing the noose tightly round the bird's neck and securing it.

It looked to me like a totally obvious trap, unlikely to fool even the most dim-witted and careless bird. Still, after my own method had failed so miserably, I thought it was worth a try. So on the following day, under the guidance of our Batawana tutor, we set up five of these traps, baiting each with a portion of the meat. As before, we then retreated into the cover of some nearby bushes, and watched the slow suspicious assembly of the vultures and the marabou storks. Some perched doubtfully on a rotten tree nearby, hunched up like witches, before landing heavily: soon quite a number were approaching the carrion, their wings still outspread, their gait still with that awkward prancing character. They did not all come at the same speed. There were poor-spirited specimens which hung back, and there were bolder spirits that pressed forward. It was one of these, naturally enough, that first touched the bait; and the trap sprang itself at once, the noose tightening so that the bird was firmly tethered.

I sprinted forward and seized it, despite its struggles. At once the other birds launched themselves into the air, some of them lightening themselves for easier flight by vomiting up the heavy mass of food that they had already eaten. I grabbed my vulture's neck with my right hand and got its flapping wings under control with my left; then I tucked it firmly under my left arm with its head to the rear, released the noose, and made the bird helpless by holding its legs together.

This was a considerable moral victory for our Batawana guide: I decided to consult him in future about all questions of trapping. Back at our camp I handed the now quiescent bird into June's tender care, and John and I set about making a cage for it. We fixed six of our medium-sized wire frames together, lining all but the bottom and the front side with a protective padding of hessian; and across the middle of this cage I arranged a perch, devised to suit the width of the vulture's talons, so that he could take his ease in his own familiar way. We put this cage on top of a rough table that we had already constructed from branches, and I took the bird from June and slid it inside. At first it lay motionless on the floor as though dead. Then after a few minutes it got up and rushed at the padded sides repeatedly; then, realising that it was trapped, it climbed on to the perch and sat there in a posture of hunched resignation.

I consulted my reference books and decided that this was a specimen of the white-backed vulture, which was common in the tropical savannah bushveldt. Its whitish head was almost devoid of feathers, and its neck resembled that of a partially plucked turkey. Vultures' feet are not adapted to the holding of a live victim, as are those of most birds of prey; their great weapon is the powerful beak, which is perfectly adapted to the tearing of skin and flesh from dead carcases. In some of the regions where they live carcases have become scarce owing to the establishment of European farming methods; and in that situation, being desperate, vultures have been known to attack live sheep. But they have only succeeded in injuring the sheep, not in killing them: unlike the eagles, they are quite unpractised and incompetent in the art of killing.

During the next ten days I concentrated on catching as many different species as I could. The traps succeeded wonderfully, perhaps because they were made wholly out of materials that the birds were accustomed to seeing every day, whereas their keen eyesight would lead them to avoid my fish-gut or anything else unfamiliar. I thus caught two more of the white-backed variety, and then – on a single morning – two specimens of the smaller white-headed vulture. I didn't want too many specimens of any single variety, however, and this meant that I had to release a good many of the birds I caught. This was never understood by John and the other Africans: there I was, spending laborious days in the hot sun in order to catch birds, and then releasing most of those I did catch. As at many other times, my activities must have seemed somewhat crazy to them. The moral is that we should not pass hasty judgement when other people's activities seem crazy to us.

Beyond any doubt the prize of my vulture collection was a fine eared or lappet-faced vulture, the largest species to be found in this area, with a wing-span of over nine feet. June named him after Helen of Troy's Paris, since in her estimation he looked so magnificent. This is a relatively unsociable species, found in twos and threes where others gather by the score; but even so they dominate, driving off competitors until they have chosen the best parts of a carcase, and then standing back to allow the lower classes their turn.

Soon there was a line of cages on that table behind the DUKW. The spaniels gave it a wide berth, no doubt thinking it beneath the dignity of pedigree dogs to associate with such scruffy birds. Chinky also seemed a bit negative about them. They were usually downwind from her truck, so that she couldn't smell them, but if I came straight from handling them to be sociable with her, she would utterly refuse to lick my hand or play patty-paw. Robert felt similarly: he found these carrion-eating birds entertaining but smelly, and moved his camp-bed to place the greatest possible distance between himself and their cages.

With so many large birds on hand we soon ran out of wire frames and hessian, and had to improvise cages, using the straightest branches we could find in the adjacent bush. We allocated ten days to this part of the expedition, and before our time was up I had caught three marabou storks and – an unexpected guest – a tawny eagle. He was nasty to handle. I had no difficulty in extracting a vulture or stork from a trap, but when I came to remove this eagle, he was in an angry mood and lay flat on his back, using his sharp-taloned claws to dangerous effect. Before I could release him and bring him under control, I had to tear off my shirt and press it upon him, so as to give those fierce talons something to hold.

Unfortunately I had not observed the tawny eagle among the vultures before it was caught: I did not know whether it had come along for a share in the meat, or to attack the vultures. I knew that such birds will often attack other birds, as well as hares and small antelopes and other mammals; I had not heard of them attacking carrion-eaters, but I did not want to take risks, and so I housed my eagle separately, well away from the vultures and out of their sight, close to the crocodiles and Albert the tortoise, all of which seemed quite indifferent to their neighbours.

This excellent collection was endangered by a tendency, on the part of some of the birds, to go on hunger-strike. I eventually persuaded them to eat by hanging gory meat in festoons from the roofs of their cages, so that it brushed against their faces and beaks: this irritated them, they snapped at it, found it edible, and fed themselves at last. When they had eaten, the crop of each bird would bulge as though it had swallowed a cricket-ball. When they were in that state, it was important not to disturb them: if they were frightened, their hunched forms would lurch up and down and they would regurgitate their rations in a definitely un-beautiful way. I soon learnt this lesson, and learnt also to feed Chinky and Timmy before the vultures. At first I failed to do this; and just as I was congratulating myself on persuading the vultures to eat at last, Chinky gave a loud hungry roar, all the birds emptied their crops in alarm and shook their cages in fruitless attempts at mass flight.

At the end of the fourth week, we saw rain clouds gathering darkly and mountainously on the horizon, and we realised that the first storm of the rainy season was at hand. I got John to cut me a stack of reeds to be spread out on top of 'Death Row', which was June's name for the line of vulture-cages, and also to cover the accommodation of the marabou storks, the crocodiles, and Albert the tortoise. We brought Chinky's truck closer to the fig tree, as well as Timmy and the grey horse, arranging the three animals in a triangle around the DUKW: and Robert erected a canvas lean-to against the southern side of the DUKW, so that our table and our camp-beds would have some shelter against the expected downpour.

Just before the storm broke, everything became still and breathless: a silence like that of a crypt hung over the bush and the veldt and the reed beds, broken only by Chinky as she swayed to and fro in her restlessness. Then a gentle breeze fanned the ground, throwing up eddies of dust and bringing with it the first big spots of rain; then a clap of thunder from the north-west heralded the full darkness and power of a tropical storm. Vast inky clouds moved over us, releasing their torrential loads, splashing the red soil around and piling the water up on the hard soil before it could soak away, until streams of mud ran under the DUKW to where we were sitting under the canvas lean-to, flooding and dirtying everything that was not on the camp-beds or the table.

The thunder crashed and rumbled away, and the lightning

lit up the countryside in vivid erratic flashes. The spaniels huddled nervously under one of the bunks in the DUKW; the lions lay crouched; the big birds hunched themselves up on their perches; the crocodiles lay as motionless as ever; and the grey horse remained fairly calm, since Robert had blindfolded it as a precaution against stampede and flight. If it had run away, its chances of survival would have been small.

It was, I suppose, an inconvenience to be thus flooded and muddied out. But the storm was spectacular, a wonderful thing to experience; and when it was over, the rich moist smell of the earth – after the dusty aridity of the dry season – was a sensuous delight to the nostrils.

CHAPTER 8

A Bush Camp Easter

THROUGHOUT this expedition Robert had been in regular
radio contact with Maun. Now, by that means, he heard that the
Smeetons had arrived from Francistown and wanted to join us
at our camp on the Kwaai. They had been expected, but not
until the end of the month. So the District Commissioner
agreed to bring them up to where we were, with the help of
his own guide, so that they could join us for the Easter weekend that was approaching. He also was interested in seeing
what animals I had managed to trap.

The Smeetons and their travels were well known to me by
reputation. I had read about Beryl Smeeton's extensive journey-
ings through China, Japan, Persia and Russia in pre-war days –
about how she had ridden over the Andes into Patagonia, driven
a van through much of the United States, and walked through
Burma during the monsoon; I had read about Miles Smeeton's
life in India, where – as a regular army officer – he regarded
pig sticking and big-game hunting as better training for jungle
warfare than most of the official training exercises. I also knew
about the somewhat light hearted attempt that they had both
made, with Sherpa Tensing, to climb the 25,460-foot Tirich
Mir in the Himalayas. But the thing that had really captured
my imagination was Miles's book *Once Is Enough*, in which he
described their two epic attempts to sail round Cape Horn,
their yacht *Tzu Hang* being turned over and smashed up on
each occasion. I am not trying to suggest that I envied them
this experience: on the whole, I prefer to keep my feet on

dry land. But the Smeetons had been stretched to the full, both mentally and physically, on their first attempt; and after its failure they had been game to come back for a second attempt. I admired that. I felt that we were now to have among us travellers of the epic sort, straight from the pages of the old pioneering books. So I tried to follow the example set by their perseverance and work extra hard, so that when they came they would find a notably better and more comprehensive collection than I had achieved so far.

I took thought, therefore, and remembered that a sandy riverside beach nearby was the daily rendezvous of a pair of hamerkop or hammerheaded storks. Here, where various game had trodden the reeds down on their way to the water, they would arrive each morning, but always separately, as though trying not to attract attention: then they would strut up and down in the shallows, picking up small fish and insects in a somewhat fastidious manner. They were small brown birds, the backs of their heads having a shaggy appearance, suggesting the more hirsute sort of hippie.

So I erected my last mist-net parallel to the water-line along this beach, and hid in the reeds on the opposite side of the river: at this point it was shallow enough to be waded across if I made a capture. The two hamerkops arrived within five minutes of each other, and were apparently not in the least put out by the presence of the two tall aluminium poles that supported my net. They drank and ate as usual, and then waded up and down before the net, as though they were on guard duty. Then they stopped for a siesta, each balancing on one leg within a foot of the other, heads comfortably tucked beneath wings. This gave me my chance: if I rushed at them now, from across the river, they would obviously fly away from me and so collide inextricably with the net. This crafty plan was no sooner devised than put into execution. Unfortunately, instead of flying away from me, the hamerkops flew vertically upwards, missing the net altogether and disappearing upstream at a low altitude, uttering a peculiar squeaky whistling sort of cry as they went.

I was sorry to lose them; but it was nice to think that they could now continue undisturbed with what I suspected was an impassioned love affair.

I turned back to the net and saw that I had not failed completely: a giant kingfisher was caught in its central fold. It was a handsomely marked bird, its white chest speckled with chestnut, and it did not at all like being handled: it uttered a loud cry when I took hold of it, though I was very gentle. I took it back to camp and placed it carefully in a sheltered cage. It appeared to settle down immediately: it sat there on its perch looking placid and plump and deeply thoughtful.

It had to be fed; and John's duties, which grew heavier as my collection grew larger, now included the finding of some minnow-sized fish. We put these into a bowl and offered them to the kingfisher, but he wouldn't touch them. When this had happened a few times we realised that forcible feeding was going to be the only way of keeping him alive.

So I asked Robert to hold the bird firmly but gently in both hands, and then I tickled the sides of its beak with a struggling minnow. I hoped that he would grab at it, if only in irritation. But soon the minnow stopped struggling, and I had to put it back in a bucket of water to recuperate. Then, holding the base of the upper mandible with one hand, I slowly forced down the lower mandible and slipped a worm into the kingfisher's mouth. This infuriated him: he didn't merely spit out the worm, he also nipped one of my fingers with his beak, and very painfully, to teach me better manners. An uncontrollable reflex made me wrench my hand away, so sharply that I inadvertently pulled the bird right out of Robert's grasp. My finger was thus set free, but so was the bird: in a second it was lost among the reed beds, gone for ever, another specimen destined to escape my collection.

Robert was sympathetic. 'What about the springhare?' he said. 'It's a handsome beast, and it isn't often seen in European zoos. I'll take you out this evening to catch some.' He said this over lunch, and very casually. These animals, he explained, are easy to catch: get them in the direct beam of the headlights and they'll stay fixed, hypnotised, until someone comes round behind and grabs them by the long ears. This sounded marvellously easy: I got two baskets ready, and prepared for a productive evening.

We made sure that June had a Verey pistol loaded and ready, in case we had to be summoned back for some emergency, and we took the diesel truck and drove off to the rear of the camp until we came to an area of open short grassland, where the soil was particularly sandy. There were no spring-hares in sight. Robert stopped the truck and told me that they had almost certainly been there, but had bolted down their holes when they heard us coming. If we kept quiet for five minutes, he said, and then switched the headlights on suddenly, we would be sure to see a number of them grazing by their burrows. And so it turned out. We waited in silence: the night air was damp with the moisture that rose from the hot earth, and we heard an owl hooting nearby as it went about the night's hunting. Then Robert pressed the switch, floodlighting the grassy area in front of us and illuminating the kangaroo-like figures of two springhares, which stood there mesmerised and immovable. Silently I slid down from the cab and circled round to approach one of them from behind and also from downwind: surprise would be the key to success.

You never know how uneven these apparently lawn-like grasslands of the bush really are until you try to move over them quickly and silently in the dark, and without any light. I kept stumbling over small ridges and hollows, tripping over bits of vegetation, lacerating my skin on thorny acacia bushes: twice I actually fell, just managing to hold back the loud curses that would have eased my feelings but also broken the spell that held my quarry in a kind of trance. As I rose again I could see it clearly: the cinnamon-buff pelage, the long narrow ears, the big nocturnal eyes that now reflected the truck's headlights. I came closer, losing one of my shoes in my excitement but caring nothing now for any such loss or discomfort: I was right behind the springhare, its ears tilted helpfully in my direction, and then I pounced, swooped like an eagle, and grasped it by the base of the ears and the long back legs. I had to hold it carefully away from me, or the long curved claws on the front feet could have hurt me nastily. Robert drove up, having very much appreciated the performance, and we put the springhare into one of the baskets and started to look for the missing shoe. We never found it; the bush claimed it as the price of my springhare. I had no intention of repeating the exercise in only one shoe, so we went back to camp, resolving to come back next evening to capture a mate for our new friend.

I wanted to see some of the larger wildlife at closer quarters, and I knew that one could approach them more closely on horseback than on foot. So next morning I borrowed the grey mare and set out soon after dawn. She was broad and comfortable, and proceeded in a very curious gait, half trot and half canter, a consequence, probably, of the Africans' refusal to rise in the stirrups while trotting. I was soon rewarded: wildebeest, impala, zebra, warthog, baboon, and sitatunga were to be seen in quantity, all looking as fresh and cheerful as the morning itself. I found a whole family of warthogs wallowing in a mud-bath, smiling as their American cousins, the dangerous peccaries, do: the two young ones had faintly striped reddish-brown bodies, and the parents had the characteristic crest of long black bristles, with large fleshy warts below their eyes. They emerged from their mud-bath deeply refreshed, and then the boar's acute sense of smell and perhaps of hearing told him of my presence. At once his tail flew up as a danger signal and all four stampeded off in great confusion, probably to take refuge in some deserted aardvark burrow and to consider their own rashness in allowing a human being to come so close to them undetected.

Later on, during that same day, Robert and I saw the largest concentration of game that I had ever encountered. We had driven about four miles upriver from camp when quite by chance we came upon a herd of between five and seven hundred wildebeest or brindled gnu. It is gratifying enough to see any animals in the wild state, but it was really astonishing to find a herd of this size, living their own life in total liberty, not even partly fenced in as they would be in a game reserve. This was a totally unspoilt part of Africa.

We moved in slowly towards them, and I felt rather as though I was on a cattle ranch in America's old West. The young wildebeest calves were being suckled by their mothers, and they seemed quite undisturbed by our presence: they frisked their black horse-like tails and butted greedily at the udders. The adults were bearded, and had tufts of long black hair protruding from muzzle and throat and between the forelegs: in their buff to black vestments they looked like dignitaries attending a congress of the Greek Orthodox Church. Henry was in the cab with us, and he was enchanted by the clouds of unusual smells that were coming his way: his nose twitched frenziedly, and he quite forgot to utter the bark with which he usually commented upon such situations.

We watched the herd for a good quarter of an hour, and then Robert restarted the engine and drove slowly forwards, to see how close we could advance without disturbing them. When we were about fifteen yards from the nearest of them a few of the larger wildebeest began to edge in our direction, snorting and pawing the ground in threatening gestures, Henry got the message and threw himself down to the floor of the cab in some terror. Then the herd started to move away, leaving a protective rearguard of a few big specimens which tried to keep us at bay by making menacing little charges, digging at the ground with their horns, snorting, then dashing away, then turning again to face us, their tails thrashing vigorously all the time. The sun had been very hot recently, and the earth had quite dried out after the storm: when the herd began to move more quickly, a great dust storm arose, like a desert sand storm. There must have been a real shortage of water. Wildebeest usually go about in small herds of five to fifteen, based on scattered waterholes. It is only when these dry up that they come snowballing together in search of some major water supply – in this case, the main streams of the Okavango swamps.

On our way back to camp I spotted the large form of a

leopard tortoise. We stopped the truck and took it on board: this was one capture which succeeded without any speed on my part. It was about one and a half feet long, and when I looked at it closely, I saw that it must have been involved in a bush fire at some time: the horny plates or laminae covering the carapace on the left side, had been burned off, exposing part of the undershell. I decided to take it back to camp to see if it could be a companion for Albert. Henry was nervous about having it in the cab, but took some comfort when his challenging growl brought no counter-challenge.

And so we came home, and attempted to repeat the previous evening's success with the springhare, but without success: when we switched on the headlights, after the same five minutes' wait, there was not a specimen to be seen. We knew that they were around, since we had seen them momentarily on our drive out to the place, appearing before us and vanishing at once. But they didn't seem anxious to fall for the same method. Maybe the word had got around.

I was very much enjoying my stay out in the wilds, but I noticed that John was unhappy: compared with what he had been used to it was a lonely existence for him. He used to follow me around like a devoted disciple, and always looked anxious when I felt the camp without him. But he had settled down well to his duties, which he had restricted to the preparation of the vultures' food, the cutting of reeds for Chinky's flooring, and the catching of a few fish. He was willing to feed the tortoises with greenstuffs, but apart from that he left the feeding of the livestock entirely to me, himself keeping apart and well away from any possible danger. He was homesick, which would not have surprised me in a town-dweller, but did surprise me in him, since he came from a very similar countryside: during the last ten days of our stay by the Kwaai, he seemed to ask me every day when we would be going back to Mazoe.

For my part, I would have been ready to spend any amount of time there in the Okavango, observing the wildlife and its infinitely varied behaviour. A morning ride on the grey horse was now part of my daily routine, and a very enjoyable one: it made me feel as close to nature as I could possibly get, and filled me with tranquillity and satisfaction.

There was always something new to see. Sometimes I would come across a small collection of the dull greyish-brown sitatunga, feeding among the reeds on sedges and swamp grasses: they fed partially submerged in the water, and the blobs of white on their shaggy coats acted as remarkably effective camouflage. I noted the great elongation of their hooves and the peculiar flexibility of their foot-joints: distinctive structural characteristics which adapted them very well for this practice of swamp-grazing. The species of sitatunga to be found in the Okavango swamps is the most southern form of the three races, and was named after the famous explorer and hunter, Frederick Courteney Selous. As with the other two species the females are without horns, more conspicuously striped, and smaller than the males. When surprised, they can immerse themselves in the water and submerge entirely, with only the tip of the snout protruding above the surface. They often spend the heat of the day in the water. On dry land, their long hooves make them run a little clumsily.

Sometimes, again, I would come across impala, which would leap away to cover in a curiously erratic and unpredictable sort of way. If I disturbed a group of them – a stag, say, with the four or five wives of his harem, as they drank at a watering-place – they would often collide with one another in their efforts to spring away to safety, then apologising (or so it seemed) and moving off in those remarkable high bounds, even though there were no obstacles to clear. I tried to avoid disturbing and frightening animals wherever possible: it is not much to the credit of the human race that when we meet them most animals think it wisest to run.

Then, on one of these rides, I came across a troop of the Chobe chacma baboon – about twenty-five of them, strolling through the long grass on the west side of the river as I came riding up on the east side. They noticed me, and one large adult male acted as look-out, keeping me under constant observation, but without ceasing to grab bits of vegetation, bite at them, and wastefully cast most of them aside. He even ventured into the shallow waters of the riverside, yawning in apprehension at the unfamiliar sight of my binoculars. I saw some newly born infants, small and dark, riding on their mothers' backs and clinging on with the determination of jockeys. Some of the half-grown members of the troop – the bold adolescents – kept breaking their ranks in order to get a better look at me, but this was frowned upon by adult authority. Perhaps I was considered an unfit spectacle for the young to see, or perhaps there was an apprehension of danger. If one or two brave teenagers had crossed the river and fallen into my clutches, the troop would have been hard put to it to rescue them.

Baboons have their ways of asserting themselves against the human race, even so. One night Robert and I made a third – and still unsuccessful – attempt to catch a second springhare, and we went by foot to cause less disturbance and give less warning. On our empty-handed way back we were walking through a copse of acacias when we suddenly heard the shrill bark of a mature baboon overhead, and at the same moment a shower of faeces fell all about us, as thickly as cherry blossom in a springtime wind. We were not aware of sustaining any direct hit, or not at the time; but the smell of manure clung to us unpleasantly, and Robert found later that his bush-hat was liberally anointed. After that he made a great point of never forgetting to wear it when he went out in the bush at night. This was not the most gentlemanly way of repelling intruders, but it made great sense from the baboons' point of view, since it was likely to deter predators. In particular the elegant leopard – who is one of their chief enemies – would think twice before getting his velvety coat sullied in this way.

We only had two days now until the Smeetons and the District Commissioner were due to arrive, and we wanted to have plenty for them to see. So Robert made a slight alteration to the crate in which Chinky was to travel, thus converting it into a trap. We had seen a spoor in the light cotton soil some four miles to the north, and both Robert and June were convinced that it was the footprint of a cheetah. This was an exciting thought: I had found a fiancée for the Dublin-born lion back in the Jersey Zoo, and if I could find a mate for Paul, our cheetah, it would be a great triumph.

So we took this large heavy trap to a suitable site and covered its floor with soil, smoothing this across the threshold so as to make a continuous surface with the ground outside, and making sure that everything was firm and solidly mounted: we did not want any animal that might enter the trap to feel any suspicious movement underfoot, or to suspect that he was not still on ordinary ground. We also didn't want him to smell our human presence, and so we smothered the sides of the trap with wildebeest dung, then camouflaged the whole arrangement, except for the entrance, with branches. Robert fastened a piece of freshly killed meat to the far end of the trap and I crept inside to test the mechanism. Robert lubricated the grooves of the sliding door with fat and held it open with a small piece of metal, attaching this to a long piece of wire that ran along the top of the trap and round to the bait. Lying inside, I pulled at the meat gently, and at once the door slid down and closed with a thud. Robert then let me out: I was rather glad when he did. I might have been able to get out by myself: it's just possible that a chimpanzee could. But any large and less intelligent animal would be trapped securely.

Finally we trod in some wildebeest dung and spread that odour around the trap to mask our own, also brushing the ground with a branch. Then, leaving the trap carefully set, we returned to camp, with the intention of returning at first light next morning.

Excitement made sleep impossible for me that night. In the small hours of the morning, still wide awake, I rolled off my camp-bed and went over to Chinky's truck for a word with her: she too seemed to be restless, and I told her all about her travelling crate, and what we were now doing with it, and what we hoped to find in it in the morning. I also held forth on the charms of the Dubln-bred fiancé whom she would find at home. She seemed to be deeply interested in all this.

Just before dawn we were on our way, scattering several early foragers as we drove to the trap, swerving in this way and that to avoid the many potholes and the abundant vegetation. Robert, who was usually calm, appeared to be excited for once. We both felt sure that we would have caught something, even though my past experience hardly justified such optimism, and I dreamt gloatingly of my success. Would it be the longed-for cheetah? Or, failing that, a Delande's or bat-eared fox, or a specimen of the lynx-like caracal? It would be something marvellous, at all events.

In our impatience to find out we accelerated and covered the last quarter of a mile at high speed, scattering antelope and wild pig as we went on, still on, then past a final copse of mopane, and there it was – our trap, and yes, there was an animal inside it. We flung the doors open and tumbled out of the cab and saw – not a cheetah, but the wretched skulking form of a spotted hyena, just like the one I had seen with Captain Boathby at the Umtali Museum. It crouched at the far end of the trap, growling.

It looked a terrifyingly powerful animal, with jaws and teeth and muscles surpassing those of the larger carnivores. These hyenas can crack the leg bone of an ox as you or I would crack a match, and they can completely demolish the largest bones of the hippo and even of the elephant. Even so, while this one had damaged the sliding door of the trap in its efforts to get out, it had not bitten its way out. This said a good deal for the strength of the trap, and for Chinky's security in it during her voyage to England: it was a comfort in its way, making up in some degree for our disappointment.

It was a disappointment: I had no way of housing such an animal in my collection due to a hyena's strength, so we decided to write off the night's work and release it. We tied a rope to the top of the sliding door, brought it across the branch of a tree and across to the truck, so that we could

open the trap from the safety of the cab. The hyena soon
realised that it was free: it emerged, and its large form lum-
bered out and away, across the rough ground behind us, at a
quite astonishing speed.

Unlike the striped hyena, the spotted hyena travel in large
packs, and they eat on the spot rather than dragging the provisions to their lairs. They will attack a lone unarmed man at
times; and they will always attack anything injured or small,
a child or a small animal, domestic or otherwise, if not protected. They are unattractive beasts, both cowardly and aggressive, and in the worst sense of either word. Even so, I would
like to have kept this one to show the Smeetons when they
came, if only there had been another crate suitable for keeping it in: those bloodcurdling howls and growls and barks,
so often ending with insane laughter, would have combined
with Chinky's very different music to provide a fine orches-
tral accompaniment to our visitors' stay.

Our Batawana guide now came once again to give me aid
and comfort in my hour of tribulation: for the rest of the
morning, he showed me how to make and set small grass
nooses, so as to catch such birds as might run through the
thickets nearby. By sundown I had thus caught five red-billed
francolin: this is a small grey grouse-like bird with an impressive deep red beak. I had not seen this species in zoological
collections previously, and as they seemed easy to catch I
decided to take a good basketful home. They differ from some
species of pheasants, to which they are related, by the fact
that the two sexes are alike; but the cock francolin, like the
cock pheasant, can be distinguished by the spurs on his red
legs. Of the five that I had now captured, four were thus
seen to be cocks: I decided to catch three more hens to make
a balanced collection of four couples.

Our guide's primitive methods seemed to work. By contrast, the small wire trap that had been so successful in Rhodesia, with the slender mongoose at least, failed completely
with the Okavango fauna. I would set it regularly: it was always sprung but never occupied. Apart from one springhare

and Chinky and a tortoise or two, my local collection was mostly a bird collection. Just before the Smeetons came I augmented it with a couple of ducks. This happened while I was taking the crocodiles down to the river in their wire box so that they could have their daily sulk in the water: I saw, a whole family of waterfowl and gave chase at once, almost dropping the crocodiles in my excitement. The mother duck broke cover and ran off, followed by eight ducklings stumbling confusedly after her: the last two took the wrong turning and came up against an impenetrable tussock of grass, thus giving me time to come up to them and catch them, while twenty yards in front I could see their mother feigning injury in the hope of distracting my attention, ready to sacrifice herself for the sake of her babies. I apologised to the crocodiles, took my ducklings back and put them into one of the baskets: within an hour they were accepting my offered pellets of broiler mash, mealie-meal, and munga seed, swilling this tasty food down with gulps of water.

I searched through my reference books to identify the species, but all the illustrations were of birds in adult plumage. I had seen the parents, but only briefly, since my mind was concentrated on the ducklings: I hadn't yet learned the importance of developing a photographic memory for wildlife, which is often seen for the shortest of moments and then not again.

This episode with the ducklings distracted me from something of the utmost importance – the importance of appearing smart and regimental when we had distinguished guests. So I embarked upon a quick shave; but just as I was dipping my safety-razor into a canvas basin of lukewarm water I heard the distinctive sound of a diesel engine, making heavy weather of the rough ground to the south-east of us. I shaved as hurriedly as I could, but it wasn't possible: before I had sorted myself out to receive company, a truck drove up alongside the DUKW and out stepped the District Commissioner and his wife, splendidly dressed and majestic in their bearing, every inch of them making it clear that they represented the British Crown in this part of colonial Africa. So I rubbed the remaining soap off my face and tried to rise to the occasion. Behind them, I saw two tall and youthful figures which were obviously Miles and Beryl Smeeton: even before we were introduced, I could sense their friendliness and their keen interest in everything they saw. After them the DC's guide emerged from the truck, and finally the total answer to the prayers of any young man who was ever in wild lonely places – two blonde girls, who at once descended upon the spaniels to envelop them in affection.

Robert and June handled the occasion with bush-camp informality but also with full observance of true British conventions. They made tea, and they also produced a tin of assorted biscuits that had often been discussed and hesitated over but not actually broached. Tea and sweet biscuits! We might have been in the cathedral close at Barchester.

Almost at once we were plunged into business by the taller of the two blonde girls, who turned out to be Clio, the Smeetons' only daughter. 'Come on,' she said, 'we're dying to see what you've collected!' So I thought quickly, and asked Robert to introduce the visitors to Chinky, our prize specimen, while I darted backstage to take a very necessary precaution. I went and terrified the vultures with loud noises and gestures. If there was going to be any regurgitation I thought it had better take place before these distinguished and sensitive guests arrived, rather than in their presence.

The animals performed well. Chinky enacted her fondness for Robert as fully as any theatrical producer could desire: she played patty-paw with him and licked his arms and face most impressively. Then Timmy staged a dramatic entrance from under the shade of the fig tree, scattered the brown hens, and took a nearly successful swipe at the terrified Henry. Thus both sides of lion character were displayed: the kittenish and affectionate, and the wild and predatory. 'You'd better watch Timmy when you're walking about camp – he's a little boisterous at times, and likes to grab people by the ankles': Robert uttered this warning quite seriously, but the

DC's wife seemed to take it completely in her stride. As for the crocodiles, they refused to move an inch: they looked exactly as they would if dead and stuffed. I explained that they were very much alive, and were in fact taken down to the river daily. They had not eaten any of the food that I had offered, but they had probably captured such small fish as swam foolishly into their cage when it was immersed.

The party now approached the row of vultures' cages, from downward as it happened, and just as a gust of warm air seemed to whirl around the cages and gather up all the scattered odour and roll it all into a ball and fling it at our visitors' nostrils. The DC responded in the highest traditions of Empire by making no response whatever: I did notice, though, that his moustache wilted as though sprayed with a powerful corrosive. His poor wife gasped, but soon rallied; and the Smeetons lived up to their reputation by pressing on, walking enthusiastically up to the origins of this appalling smell undeterred. Robert made hasty apologies for our odorous friends: they were not used to so many people approaching them at once, he said. And in fact they did not behave too badly: at least, thanks to my wise foresight, none of them regurgitated during this official inspection. I showed them off proudly: the eared vulture to begin with, whom we called Paris, then such lesser birds as the tawny eagle, the marabous, and the minor vultures.

We now came to the two ducklings that I had captured so recently, and the DC – having recovered from the gas attack – was able to identify them as members of the comb or knob-nosed species of duck. If either of them was a drake, he explained, he would develop a comb on the base of the upper mandible. They are quite plentiful in the Okavango, though he hadn't seen such young specimens for a long time.

I then showed off my red-billed francolin, and one of them nearly escaped: it had wriggled between the lid of the basket and the protective hessian lining, and flew up as soon as the lid was opened. I moved as smartly and effectively as any wicket keeper, and fielded it securely before it had taken more than one flap of the wings. There it was in my hands, its red beak gaping at our visitors. The DC's wife commented that francolins are very good to eat: an approach to wild-life that was not quite my own.

The tortoises came next: Clio picked up Albert and nearly dropped him, thus alarming him so seriously that he with-drew into his shell and raised the drawbridge and quite re-fused to be sociable. He thus gave a false impression of himself. For the last few days he and I had become very friendly: perhaps he thought that since I was so obviously a friend of those fearsome lions, it would be as well for him to keep on the right side of me.

The sun went down, the pale stillness of the brief tropical dusk came upon us, and the diurnal part of the local wildlife settled down just as the nocturnal part woke up: the camp fire crackled briskly, its noise blending in with that of the frogs and toads in the swamps nearby, its heat and glare keeping the mosquitoes away. All at once, Fig Tree Camp took on a different atmosphere. From a cellar deep in the bowels of the DUKW, Robert and June brought up an assort-ment of bottles, and soon we were sipping aperitifs from antique glasses. We even changed for dinner, feeling that the occasion warranted a special turn-out: that is to say, the men put on ties or silk scarves. In respect of manners, food, drink, and conversation, we ceased to be pioneers in the wild and became a weekend party in an English country house. But when the meal had come to a leisured end with coffee, the liqueur brandy came out, to warm and loosen our tongues and direct our conversation back to the one subject that was in all minds, the one question that was res-ponsible for our being here – the subject of animal conserva-tion.

There were several different points of view. Like so many naturalists before him, Robert had approached this subject by way of an original passion for big-game hunting. He had shot in Tanganyika, Rhodesia, and Mozambique, but now his chief concern was for the conservation of wildlife here in the Okavango. It was not that he had suddenly revolted against all killing of animals: in one sense he was still a hunter at heart, as became obvious when one saw him on the trail. It is one thing to kill for the pot. But it is quite another thing to stand by while the unbelievably rich fauna of Africa are systematically and irreplaceably destroyed with further unforeseeable consequences; and Robert was determined that at least this large inland delta of the Okavango should be saved from the greedy attentions of the safari firms, which were already seeking fresh killing-grounds for their rich clients.

June saw the question through the eyes of a journalist, and perhaps more emotionally, especially when she was involved in direct contact with the animals concerned. The steel gin-traps that were on sale in some of the trading stores near Maun infuriated her: whenever she saw one, she had visions of one of her beloved Bambis getting his legs caught and mangled in the jaws of such a trap and then dying slowly in terrible pain. I was with her in the Okavango for nine weeks, and during the whole of that time she was pounding away at her typewriter as though possessed, working without pause at the propaganda that was necessary if cruel traps were to be outlawed and if proper game reserves were to be established, safe from human exploitation.

The DC was a colonial administrator of the old school, scrupulously fair, wholly dedicated to the task of doing what he thought best for everybody and everything in the territory. N'gamiland was heavily subsidised, like the rest of the country, and it needed every penny it could get hold of: shooting licenses were a most useful form of revenue, and although little had come in so far – mostly from a trickle of South African hunters – there was promise of a great deal more. These safari firms in East Africa were deeply interested; the sporting concessions they sought would bring great wealth to the area; they were even proposing to improve the airstrip at Maun at their own expense for their customers' sake, but inevitably to the advantage of communications generally. This would benefit the European administration and people, and the authorities and tribesmen of the Batawana as well. Given the nature of his responsibilities, the DC was bound to take these considerations into account. But he recognised the importance of conserving the territory's wildlife, and suggested that this could best be done by restricting the number of licenses to be issued. With this approach to the matter, his wife was in wholehearted agreement.

Miles Smeeton had been a devotee of field sports for as long as he could remember, and fox hunting, tiger shooting and pig sticking had been his favourite pastimes when he was stationed in India. The more cunning the fox, the longer run it gave, the more elusive the tiger, the more ferocious the cornered wild boar, the better Miles was pleased with the hunt. But he saw the other side of the matter too. In the course of their travels, he and Beryl had seen the consequences of indiscriminate slaughter: at the very least it was necessary that a close season should be strictly observed, so that the game would be able to breed in peace, and if some area like the Okavango could be set aside as a reserve, so much the better. They would do everything in their power to support such a scheme.

It was a sound scheme. N'gamiland was an area large enough to support the game independently, without its having to move outside upon occasion for food and water, as with the Serengeti Reserve in Tanganyika. Safaris could continue, though with camera instead of gun; and scientific game-cropping could provide protein food for the indigenous population in those areas where the tsetse fly made it impossible to keep domestic cattle. Trapping for skins could and should be outlawed.

And so we talked on, over the coffee and brandy, trying always to make the DC fully aware of the urgency of the matter, until we were interrupted by a sudden clap of thunder. We felt that we had got somewhere. But the DC, being a practical administrator, was plainly worried by the obvious and inescapable question – who was going to pay? Robert and June had made a practical start, launching the whole idea of a game reserve and a N'gamiland Fauna Preservation Society; they had met with some success, but the money was still to be found. It was less than the cost of a single one of the jumbo jets that most modern nations seem to buy so freely.

The camp fire sank down to a hot glow, and we thought of bed. But sleep was not very attractive to us: we were too much taken up with this dream of a game reserve, and, long after the others had retired for the night, Robert and I sat up over the dying fire, dreaming and planning and hoping on lines which – as the night drew on – became less and less realistic.

But it was, and remains, a good dream.

CHAPTER 9

By Truck, Train and Plane

ON Easter Monday the DC and his wife left us, possibly to take part in the holiday festivities of their administration. But the Smeetons stayed with us at Fig Tree Camp for the last few days of our stay there, and soon came to share our absorption with the animal kingdom, both inside the cages and in the country around.

The two girls were extremely helpful in the daily tasks of looking after the animals: their nimble fingers were particularly good at a task which now became necessary: the weaving of reeds through the walls of various cages, so as to provide padding for the journey south. Their devotion to the animals was extreme, and it wouldn't have surprised me to find the vultures and marabous with their talons manicured and their beaks polished.

By now there was an end of term feeling in the air. John had discarded his previous gloom and now wore a water-melon smile constantly, aware that he would be going home soon. We set about our preparations. First of all we gathered up the dry branches with which we had built a kind of laager around our camp, and piled them all up to make a huge bonfire: it burned wonderfully, its great flames seeming almost to lick up to cloud level. Then there was the question of garbage. We wanted to leave the site as we had found it; so we thought it wise to dig a very deep trench and bury all our miscellaneous refuse beyond the reach of any inquisitive hyena. Shallow burying would not suffice: with our strong feelings about conservation, we did not want to feel responsible for the ugliness that would follow if our waste and mess were to be dug up and scattered around.

During our last night at the camp Chinky gave a last performance of her damsel in distress routine, but if the local lions heard it, they were not fooled by it: she was obviously some kind of collaborator or traitor. We rose an hour before dawn so as to make a daybreak start. We must have looked like a travelling circus or a gipsy encampment on the move. The DUKW was piled high with equipment and with vulture-cages, these being arranged to face outwards as a precaution in the event of regurgitation. June's diesel truck accommodated the bulk of the smaller cages, some inside and some on top. Chinky's truck had the aluminium dinghy strapped on top of it as before, and she herself lay in her reed-upholstered quarters in great state and spaciousness. Miles Smeeton travelled with Robert in the DUKW, Beryl Smeeton with June in the diesel, and the two girls – each with a spaniel on her lap – squeezed into the cab of Chinky's truck, leaving very little room indeed for the poor suffering driver, who was (of course) myself.

The first light of morning was just making the dew sparkle as we moved away from the fig trees in procession, grinding slowly forward to the place where we would be able to ford the Kwaai and thus reach its southern bank. Thereafter it was quite easy for us to retrace our steps southwards: even after six weeks the deep tracks made by the DUKW on our way north could be seen plainly, as could also the occasional branch that we had broken in our passage that was still hanging by the roadside. We had to keep to the old track, though certain short cuts were available and had in fact been used by the DC and his guide: these would have shortened the mileage, but were so rough that they would have seriously slowed us up. Even on the established track we were often reduced to a walking pace by the absolute necessity of not disturbing my collection too much.

I felt a good deal of anxiety about how easily all these

animals and birds would adapt to the traveller's life: they had a long journey ahead of them. So when we stopped for the night, I scrutinised their response to the idea of food. Chinky, Timmy, and Albert accepted food gladly, but the birds and the crocodiles and the springhare rejected with total finality the dainties that we offered. This worried me. But water was the main necessity, and I filled all the drinking troughs in all the cages from the supply kept in the DUKW: naturally enough, the rough journey had emptied them all, splashing water around in a way which only the crocodiles seemed to appreciate.

Another early start enabled us to reach the basecamp by the Thamalakane in the late afternoon of the second day of our travelling. Three hours later the whole collection had been offloaded: I conducted a minute inspection and found them all in as good condition as before, with the exception of Albert, who had once again been dropped by Clio.

I now had to wait five days until the Riley's Transport truck would take me and my collection to the nearest railhead in Francistown. I could not leave at once and on my own in the old three-quarter-ton pick-up: it was not nearly big enough, and I would have to sell it for whatever it would fetch. Meanwhile there was plenty to be done: in particular, there were permits to be obtained before I could take my collection out of the country. I also hoped that I might be able to get some more animals, and of course there was the feeding of the ones I had already. In all these matters I was helped wonderfully by John and the two girls.

It seemed that the DC was taking a great interest in my collection and talking about it in many quarters; and so I came to hear of the possibility of a second ostrich, a mate for the one already promised by the Greek trader at Sehitwa. This second specimen was owned by a member of the South African weather service, which had a station on the outskirts of Maun: it had reached the age of starting to be pernickety about people, of being friendly with some and aggressive towards others. It lived in the high fenced enclosure of the weather station and took a poor view of the meteorological staff, so that they could not get to work without being chased and attacked in a definitely dangerous way. To this situation I was the heaven-sent answer.

Miles Smeeton, Robert and I drove over to the weather station to size up this ostrich, so that a travelling-crate could be made for it. As we approached the nine-foot wire of the compound, it came strutting up and peering at us defiantly, as though daring us to come inside. It was about five feet tall and still carried its brown juvenile plumage; its large eyes were overhung with exaggeratedly long eyelashes, as worn by the more seductive type of cabaret artist. Its neck was like a pipe cleaner, its body was like a powder puff, its bony legs were like stilts, and its feet were murderous: when an ostrich attacks, it raises one leg and then strikes down, often disembowelling the enemy with the sword-like middle toe. If we made a crate for this one, it would need to be a small crate, in which it would be forced to crouch and would be prevented therefore from striking that kind of blow. It would also need to be well padded. As for the problem of how to get the dangerous bird into the crate . . . well, we would deal with that one when we came to it. I made up my mind, spoke to the ostrich's owner by field telephone – I didn't want to go into that enclosure unnecessarily – and said that I would be back that afternoon to collect it.

After lunch John and I cut some branches and set about making frames, covering them with wire-netting, and assembling them into a cage. It stood about 4 ft high, with an 18 in open-roofed extension on top, a kind of attic or penthouse for the ostrich's head. The sides were well padded with grass and hessian, and the floor was reinforced so as to carry the full weight of the bird when lifted.

We had a cup of tea, recruited a definitely unwilling John, and went back to the weather station. The ostrich greeted us as before, but the field telephone was silent. So we shouted loud and long, through the wire and across the enclosure and towards the neat white bungalow that stood there beneath its weather masts and wireless masts. Eventually two beefy rugger types appeared on the verandah, and we debated the problem in bellows. I was very reluctant to run the gauntlet across the enclosure to the bungalow: I didn't know yet whether the ostrich would treat me as friend or enemy, and at this stage of my collecting trip it would cause great difficulty if I were to be laid up, even by some injury much slighter than an ostrich can inflict when it tries. From the bird's truculent manner it seemed certain that if we all went in, it would go for at least one of us. What could we do?

The problem was solved for us by one of the two weather men: he seemed to be less popular with the ostrich than the other, who was its owner, and he ran down and attracted the bird's attention and then ran from it into a small outhouse. The ostrich pursued him inside very angrily, and he escaped through the window of the outhouse just in time, and just as the owner came dashing up and slammed the door from the outside. We all breathed a little more freely, but the task of getting the bird into its cage remained. The compound gate was opened and we all drove in; then we took the cage down, opened it at one end and located it as close as possible to the door of the shed. Then we flung that door open and at once clapped the cage firmly to the doorway: the ostrich was out at once like a rocket, hitting the padded far end so violently that he nearly knocked the whole thing over. We managed to steady it and close the opened end, thus securing an ostrich that now seemed perplexed rather than angry; but its feelings were still strong, as John discovered when he forgot for a moment that it was able to stick its head out through the open end of its penthouse roof. One of his fingers sustained a nasty peck; and from that moment on he had a healthy respect for the ostrich, regarding it as yet another creature that was best avoided.

We now asked him to make another ostrich cage, similar to the one which had succeeded so well; and next morning, after all the livestock had been looked after, Robert, Miles Smeeton, the girls and I set out for Sehitwa to repeat the operation. Robert negotiated the fifty-odd miles of sand-track road in record time, and we soon jumped down on to the hard cracked mud in front of the Greek trader's store. The trader himself was nowhere to be found: his numerous children were there in quantity, but they refused to go and find their father, much preferring to stand there and feast their eyes on the amazing sight of us. Eventually the Greek did turn up, and dashed our hopes by saying that he'd changed his mind. The ostrich kept his poultry safe at night, and he didn't want to part with it.

Robert therefore embarked upon the diplomacy at which he excelled. We had made tremendous efforts, he explained, to find a mate for his ostrich, and now we had one. The trader seemed unimpressed. Moreover (Robert went on) we had achieved this through the good offices of the District Commissioner, who very much wanted my enterprise to succeed. This mention of authority did the trick at once: the trader was all smiles and helpfulness at once, and we all set to work much as before. To clinch the matter, I told him a true story about how a lion had recently been disembowelled by an ostrich, and asked him whether he really understood the danger to which his children would soon be exposed if the bird grew just a little larger while still a member of his household. He took the point, which was a valid one, and by the time we had the ostrich crated successfully, he seemed very glad to see it go. His poultry would have to be protected in some other way.

Before we went I asked him what had happened to the young impala that we had seen on our last visit. His children answered by laughing and pointing down their throats.

Back at the basecamp June greeted me with the exciting news that the larger of my two wire traps had caught a young vervet monkey, and was I going to keep it? I went to look. There it was, running to and fro on the platform in the middle of the trap, quite unable to see why it couldn't get out and rejoin its family and friends. It was a remarkably pale specimen as compared with the much darker vervets that I had seen at Mwanza and in the Vumba Mountains. Its body was olive grey with black speckling, its arms and legs were slate grey, its underparts were snowy, it had a pale nose, a charcoal-pencilled moustache and a grey muzzle. It was, in fact, an excellent example of environmental adaptation. the relatively pale colouring served as first-class camouflage in this sandy veldt country, in which the darker specimens would have been much more conspicuous.

Only two days now remained to me in N'gamiland, and I went into Maun to send a cable listing the collection of animals for which I needed transit permits. Most of their names were unfamiliar to the post-office orderly, and it took him an arduous half-hour before my own list could be copied out in his own handwriting – something that was unaccountably necessary before the cable could be sent off to Francistown. The episode tried my patience somewhat, and when it was over I went across to the small hotel in Maun to have a sandwich and recover my wits and do some thinking. But while I sat at the bar pondering, the sandwich was suddenly snatched out of my hand from behind. I spun round, thinking that I had some kind of bar-room fight on my hands, and there on the next stool sat a long-haired baboon. I was furious, and tried to snatch my sandwich back, but hesitated when she flattened her ears and bared her teeth like an aggressive dog. I just had to sit there while she bobbed up and down on her stool and rammed my precious sandwich down her own undeserving throat. Then the barman returned and told me that she could very easily be bribed into eternal friendliness by gifts of food. I had lost a sandwich but gained a friend.

It turned out that she belonged to an African truck driver who worked for the tsetse-fly control department: he would cycle to work each morning from his kraal, with the baboon on his back like an Indian papoose. Until recently she had accompanied him on his working travels, riding with him in the cab of his truck, but now the authorities had forbidden this: on one occasion she had seen something that interested her on the other side, and had leapt across to get a better view, grabbing at the steering wheel as she went. The result was a sudden swerve, a collision with the concrete-like bulk of an ant-hill, and a few unproductive days in hospital for the damaged truck.

Forty minutes later, having lost my first sandwich to this baboon and shared my second with her (but on my own terms), I walked out of the bar leading her proudly on a string with the air of someone who owns a pedigree dog. In a moment of infatuation I had paid five pounds for her. But I couldn't regret this: she was irresistible.

This new acquisition meant that my cable was out of date, so I went back to the post office to send another. But I found the orderly still puzzling over the first, apparently daunted by the task of sending it; so I added the name of my new girl friend to the list and stood over him until he had actually sent it.

Back at camp I made introductions all round, and then tied the baboon to a tree, using a rope which I fastened to a collar, this going round her thin waist rather than her neck. I then checked up on all residents. Both of my ostriches had taken well to their diet of fruit and vegetables: they had their heads out of their penthouse windows and were eyeing each other meaningfully. Maunensis, the vervet monkey, was eating particularly well, plainly enjoying a diet more varied than he had ever known in the wild. My only trouble was the loss of my Bechuanaland gerbil. I wanted to transfer him from his large cage to a smaller travelling-box; I couldn't find him, and ruffled through a big pile of his food in case he might be hiding beneath it. Finding nothing I looked up, and was just in time to see him leap out from behind the cage door and make a dash for freedom, in just the direction of the place where I had found him seven weeks earlier. I grabbed at him wildly and unsuccessfully: he would soon be at home. What travellers' tales he would have to tell his cronies! How unlikely they would be to believe him!

This loss was counterbalanced by the acquisition of three green tree squirrels in the smaller wire trap. I soon had them in exceptionally well-padded boxes: the other squirrels had damaged their heads on the wire, and I didn't want this to happen again. I thought of sending a further cable to bring the catalogue up to date, but my patience was not sufficient: these squirrels would have to travel as contraband.

On my last afternoon I had calls to make. First I went and paid my respects to Mahumahiti Moremi, and thanked her for allowing me to make an animal collection within her realm. I gave her my list, which she read through rather as though it was a menu, selecting one or two animals at random for gracious comment and question. Then one of her entourage broke into our conversation with the bare words 'Twelve pounds!' I took this to be the assessment of the tribal levy due on my collection, and I paid it over to the Queen Regent's treasurer without comment upon its somewhat arbitrary character. Then I shook hands with her and backed out of the room, so as not to turn my back on her: this I took to be the correct protocol for royal occasions. The effect was rather spoiled when I tripped over a dog.

My next call was on the European administration. The Veterinary Department gave me the documents that were necessary to take live animals out of N'gamiland to Francistown: there I would need to get a further veterinary permit before I moved them to the Rhodesian border. The DC's office stamped my collecting permit with a very impressive blue and red stamp, filled out an export permit in triplicate, copied the details from my passport into a visitors' book, and finally handed all these assorted documents to me in a big brown envelope that was boldly printed with the words ON HER MAJESTY'S SERVICE – BRITISH BECHUANALAND PROTECTORATE, so as to leave one in no doubt at all.

On my way back to camp I collected Miles Smeeton from the post office and we called in on the Calvers to pick up my spur-winged geese. The flower bed that had once been ravaged by the aardvark was now a mass of lovely blossom, and the geese had grown prodigiously. We carried the basket into their enclosure, and Miles and I set about catching them. It should have been easy: at least they couldn't fly away, since the primaries of their wings had been clipped. But they evaded us with surprising agility, until Miles lost patience and flung himself upon the gander in a high-speed rugger tackle, regardless of his own cleanliness. I should have shown such decisiveness myself, and I felt guilty when I saw the horrible mess that now covered his bush-shirt and trousers. But at least the goose was now easy to catch: she heard the indignant squawkings of her husband in the basket, came in wifely manner to help him, and was in our hands.

By now Robert had transferred Chinky to her travelling-cage. It had been well cleaned out previously, purged of its unseemly odours of wildebeest dung and hyena capture: she lay in it quite contentedly, stretched out on her mattress of freshly cut reeds, but her eyes were narrower than usual, and she kept vigilant watch upon the movements of June and Robert, being obviously aware that the immediate future was going to be different and unsettling. There was emotional stress on their side too: Chinky meant a lot to them, and would leave a painful gap in their lives when I took her away.

Last-minute visitors started to come: the Calvers, the DC and his wife, and a few others, all anxious to wish me well for a safe journey, while at the same time satisfying their curiosity. I acted as their host and guide as well as I could, but my attention was taken up by a hundred small adjustments to the cages and the other arrangements, and also by the necessity of giving the animals a big feed before the journey started. When it began it might well unsettle some of them and put them off their food: I wanted them to be well fattened up against this possibility. The tasks were small but endless in ways that can hardly be imagined unless you have had charge of animals, or perhaps of small children in quantity: the two girls helped most cheerfully, being motivated by their natural love of all animals, and John helped as well, with equal vigour but with different motivation. He wanted things to go smoothly so that he could get home quickly.

It was our last night. The guests had all gone, and we sat

back in camp chairs, our tasks accomplished for the moment, to enjoy one of Robert's rare and splendid curries. He really put himself out on this occasion, and produced a masterpiece to warm the stomach and comfort the soul. The night was chilly, but we had a good fire to warm us as we sat back in the verandah of our tent and looked down across the sloping ground to the Thamalakane. Around us, strange shapes loomed up in the firelight: the hessian-cloaked cages of the vultures and marabous on our right; the four baskets of water fowl and francolin by the water's edge; the cage of the vervet monkeys; the boxes of the crocodiles, the springhare, and the tortoises; and in the midst of all, the form of my friend the baboon, looking like a sentry who has fallen asleep at his post. It was as though we were all waiting for old father Noah to come and let us on board the ark.

The stars circled slowly and we talked beneath them – of my hope of returning to the Okavango some day, and of Robert and June's hope of establishing a game reserve there, so that for years to come other people would enjoy the privilege which had meant so much to me recently: that of seeing animals safe and unmolested in their natural setting. And as we talked I worked through the final stages of a task that had occupied me off and on all through my visit: the task of grooming the spaniels, of getting the tangles and the matted lumps out of their coats and ears. Now, at this last moment, I finished the job; but small thanks did I get from them.

The morning of departure came. The Riley's Transport truck was supposed to arrive at our camp between eight and nine: by the standards locally prevailing, we had to see great punctuality in its actual arrival at about ten fifteen. The driver appeared to me to be in no fit state to drive. But there was no alternative, and I embarked on the big task of loading.

This was complex. Each cage had to be accessible, of course, so that I could keep the animals fed and watered throughout the fifteen-hour journey; furthermore, it was important not to put any predator next to a possible victim. The four stony eyes of the crocodiles could not be allowed to frighten the already agitated Maun squirrels; the long coils of my python must be kept well away from the terrified and crouching springhare. Chinky's cage was located about half way along the right-hand side, and the two ostriches were put against it on the opposite side. The vulture cages were arranged in a row on top of some provisions, with the marabous alongside: I arranged my own sleeping-bag by the sliding door of Chinky's cage, just in case, with the waterfowl baskets opposite. As for the baboon, I tethered her at the back of the truck, just out of grabbing distance of any food or damageable cage: she would best enjoy the journey there, I thought, while also keeping guard if I had to leave the truck at any of the numerous stops between Maun and Francistown.

John's face shone like the morning sun as he said goodbye to his friends and got into the cab of the truck a good half hour before our take-off time. He wasn't going to risk being left behind. As for Robert and June, they climbed down slowly and reluctantly, after making their almost tearful farewells to Chinky. She was now my sole responsibility, and I was very glad that she liked and trusted me. Had any animal-gathering expedition to southern Africa ever come out with a more endearing and remarkable specimen?

Clumsily, with a genuine lump in my throat, I expressed my grateful farewells to Robert and June. They had been the best and most considerate of hosts. I was anxious to get my collection home; but I was also very sorry to leave them, and to part from a region and a style of life that I had grown to love.

But all things come to an end, and moments of departure are suddenly upon us. The green canvas awning was tied down on both sides, leaving the front and back open for ventilation, and the engine of the truck shuddered into noisy life. One of the marabous immediately and messily regurgitated its breakfast. Then, as Robin and June waved and as the baboon barked a farewell, we lurched forward and drove out of camp.

We crossed the creaking timbers of the Maun bridge, and I gazed for the last time upon the clear cool waters of the Thamalakane, the forests of reeds, the swamps of the Okavango. Then the truck gathered speed and away we went, bouncing over the rough road to the eastern boundary of N'gamiland, and then on through Bushman Pits, Kanye, Oudiakwe, and Nata, towards our destination of Francistown. At sundown the truck stopped, and we gladly accepted the invitation of the driver and his mate that we should join them in an evening meal; I took this opportunity to look after my charges. I replenished the seeds and water of the waterfowl and the francolin, which were duly grateful; I cut up some water melon and bananas and figs and fed them to the hungry ostriches; I raised Chinky's slide and gave her some fresh water, which she lapped up and then licked my arm with her rough tongue. I knew perfectly well that the marabou storks, the vultures, the tawny eagle, the crocodiles, and the python would be in no mood for eating. But Albert obliged me by sampling some lettuce and a slice of water melon that had been rejected by the smaller ostrich; and the Maun squirrels disentangled themselves from one another and from their connubial bed, and came forward to drink some water and nibble at some figs, their tails twitching in apprehension meanwhile. My friend Maunensis bobbed up and down at me while I was placing fruit in his cage, and then ate it all like a hungry soldier.

As for my new baboon – but she needed to have a name, she couldn't be just 'my baboon' for ever. I had thought of this before I left camp; and I had suggested to Clio Smeeton that in view of her gallant service and her devotion to duty, she might have this animal named after her. Clio agreed with enthusiasm, recognising this for the honour that it was: how many English girls can claim to have had baboons named after them?

I can therefore say that having checked the rest of my collection, I untied Clio from the back of the truck and took her along the sandy track so that both of us could have a little exercise. She led me a fine dance, ending up at a pool of stagnant water which she insisted upon sampling.

Then we journeyed on through the night, very much as

I had come, but in greater comfort and with less cramp. My mind was far too active for sleep, so I stayed alongside Chinky's cage, loving her through its structure, and meditating upon the past life of each of these animals and also upon the future that was in store for them. Freedom and danger then, captivity and safety now: it raised some thorny questions of the ethical sort, and about these (not for the first time) I brooded.

As the night and the bouncy journey continued, I became more and more afflicted by the continual sandstorm that blew in from the front; and I tried to close the canvas, to reduce its impact, but with doubtful success. My animals, however, seemed all right. Exhausted, the ostriches and the marabous had crouched down on their haunches and gone to sleep; by the light of my torch I could see the vultures gripping their perches tightly with their immensely powerful talons, and thus steadying themselves against the joltings of the truck. My dear Chinky had pillowed her great head down on to her broad paws, but she was not asleep: she kept opening her large friendly eyes, to check up on me and make sure she had not been deserted.

In the very early morning there was a completely unexplained hold-up of a whole hour, in some completely unidentifiable place. Despite this we drew up in the goods yard of the station at Francistown almost exactly at the scheduled time. They knew about me and were ready. The Afrikaans station master had allocated us a spacious closed-in wagon, and this was parked all ready in a siding, and he issued us with two fourth-class tickets so that John and I could travel in this wagon with the animals. We now faced the task of transferring them from the truck to the wagon, and a large crowd assembled to enjoy this spectacle, with many a helpful but noisy comment which did little to soothe my collection. I was fretful with lack of sleep, and I was glad to speak up on their behalf and call for a little peace, but without much effect: soon I felt an ignoble temptation to set Chinky upon them as a sobering influence.

This would hardly do, but Clio managed at least to keep them at a distance.

We completed the transfer, and I left John and Clio to guard the wagon, making it clear that nobody except the station master was to be admitted. I had watered and fed my stock, and I now wandered off into the dry heat of Francistown – it was well into the nineties – in search of provisions and fresh permits.

I found a fine old confusion. The Veterinary Office had not received word from Salisbury to authorise the transit of my collection through Rhodesia; it was now after noon, and for the next two hours it would be impossible to phone Salisbury; I would therefore miss the mid-afternoon train that was supposed to be taking me and the animals northwards; the cable that I had sent from Maun some forty-eight hours previously had not arrived. So, in resignation, I bought some fresh fruit and some meat and returned heavily burdened to the station.

There I found two somewhat bombastic Afrikaans policemen waiting for me; John had managed at least to keep them out of the wagon by saying that Clio was dangerous and quite uncontrollable. Thus thwarted they released their anger in a display of petty officialdom. They inspected my passport closely, also John's entry permit, disturbed all the animals by a pointless scrutiny, and then tipped out the contents of one of my cases on to the grubby floor of the truck. Sighing wearily, I produced receipts to show that I had paid tax, and permits to show that I was authorised to transport my collection. It was all very boring, but the story has a happy ending: one of these junior policemen was rash enough to put his hand where the older and fiercer ostrich could get at it, and was powerfully nipped, to my extreme gratification.

Thus the afternoon passed in the hopeless war against bureaucracy, and by night-time I had received the necessary authorisation to take my collection into Rhodesia, together with a fresh veterinary certificate from the authorities at

Francistown. The station master told me that a goods train would come and pick us up later on in the evening, at a time which could not be predicted, so that we would do well to remain on board the wagon. So we did, and eventually we felt a terrible jolt that knocked most of the birds off their perches. After that, however, things went much more smoothly; we were coupled on to the train and then proceeded in what seemed – by contrast with the previous night's travel – the most velvety and luxurious fashion, even though the train had to fight its way up the steep incline into Bulawayo.

The vultures celebrated their arrival in Rhodesia by greedily accepting some of the meat that I had bought in Francistown. Chinky was also willing to eat, provided that I cut it up and fed it to her by hand. She needed attention, she wanted to be looked after: the parting from Robert and June had been a shock that she could not have expected and could not now understand.

I kept the broad door of the truck permanently open, as there was no other ventilation. Whenever the train stopped in Matabeleland I would jump down alongside the track and pull up bunches of the yellow stringy grass to feed to the ostriches, gathering its roots as well for the springhare. Clio was housetrained and needed to be excercised at these whistle-stops for personal reasons: it must have provided an unusual spectacle for any onlookers when a baboon with a European in tow was to be seen jumping on to a goods wagon.

We arrived at Salisbury in the early hours of the morning, and our wagon was detached and shunted into a siding. There was nothing that I could do now until the city came to life, so I fell asleep by Chinky's side, my snores doubtlessly counter-pointing hers.

I woke up when the morning was well advanced, and secured from the Veterinary Department a permit to take my collection out to Glendale for the three days that remained before the Africargo flight to London upon which we were all booked. A transport company supplied me with a sufficiently large truck, and so we went forth on the familiar road to Douet Farm.

John was in his glory, and as we went past Mazoe Dam he took on the role of a returning and triumphant Caesar, waving to every African by the roadside, his cheeks blossoming with goodwill, his confidence expanding with every mile.

And so we came back to Douet, and to a tumultuous welcome: I quite expected the boss boy to come out and put a garland on John's head. It was good to see Robin and Pris again; they saved me from the throng and helped me to unload everything into the old tobacco barn, which still smelt slightly of hunting dog and jackal. Chinky had a private suite – the garage to be precise – and the tractor had to live outside for the time. The whole collection made a wonderful impression: Roselle fell in love with Maunensis above all, while James – bold as ever – decided that Chinky was for him.

Once again I had a problem of accommodation. For the spur-wing geese, which had been seriously cramped in their basket, I took over one of the poultry pens. As for Clio, I tethered her to a tree in front of the farmhouse, so that she could perform her various tricks within sight of the children. But she interested other people too; and one day, while she was deeply engaged in inspecting the long coarse brown fur of her back, a crowd of Africans gathered and were soon laughing at her. She could not endure this mockery, and strained at her leash for revenge: this increased the laughter and made it more hostile, and she strained more violently, until by a happy chance the catch on her chain broke. The jeering became a collective shriek of terror, and the unkind crowd dispersed to the four winds: the worm had turned, the fox had bitten the hounds.

New acquisitions still came pouring in. The Smoelkes presented me with three leopard tortoises, which I was glad to have, though Albert was somewhat put out by this competition. Then, thanks to a news item about the departure of my Rhodesian collection, Robin had been contacted by a bird fancier in Livingstone, who wanted to know whether I would like to have a fish eagle and a martial eagle. He had accepted on my behalf. The fish eagle was the replica of the one that had foraged for food near the DC's house in Maun; with its white head and neck establishing its adult status, it looked thoroughly proud and arrogant. The martial eagle, with its magnificent crest, had been shot in the left wing by some trigger-happy European; a Mr Oxenham had rescued it and mended its wing as well as he could, and it now looked extremely healthy, though when it perched its left wing would hang slightly, the primary feathers not tucking up to the tail feathers as they should.

The weekend passed rapidly. The animals were all eating well, except for the crocodiles, which had renewed their hunger-strike. John and I basked in glory. He had acquired the reputation of a fearless hunter, and this was useful to me, since it meant that he worked very hard to live up to the prevailing image of himself. As for me, I was written up in the *Salisbury Press*, after a reporter's visit to Douet Farm, and I was given the undeserved titles of explorer and zoologist. In fact I was neither. But I was glad of this article, since it gave useful publicity to the conservation work of Robert and June in the Okavango, and also to the work of Gerald Durrell at the Jersey Wildlife Preservation Trust.

With the animals well rested and well fed, we departed for Salisbury for the last time, after brief but exceptional hospitality at the farm. As I drove past the wooded kopjes and the uncultivated part of the land, which was now pretty well devoid of animals. I thought how splendid it would be to liberate my collection in just such a place, in order to recolonise it – if only it would be safe from human persecution.

Chinky saw the broad waters of the Mazoe Dam, and perhaps thought that she was back in the Okavango. The ostriches fluttered their eyelashes at one another foolishly. Clio sat unhappily in an uncomfortable box: she was a seasoned traveller, familiar with trucks if not with aeroplanes, but the airline had insisted that she was not to be loose on the plane.

The Game Department gave me an export permit, and the Veterinary Department passed the whole collection as being free – as far as they could detect – from contagious diseases. As we passed down First Street in Salisbury, a press photographer took a picture of Chinky, which appeared in the evening paper with the caption 'Lion Roars in First Street!' In point of fact Chinky hadn't uttered a sound since we left the northern regions of the Okavango. Never mind: it made a nice fantasy for the readers, to think of a pride of lions invading the urban streets of Salisbury.

And so we came to Salisbury Airport, where I had great difficulty in controlling the porters, who swarmed like ants over the truck in their anxiety to see what was in these different cages. If they had been left to their own devices, most of the cages would have been hauled off the truck in any old fashion, upsidedown or sideways, to the great detriment of the occupants. I had to keep control. But at least we got the publicity. A television man brought a bloodshot eye up to the squint-sights of his camera and took a series of shots while the collection was being weighed, incessantly distracting me from the job with requests for a cheesy smile. And as I stood by Chinky's cage, a small boy came up and asked me for my autograph. But here I may have been sought out under a misapprehension: the British Lions rugby team had arrived in Rhodesia that very afternoon, with their mascot, and this boy may have supposed that I was one of them. I had no such glory.

Now it was time for the empty lorry to go back to Glendale, and this meant that I had to say goodbye to John, who was going back with it. This also was a parting which grieved me. Ours had been an odd relationship, more deep-rooted than it seemed, rather like the relationship between a school prefect and a fag. He seemed very cheerful and confident about his own future: with the money he had earned while he had been with me he proposed to seek out and buy a good hard-working wife. I told him that I would be coming back to Africa next year on a similar quest, and that he would be the first person I would wish to employ. He grasped my hand emotionally, and so we parted. What stories he would have to tell, back in the home kraal, of intrepid hunting and of ferocious animals boldly captured by himself!

The aircraft was a DC6 freighter; I was the only passenger, listed in the flight manifest as an animal attendant – yet another new title for me. I checked that all the cages were held firmly in place by the straps provided, and I blocked up a small hole in the wire door of Clio's cage: she had been busily at work enlarging it so as to get a better view around the aircraft. I had brought a good supply of tranquillisers to administer to Chinky if necessary, but she seemed very peaceful, and so I did not give her any, feeling that my own presence, close at hand, would soothe her better than any chemical. These tranquillisers are often very useful on a short-term basis, but when the effects wear off, the animal tends to be under worse stress than if it had received no medication at all. And we had a long journey: I had to take the long-term view.

The piston engines of the DC6 spluttered into life and were then run up and tested, to the astonishment of the passengers: the crocodiles tried to submerge in some non-existent water, and the ostriches stood petrified. Chinky lay flat on a mattress of wood-wool, her ears flickering; she was disorientated and bewildered by the alien noise, and her eyes were narrow and uneasy. I raised the sliding door of her cage slightly so that I could scratch her reassuringly under the chin. She seemed grateful for this, and lowered her head on to her paws, with my hand caught between them as I lay alongside her cage. It was in this position – which is not what stewardesses usually recommend – that I experienced the taxiing of the aircraft, the slow turning on to the runway, the roar of full power, and the swift rough acceleration of the take-off.

Soon we were at cruising height, and the engines settled down to a steady quiet roar. Chinky felt better now – after all, even the most experienced air traveller feels a shade nervous during the take-off and the initial climb – and she started to sandpaper my bare arm. We both took up more relaxed positions. Soon, in defiance of orders, I succumbed to Clio's entreaties and took her out of her travelling-box, so that she could inspect the tubular interior of the DC6. I kept her firmly under control by her waist-collar; she seemed beside herself

with exitement when she happened to look out of a window
and see the vast immensity of the land beneath her. It amazed
me too, especially when I saw the snow-capped heights of
Mount Kilimanjaro, gleaming in the sunshine like a diamond-
studded snowball in a desert. The fact is that Clio enjoyed
air travel, finding it much more exciting and spectacular than
anything she had experienced in the cab of that tsetse fly control truck. I had the greatest difficulty in getting her back into
her cage.

Our first landing was at Nairobi, where we took on board
some further animal cargo, unconnected with myself. There
were ten plywood boxes crammed full of Fischer's lovebirds,
which abound on the slops of Mount Kenya: they had been
netted and packed like sardines for shipment to a dealer in
Holland. There were also two domestic dogs. One was an
angry Scottish terrier who seemed most reluctant to leave the
warmth of Africa for his own damp misty homeland: the
other was a miniature pug, who yapped hysterically until
silenced by a well-timed roar from Chinky. Clio put on her
dog voice and barked a little at these newcomers, but received
no reply. Perhaps they were petrified.

When we next landed, this time Khartoum, I noticed that
the ostriches were running out of green food: they had been
eating it greedily during the flight, and now there was none
left. I descended from the aircraft and went across to the airport building, which was guarded by a real forest of bayonets.
Through these I managed to see a civilian wearing the white
smock and red fez of a waiter, and I got hold of him and
ordered two dozen lettuces. After about twenty minutes he
came out to the aircraft, escorted by a Sudanese soldier who
was carrying his rifle in a distinctly threatening manner. I
was given four cardboard cake-boxes. I opened one of them
and found six small lettuce hearts, denuded of the more accep-
table and nutritious outer leaves. I tried to explain that they
were for my ostriches and not for myself, and that if this
chap wanted me to pay his hefty bill he would have to find
the outer leaves too. He didn't *want* to understand, and the
soldier fidgeted with the trigger of his rifle in a more and

more pointed way. So I stormed across the tarmac, pushing my way boldly past the soldiers, and found the kitchen, where I accosted someone who must have been either the manager or else the cook. Whoever he was, he pretended not to understand my perfectly simple request for the outer leaves of those lettuces to serve as ostrich food. It was almost as though he had never met such a requirement before. But as is often the case with foreigners, violent gesticulation did the trick; and soon I was back in the aircraft with a big polythene bag full of what I wanted. The ostriches were duly grateful, or greedy at least.

Here at Khartoum the heat was quite suffocating, though it was after dusk. I kept myself busy by watering the whole of my collection, dampening the waterfowl baskets continually, and even pouring water over the unresponding forms of the apparently mummified crocodiles. Chinky was restless now, and paced up and down fretfully: the ninety-minute stop seemed like half a day, and I was extremely glad when we took off again into the cloudless night sky.

We touched down at Malta in the early hours of the morning for the third refuelling and the second change of air-crew. The animals were all still in good shape, though Chinky became nervous once again as take-off approached, and insisted on being scratched and fondled and then upon holding my hand, just as when we first left Salisbury.

And so the great journey moved on to its ending, until we bumped down on to the runway at Heathrow and taxied to the terminal building. I was greeted there by a horde of officials who seemed to be much more interested in my collection than in their proper bureaucratic task of checking my documents.

I had meant to carry on to Jersey immediately. But my return happened to coincide with a lightening strike of airport engineers, so that all domestic flights were grounded. For three days my collection had to be accommodated at the RSPCA hostel at Heathrow, where every possible attention and comfort was provided for them.

Meanwhile there were the newsmen, and my story ends with them. I knew already that when I reached Jersey I would be met by a BBC television team, who were collecting film for one of Johnny Morris's children's programmes. They wanted to film Chinky's first meeting with her fiancé, the Dublin-born lion called Leo. Since this was now impossible because of the strike, they wanted to record her great friendliness towards human beings, which had already been the subject of a press release. So I was asked to demonstrate here in London.

This was a somewhat unnerving prospect. Chinky had not been out of a cage for nearly six months, long before my arrival in Bechuanaland. She had certainly shown many signs of goodwill and affection towards me, especially since parting from Robert and June, but this had only been a matter of holding my hands and washing my face while she was securely caged. I did not really know how she would behave when given the chance of some wider relationship; and after all, she was a lioness, not a kitten.

The time came for the filming to take place. She was released from her travelling cage into a large indoor den, where she looked larger than ever. The producer and the cameramen, from a safe place outside, gave me the signal that they were ready. Slowly, apprehensively. I put on a thick duffle coat by way of extra protection, and went in.

I need not have worried. Chinky sprang to her feet in obvious delight, curled her lips in a smile, gave forth a gentle cub-like roar, and jumped up to put her big paws on my shoulders, thus flattening me against a wall, and then joyfully sandpapering my cheeks with her tongue. I felt utterly smitten with guilt at having doubted her friendship, and I hugged and embraced her like the sweetheart that she was.

I had travelled many miles. But a man could journey over the whole of this wide world, meeting animals and men of every kind, and still never meet such a friend as she. I was lucky.

Postscript

FINANCIALLY, my African journey was a disaster, for I found that it was impossible to regard any animal as a piece of merchandise to sell to the highest bidder. But although I had lost in credit, I had been rewarded a thousand times over with a treasure chest of unforgettable animals and events, which perhaps not even money would be able to purchase in the future.

I considered that the essential prerequisite of sending an animal anywhere was to know that it was going to be looked after properly by a sympathetic establishment. Perhaps general collections are not now really justifiable, since if a species is to benefit from captivity, it must be represented in sufficient numbers to provide viable breeding units. By captive breeding and good management zoos and other organisations handling 'exotic' animals could be almost self-supporting, and would not have to keep drawing on the increasingly depleted wild populations. However, it is almost impossible to achieve this goal, unless sufficient numbers of the same species can be collected and imported at much the same time, so that compatible pairs will result in regular propagation. A number of animal species already owe their survival to the protection afforded them in a controlled environment.

Some of the animals I collected have been kept at the Jersey Zoo, although over the years some of them have been sent to other collections, to make way for more specific breeding programmes.

The Zoological Society of London accepted a pair of the red-billed francolin, the first of this species to be represented in the Society's collection: their presence was given a learned mention in both the Zoological Record and the Avicultural Magazine.

The Royal Zoological Society of Scotland maintained the pair of cape hunting dogs in a spacious rocky enclosure; whilst Chessington Zoo in Surrey looked after the black-backed jackal.

The Bristol, Clifton and West of England Zoological Society purchased Paris the eared vulture; whilst the North of England Zoological Society, at Chester, played host to a trio of the white-headed vultures.

Flamingo Park, in north Yorkshire, accepted the ostriches; and the Welsh Mountain Zoo, at Colwyn Bay, who were specialising in birds of prey, purchased the martial eagle.

After a six-year stay in Jersey Clio left the island to take up an appointment at the Marquess of Bath's Longleat Park, to become a founder member of the baboon colony, which was in close proximity to familiar lions. Clio was also honoured by Dr W. C. Osman Hill, who included a portrait photograph of her in the eighth volume of his renowned monograph on the anatomy and taxonomy of primates; thus ensuring that Clio's presence on this earth will be preserved for posterity as the representative of *Papio ursinus chobiensis*.

The black spur-wing geese now reside in the graceful parkland of the Château de Cleres, near Rouen, France, in the collection of the famous ornithologist Jean Delacour. A dead Maun squirrel, perhaps not as fortunate as the others, is preserved in the mammal room of the British Museum, representing the only specimen of the type species, *Peraxerus cepapi maunensis*.

The Jersey Wildlife Preservation Trust recorded the first captive breeding of the red-billed francolin, and some of the progeny have been exported to England, Holland, and the USA.

The serval cat Tammy has given birth to twenty-two kittens. Some of the young have been sent to Regent's Park and Whipsnade in England; Wassenaar Zoo in the Netherlands, and to the Rare Feline Center in Florida, USA. Recently she has become a grandmother twice over.

Maunensis, the Okavango vervet Monkey, matured into a fine male, and has now perhaps created a record amongst the vervet heritage by successfully siring nine young, five sons and four daughters, in the space of seven years. It is rumoured that he is soon to become a grandfather.

Chinky and I could hardly have thought more deeply about each other: the depth of our affection appeared to be un-fathomable. Whenever she caught sight of me approaching her enclosure she would utter her 'wow' of greeting, and her golden form would trot effortlessly over to talk to me: much to my gratification and to the infuriation of her pos-sessive mate. Almost a year after Chinky's arrival in Jersey it was established that she had been successfully mated by Leo. Letters flowed between the Okavango and Jersey with the same degree of intensity as if I had married Robert and June's daughter, and was about to become a parent at any moment. However, during the final stages of pregnancy, an internal virus suffocated the cubs, and before it was possible to save her life she died.

At the time of her death I realised that there could never be a replacement in the animal world for Chinky. She had become a part of my life and had taught me so much about the true understanding of animal friendship, and the realisation of how important it was to cultivate a mutual respect between man and beast – a relationship once achieved, impossible to surpass.

Appendix: The Animal Collection

2   European red foxes

24	Assorted frogs	1	African tawny eagle
2	Chameleon	1	Martial eagle
1	Bell's hinged tortoise	1	Fish eagle
3	Leopard tortoise	3	Marabou stork
1	Rock monitor	2	Southern ostrich
2	African crocodile	1	Chacma baboon
1	Mole snake	1	Okavango vervet monkey
3	Python	3	Maun squirrel
4	Hottentot teal	1	Cape pouched mouse
4	Red-billed teal	1	Rhodesia bush hare
2	Black spur-wing goose	1	Springhare
8	Red-billed francolin	1	African lion
2	White-backed vulture	1	Slender mongoose
3	White-headed vulture	2	Black-backed jackal
1	Eared or lappet-faced vulture	2	Serval cat
1	Yellow-billed kite	1	African wild cat
2	African goshawk	2	Cape hunting dog

SPECIMENS COLLECTED — RELEASED OR ESCAPED

1	Rock monitor*	3	Double snipe
Numerous	assorted frogs*	1	Giant kingfisher*
1	Leopard tortoise	1	Coucal
1	Striped skaapstekker*	1	Long-tailed starling
3	Red-billed francolin*	1	Bechuanaland gerbil*
3	White-backed vulture	3	Maun squirrels
1	Barn owl	3	Slender mongoose*
18	Blacksmith plover	1	Blotched genet
2	African skimmer	1	Spotted hyena
1	Avocet	*	Denotes escapees

Index